Devil May Care

Devil May Care

A NOVEL

SHERI McINNIS

ATRIA BOOKS

New York   London   Toronto   Sydney   Singapore

ATRIA BOOKS

1230 Avenue of the Americas
New York, NY 10020

Copyright © 2003 by Sheri McInnis

ISBN: 0-7434-6484-2

First Atria Books hardcover edition August 2003

10 9 8 7 6 5 4 3 2 1

ATRIA BOOKS is a trademark of Simon & Schuster, Inc.

Manufactured in the United States of America

For information regarding special discounts for bulk purchases, please contact Simon & Schuster Special Sales at 1-800-456-6798 or business@simonandschuster.com

For my husband,
Mark.

Devil May Care

ONE

Be sober, be vigilant;
because your adversary the devil,
as a roaring lion, walketh about,
seeking whom he may devour.

1 PETER 5:8

"Name?"

"Sally Carpenter."

She skims the list of names with her pencil. "You're not here," she says.

"Yes, I am."

"Where?"

"There."

"*Where?*"

Sigh. I plunk my finger on the list. "There."

"Oh." She looks up at me with large blinking eyes. "Sawwwry!"

"Am I late?"

"A little," she says, shoving the crumpled scene pages at me. "But don't worry about it. They're running behind."

I exhale in relief and turn to face the broadloomed waiting area. It's filled with the shifting, murmuring figures of what must be every actress in Manhattan who could get the lunch rush off. Some are tall, some are short, some are sitting, some are pacing, some are cross-legged, doing breathing exercises on the floor. The only thing they seem to have in common is that they're all muttering the same words under their breath in a great monotonous chorus:

"Good morning, sir. Welcome to First Fidelity. . . . Good morning, sir. Welcome to First Fidelity. . . ."

It's the opening line for the part of Candace, "a buxom bank teller" who gets taken hostage during a bank robbery that goes wrong on UBN's prime-time cop drama. I'm not exactly perfect for the role, anatomically speaking, but my agent told me to explore the wide world of Wonder bras and sent me out for it anyway.

"Salleee! Sallee-hee!" I hear my name called in a breathy, singsongy whisper. I look over to see a blond woman in a pink T-shirt and A-line miniskirt bouncing excitedly up and down on the edge of her seat, fluttering her fingernails at me.

Shit. Dara Dempsey. Now I'm never going to get the part.

I tuck the script under my arm and reluctantly walk over, sitting down into the cloud of CKOne that surrounds her.

"I haven't seen you in *ages,*" she whisper-trills, tapping my knee. "How *are* you?"

"Oh, not bad, Dara. You?"

She sticks out her tongue in a little pant. "I'm so busy I can't *take* it! Did you hear I got the part on *Dusk Until Dawn?*"

"You *got* that part?" I ask innocently. "Congratulations."

But of course I know she got that part. I auditioned for it myself. Dara and I always end up on auditions together—not that it's surprising. We're both about the same age, same height, same hair color, same blue eyes (okay, well, mine are sort of grayish blue, but I put blue on my résumé because it sounds better). The only real difference between us, besides the fact Dara doesn't have to wear padded bras to "buxom bank teller" auditions, is that *she* always gets the part.

"Thanks," she says, "but it's no big deal. Just a soap. What about *you?* What have *you* been up to?"

She has to ask? Isn't it obvious from my scuffed boots and second-

(possibly third)-hand leather jacket that I haven't had any disposable income since they canceled *Melrose Place?* And definitely not since the last time we saw each other. Dara and I used to hang out. We weren't best friends or anything, but we'd sometimes find ourselves at the nearest Starbucks drinking skinny lattes after acting class. We'd commiserate over our lack of prospects, bitch about other actors getting work, and whine about being broke. When it got really bad, we even threatened to drop out of acting and find something useful to do with our lives before it was too late. She wanted to be a teacher. I wasn't so sure—maybe I'd go back to Wisconsin and finish my psych degree.

But then she got that walk-on part in an HBO movie.

And a national ad campaign.

And now the soap.

So I'm drinking my skinny lattes alone.

She's still waiting to hear what I've been up to, and I'm fumbling over the most impressive way to say "Absolutely fucking nothing!" when the casting assistant, wearing a mustard-yellow shirt and brown argyle vest, leans around the corner and consults his clipboard.

"Sally Carpenter?"

"That's me!" I say, springing from my chair.

"Break a leg in there!" Dara says. "And if you can't break a leg, whatever you do—don't break a nail!" She throws her blond head back and giggles.

I laugh like it's the first time I've heard the line, but she uses it before every audition.

I catch up to the quickly disappearing argyle vest. He has one of those abrupt, tense walks where his knees seem to lock after every step. We take a left, then a right, then another left down a long white corridor. I make a mental note of a water fountain and two rubbertree plants so I don't get lost on the way out. I always get lost after auditions at UBN. Everyone does. With its labyrinth of white hallways, closed doors, and nondescript exit stairwells, actors have a nickname for the place—we call it Purgatory.

"Wow. I'll never understand how you guys know your way around here."

"You get used to it," he says. "Hey! Wait a sec! *I* know you!" He clicks his fingers and points at me. "You're in that Pizza Hut commercial, aren't you?" He can tell by the look on my face that it's a case of mistaken identity. "Whoops! Sorry. I thought for sure it was you."

"Don't worry. Happens all the time." And it does. But Dara's the Pizza Hut girl. I, naturally, made an idiot of myself in the audition. There were about sixteen of us at the call, all gathered in a stuffy room, surrounded by stacks of pizza boxes. The casting director told us that for authenticity's sake, and to test our natural aptitude for cheese-stretching, which is essential to the success of any Pizza Hut campaign, the pies were hot—very hot. "Now remember," he said. "Forget the fat grams. Forget the carbs. This is the best pizza you've ever tasted. You're in pizza rapture." On cue, we enthusiastically sank our teeth into our slices. He hadn't been kidding about the "hot." I felt the sizzling cheese immediately graft itself to the roof of my mouth. My eyes started to water. My throat started to close up. *Pizza rapture. Pizza rapture,* I was thinking. But I couldn't take it. I gave the slice such a violent jerk that the sizzling toppings slid off the crust and flopped onto my chin, sending the production assistant running for the first aid kit. Dara got the part. And I ended up smelling like Ozonol for a week.

"So," I begin, lightly, "who am I reading for?"

I cross my fingers and look heavenward:

PleaseGodletitnotbeHazelGrippe. . . . PleaseGodletitnotbeHazel-Grippe. . . .

"Hazel Grippe," he announces.

Shit. I might as well just go home.

"Why? You know her?"

"Oh, I know her, all right," I grumble.

He opens the fingerprint-smudged door to the audition room. Like most audition spaces, the room seems expressly designed to cause as much anxiety as possible in every actor who walks into it. It's too

small, too cold, and too bright—more like a walk-in freezer than anything else. The argyle vest quickly hurries to a video camera set up in
the corner and begins puttering around it like an executioner polishing his gun.

There are two other people in the room, both sitting behind a
cluttered table. One is *Precinct*'s Emmy Award–winning director, Foster
Maclean, a middle-aged man with silver hair and a round belly. He's
leaning back in his chair, stroking his beard, his thumb hooked into a
loop on his multipocketed khaki vest. He seems to be staring with
great intensity at no particular spot on the floor. The other person, of
course, is Hazel Grippe. The most-feared casting director in the city.
Or at least the one I fear the most. With her glossy cap of red hair, her
red business suits, and her sharp little fuse of a nose, if you had to cate-
gorize Hazel as something other than a casting director, a stick of
dynamite wouldn't be too far down the list. She's furiously scribbling
on the back of someone's résumé and doesn't so much as glance in my
direction.

The director's gaze travels from no particular spot on the floor and
comes to rest in the general vicinity of my bustline. He squints and
strains curiously. I know what he's thinking:

Next!

Finally, Hazel puts down her pen. "Hello, Sally," she says tonelessly.

"H-hi, Hazel."

"Did you lighten your hair or something?"

"Uh . . . a little."

"Uh-huh," she says without approval. She reaches for her can of
Diet Coke with a menacing flurry of her red fingernails while quickly
glancing at my old leather jacket and jeans. "We asked everyone to
dress in character this time, Sally. Or at least to take an honest stab at
it."

"I know," I say apologetically. "But I was at work when I got the
call and I didn't have time to change."

She arches an eyebrow. "Well, at least you didn't wear the dress."

Wait a second. Did she say "the dress"? It can't be. She *couldn't* have said "the dress." All this time I've been telling myself that the reason Hazel Grippe hasn't hired me in eighteen months wasn't because of "the dress"—because that would be shallow and catty and unprofessional—but because I was too tall or too short or just wrong for the part. But there it is. She brought up the fucking dress.

"The dress?" the argyle vest asks.

"Last year," Hazel begins, "Sally and I showed up at a wrap party in the exact same little red Versace number, didn't we, Sally?"

The argyle vest lets out a loud gasp—the kind of hopeless, sympathetic noise people emit when they hear very young children are dying of cancer.

"It was a year and a *half* ago now," I correct Hazel, hoping to remind her it may be time to bury the hatchet.

"It was still a tad embarrassing, wasn't it?"

"It was worse for me." I laugh. I flatter. "You looked way better in yours."

"That's because *mine* wasn't a knockoff."

"That's enough," the director says. "Can we get on with this? My ass is falling asleep."

The argyle vest comes over with a Polaroid. "Say *Brie!*" he announces. The bulb flashes, eternally capturing what I am sure is the thespian equivalent of a deer caught in the headlights. Through the shifting phosphorescent images that follow the flash I hear Hazel's voice: "Okay, Sally. Knock us dead."

TWO

From his brimstone bed at break of day
A walking the Devil is gone,
To visit his snug little farm the earth,
And see how his stock goes on.

SAMUEL TAYLOR COLERIDGE AND ROBERT SOUTHEY

I bang the door to the audition room open and it slams against the wall. I mumble under my breath, storming down the hall, fighting tears. She cut me off! No, she didn't just cut me off. She pulled a Marie Antoinette on me. She dragged out the guillotine, called in Madame Defarge, and lopped off my fucking head!

This is what happened.

"May I help you, ssss—"

"Thank you, Sally. *Next.*"

"May I help you, ssss—?!" Who the hell can tell if a person is right for the part when all they get a chance to say is *"May I help you, ssss—?"*

White halls are whizzing by me. At the first rubbertree plant, I take a left.

It was probably my breasts. Maybe the director has a secret code or something he uses to get flat-chested women out of the room in a hurry. I *told* Gus this was nothing but a waste of time!

I take a right and stomp down another long white hall.

But what if it wasn't my breasts . . . ?

What if it was "the dress"? What if I never work again in this town all because I have the same taste in cocktail dresses as someone else?

A jolt of fear passes through me. What if it isn't the dress *or* my boobs? What if I'm just the worst actress in the world? What if the reason nobody's hiring me is because I have no talent? No future? No hope? Oh, damnit! That's what it is. That's *got* to be what it is. When am I going to stop making such a fool of myself and just go back to Wisconsin to finish my—

I skid to a halt in the corridor. My self-loathing dissipates for a minute. I'm standing in front of a rubbertree plant that doesn't look familiar. I don't remember that big dead leaf sticking up on top. I look around. Ominously quiet corridors stretch out in all directions. Come to think of it, nothing looks familiar.

Shit. I'm lost. Again.

I let out a big sigh, drop my tote bag to the floor, lean against the wall, and slide down to sit on my butt. I put my head in my hands.

What did I do wrong this morning?

I did my breathing exercises.

Spent the whole subway ride *visualizing* getting the part.

I even managed to squeeze in a few minutes of yoga before I left— so what if I was too tired to do Downward Dog?

Maybe I wasn't inclusive enough in my little pre-audition prayer. What if I left somebody out? My mind flashcards through a list of gods, hospitable and inhospitable both, I could have called upon for help. Maybe ignoring one of them is tantamount to forgetting to thank the studio boss in an Oscars acceptance speech or something. Maybe your career just never recovers.

Okay. *Please . . . God . . . Buddha . . . Allah . . . whoever!!! Even if I don't worship you on a regular basis . . . all I want is a little luck. . . . Is that too much to ask? I'd do anything for one lousy break!*

I stare heavenward, waiting for some indication that my prayers are being answered. As usual, the heavens are quiet. But I do see something—or, rather, *sense* something—in my periphery. A man in a black suit is standing at the other end of the hall, his arms crossed, his shoulder leaning against the wall; he's just watching me.

"Hi there," he says. His voice echoes over to me. Full. Calm.

"Uh, hi," I say, standing up, brushing my jeans.

"Need some help?"

I laugh weakly. "Is it *that* obvious?"

"I'm afraid so."

"If you could just point me in the general direction of the elevators, I'd be"—but he's already walking over to me—"eternally grateful."

As the distance between us closes, I get a better look at him. His gait is long and loose and the jacket of his black suit billows with each step. He has dark hair and dark, deep-set eyes. His face is full of angles, a jut of cheekbone, a slash of jaw, that seemed harsh from a distance but have settled into a welcoming smile now that he's close enough that I get a better look at him. He seems to have an energy that hums about him tangibly—snapping and kinetic.

"Follow me," he says.

"Thanks. . . ."

We turn down a corridor and I scissor-step after him, my tote bag jingling with makeup and keys. "This is really great of you. I don't know what it is about this place, but I always get lost in here. Actors have a nickname for it. . . ."

He gives me a sly smile. "I've heard."

We walk in silence for a moment. I find myself drawn to look at him. He has what I think you call a ruddy complexion, a kind of manly red you only see in aftershave commercials. Red from sky diving. Mountain climbing. Sailing the ocean blue. I see the flash of a platinum watch beneath his cuff. Great hair—wavy and not too fussy. He catches me staring and I look away, embarrassed.

We turn a corner and I exhale in relief when I see the bank of elevators.

"Thanks so much," I say.

"Any time." He presses the DOWN button for me. "When you get to the bottom, it's straight out the door to Fifty-fourth."

"That part I know." I turn to face the closed elevator doors. I expect him to leave. I want him to leave, actually, so I can stew in my anger awhile longer.

But he doesn't. He just stands there, watching me. It's then that I realize his eyes aren't as dark as I thought they were; they seemed almost black at first, but there's an inner glow to them, like candlelight reflected on wood.

"You waiting for the elevator, too?" I ask him.

He shakes his head.

"Oh . . . well, thanks again." I give him a little wave, as if to let him know I can take it from here. I press the DOWN button again. But he's still watching me.

"Are you okay?" he asks.

"Who, me?" I say in a too-innocent voice. "Of course I'm okay. Why wouldn't I be okay?"

"Just a feeling I have."

"I'm fine," I say. And then, through clenched teeth: "Couldn't be *better.*" I ram the DOWN button again, this time so hard that the top third of my index finger turns white from bending the wrong way. He's still staring at me, so I turn to face him. "Look, I really hate to be rude, because I appreciate your help and everything, but I've just come from a world record–breakingly bad audition and I think it would be best for both of us if I didn't take it out on you."

"Ahh—an actress," he says. "Or do you say *actor?*"

"Doesn't matter. It's past tense, anyway. I've had it. I quit. I am now going to go home and contemplate a glamorous career in, oh, I don't know—telemarketing or something."

He laughs at that and for the first time all day I actually feel good. I like the sound of his laugh. Kind of warm and relaxed, expanding a little in his chest.

The elevator dings open. He holds the doors for me—a needless, though pleasant act of chivalry—and I step inside.

"About the audition?" he says. "Forget it. I have a feeling you're going to be just fine."

"Tell that to my agent."

"Trust me. I'm a great judge of character." He gives one last smile and backs away from the doors, letting them close.

I feel a tight compression in my chest as he disappears from view. I press G. The elevator gives an unnerving bounce and starts to descend. I watch the little numbers light up and go dark one at a time.

I have a feeling you're going to be just fine. God, the confidence in his voice. It's as if he's the sort of person who actually believes that.

. . . 16, 15, 14 . . .

I wonder who he is. . . .

. . . 10, 9, 8 . . .

Very cute, anyway!

. . . 4, 3, 2 . . .

Then I remember Hazel.

The bitch.

THREE

An apology for the Devil: It must be remembered
that we have only heard one side of the case.
God has written all the books.

SAMUEL BUTLER

IN case you haven't figured it out, I haven't become independently wealthy on my acting career. I work at the Backburner, a used-book store in the Village, five days a week. The hours are pretty flexible, which is good for auditions (when I get them), and it sure beats waiting on tables.

The Backburner is a narrow, run-down, street-level shop with grimy windows and a crumbling brick facade that, judging from the color of it, hasn't been painted since the Great Depression. There's something misshapen and slumping about the place, as if it were a drunken old derelict who only remains standing through the grudging support of the broad-shouldered buildings surrounding it.

I'm about to open the dusty front door when something thonks me in the leg. I look down to see a lean black dog dashing out of the store.

"Mangy bloodhound!" I hear a hoarse voice cry. A cellophane-wrapped collector's edition of *Penthouse* (the one with Cindy Crawford in it) flies out the doorway after it. The dog yelps pitifully as the magazine catches it on the rear end. The poor animal curls around behind me, tucking its tail between its legs and shivering.

"Jeremy!" I scream. "Don't be so mean!"

Jeremy stands angrily in the doorway, threateningly brandishing a back issue of the *Utne Reader.* Jeremy owns the Backburner. He's a tall, painfully thin man in his late forties somewhere, with stooped shoulders and long, skinny arms. He has sunken gray eyes, a sickly complexion, and bristly silver hair. He wears a dingy sleeveless undershirt and baggy brown pants. The hollows in his cheeks and temples are so deep, it looks like you could rest golf balls there.

"Poor puppy dog," I coo, bending down and taking the dog's thick black head between my hands. "Poor, poor doggie."

"Jesus, Sally, it's a stray. Have you no idea what kind of diseases those things carry?"

But I ignore him, rumpling the dog's ears playfully. The dog makes a little whimpering noise in its throat. His fur is mangy. His eyes a warm golden brown. When he's wagging his tail and licking my hand happily, I decide he's okay. I give him one last pat, pick up the *Penthouse,* and go into the store. The rusted bell above the door lets out a pathetic brassy tinkle.

Jeremy's striding to the back. "You're late. *Again*. Sometimes I feel like a cheap paparazzo with nothing better to do with my time but sit around and wait for you to make an appearance."

"I'm sorry, Jeremy. They were running behind and then I got lost at the—"

But he doesn't listen to the rest of my explanation. The grimy floral curtain strung up across the doorway at the back of the shop flaps decisively closed. I let out a hopeless sigh. I know better than to disturb him when he's back there.

I pull off my jacket. As usual, the torn lining in the sleeve catches on my street-Gucci. It takes a moment before I can unhook it from the clasp of the watch. I toss the jacket in a ball under the counter and assume my position on the wooden stool behind the cash register. I sigh and look around the place. There are two tall aisles of bookshelves that stretch to the back like great, densely planted rows of beanstalks. Banks of fluorescent lights line the ceiling, but Jeremy can't stand fluorescent light, so the shop remains in a perpetual state of gloom, the only illumination provided by a few shelf lamps and whatever daylight can filter through the front windows, so thick with grime, a kid couldn't resist scratching FUCK YOU on the glass last winter and we'd need a sandblaster if we wanted to get it off. Along the window ledge, the carcasses of spiders and houseflies are turned upside down like rumpled balls of black thread and the planks of the wooden floor are worn thin in places—especially in the Erotica section and in front of the cash.

The whole place smells of dust, must, and charcoal. Charcoal. Not what you'd expect in a bookstore, but smudges of charcoal are all over the place—on the cash register keys, the counter, the light switches, the phone—like blasts of black gunpowder from Yosemite Sam's gun. The charcoal's from Jeremy. He's a sketch artist. He spends most of the day holed up in his back room working on his beloved charcoal nudes. He only does nudes. Nude men. Nude women. Nude "ideas," as he sometimes calls them. His sketches are extremely explicit. They have the same disquieting effect on me the drawings in *The Joy of Sex* did when I first saw them: They kind of gross me out and make me horny at the same time. All those half-closed eyes and hairy triangles and things disappearing into holes I thought were there for other reasons.

Jeremy doesn't have much luck selling his work, but he doesn't care. He says true artists are only appreciated after they're dead. And he should know. He's a genius, after all. An official genius with a 160 IQ and everything.

Suddenly the phone rings. A stray prayer shoots through my head. *Pleasepleasepleaseletmegetthepart!* "Backburner Books?"

"Okay, calm down. It's only me."

"Oh, hi, sweetie," I say, letting the tension out of my breath. It's my boyfriend, David; we met in an acting class three years ago and we've been going out ever since.

"So? How'd it go?" he asks.

"Don't ask," I say.

"Did you have to read for Hazel?"

"I said, don't ask."

"Shit. You had to read for Hazel. What happened?"

"She cut me off."

"Oh *no* . . ."

"I knew she was still pissed about the dress."

"Don't say that, Sal. There's no way that dress could still be—"

"Oh yeah? Then why did she bring it up?"

"You're kidding? She brought it up?"

"Yep."

"Shit." A note of awed hopelessness wavers through David's voice and I know he's digging through his own shallow well of confidence for something to buoy my spirits. It takes a moment, but he finally comes up with our standby: "Don't be too down about it, Sal. Remember, Danny Aiello didn't—"

And we both finish the rest in unison: "—get his big break till he was forty."

"Yeah, I know, David." I sigh forlornly, punch in a customer who's bought two copies of the same Piers Anthony book. Questions like that, like why someone would buy two copies of the same Piers Anthony book, used to intrigue me when I first started working here. They don't anymore. Questions get kind of pointless when you know you never have a shot at the answers.

"It was just one thing after another," I tell David, sending the Piers Anthony guy on his way. "First of all, Dara Dempsey was there. Being all sweet and sappy like we're best friends or something. Then Hazel did her hatchet job on me. Then—naturally—I got lost in the halls." I have a brief urge to tell him about the guy in the black suit, but I stop myself and don't know why.

David says, "Maybe we should go out tonight. Drown your sorrows. I get off at eleven." (David's a waiter on the side the same way I'm a bookstore clerk on the side.)

"Nah. I'm gonna crash early. The sooner I'm unconscious, the better."

"How about I swing by later? I'll bring my key in case you're sleeping."

"Sure."

"Take it easy, Sal. I love ya."

"I love ya, too."

I hang up and give the phone an angry squeeze. *No more false alarms, you bastard!* I flop back onto my wooden stool, glaring at the phone one last time. It seems I spend half my life waiting for the phone to ring. Waiting for calls from my agent. Calls from a casting director. Calls from anyone who could tell me that I'm not wasting my time, my youth, my entire *life,* trying to become an actor in New York. Do you know that I read somewhere that professional actors are so rare that they're statistically nonexistent? They're mythical beings. Like angels or unicorns or gods.

Suddenly I hear loud, prolonged crashing from the back of the store. There are a few screams. More banging. A distinctly harsh *"Bleeding tarts of the sea!"* as Jeremy kicks away at his easel. The few uncertain customers in the store look to me nervously, then to the curtain, which billows and puffs. Jeremy's gaunt face pokes out from the dingy floral fabric.

"You're going to hear the chair go over in a moment," he says breathlessly, "then the snapping of a rope. Give me twenty minutes, then call the morgue." He disappears back behind the curtain.

A customer looks at me uncertainly. "Don't worry." I shrug. "He does this all the time."

The person frowns, looks to the back of the store, where there's more banging and crashing. There's a moment of silence. Then a triumphant howl.

"Never mind!" he calls. "I'm a *genius!*"

I raise my eyebrows at the customer. "See?" is all I say.

By eight o'clock, the early September sky is pink and blue and mauve, all fused together airily like spun-sugar remnants in the bottom of a cotton candy drum. I call good-bye to Jeremy, but he ignores me. Strangely, the black dog is waiting for me when I get outside. It's sitting beside a parking meter; its slightly flea-bitten tail wags when it sees me.

"Hi, there," I say curiously.

It stands up and shifts its weight excitedly from foot to foot, looking behind me, as if checking to see whether or not it's going to take another *Penthouse* in the rear. I get down beside it, taking its dark head in my hands again.

"Are you lost or something?" I look into its eyes. The light brown color seems to drop away into the black pupil as if into a deep hole. It makes me slightly uneasy. I stand up and begin to walk away from the store. I hear its nails clicking on the dry sidewalk behind me. It falls in beside me, then trots on ahead a little, sniffing at lampposts, storefronts, parking meters, occasionally looking back to make sure I'm still there.

"Poor thing," I say, half to myself. I notice it doesn't have a collar and its coat is nicked here and there with welts. I can't believe there's any affection left in it at all. Dogs. Such stupid creatures. You can beat them half to death and they always come back with their tails wagging. I guess people are that way, too. Actors especially. I mean, look at me. Since I came to New York, I can count the number of paying gigs I've had on one hand, but I still stick around, waiting to get slapped down one more time.

I'm originally from Tecumseh Falls, Wisconsin; it's a suburb of Milwaukee. My mother still lives there, in the same run-down little bungalow where I grew up. She has the same job she's had for as long as I can remember, working as a clerk in the forest of beige legs that is the women's hosiery department of the local JCPenney. And although I

haven't seen her since the Christmas before last, I'm sure she's still dye-
ing her hair the same shade of Nice 'n' Easy brown she's been using for
twenty years. We don't talk much. Maybe once a month. She doesn't
like the fact I'm living alone in New York trying to act. She never
misses an opportunity to tell me that I should do something safe and
normal with my life—like my older brother. He works on an oil rig
off the coast of Alaska. I guess anything's safer than trying to be an
actor in New York.

You probably haven't heard of Tecumseh Falls. Its main claim to
fame is its ice cream, which has won gold medals at international ice
cream competitions every consecutive year since 1936. Except, of
course, for 1969 and 1970 after hippies on a local commune broke
into the dairy one night and let all the cattle go as a protest against eating red meat. When they realized you don't actually *eat* dairy cattle,
they apologized, but still, the damage had been done. The two empty
spaces on the plaque wall at City Hall are a constant reminder of the
cruel hand of fate.

The other big industry back home, of course, is Milwaukee's
famous breweries. I always thought it was strange to come from a place
known for its ice cream and its beer. I wondered if it didn't cause some
kind of permanent rift in the souls of the people who lived there—a
sort of confusion about what was right and wrong. It was an irony that
certainly wasn't lost on my father, who drove an ice cream delivery
truck by day and went above and beyond the call of duty to support
the local breweries at night. I was ten when the accident happened
and everything changed after that. Everything. It's one of my *Enquirer*
"Dark Secrets." One of the things that, if I ever get famous—*Please-
pleasepleaseletmegetfamous!*—the paparazzi will taunt me with.

"*Sally! Hey, Sally!*" they'll scream. "*Is it true about your father?*"

"*Tell us about it, Sally! What kind of gun did he use?*"

And I'll batter my way through them: "*Leave me alone, you parasites!
Have you no shame?*"

It started out as just another average June evening. My dad had finished his deliveries early and had stopped at the bar for a couple of "cool-me-downs," as he called them. Then he had a couple more. He left around 8:30, as far as the bartender could figure. He didn't seem too drunk to drive. At least not more than usual.

It was a beautiful night and most of the neighborhood kids, including me, were out on the street, playing hide-and-seek or sneaking cigarettes. Tommy Bishop was out that night, too. He was six years old. He had just gotten rid of his training wheels and was so excited that at all hours of the day, and well after the streetlights came on, you could see him pumping his little bicycle up and down the block. Tecumseh Falls was the sort of place where kids could play until after the sun went down. A neighborhood of families and friends.

My dad's ice cream truck swerved onto the street about 8:45, as witness statements showed. Apparently he didn't see Tommy on his bike. He said it was dark, that the streetlight was broken, that the kid was too small to be on a bike anyway. But none of it really mattered because he blew point fifty or something like that on the Breathalyzer at the hospital two hours later. He didn't know he'd hit Tommy. He didn't know anything was wrong at all, in fact. He dragged the boy half a block before the frame of the bike finally ground into the gears of the truck and brought it to a stop. Tommy Bishop died in the hospital later that night.

His parents wanted to charge my father with Second-Degree Murder, but would settle for Willful Negligence Causing Death if it meant putting my father behind bars where he belonged. The dairy had to suspend my father for the duration of the trial. The stress was incredible for him. He stayed home with the curtains drawn all day long while my mother went to work. He opened beer bottle after beer bottle and chain-smoked cigarettes until his fingertips turned the same color as caution lights.

It was two days before the trial when something in him just snapped. I don't know. Maybe the ice cream side of his soul took over or something and he couldn't take it anymore. I was coming home from the grocery store—I was running a lot of errands for my mother that summer, trying to help her around the house—when I saw the police cars parked outside our bungalow. Although cruisers and news vans had been a normal sight on our street right after the accident, it had been a while since I had seen so many of them. I knew something was wrong. Another funny thing was that the ice cream truck was in the driveway. I knew my father wasn't allowed to drive the ice cream truck anymore and I hadn't seen it in almost two months. I'm not sure how I managed to scramble through the legs of all the neighbors and police officers. I only know that when everyone saw me standing there beside the ice cream truck, they started screaming and pulling me away. I wasn't sure what had happened, only that there was a splash of bright red gunk on the driver's side window of the truck. It looked like ice cream really, a strawberry ripple sundae with crushed walnuts, all smeared against the glass. The police dragged me away before I saw anything else. They carried me to sit with my mother, in the stale living room, where she was hunched over, clutching her rosary beads in her hands, crying even harder than she had all those weeks since Tommy Bishop died.

It was hours before the police took the ice cream van away. So long in fact that the ice cream in the back melted into a great pool that ran in a sweet river down the driveway to the gutter. Children played in it, dragging sticky footprints and bike wheel ribbons across the pavement. Neighborhood dogs came to lap at it. It seemed days before it rained and the smell of melted ice cream was totally washed away from the neighborhood. More than anything else, the smell is what I remember. Ever since it happened, I've never been able to stand the smell of melted ice cream on a hot summer day.

FOUR

And the Lord said unto Satan, Whence comest thou?
Then Satan answered the Lord, and said, From going to and fro
in the earth, and from walking up and down in it.

JOB 1:7

I live in an ancient six-story walk-up above a convenience store on a corner of Sullivan Street. The brickwork has been painted over so many times in shades of rust, green, and gray that the mortar of the place has all but disappeared and the entire facade ripples gloomily as if layer upon layer of medieval candle wax has melted, dried, then melted again. It doesn't help that the fire escapes bristling along the front of the building have been painted with so much thick black enamel that the place gleams with perpetual wetness day or night. When I first moved here, there used to be a great view of the World Trade Center from the roof. Not that I usually looked at the World Trade Center. If I was up there for a barbecue or tending to my (ill-fated) herb garden or watching Mr. Kellock, the nice old man from the second floor, feed his pigeons, I always faced my lawn chair north, so I could see the Chrysler Building or the Empire State. Now I face south sometimes, and stare at the empty space, and try to remember. . . . When I can't take it anymore, I turn the lawn chair around and face the other way.

The building sits directly across from an old church, St. Francis de Sales, a large pale-bricked cathedral of a place with dark archways and heavy wooden doors. The center arch strains higher than the others and above it, overlooking the neighborhood like the eye of a giant Cyclops, is a single stained-glass window that is dark and sleeping during the day but that glows like a giant disk of fire at night. Adding to the otherworldliness of the place are the figures of nuns, in their black-and-white habits, floating quietly up and down the street between the church and the convent that sits a block deeper into SoHo.

I shouldn't be able to afford a place in such a great neighborhood. With my income I should be relegated to a building several subway tangles out of Manhattan itself. But the apartment finder I hooked up with happened to have the same last name as mine, so she put me at the top of the waiting list for a rent-stabilized place that hadn't come open since the Nixon administration (the old woman who used to live here had finally gone into a rest home).

I jingle my keys into the lock of the front street-level door. The dog bats his front paws back and forth on the sidewalk.

"Bye for now," I tell him. "Go home, boy. Go home." But he paces excitedly back and forth, wagging his tail, making squeaking noises in his throat, in a pitiful attempt to keep me from leaving him alone.

I feel the weight of happy resignation. "Okay. You can stay if you want. But just for tonight." I open the door and he hurries in past my legs, running into the cramped lobby.

The place smells of mildew and dirty mops. I check my mail slot. A bill from Bloomingdale's, a letter from NYU reminding me I owe them money for a night class I took in *commedia dell'arte,* and some junk mail, the last of which I toss in the small recycling bin in the corner.

I am surprised when the dog dashes on ahead of me, up the stairs two flights, then crisscrosses back and forth, smelling the worn carpet, before he comes to stop directly in front of my door on the third floor.

"Good boy," I say, oddly impressed. I unlock my door and he squeezes by in front of me.

The place is officially called a "junior one-bedroom" in that other than the living/bedroom area, there's a separate kitchen that's just big enough for the appliances and a two-seater beat-up Formica kitchen set that I almost never use. The main room contains a navy futon from Futon Joe's that rolls into a sofa during the day (when I bother to roll it up, that is), a beat-up trunk that serves as a coffee table, a couple of odds and ends to sit lamps and books on, and my small black-and-white portable TV. I ragged the walls myself in a blue-green combination, hoping for a marbleizing effect; what I got was distinctly closer to mold. The bathroom is tiny (shower, no tub), with original black-and-white tiles that have settled and sagged so badly over the years that they swerve off in different directions, creating the optical illusion that the room is shrinking in one corner and expanding in the next. The place smells like me: instant coffee and dirty jeans, cheap Chilean wine, and the occasional cigarette. The dog doesn't seem to mind any of it, sniffing around from one tiny room to another, then back again, his claws catching awkwardly on the aged brown indoor-outdoor carpet.

I pour him a bowl of water and look in the fridge for something for him to eat. A couple of slices of veggie bologna past their best-before date. I rip them up and put the pieces on the floor next to the water. He munches them happily.

The answering machine is flashing; I hit REWIND and recognize my agent's gravelly voice in reverse. *Damn.* She's probably calling to give me shit for screwing up the *Precinct* audition. Fifteen percent of nothing doesn't buy a lot of loyalty in this business.

"Sal? You there? If you're there, pick up." Gus waits a few beats. "I know for a fact you don't have a life, so where the hell could you be? Awright, awright, give me a call as soon as you get in. You're not gonna believe this—because I sure don't—but you must've done something right at the audition. I just got a call from Hazel Grippe." Her voice tightens excitedly. "You got a callback, Sal! They want to see you again tomorrow!"

I stare, dumbfounded, at the answering machine. Then clasp my hands together and look heavenward.

Thankyouthankyouthankyou. . . .

Nowpleasepleasepleaseletmegetthepart!

FIVE

The Devil never sleeps.

ST. CATHERINE OF SIENA

THE room is a swarming sea of blue-blackness when I wake up to the sound of a dog barking. First in a dream. And then echoing off the walls of my apartment. The dog's barks warp and twist in a throaty, metallic way. My heart hammers in a panic when I see the oblong of light coming in from the hall. The door's open. Someone's broken in! *Oh, I knew it! I knew it!* My mother always said this was going to happen to me! Hacked to death in my own bed! *Raped first probably and then stabbed—oh, I don't know how many times—twenty-six, twenty-seven. . . .* I'm thinking all this in the split second it's taking me to reach beneath the edge of my futon and find the wooden handle of a butcher knife I keep there for just such an emergency. I picture the guys from *Law & Order* standing over my body with sober expressions on their faces: *Such a mess—he must've really had it in for her.* My hand closes down on the knife handle and I slide it out. In a flash I remember a self-defense manual I read about how to hold a knife if you don't want it used against you, when I recognize David's voice: "Sally! Jesus! Help me!"

I reach over and flick on the light. David is plastered up against the far wall, his lips trembling, his ponytail shaken loose. He's holding a greasy take-out bag over his head. The dog is two feet in front of him, barking and growling.

"What . . . the . . . fuck . . . is *that?*" David stammers.

"A dog."

"I can *see* that." There's a vicious snarl. Saliva drips from the dog's jaws. "I mean what's it doing here?"

I put down the knife and scramble off the bed. "He followed me home." I crawl over to the dog slowly, not wanting to make any sudden movements.

"Sally, be careful!" he says. I can see his knees trembling beneath his baggy cargo shorts. David is tall (ish) and quite slim (from running four times a week), with a pale complexion and long, wavy brown hair he usually wears in a ponytail. He used to have a goatee and a nose ring, too, but his agent was always on his back to change his look because it was limiting his appeal in auditions. David didn't want to cut his hair, so he and the agent compromised. He lost the nose ring, shaved the goatee, and gave his agent an extra 5 percent. The hair stayed.

I move toward the dog and slip my hands around his neck. "Shh, boy. It's okay . . . it's okay, sweetie. . . ." The dog whimpers softly. He licks my face. "It's just David. He's not going to hurt me."

"That's right, boy, I'm not going—" But the mere sound of David's voice aggravates the dog and he starts barking again. I feel the hoarse vibrations in his body. I'm shocked by the strength rippling in the muscles beneath his fur.

"Maybe he wants this," David says, holding up his greasy take-out bag.

"Try it."

David tosses the bag to the floor, kicking it over. But the dog barely registers it, growling more menacingly than ever.

I can't help but laugh. "Okay, so it's not that."

"I have a real way with animals, don't I?" he says.

All at once, I can't control the dog anymore. He slips from my grasp and lunges at David, who slides against the wall and out of the way just in time. The dog gives one last angry howl, then dashes out the still-open doorway to the hall.

"Did he get you?" I ask.

"I don't think so." He inspects his limbs just to be sure. "You better go get him, Sal. Before half the neighborhood needs rabies shots."

I tiptoe into the hall; I'm only wearing my pajama bottoms and an old tank top. "Here, boy," I whisper. I whistle softly, so as not to wake the neighbors. "Here, boy. . . ."

I pad barefoot down the stairs to the vestibule and am relieved to see him standing by the front door, panting patiently.

"You wanna go out?" I ask him. His tail wags once. He seems as sweet and harmless as he did this afternoon. "Okay," I say, curious and maybe a little hurt. I unlatch the door. He slips out quickly. "Good night, boy," I say. I watch for a moment as he crosses the street. He looks back once, then disappears into the night. I feel a pang of regret. Like I might miss him.

I hurry back up to my apartment, locking the door. "Sorry about that. I don't know what happened. He was . . ."

But I stop. I hear a distinct *pop* from the kitchen. I move to stand in the doorway. I see David pouring two glasses of champagne. He gives me a sly grin.

"Hope Cujo didn't ruin the mood," he says, "because *we've* got some *celebrating* to do."

I groan tiredly. I left him a message with my news. "David, it's just a *callback.*"

"So? When's the last time you had a callback?"

"Don't remind me."

"Here." He hands me my glass. "Let's toast. To Sally—who's going to support me in my old age with her royalty checks. Come on. Drink. It's the best champagne money can buy."

We both take a sip, smiling at each other. But our eyes go wide. Our cheeks are puffed out. We stare at each other helplessly for a moment, then bend over, spitting into the sink.

"I should've specified," he says, tasting his tongue. "The best champagne *my* money can buy. At least there's *this.*" He holds up a partially crushed Styrofoam container containing some soggy fries and what looks like it might have started out life as a cheeseburger.

"I shouldn't," I tell him. "I'll probably retain every ounce of water I drink for the next twelve hours." But the aroma of the fries wafts up to me. "What the hell." I grab the ketchup bottle and we both go into the living room, sitting cross-legged on the futon, the container between us.

"You nervous?" he asks, holding the mashed cheeseburger. He comes at it from a few angles, figuring out how best to eat it. A disk of tomato slides out.

"Who *me?* Nervous? *Pshaw.*" I flap my hand in the air. I pick at the fries. "I wonder if Dara got a callback. Did you hear anything?"

"Beats me. They don't let us talk to the *real* actors."

Besides being a waiter, David has a part-time gig on *Dusk Until Dawn*—the soap opera Dara is on. He's a background player in the restaurant scenes (in other words, he's an "extra"). When he got the part six months ago, he thought it was going to be his big break. Unfortunately the show refuses to pay him for a speaking part so he has yet to utter a line. He just walks around opening fake wine bottles and quietly taking orders from other background players. Most of the time you don't even get to see his face.

"Guess how many lines I had today?" he asks rhetorically. Then makes a big "0" with his thumb and forefinger. *"Nada.* Zippo. Zilch. But . . . guess how many tables I waited on?"

"How many?"

He looks up, as if pretending to count. "Well, let's see. Thirty-three at the studio today. And twenty-one at the restaurant tonight. How is it possible that I can wait on more tables as an actor *playing* a waiter on

TV than I do as an *actual* waiter in real life? Stanislavsky would be proud of me. I'm *in the moment*—all day."

I laugh. He gives up on the cheeseburger, dropping it back into the box. Then he looks at me, a suggestive smile on his face. "The celebration isn't over yet," he says. He starts crawling over to me.

I back away, my voice wary. "David . . ."

"Come on, sweetie. . . ."

"Not tonight . . . I have to be up early . . ."

He pulls out his ponytail, shaking his hair free. I laugh a little as his cold lips touch my neck, sending goose bumps along my skin. "I'm too tired . . ."

"Come on . . . it'll help you sleep . . ."

"Please, David . . ." I try to push him away, but every time my hands go over, his go under; every time mine go under, his go around. It's as if men have the surefootedness of mountain goats when it comes to a stubborn female libido.

"David . . . come *on* . . . I said *no*. I need my sleep."

But a little voice is easing its way into my consciousness: *Sally, don't be so selfish. This is your boyfriend—your lover. He's happy for you—he just wants to make love. What's wrong with that? What are you—FRIGID?*

I glance at the clock.

1:23.

Oh, all right. The sooner I get this started, the sooner I can get back to sleep. I slip my arms around his neck. We lie down together. He moves on top of me, his elbow hitting my chin.

"Sorry," he whispers.

" 'S okay. . . ."

We're still kissing as I bat around on the end table for a condom—I could've sworn I saw one there today. Ah, got it. There are more moans, more kisses, I feel the surface of my skin get hot, my eyes close very deeply, and I move toward the darkness . . .

But by 1:28 it's over. My heart rate is up and there's sweat on my forehead, but that's about it.

By 1:36, he's sound asleep.

And I'm staring at the ceiling craving more of those fries.

Damn.

I get up and begin searching for a cigarette instead. I don't smoke all the time. Just when I'm anxious. Unfortunately for my lungs, I'm anxious a lot. I find a crumpled package of Marlboro Lights in the bottom of my tote bag. I shake out a cigarette and put it between my lips, lighting it with a match that burns so brightly I have to squint against the flame. I move to the window and exhale into the night. I see the darkened stained-glass window of the church.

PleasepleasepleaseGodletmegetthepart.

I don't want you to get the impression I'm a religious freak or anything, always praying to God to help me in auditions. But you know what they say about "no atheists in the foxholes"? The same adage holds true for audition rooms.

Besides, it was a little hard not to be affected by my mother's Catholic roots when I was growing up. Despite the fact my father wasn't religious *("Nothing but a bunch of superstitious claptrap for people with weak minds"),* my mother was. She considered herself a "good Catholic." She said grace before every meal (even if it meant doing it by herself and very quickly), went to confession once a week, and even managed to drag my brother, Paul, and me to church sometimes. Christmas, Easter, and the odd Sunday morning when my father was too hungover to put up a fight. It was funny to come from a home where two people could have such opposing ideas about God. It made me think that God wasn't the Absolute in our house he was in other families. It was almost as if God were a relative—an in-law, perhaps. My maternal grandmother, for instance, got much the same treatment in our house.

I never told my father, but I was always on the *"There is a God"* side of things. I liked the idea of God watching over us, sort of like a year-round Santa Claus who could always tell if we were being naughty or nice. I also enjoyed going to church with my mother. I liked to watch her cross herself and count her rosary beads and respond to the priest on cue . . . *And also with you* . . . like all the other grown-ups. Outside of church, the only thing she seemed to be so comfortable doing was working in the kitchen—and in the late seventies and eighties that was starting to get square.

I also think I had a special connection to God because of the plastic Jesus. My mother had a plastic Jesus on a shelf in the kitchen next to the stove. (She also kept a crucifix above her bed, but that just scared me.) I remember sitting in the kitchen every morning, eating my Froot Loops and staring at the plastic Jesus. He was about the same size as Barbie and Ken—I know this, because I took him down a few times and let him ride around in my Malibu Barbie Camper. When my mother caught me, she gave me the hardest slap on the butt she ever had. "That's not a *toy!*" she said, putting it back in its place on the shelf. But the connection was already made. Me and the plastic Jesus had a special relationship. I couldn't help it. With his long hair and beard, he just seemed cooler than Ken, and I was too young to comprehend just how inappropriate it was to feel this way. Nobody else seemed to pay much attention to him. Certainly not my father, who always sat with his back facing that wall because he thought the statue was "creepy." My brother, Paul, who usually skipped breakfast altogether, only briefly popping into the kitchen to swig orange juice from the container while three separate applications of Final Net Ultra Hold dried on his Eddie Van Halen hair, didn't seem to notice Jesus either. Not even my mother paid much attention to him. She was always too busy making our lunches or fixing breakfast or getting ready for work herself (a process that included much yelling at my brother to *give her back her hair spray!* and applying such a garish combination of green eye shadow, coral lipstick, and white under-eye concealer that, in certain lighting, she bore a distinct resemblance to a faded Italian flag).

But I liked the plastic Jesus. He seemed so peaceful and happy, standing with his arms gently outstretched and the hem of his blue

robe parted to reveal one sandaled foot. I had been to church enough
to know that Jesus had sacrificed himself for our sins. That he taught us
to do unto others as we would have done unto ourselves. And that he
said things like *"Thou shalt not kill."*

Shalt.

Unto.

Sacrifice.

These were all grown-up words. Whenever I asked my mother to
explain them to me, she told me it just meant I had to be "nice."

Of course, my ideas about God changed a lot after Tommy
Bishop's accident, and then even more after my father died. But everything changed that summer. . . .

I feel an unpleasant tug on my conscience. I try to shake it off.

*Don't think about it, Sally. You've got enough to worry about with the call-
back.*

I exhale the last of my cigarette and mash it into the ashtray. I
crawl back into bed and, with one last silent prayer into the ether—
Pleasepleasepleaseletmegetthepart—I fall asleep.

SIX

Even Satan disguises himself as an angel of light.

2 CORINTHIANS 11:14

UBN is situated on a sunless, windy block in the very hub of network land. It's a tall, sleek building that soars up into the sky like a great black monolith, neither reflecting nor absorbing the light. In the last few seasons, UBN has catapulted from fifth to second place in the ratings. Some say it's because of Emmy Award–winning hits like *Precinct;* others say it's because they snagged the rights to Yankee baseball last year; still others think it's because they stole the *Friends* spin-offs from NBC. Whatever the case, the building no longer feels like the makeshift home of a scrambling underdog. It has a mystique all its own. Every actor who passes beneath the imposing logo over the front door now automatically stands a little taller and starts breathing straight from the diaphragm.

Half an hour early for my callback (I wasn't gonna be late this time), I'm pacing back and forth outside the building, fighting the urge to have a cigarette and going over my lines in my head.

Good morning, sir! *Welcome to First Fidelity. . . . May I help you? Good morning, sir. . . .*

Hazel will be happy to see I dressed in character today, in a slightly outdated navy suit I bought at a thrift store two years ago and a pair of cheap black pumps from Payless. It's my standard Office-Worker-Audition ensemble and the closest thing I have to what a bank teller might wear—or what I *think* a bank teller might wear, having not actually stood in line at a bank since the invention of ATM cards.

Good morning, sir. . . . Welcome to First Fidelity. . . .

Good morning, sir. . . .

Well, maybe just *one.*

I dig through my tote bag for the package of Marlboro Lights. I try to get the cigarette lit, but the wind is so bad, the match keeps blowing out. I sidle up close to the building to find a pocket of still-ness. Three matches later, I take a big, calming inhale. *That's better.* I catch a glimpse of my reflection in the glass doors to the lobby. I lean forward to straighten my hair a bit. I falter when I see a dark shadow between my eyebrows. I narrow my eyes and take a closer look. *Damn!* It's not a shadow! It's my frown lines. I massage them furiously, trying to get them to relax. I've got to stop frowning so much when I'm nervous. Wrinkles will come and that's fine. Little lines around your eyes? Laugh lines? Like Michelle Pfeiffer or Sharon Stone? No prob-lem. But *frown lines?* Evidence that you worry? Concentrate? Have negative emotions of any kind? No way. You can grow old (a little), but what was it they used to say in that deodorant commercial? "Never let 'em see you sweat."

"Salleee!!" I hear a lilty voice. I turn to see Dara Dempsey getting out of a cab.

Damnit! She *did* get a callback. I wish she'd get some debilitating disease or something and let the rest of us have a chance.

She leans in the passenger-side window to pay the driver, the hem of her mini-skirt flapping in the wind. Then she turns and tiptoes over to me. I can see the telltale crumples of her push-up bra beneath the thin fabric of her blouse. Doesn't it piss you off when women who don't *need* push-up bras wear them? Kind of ruins the effect for the rest of us.

"Oh, goodee! You got a callback, *too?*"

"Yep." I shrug as if I'm stunned, which I am.

She puts her small hand in my elbow and swerves me an air kiss. "We didn't get much of a chance to talk yesterday. We *hafto-hafto-hafto* get together more often."

"Absolutely," I say, but I'm thinking, *Yeah, right. I bet I don't have enough SAG credits for you.*

"What are you doing after the callback?" she asks. "You want to go for a coffee or something?"

I shrug. "Sorry. I have to work."

"Too bad." She *tsks,* softly. She twists her slim wrist to glance at her watch. She's wearing a Gucci, but I know it's a *real* one because the battery died during improv class one night and she had to leave early to get to a jewelry store—an actual *jewelry* store—to buy a new one before it closed. When my street-Gucci runs out of juice, it's cheaper for me to just throw it out and buy a new one from a vendor on a corner somewhere.

"Well, maybe next time," she says. "I better go or I'll be late. Break a leg in there. And remember, if you *can't* break a leg—"

"Don't break a nail!" I chime.

She throws her head back and giggles. "That's right! *Ciao!*"

I watch as she swivels away and disappears inside the building. I feel a flutter of guilt. Okay, maybe she's not *that* bad. But she's still going to get the part, isn't she? She's not even a very good actress. I catch myself. I used the word *actress* again. I never know what to say. Actresses seem as if they should have inflatable casting couches in their purse. But actors should be able to break into iambic pentameter at the drop of a hat. I usually settle on "I act."

I sigh forlornly and go back to my cigarette.

Good morning, sir. Welcome to First Fidel—

"You're back." I hear a voice behind me. Full. Warm. Deep.

There's a tall man in a black suit standing behind me. I feel that horrible smile of mine—the one that quivers between the recognition of someone I should be nice to and *Who-the-fuck-are-you?*

"I like a person with determination," he says. Then he gives a sly grin.

"Oh, it's you!" I say. I almost say, *"My knight in shining armor,"* but I settle on: "The guy from the hall."

"The guy from the hall," he repeats, as if he's amused by the title. He extends his hand. "I'm Jack."

"Sally Carpenter," I say, reaching to give him my practiced, confident handshake, the one that clicks in at 100 RPM and is supposed to make people think I believe in myself. But as our hands meet, I feel myself overwhelmed by his own energy. It's warm and slow and pulsing, like a muscle constantly flexing and relaxing. When we release hands, my whole arm feels tingly and numb.

"Another audition?" he asks.

"Actually, I'm on a callback for that audition yesterday." I stand a little more proudly.

"Told you you'd be fine."

"Yes . . . you did."

"I see we have something in common." He reaches inside his suit jacket and retrieves a silver cigarette case.

"Oh, right. I'm trying to quit, but I'm always so nervous before an audition, I can't resist."

I watch as he puts a cigarette between his lips and bends to light it with a silver Zippo.

"That's not going to work," I tell him. "It's much too . . ."

But the flame ignites easily, barely wavering within the shelter of his cupped palms. He snaps the lighter closed and exhales. "Sorry?"

"Uh, nothing. Just that it's a little windy today." I'm pressing down the hem of my skirt. "Why is it always so windy around here? And there's never any sun. I'd go crazy. I think I have that disease. What do they call it? Seasonal affective disorder?"

"There's sun," he says. "You just have to know where . . ." His voice trails off as he notices something behind me. I turn to see a homeless person shuffling toward us. He has matted gray hair and a long salt-and-pepper beard; he's wearing a gray overcoat that's so tattered you almost can't tell where his beard ends and his clothing begins. By the time he holds out his shaking hand, I'm already digging for my wallet.

"Here," I say, planting my spare change in his upturned palm. I get a whiff of him—a thick, sweaty staleness—when the wind turns. He grumbles a thank-you and turns his hand toward Jack. Jack is just watching us, smoking his cigarette, as if not understanding what's expected of him. I give him an admonishing nod of my head.

"Oh, sorry," he says. He slips his hand into his pocket, pulling out a money clip. He peels off a twenty and hands it to the guy. "Sorry. No change."

The man grunts as if to say, *You think I got change, buddy?*

Jack lets out a small laugh. "Just keep it," he says, as if he weren't going to take it back once the old guy touched it anyway.

The old man pockets the money and hobbles down the sidewalk, scattering pedestrians like a zoo animal on the loose.

I take a deep, contented breath. I'm proud of myself for having made this guy in what is obviously a $3,000 dollar suit fork over a few bucks.

"Do you always do that?" he asks.

"Sure. If I've got the change."

He's watching me in a sort of assessing way. "How . . ." He seems to be searching for the word. " . . . *nice.*"

I smile, a little awkwardly. "You make it sound like an insult."

He just laughs.

"So, what do you do around here?" I ask him. "Are you a producer or something?"

"Not really."

"An executive?"

"Something like that."

"Ahh. A deal maker. I see."

I feel a sudden heat in my fingers and I realize the ember on my cigarette has burnt down to the butt. I quickly throw it away. When I look back at him, he's staring at my forehead.

"Before you go in, you should do something about—"

"What?" My hand slaps over my frown lines.

"You've got something—"

Oh, my God! I can't believe it! A perfect stranger is commenting on my frown lines!

"Relax, Sally," he says with a soft laugh, gently pulling my hand away from my forehead. "It's just some dirt or something. I think it's ash from your cigarette."

"Oh." I must've gotten it there during the little minimassage. Relieved I don't have to inject myself with Botox (at least, not immediately), I lick my fingers, rub them clean on my skirt, then bring them to my forehead, stroking feverishly. I look at him with raised eyebrows. He shakes his head.

I rub more. He smiles. "Perfect."

"Thanks," I tell him. "There's no way I would've gotten the part if I'd gone in there to read with dirt on my forehead. I owe you one."

"Promises, promises," he says.

"Well . . . I should be going in. . . ." I start backing toward the doors. "Nice seeing you again. *Jack* . . . right?"

"Jack," he says.

Jaaaaaccccccckkkkkkk. Like an arrow whizzing through the air, hitting something soft.

I'm still backing up. Where the hell are the doors? Finally, I feel the slab of cold glass behind me. Before I duck inside, some witty parting words occur to me. "I'll leave a trail of bread crumbs this time—so I don't get lost."

"Don't worry," he says with a smile. "I found you once. I'd find you again."

THE audition room is more crowded than it was yesterday. Foster Maclean is there, staring at the floor again, stroking his beard. The casting assistant is there, too (in a different argyle vest). Two other people are watching me with such intensity, I feel like I've just walked into a police lineup. The casting assistant introduces them (needlessly) as Griffin Hughes, the executive producer of *Precinct*—he's a slope-shouldered, curly-haired guy with glasses so thick they make his blue eyes appear as if they're farther away from you than the rest of his face—and Marcy Kornfeldt, the show's head writer, a slim-boned woman with brown eyes and the kind of rotini-tight dark curls that make her look beautiful without really trying. Of course, Hazel Grippe is there, too, monopolizing the biggest patch of the table with her head shots and résumés. But this time, when I walk in the room, the strangest thing happens—she puts down her pen.

"Hey, Sally," she says. She leans back. "Whenever you're ready."

Jesus. Hazel Grippe can actually be *civil*?

I take a deep breath and close my eyes, trying to focus. But the more I strain for my concentration, like a drowning victim flailing for a life preserver, the farther away it drifts. Oh, what the hell. Here goes:

"Good morning, sir. Welcome to First Fi—"

"Thanks, Sally." It's Hazel's voice.

What? Are you fucking kidding me? I came all the way in here just to get to *"Fi—"*?

"We'll call you if we need you," she says. "Next."

I grit my teeth, pivot on my Payless pump, and leave the room. I'm fully prepared to get lost in the halls again, but Dara Dempsey is waiting for me outside, holding one of her soap opera scripts against her chest like a high schooler with an armload of binders. When she sees me, a smile alights on her face. "How'd it go?"

"She cut me off. *Again.*"

Dara *tsks* sympathetically. "You sure you don't have time for that coffee? My treat."

I'm surprised she was serious about the invitation. I glance at my watch, shrug *Sure.* She tucks her arm in mine and we head off through the white halls together.

WHILE we're in line at the Starbucks across the street, waiting for our low-fat lattes and a piece of chocolate layer cake to share, Dara is talking about her stint on *DUD*. (That's what they call *Dusk Until Dawn* in all the soap digests. *Y&R, AMC, GH, DUD.* As unflattering as the moniker seems, it stuck.)

"I play the part of Meridien," she's saying, "the nun who gets found by her long-lost parents?"

I nod, feigning polite curiosity—even though I know all about the role from the scene pages we got before the audition.

"Kinda hokey, I know," she says, rolling her eyes as if to say, "But what do you expect from a soap?"

We find a table on the patio amid the exhaust fumes and tarry wind. We put the chocolate cake on the table between us and start tag-teaming it with two forks.

"Not that I'm a snob about soaps or anything," she's saying. "It's great training ground. Some of the best actresses of all time got started there. Demi Moore. Sandra Bullock. Meryl Streep."

I think of correcting her on the Meryl thing; I'm quite sure there are no daytime dramas on Ms. Streep's CV, but Dara doesn't leave enough of a breath pause for me to interrupt, and by the time there is one, I've either forgotten about Meryl or don't care.

"I'm just glad that they don't have me on an exclusive contract," she says, "so I can try out for other parts. Like this bank teller thing." She smiles sweetly and sips her latte, going on to tell me how *"bizzy"* she's been.

I know other people think that Dara and I look alike. But as far as I'm concerned, how much we resemble each other physically only seems to emphasize how different we really are. It goes way beyond the Gucci. Or even the blond hair: Hers is the kind that takes a lot of money and several hours in a stylist's chair every month to achieve; mine, on the other hand, comes from lemon juice stints I do on the roof. The real difference between us is that Dara looks successful and happy.

And I don't.

I mean—*look* at her. Bubbling and burbling away. (I forgot how much she likes to talk.) Her clothes are perfect. Her makeup is perfect. Her nails are freshly manicured. My eyes travel up to the patch of skin between her perfectly waxed eyebrows and I embark on a quick hunt for her frown lines. Nope. Not a crimp. Not a crinkle.

Maybe she's had them Botoxed.

I've considered getting it done myself. Just injecting a couple of nanograms of food poisoning into the damn things and numbing them into submission. But then I think, How could I ever be a really good dramatic actress without frown muscles? How could I ever play Blanche Dubois or do *Taming of the Shrew* without the muscles I needed to form a frown? I'd end up being relegated to Pizza Hut commercials and soap operas for the rest of my life, like Dara here, who's still prattling on.

Sigh.

Where *are* her frown lines? How is it possible for a woman in her late twenties to not have even a hint of frown lines? Maybe she's just never had to frown a day in her life. Do you think there are people like that? People who are so happy their frown muscles atrophy from lack of use?

She leans forward over the now empty cake plate, swirling designs with her fork in what's left of the icing. "Plus," she says, "I've met someone."

"Really?"

"You should *see* him, Sally. *Whew!*" She fans herself.

"Who is he?"

She looks down sheepishly. "I shouldn't say. I'm sort of pulling a Monica Lewinsky."

I think about it and squeal playfully, "You're bonking George Dubya?"

She rolls her eyes. "As *if.*"

"You mean"—I lower my voice disapprovingly—"he's married."

She slaps my arm. "I'm not stupid, Sally."

"What, then?"

"I mean he's *powerful.*" She widens her eyes for emphasis. *"Extremely.* powerful." She starts dragging a heart design through the icing with the tines of her fork. "Sally, what would you be willing to do to get ahead in this business?"

"I just finished a night class on Shakespearean tragic heroines with Angie Dickinson's understudy. Obviously the sky's the limit."

"That's not what I mean."

"You mean . . . would I sleep with somebody?"

She's cagey now. But she doesn't answer.

"Dara, I don't give a shit if you're sleeping with somebody to get a gig. I mean, *I* wouldn't do it. But it's your choice."

My philosophy on women (or men, for that matter) sleeping with someone to get ahead is that if you're talking about a woman who *would* sleep with someone to get ahead, and who is, in whatever sense, desirable enough *to* get ahead just for sleeping with someone, *and* someone who *would* consider casting/hiring/promoting a certain woman just because she *would* sleep with him, rather than rip up her résumé and throw her out on her ass for what it says about her character, then you're probably talking about two such supreme jerks that appealing to their better nature by citing *The Feminine Mystique* would not likely do any good.

"It's not that," she says. "It's just that I've never met anyone like him before. Sometimes I think he could give me anything. Anything I want. All I'd have to do is ask."

I crack a grin. "Hope multiple orgasms are on the list."

She watches me evenly, not smiling. "I mean *anything*, Sally."

I must admit, her uncharacteristic seriousness has piqued my curiosity. "Go on . . ."

She narrows her eyes at me, as if judging how much she should say. For a moment she seems so different. Her face is unsmiling; her eyes are in shadow.

"Don't leave me hanging," I urge her.

She seems to think about it a moment longer, then tosses her head. "Never mind. Forget I mentioned it," she says, shrugging off her dark mood as if it were a black cardigan on a hot summer day. "Enough about *moi*. What about you? How have things been with you?"

"Okay, I guess."

"What about Michael? I don't get a chance to talk to him very much on set."

"David."

"David."

"He's fine."

It's my turn to start twirling designs in the leftover icing as I catch her up. I don't get very far before I notice that her eyes have gone out of focus somewhere over my left shoulder. I turn to see that she's staring at the mannequins in the Banana Republic window across the street. When she actually yawns out loud, I take that as a hint. "Anyway, I should get going," I say. "Jeremy's going to fry me if I'm late."

She smiles vaguely. "I should go, too. Just let me fix my lipstick." She reaches for her purse. She rummages around for a moment or two and then lets out a little shriek. She stares at me in horror.

"What is it?"

Very slowly, she pulls her hand out of her bag. She turns her fingers upward, facing me. I blink a few times as if to clear my eyes. Because the unthinkable has happened.

Dara Dempsey has broken a nail.

SEVEN

The Devil's children have the Devil's luck.

PROVERB

"Gus, *you're kidding! I got the part?*" I'm jumping up and down in little circles at the Backburner. "I actually got the part?"

"Told you Hazel wasn't pissed off about that dress. She's too much
of a mensch to let something that stupid bug her."

"But she cut me *off.*"

"She must've known you were right for the part and didn't want
to waste everyone's time." Her voice natters on with the details about
my call time. I jot them down. When I hang up, I lean forward and
plant a big kiss on the charcoal-stained phone. Someone in the True
Crime section gives me a "look."

"I got the part," I say by way of explanation.

I race to the back of the store. "Jeremeee!" I call, hammering on
the grimy pink and green curtain slimed through with charcoal.
"Jeremy! I got the part!!"

Nothing.

"Jer?" I swish the curtain a little more. I know I'm not supposed to
bug him when he's back there, but common courtesy can't contain my

excitement. I haven't made a lot of friends since I came to New York—everyone's too busy with auditions or classes or day jobs—and I've lost touch with the girlfriends I used to have because most of them stayed in Wisconsin or moved to another suburb somewhere. As a consequence, Jeremy has become one of my closest friends (next to David, of course). Being an artist, I think he can relate to all the sacrificing and rejection I have to endure as an actor. I can't wait to tell him *good* news for a change!

"Jeremy!" I shake the curtain again. "Did you hear me? I got the part!"

Suddenly, the curtain thrashes open and Jeremy stands there in the doorway like a great crane with its wings spread. He glares at me.

"Am I supposed to be *happy* for you?"

"Well, I was kind of—"

"When are you going to *learn,* Sally"—he begins to circle me—"that a few lousy walk-on parts are not going to guarantee you immortality?"

"Jeremy, I—"

"I suppose you want to go out and *ce*lebrate or something depressing like that."

"Not really, I just—"

"All right, fine, let's go for a drink, then. I should try to talk some sense into you anyway."

He swoops back into his workroom, grabbing his baggy tweed coat. I catch a glimpse of his easel with its big vanilla-colored sketch pad, the floor full of smashed charcoal nubs, like gum on a subway platform, the walls plastered with the rumpled nude sketches. The arms. The legs. The indiscreet triangles of hair. I feel a heat rush over my cheeks. He closes the curtain in front of me.

WE hang the BACK IN 5 MINUTES sign on the door and go to a dingy, narrow pub a block from the store (incidentally, we're never back in five minutes). The place doesn't really have a name, but everyone calls it Pab's because the only discernible way to identify it is by the old, half-lit Pabst beer sign in the grimy front window. The clientele runs mostly along the unemployed/war vet/wino line. Their gray heads glow like patio lanterns when we get inside.

Jeremy drops himself into our favorite booth at the back and stares at me with reproach. The dim, orange-shaded lamp makes the hollows of his face look even deeper. The bartender comes over with a pitcher of cheap red wine. Jeremy pours us each scratched highballs full, then lifts his glass between us with a dramatic flourish.

"To the inevitable corruption of Sally Carpenter! My onetime friend and colleague!" He takes a big swallow, his Adam's apple bobbing loudly. He slams his glass down, wiping his mouth with a sweep of the back of his charcoal-stained hand. He leaves a smudge of black on his cheek, but I don't bother to tell him about it. He'll call me "bourgeois."

"Thanks, Jeremy. That was . . . touching."

He sighs at me. "What do you expect? You know how I feel about this. How many times have I told you, If you absolutely *must* act, then take to the stage where the energy is *transferred* and . . ."

"Yes, yes, not merely *inferred*. You've told me a million times. And I've told *you* a million times that most of the work is *in* television. If I want to be an actress, I have to work in TV!"

"Even when you know what's happening to the prefrontal cortex?" he says, tapping impatiently at his temple.

"I know about the prefrontal cortex, Jeremy."

"It's the most recently developed layer of the human brain, Sally," he says, as if he hasn't plunged into this particular diatribe a hundred times before. "Responsible for *all* of man's higher thought processes. Language, art, music, philosophy. In other words, without the prefrontal cortex, we'd all still be peeling bananas! The problem is"—he glances around conspiratorially—"they've been conducting top-secret tests and they've found that the prefrontal cortex is actually point-two-two-two nanometers thinner than it was a century ago. The prefrontal cortex is shrinking, Sally! It's actually getting smaller! And do you know why that is?" He allows for a dramatic beat. *"Television!"* he says with considerable derision—and more than a little spit. "It's narcotizing us! It's turning us all into a race of slobbering, catatonic vegetables!"

"Precinct's not like that, Jeremy. Have you ever even *seen* it?"

"Of course not."

"It's a very good show. It deals with hard-hitting issues. It won three Emmys last year!"

"And that's supposed to *impress* me? Everyone in your business gets nominated for some award or another. Do you see doctors handing out trophies for what they do? *'And the winner for the best Triple Bypass of the Year is . . .'?* No. Of course you don't. Because doctors don't have to legitimize their profession by accessorizing it with little statuettes."

I sigh helplessly. "So what am I supposed to do? Drop out? You think I have a *choice?* You think I *like* rejection? You think it's *fun* for me? Are you *kidding?* I *hate* it. But I can't help myself. Acting is the only thing I've ever wanted to do with my life. Ever since I was a little girl, I've always—"

"Brava!" He interrupts with three bored claps of his charcoal-stained hands. "Bravissima! What a moving portrayal of a helpless young waif struggling to make her dreams come true in the big city." He wipes at a mock tear in the corner of his sunken gray eye. "Maybe there's hope for you after all."

I give him a wimpy snarl.

"What's the part *for* anyway?"

"A bank teller," I grumble.

"Who gets shot during a holdup, I bet."

I flush—because he's right.

"Why don't you really take a look at what's on television some night, Sally. Why don't you see how many young actors and actresses get stabbed, murdered, raped, then forgotten in prime time every night? Last week's *TV Guide* blurb. That's all you are. Fodder in the war against art." He flaps a hand at me, as if I'm a hopeless case. "Oh, how can I blame you for all this? You were raised in an era where Aaron Spelling was the chief disseminator of moral values. You're predisposed to believe in happy endings. But that's not the way life is, Sally. Problems don't go away when the credits roll. Life is hard. Bloody well hard. And it gets harder every year. Trust me. I *know* what I'm talking about. I'm a genius."

A sigh. "Yes, Jeremy. I know you're a genius."

"So why don't you listen to me? Are *you* a genius? Nooooo. You're an *ack*-tress!" He grabs his neck as if choking. "A dreamer! Someone who makes a profession of being sheltered from the truth! Well, I'm not going to help you do that, Sally. I'm the one who's going to be honest with you. I'm the one who's going to be there to pick you up when the director yells 'Cut!' and the phone stops ringing again. I'm the one who'll tell you the cold, hard facts of it. Because that's what friends are for." He pats my hand. "Now—let's order some more swill, shall we? I can see you're feeling better already."

"Sure." I manage to smile stiffly before the bar blurs with tears.

EIGHT

He who sups with the Devil must use a long spoon.

PROVERB

THE September wind snaps at my hair as I approach Gus's building off Columbus Circle. Gus (Augusta) Koniklouris has been my agent for almost three years. Her office is on the fifth floor of a half-vacant, undesirable building whose true color can't be distinguished for all the years of exhaust grime that has built up on the brick. When she hears my knock, she throws the door open, beams a big smile at me, and buries me in an unexpected bear hug.

"Am I glad to see you!" she says.

She plants a thin orange-lipsticked kiss on my cheek, then rubs it off with her thumb, smiling maternally at me. I give her a wary look. Gus usually isn't so nice to me. In fact, we're sort of on a five-to-one call-back ratio. I call her five times for every one time she calls me back.

She releases me and squeezes around her desk. Gus is the sort of woman who shops at places that proudly declare "Big is beautiful." She always wears brightly colored suits and blouses (right now she's in peacock blue) and jewelry that clatters when she moves. Her hair is wavy, chin length, and magenta-colored. At least, today it is. Sometimes it's mulberry, chestnut, or some variation of henna. It all depends on which hairdressing school she's patronized this month. But no matter which shade she's chosen, there's always this stubborn streak of white that won't take the dye and eventually shows through, running from the left side of her forehead up over the top of her head. It doesn't seem to bother her, this modern Bride of Frankenstein "do"; in fact, I think she's kind of proud of it. It's a bonus in this business to have the reputation of a monster—to actually bear physical resemblance to one is like money in the bank.

"Siddown, siddown," she says. "There's the script. They want you in makeup at seven thirty."

"Okay." I sit down in front of the rather hefty-looking document.

"I highlighted your lines," she says.

"You *did?*" I flip through the script. Sure enough, Candace's (scant) lines are traced neatly with green highlighter. "Why?"

"Anything to help my favorite client," she says, smiling.

Favorite client? Since when?

It's then I notice something amiss in her office. Gus has a roster of an undisclosed and constantly changing number of B-movie, off-off-Broadway, and TV bit actors, whose framed head shots she displays on the wall next to her desk. The position of an actor's photograph is in direct positive or negative correlation to the number of gigs he or she has been getting. The more successful the actor, the more likely he or she is to find him or herself near the prestigious center of the middle row; the less remarkable a person's career, the more the photograph tends to gravitate toward the outer edges. Some actors' situations get so abysmal that, as if moved by the show business law of inertia, which dictates that a career in a downward spiral tends to remain in a downward spiral, their photographs disappear altogether, leaving ominously blank spaces upon the yellowed plaster as the only evidence of their existence. Gus lets the spot sit empty for a while as a warning to the rest of us: There's nothing scarier for an actor than to disappear without a trace.

My spot upon the wall has been anything but impressive of late. The head shot (a horrible, tense-looking photograph of me in a black sweater with the kind of smile usually reserved for female acrobats who swing sixty feet above the ground from jaw apparatus) has been in the very bottom left-hand corner for the last year. More recently, it's even threatened to fall off the hook. But this morning my strained smile has moved from the sixth to the third row.

What's going on? She can't be doing all this just because of one lousy walk-on.

"So, Sal," she begins, in a syrupy voice. "I didn't know you knew Jack Weaver."

"Who?"

"Jack Weaver," she repeats, her smile faltering a bit.

"Jack Weaver . . . Jack Weaver . . ." I shrug, clueless. "Isn't he the guy from Fox?"

Her smile evaporates completely. "You let your *Variety* subscription lapse again, didn't you? Goddamn you people. How do you expect me to earn a living off you if you don't do your homework? No—he's *not* the guy from Fox. Jack Weaver is the president of Network Programming at UBN," she says sternly. "A.k.a. God to you and me."

"Oh, yeah, right!" I say, clicking my fingers.

"Oh, yeah, *right,"* she mocks me. "Christ, Sally, you're going to give me a migraine." She starts digging through her drawers, clattering half-empty bottles of Imitrex and Excedrin. "So—*do* you know him or not?"

I let out a small, incredulous laugh. "Of course not. What made you think I *did?"*

"Hazel asked me about it when she called to tell me you got the part."

"Hazel asked you if I knew Jack Weaver?"

She nods. "I didn't want to let her know that I was out of the loop, so I made some joke about how my clients have lots of friends in high places. But I made a mental note to ask you." She taps her skull. "So—dish. How did you guys meet?"

"I'm telling you that I *don't* know who Jack Weaver is and if I did, I'd . . ." But my voice trails off. Suddenly, it dawns on me. I remember the guy in the black suit reaching to shake my hand. *"I'm Jack . . ."* I slam forward onto her desk. "Gus, *that* was Jack Weaver?!"

"What the—" She has to lean back out of the way.

"Gus, *tell* me that *wasn't* Jack Weaver!" I stand up and start pacing the room. "That *couldn't* have been Jack Weaver! Is he kinda tall?"

"Yeah."

"Dark?"

"Yeah."

"And—"

"Drop-dead sexy?" she finishes for me.

"Yeah!"

"That was him, all right."

I'm still pacing, raking my hands through my hair. "But he was so *nice.* He was so *helpful.* Shouldn't he have been surrounded by a group of assistants or something? How the hell was I supposed to know it was him?"

"Because it's your fucking job, that's why," she says, clearly not impressed.

I suddenly grip my head, feeling a wave of retro horror as I remember practically twisting his arm so he'd give the homeless guy some money. I flop back into the chair. "Jesus, Gus. I am *such* an idiot."

"You're not getting any arguments from me."

"So is that what this is all about? The coffee? The marked script? You think I'm pals with a network head?"

But she ignores the question and leans forward, eyes gleaming, as she asks me to tell her how we met. I reluctantly explain that he helped me find the elevators in Purgatory and that we blew a smoke together outside the building the next day. She listens with rapt attention to every word, then taps her chin. Eyebrows that have long been plucked away and replaced by auburn pencil lines frown thoughtfully. "Hmmm. . . . I just thought of something," she says.

"What?"

"Maybe he put in a good word for you with Hazel."

"What makes you say that?"

"What else would make her do such an about-face on that dress?"

My eyes widen. "I thought you said she wasn't mad about the dress."

"Are you kidding? She was pissing vinegar over it."

"You told me I was just being paranoid!"

"And you were." She smiles and crosses her hands on the desk. "But you were also right."

"So you're saying *he* got me the part?" I squeal. "You think he called Hazel and told her to hire me?"

"All I'm saying is that something has given her a change of a heart. And that's quite a feat, considering my money was against her even having a heart in the first place."

"Shit!" I punch the arm of the chair. "I knew this was too good to be true! I knew something was up! First gig I've had in almost two years. Well, I don't need some slimy television executive doing any favors for me. I can get parts on my own!"

"Not according to *my* bank statement, you can't," she says. "And by the way, watch how you're referring to people who can make or break your career. 'Slimy television executive' might not be the most flattering term. Besides, he's not doing you any *favors*. He's doing *business.* You've been unemployed so long, maybe you forgot how things work. Sally, what's wrong with you? You're acting like this is a bad thing. But it's not. There are a hundred thousand actors in this town and ninety-nine point nine percent of them could drop dead beneath their drink trays and he wouldn't even bat an eye. But you—for whatever reason—he's noticed." She stands up and comes around the desk, sitting on the edge of it. "This could be a big break for you, Sal. Jack Weaver is a very important man in this business. He could really make things happen for you." She picks a nonexistent piece of lint off my shoulder. "If you play your cards right . . ."

"Play my cards right? What's *that* supposed to mean?"

"You know . . . be nice to him the next time you see him."

I cross my arms angrily. "You want me to drop to my knees and give him a blow job right then and there?"

She thinks about it. Cracks a grin. "Only if you give a decent one."

"Gus!"

"I'm just kidding! Be polite, that's all I'm saying! At least let him know you know who he *is* next time you see him. And here." She grabs a stack of trade papers—*Daily Variety, Hollywood Reporter, Back Stage,* and the like—from her desk and drops them in my lap. "Do your fucking homework."

I'm sitting at the kitchen table watching the sun going down. Red, orange, and yellow light spills across the rooftops of the other brownstones, like lava pouring through the neighborhood, melting the edges of ductwork, construction cranes, and chimneys, turning everything into something else. Asphalt into the surface of a lake. Church steeples into burning trees.

I go back to my script. I've been trying to develop my character, coming up with Candace's favorite color (blue), and movie *(When Harry Met Sally),* and sign (Virgo). There aren't many lines to memorize—just a lot of screaming and "Please God, don't kill me's" when the bank robbery goes wrong. Which is why my mind kind of drifts. Sometimes. To Jack Weaver.

I can't believe I actually *talked* to him. His name is spoken with the same fear and awe people in my world associate with Moonves, Zucker, Albrecht, and a handful of others for the chilling control they have over what (and who) gets beamed into millions of American living rooms every night. There is certainly no shortage of mentions of him in the trades, particularly since he's initiating the takeover of

Geostar News, an international satellite news network based in Britain. Terms like "Machiavellian genius," "meteoric rise," and "enigmatic leader" come up a lot. Several articles also mention that he prefers to keep his inner circle small, which is why he isn't always surrounded by a pack of *Beggars & Choosers* types. Except for the odd blurb about a few actresses he's been seen with, and the fact he usually ends up on *somebody's* Most Eligible Bachelor list, there isn't much else about his personal life.

Not much at all.

I think about the man in the black suit.

"Forget it. . . . I have a feeling you're going to be just fine."

It still seems so hard to believe it was him. And that he knows *me*. It's on par with time travel. Splitting subatomic particles. Life on Mars. The *president* of UBN Network Programming knows *me*. I'm not sure how it makes me feel. Wary. Flattered. And something else. A low, stirring sensation that I can't quite separate from fear.

NINE

High on a throne of royal state . . .
Satan exalted sat. . . .

JOHN MILTON

THE morning of the *Precinct* shoot is one of those colorlessly calm days I never remember having in Wisconsin. It's as if New York is such a busy city that occasionally even the weather gets tied up in traffic and doesn't show.

They're shooting the *Precinct* robbery scene in a vacant bank in midtown. Naturally, the first thing I do when I cross the line of pylons and cables onto the set is trip. A police officer standing guard has to catch my arm to hold me up. I look up at him in embarrassment, then around to make sure no one else saw me. But sure enough, the gaggle of tourists gathered on the other side of the barricades strain their necks to see if the lady who stumbled is famous. Satisfied they don't recognize me, they go back to their vigil of the string of white trailers, looking for the real stars—people like John Monroe and Sabrina Calliope-Clark.

I just shrink inside myself. My first job is to find the third assistant director who will be my umbilical cord to the rest of the set. I grab the elbow of the nearest person in a headset passing by.

"Where's Kelly?" I ask.

The young woman holds up a finger. She's listening to her head-set, her eyes focused nowhere in particular. She's got feathered brown hair and wears denim overalls. I wait patiently, using the time to look around the set. It has the atmosphere of a small, tidy war. Young, dis-pensable soldiers dart around, sweating doggedly beneath heavy equip-ment. Every now and again a general passes by, barking commands.

The woman signs off on the headset and turns to me. *"I'm* Kelly," she says. "Sally, right?"

Before I have time to say "Nice to meet you," she shoves the script changes into my hand, sticks her arm in my elbow, and propels me toward the makeup trailer.

"We're about half an hour behind schedule," she says. *"E.T.'s* on set interviewing John." John Monroe plays Detective Hogan on the series, the dark and swarthy maverick who gets more fan mail than anyone else.

"E.T.? Wow."

"Yeah, they got an exclusive on his rehab story."

I nod in comprehension. Every entertainment magazine and tabloid paper in the country has been following John's drug rehabilita-tion with obsessive detail. On the way to the wardrobe trailer, we see a quiet clearing where two director's chairs are facing each other for the intimate interview between John and a lovely reporter from *Entertain-ment Tonight.* As we walk past them, my perspective of them changes slowly, slowly, as if they are shimmering holograms that can be seen but not touched, separated as they are from the world by their mutual fame.

". . . And were there ever times when you thought you weren't going to make it, John?" asks the reporter with a compassionate crumple-smile. But before I have time to hear the answer, Kelly has dragged me away.

She deposits me in the narrow, stuffy wardrobe trailer lined with racks of stale-smelling clothing. The clothes shuffle and puff mysteriously. "Hello?" I call uncertainly into the shadows. A moment later, the wardrobe assistant emerges from behind them—a mousy, pale woman with tiny, almost subterranean eyes. She seems to identify me with only a sniff of her little pink nose. "Candace," she concludes. She momentarily digs back through the clothes and returns with a hanger containing a dress and a clear plastic bag of shoes. The Polaroid photograph of me from the audition is stapled to the bag. My measurements, height, weight, shoe and dress size are scribbled on a Post-it note. It feels odd to me that this information is public knowledge.

I duck into a changing area with a curtain that won't close all the way and a few minutes later I emerge in the flouncy wave of a mauve-and-pink polyester dress, white plastic earrings, bubble-gum pink high heels, and spice nylons. I'm not sure anyone really dresses like this anymore. I feel like an escapee from *The Stepford Wives.* The wardrobe lady gives me a couple of foam pads to stuff in my bra to make more cleavage. It doesn't really work. She gives me a couple more.

I clatter down the metal steps to the street. Kelly sees me tottering around on the shoes, grabs my elbow, and leads me to a trailer with a handwritten sign that reads HAIR/MAKEUP in black Magic Marker.

The second trailer is brighter, lined with cluttered counters and vanity mirrors. One of the makeup chairs is so densely surrounded by a clog of hovering, bobbing assistants and makeup people that, like bees at a hive, I can't make out the mysterious center of their attention.

A bored-looking woman with heavily lined eyes and a lifeless china-doll bob sees me and separates from them, motioning for me to take a seat. She is precision-sharpening a lip liner, carefully blowing the shavings off the tip. "Got makeup on?" she asks, pushing my nose over to one side.

"Nope."

She squints at me as if she doesn't take my word for it, then plasters my face with a big gob of cold cream—emphasis on *cold*.

That's when the voice emanating from within the excited clump of bodies begins to sound familiar. ". . . I mean, *give* me a break," the voice is saying. "Who doesn't have a problem once in a while? Do we *all* end up in rehab?"

Curiously, my gaze drifts toward the other chair again. I try to determine who's sitting there, piecing together body parts I manage to glance as the hive separates and shifts. A pale upturned nose. A shock of dark hair. A slender white ankle kicking slowly back and forth. Then someone leans back and I see her reflection in the mirror. The wind goes out of me. My God. It's Sabrina Calliope-Clark! A.k.a. Det. Phyllis O'Reilly on the show.

"It's sad, really," her famous rosebud lips are saying. "If I knew I'd get that much publicity out of it, *I'd* swallow a bottle of sleeping pills, too." The hive shivers with encouraging laughter.

Suddenly the shiny dark eyes, boredly entranced by their own reflection, seem to intuit the unwelcome sensation of being recognized when she's not fully made up. She meets my gaze in the mirror. A moment passes where it's just me and Sabrina Calliope-Clark staring at each other across the great chasm of my anonymity.

"May I *help* you?" she asks, in a clipped tone.

"Sorry," I stammer, looking down.

With several judgmental *tsks,* the hive protectively closes in around her.

When my makeup is done, the hair guy sashays over. He's wearing a tight black T-shirt and studded jeans. He's so tall, he has to hunch his neck and shoulders to not bump the grilled lights on the ceiling. He licks his finger, then touches a large curling iron, making it sizzle. He takes pieces of my hair, curling them up in great loops, which he holds in place long after I smell something burning.

Sabrina continues to flit from topic to topic, like a butterfly in a field. Galas. Restaurants. Spas. Every minute that goes by reminds me just how much I don't belong here.

Finally, Kelly stomps up into the trailer with her clipboard. "They're gonna do a run-through. You ready?"

"I think so," I say. I look uncertainly at my reflection. My lips are frosty pink. My eyelids are caked with shimmering blue. My hair is flipped back in frothy waves. I look something like a young Farrah Fawcett if she had taken up a career in country-and-western singing.

I totter out of the trailer and down the steps. Kelly leads me across the cable-infested sidewalk into the bank. The bank is a large, brightly lit space that reverberates with the sound of voices and banging equipment. Technicians run back and forth mumbling and yelling. The place crackles with the sound of walkie-talkies. Dozens of extras are corralled in the holding area, drinking coffee, eating donuts, and watching the commotion like cattle gazing at traffic from the other side of a fence.

Foster, the director, is standing behind the camera, one thumb hooked in his vest, the other stroking his silver beard. When he sees me, his face lights up. He hurries over, taking my arm.

"Sheila, you look marvelous!"

"It's Sally."

"Sorry. Sally."

"We're going to do a camera rehearsal first," the first AD tells me.

The audio guy, a stout man who needs a shave, says, "Scream for real. We want to know where to boom you."

I nod. *No problem there. I'm so nervous, I'll be screaming for my life anyway.*

Someone yells, "One minute, everyone!"

"Places!"

"Quiet on the set!"

"Quiet, please!"

A bell rings.

"Roll film!"

"Rolling!"

"Speed."

"Precinct. Episode four. Scene three."

"Background!" The extras start to move and chatter.

Claaack.
"Aaaand, action."

3. INT. BANK—DAY

It's a sunny afternoon in a busy midtown bank. The bank machines are full. There's a long line for the tellers. Behind the counter stands a pretty blond woman in her mid-twenties. [I notice they removed the word *buxom* from the final draft.] *She looks up at a customer who approaches the counter. Reese is a tall and wiry man in a torn black leather jacket and jeans. He's holding a* GYM BAG. *He seems nervous.*

CANDACE
(smiling)
Good morning, sir. Welcome to First Fidelity. May I help you?

Reese slides a NOTE *over the counter to Candace. The smile on her face fades as she reads it. As if in a daze, she drops the note, backs away from the counter; her hand presses the silent alarm. Reese sees that it's going wrong. He leaps over the counter, pulling out a* GUN. *He runs up behind Candace, putting the gun to her head.*

REESE
(yelling)
Everybody down and nobody gets their heads blown off!

The bank erupts into chaos. Customers drop to the floor, whimpering and crying. An aging security guard at the door reaches for his gun, but Reese gives Candace a good squeeze. She screams.

REESE
Drop the gun or the girl gets it!

Reluctantly, the security guard drops his gun. Kicks it over to Reese. He gets down on the ground.

CANDACE
(whimpering)
Please God, don't kill me! Don't kill me!

REESE
Open your till and shut up.

He gives Candace a good shove toward the counter. As Candace is emptying the till, the air fills with sirens. Reese looks up to see police cars screeching to a stop outside the bank. Officers pile out into the street, assuming offensive positions behind doors and bumpers.

4. EXT. BANK—DAY
PHYLLIS
Don't try anything stupid, Hogan. He's got a hostage.

Hogan shrugs his shoulders in fake innocence. They hurry into the bank.

5. INT. BANK—DAY
PHYLLIS
Let the girl go so we can talk.

REESE
Are you kidding? She's my security deposit!

He jerks on Candace, who screams.

CANDACE
Please don't hurt me!

[This is basically what happens for a while: I scream a lot and the rest of the characters negotiate, while Reese chews up the scenery trying to be Al Pacino in *Dog Day Afternoon*.]

6. INT. BANK—DAY

Hogan quickly makes his way his way through the bank, ducking behind desks and counters, unseen. Reese swings the girl back and forth, yelling for people to stay down. Hogan sets his gun sight on Reese's back. A shot rings out. The sound echoes off the walls of the bank. People scream. Reese releases the hostage. There is a moment of relief. The camera pans from one shocked expression to another, then widens to reveal a growing blotch of red on Candace's dress. She looks around fearfully. Then drops to the ground.

END OF ACT I

THAT's my big opportunity: dropping to the ground like that. And the last serious challenge to my acting ability, because I spend the rest of the episode in a coma. The story line is really about how Hogan goes through all this macho Dr. Phil angst for having shot a civilian. The only opportunity I have to shine is at the end of the day when I finally go into cardiac arrest and die—lots of eyelash fluttering and trembling—but I have no more spoken lines. Like Jeremy says, just another prime-time damsel in distress.

WE'RE shooting the rest of the scenes up at the *Precinct* studios at UBN, so, still in my bloodstained dress, I pile into a production vehicle with some of the cast and crew and we head slowly back up through traffic. Sabrina and John get taken in separate limousines.

At the building, I navigate the long white corridors looking for Makeup. The smell of the place, the endless white halls—I keep expecting to see him again.

But I don't.

In Wardrobe I take off the bloodstained dress and carefully remove the squib taped to my stomach. The blood looks very convincing, but there is no center to the gore, no wound. It has a sweet chemical smell to it. I wipe myself clean with paper towels and the blood clears, leaving a soft pink stain on my skin like a sunburn. In Makeup the lip gloss and frosted eye shadow are replaced with the sickliest pale beige Pan-Cake you could imagine. The wardrobe lady with the subterranean eyes gives me a green hospital gown, which I wear over a bodysuit. Somebody runs Vaseline through my hair.

I head over to the studio and crawl into the hospital bed, trying to get into character. We do several takes of a scene where Hogan sits at my bedside, gritting his teeth and running his hands through his hair. When he's finally able to blurt out three fat tears, with the aid of a little glycerine, Foster yells: *"And cut!"*

"Reposition for scene twenty-six," shouts the first AD.

"Wait, can we record a minute of ambient?"

The AD puts up his arm, looking at his watch. "A minute of room tone, everybody! Nobody move . . . starting . . . *now!*"

And suddenly the banging and shouting stops and there is complete silence. They're recording ambient noise to make editing easier. Everyone looks from the clock on the far wall, to each other, then back again. Waiting. The second hand moves down around thirty seconds . . . thirty-five. . . . In the dull stillness around me I sense something moving—a dark, stealthy figure, threading his way through the crowd. People move quietly out of his way. He steps into the pool of light surrounding the set. My heart begins to thrum.

Jack Weaver.

And he's staring right at me, with a sly smile on his face. I try not to swallow in case the mic picks it up.

"That's great, folks," the AD says. "Everybody back in twenty."

The studio is suddenly cacophonous with banging equipment and raised voices. I quickly sit up, feeling vulnerable in the prone position with Jack Weaver around.

He strolls up beside the bed. "You know, Sally, when people tell you to break a leg, you shouldn't take them so seriously."

I laugh, or at least try to laugh. I am painfully aware of how horrible I look: greasy hair, pale complexion. I quickly slide off the bed. My hospital gown rides up as my feet touch the floor and I have to hike the hem down quickly.

"You have a minute?" he asks. "There's something I want to show you."

"Wh–what is it?"

"Come on." He gives a cock of his head.

"Uh . . . I'm not sure I should."

"Don't worry. I'll have you back before anyone flatlines." He motions to the fake monitors.

"I really don't think I . . ." But my voice trails off. He's walking backwards, nodding his head as if to coax me to follow him. Reluctantly, and against what feels like my better judgment, I do. I grumble to myself: *Arrogant prick . . . probably thinks just because I'm an actor, I'd do anything for him.*

Well, bullshit. I've got more pride than that.

Of course, this conversation is taking place in my head. And I *am* following him.

We make our way across the darkened studio. People separate for us, staring. I know what they're thinking: What the hell is the president of Network Programming doing talking to a little schlep like her?

I'm thinking it, too.

We move out into the long, brightly lit hallway. "So where are we going?" I ask, trying to keep my voice casual.

"You'll see."

We stop at the elevators and he presses the UP button. Our eyes meet a few times. He smiles at me. I don't smile back. "I guess I owe you an apology or something," I say, my tone somewhere between grudging and resentful.

"For?"

"For not recognizing you the other day."

He shrugs, as if it doesn't matter.

"The least you could've done was *tell* me, you know. Instead of letting me make a fool of myself."

"You didn't make a fool of yourself," he says. He seems genuinely surprised I would think that. "And I *did* tell you who I was."

"You told me you were *an* executive. You didn't tell me you were *the* executive."

He smiles. "I didn't exactly lie." The elevator dings open. "After you."

As I step on ahead of him, he puts his hand on my back. It shocks me. The heat and pressure of his hand. It sends a sweet rush through my body. Throbbing. Spreading. Even when he takes his hand away, I still feel the warmth on my skin, as if I'm burning very slowly from the inside out like the old map in the opening of *Bonanza*.

The doors seal closed. The elevator shudders a bit and starts going up . . . up . . .

"My agent was pretty pissed at me," I tell him. "She says I should be *nice* to you from now on."

He smiles, that deadly smile. "I like your agent already."

The panel of buttons ascends higher. 51, 52, 53 . . . My ears pop slightly. I am aware of a different pressure in my head as the elevator stops on the very top floor. The doors open. The first thing I see is a big sign that reads: AUTHORIZED PERSONNEL ONLY.

"You sure we're allowed to do this?" And then I feel silly. Of course he's allowed; he must be allowed to do anything around here.

He puts his hand on my back again and I step into a long white corridor that has the aura of only being used by custodians. There are buckets here and there, pieces of board, empty paint cans stacked against the wall. We head toward a door at the end of the hall. There's a large red stencil painted on it: DO NOT ENTER. But he disregards it. He gives the door a good shove with his shoulder and it pops open. Suddenly a gust of wind rushes in, blowing my hair, whipping my hospital gown against my legs. I have to blink against the oblong patch of bright light.

"This is what I wanted to show you," he says. "You said there was never any sunshine around here. But there is."

With renewed wonder, I look around the roof. Sunlight pours across everything, bleaching it evenly. The sky is blue and endless, uninterrupted by buildings, bridges, or cranes; pale clouds tumble lazily about, seagulls drift and dart. He takes my arm, but I resist a little.

"You afraid of heights?" he asks, noticing my discomfort.

"No . . . just death."

He laughs at that. "I won't let anything happen to you."

And I should believe you?

I suck in a breath of air and step over the threshold of the door out onto the tar-and-cement surface of the roof. The city swims around us. To the south are the Chrysler and Empire State Buildings. To the north, the most famous collection of trees in the world. Then I notice something that always unsettles me when I see it—a red neon sign with three numbers on it, all sixes, on the top floor of a building on Fifth Avenue. I wonder if it creeps out everyone else as much as it does me.

"This way," he says, motioning toward the center of the roof.

I keep walking. I hear the distant roar of construction and car horns meshed with the sound of the wind. He stops at what seems like a large white air duct or an anteroom of some kind, with a slanted roof. He puts one foot up on the slope and climbs with the agility of a teenager. He reaches down to get me, but I just lean against the low wall.

"No thanks. I'm fine here."

"Come on up. It's a great view." He holds out his hand. *Come on.* I relent and am surprised by the strength that seems to materialize in him as he pulls me up. If a hurricane swept by this instant, it seems the safest thing to do would be to hold on to him. I sit down, but not too close to him, hugging my knees into my chest. He stretches out, leaning back on one elbow. There's a masculine grace to the way he moves, a sort of fluid strength—as if the world, the air molecules, even gravity, provided just enough resistance for his body. He reaches inside his jacket, pulls out his battered cigarette case, and offers me one.

"Thanks," I say. I slide out a cigarette and lean toward him as he tries to light it. But the wind is too strong.

"Let me." He takes the cigarette back and puts it between his lips. When it's lit, he hands it to me. I stare at it uncertainly. It seems like an intimate thing to do—put a stranger's *cigarette* in your mouth. He motions with it again. *Take it.* And I do, inhaling shallowly. It's a stronger brand than I'm used to and it burns my chest. But it feels good—a familiar burn encroaching on an unfamiliar one.

He quickly lights his own and leans back a little farther, stretching out his legs. He looks out over the dense gray mountain range of buildings surrounding us. I'm surprised by how comfortable it is to be with him. The tension about being fifty-plus floors above the street has left me now. I feel as much a part of the sky as the earth.

"You're right," I say. "It *is* nice up here."

"I come up here all the time. The cell phone works great. And no one can pitch me."

I laugh awkwardly. "And here I was—not only didn't I pitch you—I didn't even know who you were. I'm probably the only actor you've met who hasn't dropped to the ground and started kissing your feet."

He smiles at that. "Close."

I let a beat pass. "What's that like? When everyone's so *nice* to you all the time."

"People aren't nice to me. They're afraid of me. Or they want something from me. There's a difference."

"How do you know who to trust, then?"

"You learn. In my business, it's important to know who's loyal to you."

I chew my lip, thinking about that. We're quiet for a moment. I watch pale clouds whip across the white sun.

"Do you mind if I ask you something?"

"Not at all," he says. And of course he doesn't mind. He doesn't seem to mind anything.

"Did you have anything to do with getting me this part?"

"Would it matter?"

"It would to me."

"Why?"

"I just want to know. I feel a little uncomfortable about it. I don't like being indebted to people."

"What makes you think you'd be indebted to me?"

I laugh a little warily. "Just a feeling I have."

"You deserved the part, Sally."

"So you *did* get it for me?"

"Yes," he answers simply.

I absorb that for a moment. "But *why?*"

"It's my job."

"Your job is to find struggling actors bit parts? I thought it was your job to . . . I don't know." I wave my hands. "Do whatever it is you TV types do. Have power lunches. Take over the world by winning November sweeps or something."

"It's my job," he says, "to help people get what they want."

"And you want to help *me?*"

"I'd like to. Yes."

"What makes you think I need your help?"

"I'm not saying you do. It's up to you whether you take it or not."

"Well, I *don't*. Thanks very much for the gig and everything. But it's not like I *asked* you for it. I didn't even know who you were when I said that I wanted it. I was just talking."

"To the right person."

"Or the *wrong* one."

"We'll see about that." He tosses his cigarette away in an arc, then looks back at me. "I was right about you, wasn't I?"

I narrow my eyes, uncertain what he means.

"I've never met anyone like you before. You're not . . ." He seems to think about it for a moment. "I don't know how to say it. You're just different. You're not . . . *easy. . . .*"

I feel a surge of resentment. "Why? Because I'm not going to pledge eternal allegiance to you for getting me a lousy walk-on part?"

"Not impressive enough for you?"

"That's *not* what I'm saying. If you want to go around doing me favors, that's fine. But it's not like I *owe* you anything for it. I just want to make that clear."

"And it is."

"Good."

He laughs again, then lies down on his back, putting his hands behind his head. "Lousy walk-on part," he repeats, half to himself. "Maybe I should try harder next time."

"Don't bother," I say. I grumble inwardly for a moment, then glance over. His eyes are closed, so he can't see me. My gaze automatically travels across the breadth of his chest, down the length of his long legs, over the calm features of his face. I feel my bitterness toward him start to fade. He seems so relaxed, so at ease with himself even here, hundreds of feet above the world, lying on his back in a suit that was never meant to touch anything but a boardroom chair. He just seems so *unafraid* of life. I wonder what that must be like.

I am jerked back to reality when the sound of several horns honking wafts up from the street. The break was only twenty minutes long. I go to glance at my watch, but it's not there. I panic. *Was it stolen? Did I lose it?* But then I remember taking it off for the scene. I rub my bare wrist, feeling disoriented and uncomfortable alone with him and not knowing what time it is.

"Don't worry," he says. "We have plenty of time."

And I wonder how he knew that. With his eyes closed.

TEN

The devil is most devilish when respectable.

ELIZABETH BARRETT BROWNING

I'M sitting in Gino's waiting for David for our regular Tuesday night pizza. I must've been here a million times, but tonight it seems completely changed. The flowered plastic tablecloth, the wagon-wheel chandeliers, the staticky television tuned to a baseball game over the bar. The place seems so different, the colors all separated and fresh, as if the whole room has been dipped into a vat of one of those miracle cleaners they advertise on late-night TV.

Is it because of Jack? It must be. I can't stop thinking about him. Ever since I went back to the set, he's been in my thoughts. I'm grateful to him for getting me the part—but I'm also a little uneasy. There's something about him I don't trust—he's too smooth.

My thoughts of him evaporate, at least temporarily, when I see David turn the corner, his knapsack slung over one shoulder, his hands shoved deep into the pockets of his baggy jeans. He sees me at our window table; he gives a smile and a little wave. I wave back. He traipses into the restaurant, saying "Hi!" to the cashier.

"Sorry I'm late," he says, giving me a small kiss. "We had to go over my lines."

"You got lines?" I exclaim happily.

"Kidding." He grins. He throws one leg over the chair and sits down across from me. "We were held up in studio. Had to reshoot a scene. Wait till I tell you what happened."

The waiter, a skinny guy with a tattoo on his forearm, comes by with a 16-ounce mug of beer for David. "You guys want the usual?"

"Yep," David says, taking a slurp of his beer.

"You okay?" the waiter asks, pointing to my glass of house red.

I motion that I want another. The waiter whisks away.

"So—Ms. Prime Time," David begins. "How'd it go today?"

"Um . . . interesting" is all I say.

"Were you brilliant? I bet you blew them away."

I cross my fingers and clench my shoulders. *"And the nominees for Best Scream are . . ."*

He laughs. "What else happened?"

"Not much." But I'm thinking of Jack.

"Did you see Sabrina?"

"In the makeup trailer. She was a bit of a snot."

"Figures."

I look out the window at the blue-gray dusk, then back across the table. "David . . . ?"

"Mmmm?" He's rubbing beer foam off his lips.

"Do you know who Jack Weaver is?"

"Of course. Why?"

"No reason." A beat passes. "Okay—maybe there *is* a reason. I met him today."

"You're *kidding!*" He slaps the table. "This qualifies as an M.C.S."

Miscellaneous Celebrity Sighting. David and I are always trying to outdo each other. John Cusack getting out of a limousine. Danny Glover on the patio of Pastis. Penny Marshall waiting for a cab.

"Did he go to the studio to talk to Foster or something?"

"No—he was sort of talking to me."

He wrinkles his nose, as if not understanding. "Why would he talk to *you?*"

I let the unintentional insult pass. "I kind of met him before."

"You *did? When?*"

"At the audition the other day."

"You met a network president last *week* and you didn't even *tell* me?"

"How was I supposed to tell you? I didn't even recognize him! I mean, he's so—so—" I almost say "gorgeous," but I settle on "young."

David looks a little hurt. As all actors do, he has a thing about age. "He's not *that* young."

"Not *that* young, I guess."

He shakes his head. Sips his beer. He's still trying to process this news, but it's a square peg of information in a brain of round holes. "So what's he like?"

"He's kind of nice," I say. Though *nice* isn't quite the word. I tell him the story about getting lost in the halls. And that we had a cigarette outside the studio. I omit the part about sitting alone with him on the roof and how good it felt just to have his hand—*his hand*—touch my back.

"Huh," David says, shocked. *"I* heard he's a real snake. That he'd crawl over his dying grandmother to close a deal." He stops and pumps his eyebrows suggestively. "Anything else I should know about?"

"Like what?"

"Ah, come on, Sal. We've all heard the stories. He's banged every actress in the city. In a *couple* of cities, actually." He laughs. "Did he *try* anything with you?"

"Of course he didn't *try* anything," I say, giving him a playful slap. But I feel an unpleasant twinge. *He's banged every actress in the city. . . .* Am I actually feeling *jealous* over a man I just met?

"I'm keeping my eye on you," he says with a playful warning. He goes to take another sip of his beer and then stops. "I almost forgot. You *have* to hear what happened on set today."

I'm grateful for the change in subject.

"We're all in the studio shooting a restaurant scene. I'm in the background doing my thing." He mimics polishing a glass. "They zoom in for a close-up of Raine Brando, when all of a sudden there's all this banging. We look up and someone kind of tumbles into the studio. Choking or something. Well, not choking exactly. But kind of like not being able to breathe? Shaking and spazzing and flailing everywhere." He lets a beat pass. "Guess who it was."

"Who?"

"*Guess.*"

"Not Dara . . . ?"

He nods meaningfully.

"Oh, my God!" I put my hand on my heart. "You're kidding!"

"You should've seen it, Sal. It was awful. She was grabbing for her throat, her eyes bulging. Someone thought it must be a joke. He said: *"Hey, that's not in the script. Are we on pinks or what?'* And then, all of a sudden, there's this horrible sound, this . . . this . . ." He screws his face up. "This kind of wet, muffled crunching sound. Somebody's mic picked it up. It was the most disgusting sound you ever *heard.*"

"What happened?" I ask nervously.

"She bit her tongue."

"Ewwww!"

"Practically right *off.*"

"*Ewwww!*"

"There was blood everywhere!"

My breath is coming shallowly. I picture Dara sitting across from me, swirling designs in her chocolate icing. "But I just saw her. She seemed fine. Normal. Was it like a seizure or something?"

"Who knows? They took her to Roosevelt and she underwent some kind of emergency operation to get her tongue sewed back on. She's supposed to be 'under observation.' " He makes air quotes.

"Oh, God. . . ." A dull, cool weight settles through me.

"It was all very *Twilight Zone,* Sal. You have no idea how much a tongue can bleed. I even saw it. Saw her tongue hanging out of her mouth by a piece of thread, wiggling a little like a . . . like a fish on a hook, for crissakes!" He laughs in spite of himself, grossing himself out.

Just then the waiter brings over the pizza, setting it down on the stainless-steel stand between us, giving it a little spin. I stare at the greasy kaleidoscope of cheese and pepperoni and cover my mouth. David relents, fighting off his own queasiness, and begins hunting down a good slice.

"Jesus. . . . Poor Dara," I say. And I'm surprised by how much I mean it.

"Don't overdo it, okay, Sal?" His mouth is full of pizza. "It's *me.* I know how you feel about Dara. It's not like this is the worst thing that could happen to you."

"Don't *say* that. I had one minor problem with the fact she got every part I wanted, but that doesn't mean I *hated* her. I just had coffee with her two days ago. We had a really nice talk!"

"You told me she didn't stop bragging for half an hour."

"*So?*" I roll my eyes at him. "That doesn't mean I wanted her to wind up in the hospital."

"Yeah, right. You put a hex on her every time you saw her."

"Hey!" I slap his arm. *I wish she'd get some debilitating disease or something and let the rest of us have a chance.* "Are you saying *I* did it? Are you saying *I* made her sick?!"

He laughs and rubs his arm. "Just kidding, Sal. Take it easy. I'm just joking. You're acting weird tonight. All skittery. Is something wrong?"

I stare at him, feeling helpless. "I'm sorry. I'm just a little . . . tired."

He shakes his head at me, rolls his eyes as if I'm a little crazy. But he goes back to his pizza.

I look out the window again; it is dark now. I rub my aching frown muscles, remembering Dara's singsongy voice: *"Whatever you do—don't break a nail!"*

It makes me feel sick.

A hazy full moon settles over the peak of St. Francis as I walk home. I'm still thinking of Dara. *Maybe I should go see her tomorrow. Bring her some flowers or something.* I'm not exactly looking forward to this prospect. First of all, I hate hospitals. Secondly, I don't like the idea of seeing poor Dara with her tongue half off.

When I open my apartment door, the brightest light in the room is the flashing red signal on my clunky, old answering machine. With a strange sense of premonition, I walk over to it and press REWIND. It's Gus.

"Sal? If you're there, pick up. Oh, f'crissakes, where the hell are you? This is urgent. It's Dara Dempsey. She's sick. She's in the hospital." An excited squeal comes out of her. "The executive producer of *DUD* just called me, Sal. They want you to read for her part!"

I want to be excited, really I do. But a cold shudder of dread passes through me.

I wish she'd get a debilitating disease or something. . . .

God. What am I feeling so guilty about? This is just a coincidence. A freak of nature, that's all. But I long for the light, forgettable sensation a coincidence sends through you. Because this doesn't feel like a coincidence.

ELEVEN

The Devil looks after his own.

PROVERB

THE next morning is one of those first-day-of-school mornings. The leaves have not started to turn, but there is the smell of autumn in the air. It reminds me of new running shoes. Colored notebooks. The subtly lethal smell of lead pencils. I wish I could enjoy it. But I can't stop thinking of Dara in her hospital bed.

None of it bothers Gus, of course, who is propelling me down the corridor of the 31st floor of UBN, nattering instructions under her breath like a stage mother on speed. "Be nice. But not too nice. Smile. But not too much. Don't speak unless they ask you, but don't say nothing, 'cause then you'll just look dumb."

We find the right room, an office with one wall of bookshelves, another of soap award plaques, and one window with white venetian blinds overlooking a spectacular view of midtown. Two people sitting at a round boardroom table stand up when they see us. It's Lee Roswell and Ruben Ellis, the co–executive producers of *Dusk Until Dawn*. Lee is in her forties, with a blond bob, a taupe suit, and tired blue eyes. Ruben is a slight man with longish, thinning hair and a sparse beard. He wears a crinkly linen suit that's seen too many summers. They've been together for years, personally and professionally; they were husband and wife until three years ago, but they got divorced. The marriage was ruining their careers.

"Gus, so nice to see you again," Lee says. "And this must be Sally." She smiles at me and pumps my hand. "I'm Lee Roswell. This is my partner, Ruben. Have a seat."

We all sit down and I try to get comfortable. I expect someone to start talking, but nobody does. Instead, Lee and Ruben are just staring at me. They cock their heads one way, then the other. They lean forward to have a closer look at me, then lean back and let their eyes go out of focus. After a while, it makes me feel like one of those 3-D posters in a hemp shop where you have to figure out what's hidden behind all the dots.

"Physically," Lee murmurs, "she's the right type."

"The eyes," says Ruben.

"The hair."

"The coloring, too."

I think I detect their gazes traveling with disappointment to my bustline.

"Basically right," says Ruben.

Gus smiles like the madam in a country brothel.

Lee still has that vague, unfocused glaze in her eyes. "Only Sally has more . . . more . . ."

"More *oomph* than Dara," Ruben finishes for her.

"Yes, more *oomph.*"

"Is *oomph* good?" I ask.

"*Oomph* is great," Lee says.

"*Oomph* is what we're looking for," says Ruben.

A beat passes where everyone seems to be measuring my *oomph* quotient. "Um . . . has anyone heard anything about Dara?" I ask.

Lee's expression drops. "It's not good."

"So what happened?" Gus asks, trying to sound sympathetic. "Did they get her tongue back on?"

"They operated last night," Lee says. "No word yet. Oops. Sorry. That didn't come out right."

"Do they know what's wrong with her yet?" I ask.

Both Ruben and Lee shake their heads mysteriously.

"Poor girl," Gus *tsks,* but I can feel her squeeze my hand triumphantly under the table.

Lee looks at me. "I don't know how much you know about the character, Sally."

"Quite a bit, actually. I auditioned for—" Gus bumps me with her knee. "Not much."

"I'll give you the rundown," Lee says, leaning forward. "Meridien is an orphan. She was raised in the Sisters of the Sorrowful Virgin Convent, where she decided to become a nun."

I nod.

"She's only weeks away from taking her final vows when her real parents discover her. They have been looking for her for years. Her parents are Victor and Jacqueline Valencia." She waits expectantly for my reaction. When she doesn't get one, she says, "Our most popular couple with women twenty-five to thirty-four?"

"Oh, right." I nod in comprehension.

"They also happen to be wealthy jet-setters," she adds. "So here's where Meridien's conflict comes in. Does she join the nunnery as she always intended? Or does she give up the calling and become a fabulously wealthy socialite?"

"Sounds like a tough decision," snorts Gus.

"Well, it may not seem that way to you or me," Lee says, taking the character's plight very seriously. "But to Meridien, it's different. Because she wants to do the right thing. She wants to devote her life to God. And how can she do that if she goes to live with her wealthy parents?" She shrugs philosophically. "You know what they say. It's easier for an elephant to fit through the eye of a needle than it is for a rich man to enter the gates of heaven."

Ruben looks up curiously. "Isn't that a camel?"

"What?"

"Through the needle. Isn't that a camel?"

"It's an elephant."

"Are you *sure?*"

Lee looks around, a little perturbed. "Can someone back me up here?"

"Camel, elephant—whatever," says Gus. "A large, ugly animal that isn't likely to fit through the eye of a needle anytime soon. We get your point."

Lee gives her ex-husband a "look," then turns to me. "So this is Meridien's conflict, Sally. Do you understand?"

"I think so."

"Now, we'd just like you to do a read-through for us. Okay?" She pushes a script over to me. "I'll be the Mother Superior." She puts on a pair of tortoiseshell bifocals and consults her copy of the script. "Now, just take your time. No pressure."

"Yeah, right," I say nervously, looking around the circle. "No pressure."

They laugh. Warmly. Thoughtlessly.

My eyes move to the first line. But the gray words seem alien. Likes rocks lying on a beach. I take a few deep breaths and somehow bring a voice to my throat.

INT. CONVENT—DAY

MERIDIEN

I just don't know what I'm going to do, Mother Superior.
I love them. They're my flesh and blood.

MOTHER SUPERIOR
Yes, my child. But so is the Church. So is God.

MERIDIEN
But I've prayed for him to deliver them to me all this time.
What if it's a sign?

The scene only takes two minutes, but it's the longest two minutes of my life. When I'm finished, I look worriedly around the circle. I *bombed*. I know I bombed! I'm just about to tell them I'll do it again when Lee slumps forward onto the table. "Thank *Gawd!* She can *act!*" Ruben, too, exhales with relief.

I feel myself blushing. "Thank you." Gus is gripping my hand so excitedly, the tips of my fingers are turning blue.

"We'll run you past the director, but that's just a formality," Lee says. "Makes him think he has a say in things. But other than that, we can start talking nitty-gritty right away. It'll start with a scale contract with an option to renew after six weeks, just to see how everything's working out. After that, we can—"

"Wait a second," Gus interrupts. "I'm not sure we're available. Sal, how are we for the next few weeks?"

"Pardon?"

"There's that other thing coming up—but that's not until the end of October, right?"

"What other thing?"

"The"—she nudges me under the table— "*thing.*"

"Oh, yeah, right. The thing."

Gus looks back at Lee. "I guess we're free for the next six weeks. But brace yourself. Saviors don't come cheap."

The others laugh tightly. I notice this during meetings—that TV executives like to burst into laughter on a regular basis, even when nothing funny has been said. I guess it's like a laugh track in a bad sitcom; it lulls you into thinking you're not wasting your time. Lee shoves a stack of scripts at me, telling me there'll be a lot of pickups tomorrow. They tell me what time my wardrobe call is. Where my dressing room is. What the details of the contract are. There's much air kissing and congratulating. When it's over, Lee leans back in her chair and sighs happily.

"Well, he was right again, wasn't he?" she says.

"He sure was," says Ruben.

"Who was right?" I ask.

"Jack Weaver, of course," Lee answers, as if it's obvious. "When he found out what happened to Dara, he put your name in for the part right away. He knew you'd be perfect."

I feel a rush of vertigo.

Gus jabs her hand in my arm and drags me up. "Well, thanks, guys. See you soon." She propels me out of the office before I can say anything else. "See? I told you. Play your cards right with this guy and the sky's the limit."

"Thanks for the vote of confidence, Gus," I say through clenched teeth.

"Oh, *I know.* You're all upset because you *didn't get the part on your own,*" she mocks me. "Well, grow up, Sal. This is the biggest break of your career. I don't know what the hell's the matter with you. It's like you don't even *want* to be happy or something. Remind me to nominate you when they come up with a Best Masochist category at the Emmy Awards." She gives me one last reproachful glare, then heads off for Business Affairs; she wants to get my contract processed before the end of the day.

When I get downstairs, David is waiting for me on the sidewalk. He was working today, but wrapped early. "So?" he asks with an excited smile. "What happened?"

I shrug. Let a beat pass. "I got it," I say, kind of stunned.

There's a moment of nothingness. Just a hitch of time. Where I think David is mad. Or jealous. Or something. And I don't blame him. I know it would be hard for me if he suddenly started having all the breaks. But then he recovers; a big smile crosses his face and he grabs me, kissing me. "Congratulations, sweetie! I knew they'd love you!"

"I don't know if they *love* me. I just think it's because I have the same hair as Dara."

I don't mention a word about Jack Weaver.

"Just think—we'll be on the same show. We can have lunch together every day!"

"Yeah . . . I guess." I try to smile.

"Let's go out for a celebration drink!"

"I don't know if I should," I tell him. I motion with an armload of scripts. "I have too many lines to memorize." But then I see the look on his face; at least I *have* lines. "Well, maybe just one," I tell him, trying to smile.

As we walk away from the building, I look up from the shadows of the street to see blue sky and white clouds scurrying high above.

At the Backburner, Jeremy freezes over the easel. "You want time off for a"—he sneers— "*soap* opera?"

"It's just for six weeks, Jeremy. I'll still come in on the weekends. I promise."

The lighting in the back room is dim, cast from an old floor lamp next to the easel. All around me, the half-closed eyes of all those delirious lovers stare back at me, as if *they* were the voyeurs and not me.

"What am I supposed to do when you're not here?"

"I'm sure you can get someone else for a little while. Jeremy, really, I *can't* say no to this. It's great exposure for me."

"Do you realize that in any other country in the world exposure is a cause of death?"

I let out a helpless little groan. *"Please?"*

"Fine," he says grudgingly, "you can have the time off."

I peck a little kiss on his hollow temple. "You're the best boss in the world."

I go to leave the room but am intrigued by the sketch he's working on. The erratic black scratches have fallen together to form the image of a man and a woman. The woman is leaning back on her hands with her legs spread. There is a seductive smile on her face. Tumbling locks of dark hair. The man is crawling over to her on his hands and knees, his penis swollen, almost angry-looking. Jeremy is working on the space between the woman's legs, dotting fine pubic hairs in a wild triangle.

He sees me staring. "Do you mind? You're in my light."

"I'm sorry," I say, turning out of the room. "Th-thanks again for the time off."

"Don't thank me," he says with a sneer. "Just don't forget me on your meteoric rise to drug addiction and spiritual despair."

THAT night I try calling Roosevelt Hospital.

Twice.

The first time I hang up.

The second time I ask for Dara Dempsey's room.

"I'm sorry," says the woman who answers. "Ms. Dempsey is unable to accept calls right now."

And I wonder what that could mean? Is she just in the shower? Or maybe she can't speak at all?

"Is she . . . okay?"

There is a long beat. "I'm sorry. I'm not allowed to give out that information over the phone."

I hang up and sit amid my pile of scripts from *DUD*. A big black binder the producers called the Show Bible, a book with all the major story arcs and character outlines, is open in front of me. I'm trying to work on my character—to think of Meridien's favorite food, her favorite color, her favorite song.

But I can't concentrate. I feel guilty. Worried. Sad. And it's all mixed in with absolute elation that I'll actually have a regular paycheck for a while. It sort of feels as if I've been waiting in line for hours to get on a new roller-coaster ride, and now that I'm on it, buckled in, and just beginning to crest the first rise, a part of me wishes I could change my mind.

TWELVE

The Devil is not so black as he is painted.

PROVERB

"Everyone! Attention please!"

Lee Roswell has her arm around me and is introducing me to the cast and crew of *DUD*. We're all in on the 19th floor, where UBN's daytime programming is produced. *DUD* has three studios. The one we're in is the largest, with ceilings that soar off into nothingness, glinting with lighting grids and catwalks. Most of the room is cluttered with ladders, light stands, or errant coffee cups. But here and there, as if suspended by their own gravitational force, are small, perfectly lit, perfectly decorated little worlds. A living room. A kitchen. An office. And, of course, the pretend restaurant where David pretend-works. The crew members are mostly in jeans and T-shirts, looking tired and harried. The actors, on the other hand, are in full makeup, sparkling beneath the bright lights. It's such a study in contrasts, I feel as if I've been thrown into a fish tank where expensive tropicals and bottom feeders are expected to keep the peace.

When Lee has everyone's attention, she announces, "This is our new virgin! Sally Carpenter!" There's an eruption of good-natured laughter. Lee leans into me: "I bet it's been a while since you've been introduced as *that.*"

I see David standing behind the bar in his white shirt and black waiter bow tie, his hair smoothed back in a slick ponytail and lots of tan-colored makeup on. He waves "Congratulations!" to me. I give him an inconspicuous little flip of my hand. For some reason, I don't want everyone else to know I'm dating someone on the show—particularly an extra. And then I feel guilty for being so petty.

My hands are trembling as I meet the other actors. All the famous hairdos. All the familiar smiles. I was never really a big soap fan, but a bunch of us used to watch them in the dorm at college. It was a kind of postfeminist thing to do. We'd sit around laughing at the hokey dialogue and overwrought plotlines, swearing we'd never stoop to being in a soap opera no matter how broke we were. But behind the derision and the jokes I used to feel something else, something I couldn't deny—admiration. Admiration for these glorious few who had lifted themselves up out of the pool of anonymity and hit that ever elusive target—a regular-paying gig. I wondered what talent, what quirk, what strand of DNA these splendid mutations had that ensured they rose to the top? And—more important—did I have it, too?

Eventually Lee relegates introductory duties to a production assistant named Emma, a twenty-something girl with freckles and sandy-brown hair. She has tiny shoulders and skinny little arms; I'm sure her hips are narrow, too, but they bulge with so many fanny packs and walkie-talkies that she looks ridiculously pear-shaped and actually clanks when she walks. She shows me around the floor. Wardrobe. Makeup. Hair. Everywhere we go, members of the cast and crew move comfortably, familiar with each other—not quite like a family, because there are too many of them, but more like a house full of happy cats. Around every corner I keep expecting to see him, wandering around in his black suit, stalking the halls for other actors who can't find their way out.

"You'll be sharing a dressing room," Emma tells me. "Hope you don't mind. Everyone has to." She tells me that UBN is expanding so quickly, with so many new productions starting, that a lot of the studio floors are under construction. There are sheets of drywall being knocked out and installed and support beams are exposed everywhere.

"This is yours," she says, knocking on a gray door with two name plaques. One of them reads RAINE BRANDO.

It can't be! I'm sharing with *the* Raine Brando? She's been on the show for years!

But my excitement is tempered when I see the second nameplate. It's covered with a piece of masking tape upon which is scribbled SALLY C. in harried blue marker; the tape isn't thick enough to completely cover the name underneath, which seems to float up, a ghostly shadow of itself: DARA DEMPSEY.

From beyond the door I hear a feminine *"Come in!"*

Emma pushes the door open. The room is about the size of a small office, with rose-colored walls and low, worn burgundy velvet chairs. There's a smoked glass coffee table. A huge mirror lined with vanity bulbs and a long black counter. The room is strewn with makeup, lingerie, curling irons, racks of clothes, crystal vases filled with flowers in various stages of wilting.

A beautiful, long-legged African-American woman is in the room, facing the mirror, talking on the phone. She's wearing a silver-gray peignoir, a matching teddy, and satin mules with marabou trim. Her sleek hair is rolled up in enormous rollers. There's a lipsticky martini glass on the counter in front of her.

". . . And if it's not up two points by opening tomorrow, sell it. It's a loser." Her voice is full, delivered straight from the diaphragm. I'm a little stunned to see her in person. She's been a queen of daytime drama for years with at least three Best Villainess award nominations. She looks up and sees my reflection in the mirror. She stutters for a moment, then regains her composure. "Talk to you tomorrow," she says into the phone. It takes a couple of clumsy thunks before she is able to hang up because she's not looking at what she's doing; she's still staring at my reflection. "Shit," she says, awestruck, "you look just like her."

I shift uncomfortably.

Then, as if remembering herself, she turns on her chair and motions me into the room. "Sorry! Sorry, come in! Sally, right? Sally something?"

"Carpenter."

"Right. Raine Brando," she says, shaking my hand lightly.

"I know . . ."

She goes back to the counter. "You wanna drink?" she asks my reflection. I notice that people in television seem to prefer addressing each other through mirror reflections. It's as if television has made three-dimensional reality obsolete.

"No thanks."

She unscrews the cap of a half-empty bottle of Absolut and refreshes her glass. "I'm trying to create the perfect martini." She rolls her eyes heavenward and sighs helplessly. "So many vodkas—so little time."

I laugh.

"Make yourself at home. Everything up to here is mine." She points to a pink nail polish stroke on the black counter. "Everything over there is yours."

"Thanks." I move to my side of the dressing room. My shoe hits a small cardboard box under the counter.

"Oh, that's just Dara's stuff. I'm sure she's gonna come get it. Put it anywhere if it's in your way."

"No. It's fine." The box flaps are open and I can't help but peek inside.

A large transparent makeup case (everything expensive department store brands except for the familiar pink and green tube of Great Lash mascara). A Danielle Steel novel. A round brush with long blond hairs. A Polaroid of Dara, taken in this very room. The flash of the bulb is reflected in the mirror, partially obscuring the man who took the picture.

"You nervous?" she asks, adjusting her rollers.

"A little. It's just so wild meeting everyone in the flesh."

"In the plastic, you mean. You walk out there and you'll find more fake body parts than Madame Tussaud's. These, on the other hand"— she gives her gravity-defying breasts a shake—"are real. No matter what they say in the tabs."

I laugh. Emma leans in the door, crackling with static from her walkie-talkie. "They want you in wardrobe, Sally," she says before disappearing again.

"Lucky you. Now you get to stand around and get stuck with pins."

I smile, tell her it was an honor meeting her, and go to the door. I look right, then left, then turn right.

"Sally?"

"Uh-huh?"

She points in the other direction with a long nail. "Wardrobe's thatta way."

"Oh. Thanks."

DUD Wardrobe is a large white room lined with mirrors and sewing tables. Beige dress dummies stand around the room like stubborn sentries unaware they've lost their heads to war. The wardrobe mistress's name is Karen. She's a small woman wearing an oversized Save the Whales T-shirt and black leggings. A measuring tape hangs around her neck. A pincushion bristles on her wrist. She is so used to speaking through the row of straight pins she holds between her lips, constantly plucking and putting back the little silver slivers, that she has acquired an almost ambidextrous mouth. She's pinning a black dress on me.

"Okay—just hold for a second. One more and . . ."

There isn't much of a wardrobe for Meridien—by soap opera standards. A few dark dresses. All of them plain, simple, a little stiff.

"We can't forget this," she says. She fetches the little black-and-white headpiece with a short black veil that falls to just below my jaw and fits it on my head with the aid of a small comb. "You're not really a nun yet, that's why it's not a long one," she explains. "This part's called a wimple." She indicates the starched white headband that rests against my head. "A gay friend of mine told me. He's the one who gave me the pattern. He's a drag queen and uses one in his act." She stands back and looks at my reflection in the mirror, squinting. "There's something missing. Oh, yeah." She retrieves, a large, chunky silver crucifix on a thick chain. It's not really a crucifix, because I know crucifixes have an image of Jesus on them, and this one is simple and bare, but all crosses remind me of Jesus so I call them crucifixes anyway. I slip it over my head.

"Oh—and you need this," says Karen, handing me a large, worn black leather book. It looks ancient. The words *The Holy Bible* are embossed in peeling gold on the front cover. I open the book and am shocked—horrified—to see that it's not the Bible at all, but the *Oxford English Dictionary.* I've opened it to *N.*

Nightingale. Nightshade. Nihilism.

"The props department mocked it up," she explains when she sees the confused look on my face. "It's for effect. We couldn't find one that looked right on camera."

"Oh." I close the book and tuck it demurely under my arm, uncertain whether or not I should treat it with reverence. I look at my image in the mirror. Simple black dress. Short black veil with a band of white. Silver cross and big black Bible.

I am reminded of a childhood joke.

What's black and white, black and white, black and white?

A nun falling down the stairs.

Another image flashes through my mind. This one of Dara. Not in her pink T-shirt and push-up bra, but rolling around on a studio floor, bleeding and helpless and dressed like a nun. I remember another, more macabre version of the joke.

What's black and white and red all over?
A nun with her head chopped off.
Or her tongue.

I have four scenes the first day, including two pickups. I break every personal acting record I have. No false starts. No missed cues. No stepping on anyone's lines. Every time a man in a suit comes to stand in the doorway, I look over. Expecting it to be him.

It never is.

I feel relieved.

But strangely disappointed, too.

When we break for lunch, David and I meet in a designated spot in the hall, me in my pretend nun habit, him in his pretend waiter uniform. We head to the commissary. It's bright and noisy—not unlike a high school cafeteria and, like in a high school cafeteria, a careful hierarchy is observed. Techies sit with techies. Show runners with show runners. Extras with extras. When David and I sit down at the extras' table (the one in the corner, underneath the air ducts), I am painfully aware that I am the only person with a speaking part. As for the other actors, like the most popular kids in school, they sit at the sunny tables, flanking the windows. They laugh and gossip and reach across the table, sharing carrot sticks, low-carb tuna salads, and Zone bars with each other.

Over lunch, I don't talk much and nobody asks me anything. It seems extras make up for the contractual silence forced upon them when the cameras are going by not shutting up when the cameras are off.

When lunch is over, David kisses me good-bye and goes back to his position in the fake restaurant. I navigate my way through the halls, thankfully finding my dressing room. The door is partially ajar. I can see Raine's shadow moving around on the floor. But when I open the door, it's not Raine.

It's Jack.

He's standing at the counter, sniffing curiously at a bottle of perfume. When he sees my reflection in the mirror, his dark face immediately breaks into a smile and he puts down the perfume.

"I hope you don't mind. The door was open."

I swallow nervously. In fact, it *is* a little rude that he'd let himself in. But what am I going to do? Kick him out? I sniff a little indignantly and say, "Don't worry. You practically own the place, don't you?"

"Ouch. Sorry. I just heard you started today and I wanted to come and say hi."

A nervous beat passes. "Well . . . hi." I force myself to put one foot in front of another and go to the counter. I fuss pointlessly with things so I don't have to look straight at him.

"I like that," he says, motioning to the habit. "I hear black and white is big this year."

I give him a bland smile. I continue puttering on the counter, moving makeup bottles for no reason, shifting script copies. When I finally do speak, my tone is grudging. "I guess I should thank you. They told me you put my name in for the part. I really appreciate it, but you've gotta stop doing this. I told you, it makes me uncomfortable. There's really no way I could repay you."

He smiles a little suggestively. "Don't be too sure of that."

I hear Raine's voice in the hall. She sweeps into the room in a flounce of silk suiting. She stops in her tracks, looks from me to Jack, then excuses herself, backing out of the door.

"Congratulations," I tell him. "You just scared away a Best Villainess nominee."

He laughs at that, but it doesn't ease the tension. For something to do I face the mirror and begin taking off the headpiece.

"So, how's it going on set?" he asks. "Everybody treating you well?"

My voice is clipped: "Fine." Naturally the comb on the veil gets snagged in my hair. I twist and pull, but like a burr it holds fast, making one little rat's nest on the crown of my head. I grit my teeth in frustration.

"Here. Let me help." He leans toward to me and begins trying to untangle the comb. He's so close that I can see the texture of the ruddy flesh of his throat, his pulse moving steadily beneath his skin. It seems that I shouldn't be this close to him, so close that I can see his pulse.

"About the part," he says, *"I* should be thanking *you*. You're really saving my ass here. *DUD* pulls in our biggest audience in the afternoons." He hands me the veil. "And since the 'lousy walk-on' wasn't impressive enough . . ." He lets his voice trail off playfully.

"Hey, you know I didn't mean it that way."

"I'm just kidding. You're right for the part, Sally. That's why you have it."

"You thought I'd make a good *nun?*"

"I think you're a good actor."

I stare at him a moment. *He's joking—obviously.* But I feel the warmth of the compliment rush through my body, thawing me—just a little. "Anyway, like I said, it's a big break for me. If there's anything I can ever do for you . . . let me know." It seems like a harmless offer. After all, what could *I* possibly be able to do for *him?*

He gives a sly smile. "Well, maybe there *is* something."

"Oh?" That makes me wary.

"Let me take you to dinner."

"What?"

"Let me take you to dinner."

"Like, to a *restaurant?*"

"Uh-huh."

"Me and you?"

"And forks and knives and food and hopefully a little wine." He gives a soft laugh. "Yes, Sally. That's usually the way dinner works."

I feel my heart beating like the rain inside my chest. A network president is asking me to dinner. Jack *Weaver* is asking me to dinner.

Oh, God . . . I can't do this . . . I can't do this. What about David? I have to say no. There's no way I can go to dinner with this man. I *have* to say no. I can see the word in front of me. *No.* Gray and wrinkled and prunelike. But there sitting next to it, red and plump and juicy, is the word *yes,* and that's the word I choose.

"Sure," I say. And the second it's out of my mouth, I regret it.

He flashes a broad grin. "Great. How's Thursday?"

"Thursday's . . . fine."

Shit! What are you doing, Sally? Are you crazy?

"I'll pick you up at your place. Eight o'clock?"

"Uh . . . sure. I better give you directions." I lean over and start jotting on the corner of the cover page of my script. "It's best to come up Prince that time of night," I tell him. I can feel him watching me over my shoulder, feel his gaze as certainly as if someone were slowly pouring warm water over my bare skin. "And you'll never find a parking space. So just buzz up and I'll run down." I hand him the directions. "If you get lost, it's right across from an old church."

"I won't get lost." His voice is low and assured. He pushes himself off the counter. As he passes me on his way out of the room, I think he says something. I *think* he does. *See you then. See you Thursday. See you soon.* Just this hot *whoosh* of a whisper, but I'm not sure. I hold my breath until I see his reflection move to the door behind me; he turns back once, smiling slyly. When he's gone, I exhale a great breath of relief. I stand alone in the room with the hammering of my heart in my ears and my own stunned reflection staring back at me.

What's black and white and red all over?

A nun who's just been asked to dinner.

GOING home on the subway, I scribble notes in the margins of my script, developing Meridien's character. She's a Capricorn, I think. Her favorite movie is . . . *Agnes of God.* Maybe I should rent it for research. And *Sister Act.* And that old classic with Audrey Hepburn—what was it called? *The Nun's Story?*

I should talk to someone from St. Francis Convent, too. See if I can observe them for a day or two. I think of the nuns floating up and down the street in their black-and-white habits. I'm not looking forward to that prospect. Nuns make me a little uncomfortable. First, they make me feel grossly inadequate in the virtue department, and second, ever since I met Sister Ruth, I've been a little afraid of them. Sister Ruth was the principal of my brother's Catholic high school. She had gray eyes and thin lips (nobody knew what color her hair was—you could never see it). She seemed about seven feet tall, with the shoulder span of Batman in her black habit. She had the reputation for being the meanest, most crotchety woman ever to shake a walking stick (she had a bit of a limp and used a wooden cane with a goose head on the grip). I've never been able to forget my only encounter with her. It was the day of my first confession. I remember her floating over to me, bending down level with my height. I remember the way her gray eyes looked, the smell of her breath: "Remember, Sally, the meek shall inherit the earth." I shiver inwardly and make a note to call St. Francis.

I put the pad away and stare out the window at the passing blackness. The train rocks back and forth, making my joints feel loose. After a while I find myself relaxing.

I find myself thinking of him. . . .

Jack Weaver . . . I feel a surge of sweetness when I say his name under my breath.

Do you know what it feels like? It feels as if we were *meant* to meet. I know that sounds corny. I'm not really into fate or anything, especially when it comes to men, but that's what it feels like. That we were meant to meet. Or—maybe that's not quite it. Maybe it feels as if I already *know* him—that he's not a stranger to me. His voice is so familiar; like the sound of the rain. The contours of his face, the shadows and the light, like a cloud formation I remember shifting above my head when I was a child. It's as if he's been in my life all along, in the deepest, darkest parts of me, waiting until it was time to come forward. He was there when I was born. He was there when I learned to count. Learned to tie my shoes. Lost my virginity. He's been there all along. And it's as if I've been expecting him. Still, it surprised me when he stepped out of the shadows and showed his face for the first time. When the initial shock of seeing him has worn off, I catch my breath and smile in relief.

"So *that's* what you look like," I say.

He smiles and says, *"Yes."*

THIRTEEN

Let the Devil be sometime honour'd for his burning throne.

WILLIAM SHAKESPEARE

I dial the familiar Wisconsin number and take a deep breath as the phone rings in my ear. Part of me hopes she doesn't pick up. But then, there it is—"Yes? Hello?"—her voice.

"Hey, Mom?"

"Sally? Is it the end of the month already?"

I sit on the edge of my futon, twisting the telephone cord around my finger. "No, but I wanted to call because I have some news—I got a job."

"You're *kidding!*" she exclaims, delighted.

I'm heartened by her reaction. "Yeah . . . on a soap opera . . . *Dusk Until Dawn.* It's on channel nine there in the afternoons."

"Oh." A disappointed syllable. "Not a *real* job, then."

"Yes, Mother. I'm an actor, remember? When I get a part on a television show, it's a *real* job."

"Well . . . I guess . . . congratulations, then." She seems to have found her Christian generosity finally. "Lots of good news in the family this week. Your brother called the other night. They've increased his isolation pay again. I think he really likes it up there. He met a girl, a waitress at a truck stop . . ."

"Really?" I feel like telling her, *I met someone, too, Mom . . . his name is Jack. . . .* But I don't.

Eventually we get to the details about my role. When she finds out I'm playing a nun, she's horrified. "Sally, is that such a good idea? It sounds a little . . . disrespectful."

"I'm sure it's not a mortal sin or anything."

"Oh, how would you know?" she asks sharply. "You probably haven't even been to confession since you got down there."

I don't say anything. She's right.

"Well, I'm going to talk to Father Silvio about this," she says. "If he has any problems, you'll be hearing from me."

After I hang up the phone, I have to ride out the familiar wave of guilt, anger, irritation, and hopeless love that I always feel after talking to my mother. Almost as if to pour salt on the wounds, I slide open the drawer of the end table beside the futon and retrieve a small, folding brass picture frame. It used to sit on the bedside table in my room at home, but I don't set it out anymore. The last thing I need is to have a constant reminder where I came from.

There are two photos in the frame. On the left is one of my father (we used a blowup of it at the funeral to set next to the closed coffin). It's a picture of him wearing a beige sport shirt, sitting in a lawn chair in the backyard, grinning contentedly and drinking a can of Schlitz. (We had the beer can cropped out for the funeral enlargement, of course.)

The other photo is of my mother, Paul, and me, taken a couple of years after my father died. It was our first family vacation without him. It had been a difficult time for us. Paul took it harder than anyone, I think. He started cutting classes, smoking in the house, swearing at my mother. He had inherited my father's predisposition for mood-altering substances, and by the time he was fifteen he had discovered at least one of the many uses of the esteemed hemp plant. Not even the dreaded Sister Ruth could stop him from experimenting. She'd sent him home several times with red eyes, accusing my mother of letting him stray. But my mother could never prove anything. She was forbidden to go into his bedroom under penalty of much screaming and taking of the Lord's name in vain. I think she preferred not to know the truth anyway. All she insisted was that he let her do his laundry, so once a week a malodorous pile of Black Sabbath T-shirts and dirty jeans would materialize outside his door and eight hours later a pink laundry basket of said items, neatly folded and smelling like dryer sheets, would be sitting in the same place, waiting for him to reach his arm out of the darkness of his room and drag the basket in, like someone in solitary confinement who's grown so sensitive to light that he won't even venture outside for his tray of food.

It was my mother's suggestion that we take a family vacation. I was thirteen at the time; Paul was sixteen. She thought a Greyhound bus ride to Niagara Falls would be fun—and "not too hard on the budget." We rented a small, dingy hotel room with two double beds ("We girls can share, Sally," she told me). It was too expensive to have a room with a view of the falls, so our window overlooked the parking lot and the backs of hotels that did have a view of the falls. The first night we had dinner at a delicious but kitschy Italian restaurant where the plates of food were served on pewter chargers and all the waitresses wore long white togas that they somehow managed to keep clean throughout the night. The next afternoon we visited the falls. Paul and I wanted to go on the *Maid of the Mist,* but my mother said what they were charging for tickets was highway robbery. Besides, we'd all just get wet anyway. Instead she let us go to Dracula's Mansion, an amusement park–type establishment on the main strip. I remember clutching the back of Paul's T-shirt as we wound down narrow hallways lined with wax museum dummies with their heads cut off and dried fake blood everywhere. Sometimes we'd have to navigate through pitch-black corridors where local kids working summer jobs, no doubt, clutched at us from the darkness and dragged fake cobwebs over our heads. Paul laughed uproariously, probably stoned out of his mind, but I was petrified, moving toward cracks of light in the walls and praying for EXIT signs. At one point I screamed so loud that Paul yelled, *"Cool it, man! You're freaking my sister out,"* and a disquietingly casual voice coming from beside us said, "Sorry, dude."

Once out on the sunny street, I bent over at the waist, trying to catch my breath and waiting for my nerves to steady. I expected to feel relieved. Instead I just felt worse. I looked up and understood why. Dracula's Mansion was right next door to an ice cream stand, and like any ice cream stand in any tourist trap on a sunny day, the sidewalk in front of it was splotched with wayward drips and the melted puddles of scoops that had been accidentally nudged off the top of double- and triple-deckers. The sticky-sweet smell was making me nauseous. I actually had to cover my mouth not to throw up. No one else seemed to notice.

"I've got a good idea!" my mother said. "Why don't we get someone to take our picture?" Without waiting to see whether or not Paul or I would cooperate, she approached a family of Japanese tourists and asked them if they'd do us the honor. The man smiled politely, inquiring in broken English if we'd do the same for him. There was much cheerful agreement. I was embarrassed because when we temporarily traded camera equipment, the man had an expensive Nikon 35mm and all my mother had was this ancient Kodak Fiesta, which looked like it had seen every wedding, Christmas, and birthday party since she was old enough to vote.

"Over here, kids," my mother said, corralling us in front of Dracula's Mansion. She took her sun hat off, revealing a distinct dent in the helmet of her Nice 'n' Easy brown hair. We all smiled stiffly for the Japanese man.

When Mom developed the film a few weeks later, she insisted we all gather in the kitchen to look at the pictures together. She oohed and aahed at the images of the spectacular falls and gushed over the shot of the three of us standing in front of Dracula's Mansion. I thought it was terrible. So *depressing*. All of us squinting against the sun and look-ing miserable in our own ways. Paul, as usual, had managed to give the camera the finger without my mother seeing it at the time. She caught it now and slapped his arm lightly. "I told you to stop *doing* that."

"Gross me out," I grumbled when I saw myself standing with my knee curved in like a model in a Sears catalog and a smile so tense as to rival my head shot in Gus's office. Even though I had discovered acting, plastering my bedroom walls with photos of Michelle and Sigourney and enduring my mother's scorn over "false idols," and even though I had necked with Jimmy Saunders behind the Dumpsters on the last day of school, the greater part of me still wanted to be a "good girl." This responsibility seemed even more important now that my brother was distinguishing himself as the "wild one." But when I saw this girl smiling so eagerly in the photograph, I didn't like her. I didn't like the fact that no matter how hard she tried, she couldn't com-pletely hide her awkwardness or her sadness or the fact that only moments before she was so upset she had wanted to throw up all over the sidewalk. I also didn't like the pose my mother struck, her own smile rigid, her arms reaching out ineffectually for our shoulders, as if physically holding the family together was even too much to ask of her. It was all so . . . *phony*. It seemed as if we were trying to pretend my father's death hadn't happened, and if it did, that it didn't really bother us that much.

Paul's chair squeaked as he stood up from the table. "Those sucked," he said.

"No, they didn't," my mother said, sliding the photos back into the envelope. "I'm having copies made for both of you so you can always remember how much fun we had. We should do it again next summer. I'd love for you kids to see Disneyland before you're too old."

We didn't tell her we were already too old.

By the way, we never went on a family vacation again.

FOURTEEN

Give a thing, and take a thing, to wear the Devil's gold ring.

PROVERB

THE next morning I have to cry. In the script I mean. There's a scene with Meridien alone in her tiny gray room at the convent. The makeup woman was standing by with a splash of glycerine, just in case I couldn't do it, but sure enough, right on cue, a handful of big, fat tears went skidding down my cheeks. The crew cheered. Apparently it's a special rite of passage when you cry for the first time on a soap opera. I'm surprised I was able to do it. I'm so damn nervous about having dinner with Jack Weaver tomorrow night I can barely concentrate. *I must be crazy to do this!* David would kill me if he knew about it. Not that I've told him. Why should I? It's not like a date or anything.

Is it?

Emma comes up to me on a break. "Sally? Did you sign this?"

She hands me a large pink Get Well card with a cartoon kitten on it. I open it and read the florid signatures of the cast and crew and little notes like "Miss you, Dara!" and "Get better soon!" I immediately feel a needle of guilt. I haven't tried calling the hospital since that first night. I started to think that maybe Dara *wouldn't* want to hear from me because I stole her part.

"How's she doing?" I ask uncertainly, quickly scrawling my name in the bottom corner.

"We're not sure. Apparently she can have visitors now, though, so a bunch of us are going to see her during lunch. Just to cheer her up. You gonna come? Score some Buddha points?"

"Oh, I don't know. She probably wouldn't want to see *me*. Not after this." I motion around the dressing room.

"Sally, don't be silly. The girl just got her *tongue* sewed back on. I'm sure the last thing she's worried about is a stupid part. Will you try and make it? Lunch break? Roosevelt Hospital?"

"I'll try," I tell her. But there's no way I'm gonna go. *No way.*

I don't know how it happens. One movement just seems to jerk in front of the other in a clumsy, forced way until, *somehow*, at lunchtime, I find myself standing in front of Roosevelt Hospital holding a small bouquet of daisies, waiting for the others to show up. If *anyone* should visit her, it's me, right? To pay my respects. Apologize. Absolve myself. I've changed out of my costume, though, into normal street clothes. No use rubbing it in.

I look down at the flowers, wrapped in cellophane. They seemed fine when I bought them from a street cart, but now that I get a better look at them, I notice the petals are turning brown around the edges like burnt scrolls and they have a wafting, bitter smell to them.

Where the hell is everybody?

I look at my watch. It's almost two o'clock.

The sky is a strange grayish orange color; it's a color you don't often see, as if a storm's moving in, the kind of color that makes farmers lean on their hoes and peer worriedly up at the sky and say things like "Looks like she's gonna be a doozie."

I begin to notice darkened drops spreading on the dry sidewalk. People start to walk faster, tension creeping into their faces. I back up into the lobby. Dara is on the sixth floor. That much they told me. *Maybe they already went up.* I nervously take the elevator up to the sixth floor. The doors open on a long hallway. It's much quieter than I expected—more like *St. Elsewhere* repeats than *ER*. (In case you haven't figured it out yet, I see my whole life in terms of TV—or movies.)

There's a nurse working at the reception desk, head down, faded gray hair glowing dully in bright fluorescent lights. When she looks up at me, she's so pale and washed-out, her features seem to float up out of her face.

"Yes? May I help you?"

"I was supposed to meet some people here. We're visiting Dara Dempsey?"

"Room six thirteen," she says, pointing with the nub of a pencil before going back to her work.

I swallow and start heading down the hall. I hear a distant cough. The squeak of a bed. A television tuned to a rival soap opera. I hate hospitals. I hate the look of them. I hate the smell of them—that smell of antiseptic thrown over something foul. There's something so futile about hospitals, a kind of noble pointlessness to thinking you can take death out of the bedrooms and off the streets of the world and put it somewhere safe, a place it can't hurt you. But you can't contain death. Death seeps down through the cracks in the floorboards, out through the holes in the walls; death leaks back into the streets, and sometimes I wonder if it isn't all the stronger for the time it's spent incubating inside four walls.

Outside room 613, I stop. I listen for voices, laughter, inside jokes, the sounds a group of people might make trying to cheer up a sick friend. But I hear nothing. It's absolutely still. I push open the door, which feels leadenly cold and heavy beneath my hand.

It's a large room with walls that look dull without sunshine. The only light in the room glows from a small lamp on a stand set up between two beds. The bed closest to the window is empty. The second one contains a single, slight form covered in a white blanket. Her head is turned the other way. Her hands are resting on her stomach, crossed peacefully.

"Dara?" I whisper. But the figure doesn't move. I creep into the room, slowly coming around the bed. "Dara?" Still nothing. And then I see her face. *Her face!* A chill rushes over me so quickly it feels like there must be a draft somewhere, because it's not a face, not really— not Dara's face anyway. She's so puffy there doesn't seem to be any definition, any features, just this strange bloatedness. Her skin is pale; it's almost white, with blue-white veins marbleized beneath it. Thank God she's sleeping. It gives me a chance to adjust to this new face of hers without being caught. Her lips are ashen and seem to be held together by a thin line of black glue, but no, not glue—blood. Dried blood seals her lips together, as if her mouth itself were a wound healing in her face. I can't believe it's her. The shining, smiling Pizza Hut girl. It doesn't look anything like her.

Not even her hair looks like hers, which seems sadder than anything. No longer the airy, undefined, freshly brushed blond of Barbie, it's three shades darker than I remember it, as if she has sweated many times and not been able to shower. My hair looks that way when I'm battling the flu or when I'm so depressed I don't leave the house for two days. But hers is not messy or matted. Rather it lies in two smooth points that run over her shoulders and onto her chest, as if someone— her mother maybe or someone else who loves her—has tried to comb it in her sleep.

Then something twitches. Dara's face. I stare at it a moment. Is it becoming more normal? Or am I just adapting to the way it looks? It is as if the air is leaking out of it, the skin sinking down toward the contours of the bone, not so round and swollen, but a face, with cheeks and chin, the color changing from marbleized blue to a pale yellowish white. *Is this really happening?* The blue veins become more visible for a moment, then they too sink down, and suddenly she is Dara. Dara lying in a white nightgown with a ruffled neck. She looks like a doll, an old Victorian doll, the ones collectors go crazy for on *Antiques Roadshow*—pretty, but scary, too. *Dara. Dara. Becoming more Dara.* Her eyeballs start to flick wildly beneath her lids and her hands shift slightly on her chest. She must be dreaming. I realize I am afraid to be here when she wakes up.

Maybe I'll leave her the flowers . . . and a little note.

There is a pad of blue cloud paper and a mauve pen on the night-stand. I pick them up and flip forward to find a fresh page. I see big, loopy handwriting. The words say, "I love you . . . ketchup . . . change the chanel, PLS," only I'm sure she meant the TV channel, not the designer.

I begin writing my note: "Dear Dara . . . I came by to see you, but you were . . ." I sense something change about the still figure beside me. I look up. Her blue eyes are open. She is watching me.

"Dara!" The sight of her has made my blood run cold. It's her eyes. They have a dull film over them, like thickened tears, or something amphibian. I try to recover myself, my senses. I bring a smile to my face. *Relax, Sally, relax.*

"Hi, Dara . . . I didn't mean to wake you up."

She doesn't say anything at first. She lifts her head from the pillow and looks around the room as if just waking from a dream and trying to figure out where she is. It takes a moment, but she seems to remember, because a horrible resignation comes over her whole body. She drops her head to her pillow and closes her eyes. She swallows back a lump in her throat.

"Dara?"

She takes a deep breath, as if trying to be strong, and then turns her face to me. She manages to smile, just a small, closed-lipped curving of the black line in her face. I almost want to tell her not to smile—*Don't try to smile . . . or talk . . . don't break that black line*—I don't want to see what's inside. *I don't want to see your poor tongue, or what's left of it, inside your black mouth.*

"I—I just thought I'd come and say hi," I tell her. "So . . . how are you feeling?"

Oh, God, what a stupid question!

She quirks one side of her mouth and lifts her eyebrows in an ironic gesture, as if to say, "Could be better."

"I mean, obviously you're not great. But you're okay. Aren't you? The operation—it went well?"

Her jaw stiffens. She gives a little shrug of her shoulders as if to say they don't know yet.

Oh, God!

I try to sit, friendly-like, on the edge of the bed, but I don't want to disturb her—or touch her, especially—so I just hover above the bed with my knees bent until my thighs burn so badly from supporting my weight that I have to stand up again. "So, do they know when you're getting out?"

She looks at me for a moment. Shakes her head no.

"I'm sure you'll be out any day, though." I tap the bedspread with my fingertips. Look around the room, trying to find something to talk about. Then I see the flowers. "I hope you like daisies—because look what I brought!" I pick up the bouquet and three brown-edged petals break off and flutter to the bedspread. I brush them onto the floor. For lack of anything else to say, I opt for honesty. "I'm so sorry about what happened to you, Dara. Really I am. . . . I'm sure you'll be feeling better soon."

She sighs with a bitter strength I never would have expected from her. I try to think of something to brighten her spirits.

"Everyone's coming to visit you," I say. "They really miss you on set. They should be here any minute." I glance longingly at the doorway, wishing that they would tumble in with stuffed animals and flowers and the big Get Well card with the pink kitty on it and rescue me from this abyss, this vacuum of life. "Everyone misses you on set. They talk about you all the time."

She shifts her head slightly to look at me.

"I really feel bad it had to happen this way, Dara. I'm not one of those people who thinks as long as I get a break I don't give a shit about anyone else. That's just not the way I . . ." But then I stop. She's staring at me very deeply. She is frowning at me, actually frowning, and it breaks my heart to see that she has frown muscles after all.

My God. She doesn't know. She doesn't know I got the part.

"Oh, Dara . . . I'm so sorry. I thought someone might have told you. You're probably a *way* better Meridien than me, but they *had* to get somebody to—"

She holds up her hands, waves them as if to stop me from talking. She starts patting the sheets around her, looking at the end table.

"What is it?"

She's frustrated. Impatient. *"Unngh . . ."* She makes a gruff little grunting noise, like the sounds hearing-impaired children make, still batting the sheets. *"Unggh . . ."* The noise is just advanced enough that it pulls her lips apart and I see a deep red center where the black lines meet and then the small, dark keyhole of her mouth.

"Is this what you want?" I ask, holding out the notepad.

She nods, clumsily grabbing the pad and the pen. She flips forward several pages, over the morbid shorthand. She starts to write, holding the pen too tightly, trembling. She turns the pad toward me so I can read it. She has written one word—*"LEAVE"*—in her big, loopy script.

Oh, no. I feel the pang of rejection. "Okay, Dara. I understand— maybe I shouldn't have come." I start backing away from the bed.

"Unnnggh!" She shakes her head. *No!* Her hands reach out for me, pale grasping lilies. She grabs my arm. I feel the coldness, the hardness, the panic of her. It sends a chill up my spine.

"What, Dara? What?"

She releases me. Jabs at the pad with her pen, scratching through the page, nicking up curls of paper. *"Unngh,"* she says. *"Unngggh, unnghh . . ."*

"I—I don't understand."

She grips the pen and starts writing again. Her eyes dart too quickly in their sockets as she tries to focus on the cloud paper. She writes an *S*. She grunts again, loudly. *"Ungggh!"* It's then that I see the stitches in her tongue, flicking sickeningly, like a black housefly trapped in her mouth. Her arm is tense, shaking, as if she's fighting some force that is grabbing it away from the paper. She adjusts the pen, sticks it in her fist, and concentrates fiercely. *H,* she writes. Fighting, fighting. *O.* Suddenly her arm flings and the pen flies across the room, hitting the wall. I back out of the way not to be struck. Her eyes roll up in her head and she sinks deeply back down into the bed. There is a hideous crack. The dull crack of bone and cartilage.

"Dara?"

She's lying on her back; she should be flat, but there is a horrible bulge beneath the bedspread. She's twisting almost in half at the waist, one hip turning upward, protruding through the sheet. She lets out a helpless, agonized cry. A howl, really. Then her hip slowly begins to lower back to the bed, inch by inch, cracking all the way.

"Help, someone," I say. Then more loudly: *"Help!"* I back away from the bed in the general direction of the door.

Then the tremors overtake her. The whole length of her body starts trembling, flapping the sheet. Her teeth bang against each other. Her eyes roll up white.

The nurse with the pale face hurries into the room. "What did you *do* to her?"

"Nothing!"

She runs to the head of the bed. Checks Dara's pupils. "Dara? What's wrong?" She turns to me. "What did you say?"

"Nothing!"

"You must've said—" But she doesn't have time to finish the sentence. Dara's jaw begins to open and close, stretching and clenching, that horrible blood line doubles into two black lips and then one again as her teeth smash together and I hear a horrible crack. "No, Dara, no!" screams the nurse, struggling to get her fingers inside Dara's mouth. Dara's teeth clamp down on the nurse's hand. The nurse screams out loud, her pale face wracked with pain. She grunts, pointing to the end table. "Look in there!"

I throw open the drawer. A collection of wooden tongue depressors click out across the bottom. I grab one, throw it across the bed. The nurse yanks her fingers out of Dara's mouth. I see the pink indentation of teeth marks on her knuckles and a film of slimy, clear spit. It makes the nurse's hands slippery, fingers sliding against lips, cheeks, skin. The nurse tries to shove the tongue depressor inside Dara's mouth. There is the strange, musical clatter of wood against teeth. Dara's tongue flips out, a wounded eyeless pink worm disturbed in its lair and trying to protect it.

"Unnggh . . . unghhh . . ."

Another figure *whooshes* in the door—a tall East Indian doctor in a white lab coat—and behind him, a thick-necked orderly who looks more like a bouncer than a caregiver. They hurry to the bed and grab Dara's arms. The nurse seems relieved to have help. The doctor hands her a syringe and she takes it, shakily trying to fill it. The orderly holds Dara's arms and the doctor manages to stick the wood depressor inside her mouth. Dara's teeth crunch down immediately. I hear the muffled splinter of wood.

"Unnghhhhh!"

There is fresh red blood now forking out of the corners of her mouth, running over her chin. The nurse jabs her with the needle. Dara kicks and thrashes. "Unngh . . . unghhh!"

In the struggle I see something fall off the bed in front of me. The notepad. The blue cloud paper. The words Dara had written. "*LEAVE SH . . .*" And this horrible mass of an *O.*

Leave the show? That can't be what she meant.

I have to go. It's not a conscious thought but an instinct. *I have to go!* I spin around and dash out into the hall, running the whole length of it, hammering into the wall next to the elevator. I punch and punch the DOWN arrow.

"Excuse me?" I hear a man's voice. I turn to see the doctor walking toward me. He seems slightly winded. There's a smear of blood on the pocket of his white lab coat, as if he were a common butcher. "I'm so sorry you had to see that," he says sympathetically. "We've sedated her. She'll rest now. We thought she was doing better. She must've had a relapse. Do you think it was something the two of you were talking about?"

I shrug that I don't know.

"We think her fits may be due to psychological stress. It would help if you talked to your mother about it and—"

"M-mother?" I interrupt him in a small voice.

"Yes." He looks at me in confusion. "You're not Dara's sister?"

"No."

"My God . . . You look just like her."

The elevator opens behind me and I fold backwards onto it, straight into something furry that almost makes me scream. I turn to see a big teddy bear. Emma and the other crew members have showed up, stuffed animal in hand. "Sorry we're late," she says. "We were running behind."

I quickly trade places with them, getting on the elevator as they get off. Emma looks at me strangely. "You okay?" she asks.

I try to answer. But the words won't come out. I nod and smile. *Fine, fine.* I push the DOWN button. Emma watches me worriedly as the doors slide closed.

WHEN I reach the lobby, I bump into a man in a black suit. I'm so relieved. *It's Jack.*

"Sorry, miss," he says.

The smile on my face fades. Because it's not Jack; it's just a man in a black suit. I stumble out through the lobby into the rain. The city is indistinct, silvery and shapeless beneath the downpour. Headlights and streetlights multiply on slick pavement. I swing my arm up for a cab. *There's one!* But it drives right past me.

"Taxi!" Another cab pulls over; I open the back door to get in. The driver turns around to look at me. He's unshaven. His hair is dark. But it's not just any driver—it's Jack. He's looking at me blankly. Stunned, I back away from the car and somebody comes up beside me.

"Are you taking this?"

I shake my head. By the time I realize the driver is not Jack, the cab has pulled away and I am left staring after it.

No. Not Jack.

Why am I thinking of Jack?

I twist forward and walk quickly, head down, licking rain off my lips. Then I see Jack sitting in a coffee shop, reading a newspaper. Then wearing a hard hat, digging at a gushing hole in the road. The rain—it must be playing tricks with my eyes. I keep waiting for it to stop. Jack selling hot dogs from a cart. Jack dressed as a policeman directing traffic. Jack standing outside a building, smoking a ciga-rette. He starts walking over to me. But it doesn't become someone else. It's still Jack. And he looks so dry. The only goddamn thing on the street that's dry. How is that possible? It's only when I am beside him that I realize he was having a cigarette outside the building; that he saw me in the rain and came to meet me, soaking as I am, with his umbrella. We stand there for a moment as the wet cars and people rush around us.

"You okay?" he asks. He seems worried.

I nod, feeling numb.

"Are you sure?"

I nod again. He watches me for a moment, as if to make sure I'm not lying. He pushes a strand of my wet hair off my cheek, putting it behind my ear. "You better get inside." He walks me under his umbrella to the glass doors. He waits until I'm inside and can feel the dryness of the lobby. It's then I remember, with a small, sharp catch of my breath, that I'll be seeing him tomorrow. I remember saying yes.

By the time I have blow-dried my hair, everyone is back from the hospital, gathering in the doorway of my dressing room, demanding to know the "deets." Dara was sedated when they got to her room and resting peacefully, but there was blood everywhere. I tell them she had another fit. While the others gossip, Emma leans into me: "You okay?"

"Sure. I just needed some air," I tell her. "Hospitals give me the creeps."

An intern says they talked to the doctor and that they still don't know what's wrong with her—only that she'll need speech therapy and, even then, "she'll never be the same." Someone offers a theory: It's probably a tropical brain disease, some kind of fever she picked up in Thailand last year. She went backpacking there with a couple friends. Thailand. Yes. That seems to catch on—people listen to the theory and expand on it. They've heard that—we all have—how you can pick up parasites or tropical diseases that lie dormant for months, even years, before striking. And that makes sense to me in some way, that she's suffering from some kind of foreign, unseen malignity, green and spreading on a microscopic level. Something that has nothing to do with me. Something that's not my fault.

Yes. *A tropical brain disease.*

The words come hesitantly at first, awkwardly.

Dara has a tropical brain disease. . . . She got it in Thailand last year.

But eventually the thought begins to carve a new circuit in my brain, like a well-used path through the forest. *Tropical brain disease . . . tropical brain disease . . .* And instead of remembering Dara bleeding and screaming in a hospital bed, instead of thinking of blue cloud notepaper full of panic and warnings, instead of thinking of Jack getting out of a taxi cab or directing traffic or standing in the rain, I remember Dara in her mini-skirts. Dara with her pink angora laugh. *Tropical brain disease . . . tropical brain disease. Yes . . . a bug that's been dormant. . . . Yes, of course. . . .* until it becomes manageable, harmless, just another day on the calendar—not a good day or a bad day, but something that just comes and goes and sinks into memory: *The day I visited Dara in the hospital when she had a tropical brain disease.*

FIFTEEN

We've all of us got to meet the devil alone.
Temptation is a lonely business.

MARGARET DELAND

I T'S a still, lush, purple evening. I'm in the bathroom trying to put on mascara, but my hand is shaking so badly I glob it under my right eye—*Damn*—and I have to blot it off with a tissue.

The phone rings. For the third time. I let the machine get it.

"*Sal? Hey. Me again.*" It's David. He's been leaving messages all day. "*You there?*" A beat passes; he lets out an annoyed sigh. "*Someone picked up my shift tonight. I'm gonna go shoot some stick with Scott. Come and see us when you get in.*" There's a shuffle, as if he's about to hang up but has changed his mind. "*And Sal? I just want to tell you how proud I am of how well you're doing on the show. Everyone's talking about it. No one can believe me when I tell them you're my girlfriend.*" Another beat. "*I love you, Sal.*" Click.

A scythe of guilt swings through me. I support myself against the sink, waiting for it to pass.

See what a good guy he is? How sensitive and sweet? How could I do this to him?

It's just dinner, Sally. You're not committing a sin or anything.

If it's just dinner why am I so nervous?

The phone rings again and I turn toward it, trembling slightly. But it's not David's voice that fills the room this time; it's Jack's. His slow, sexy drawl.

"Sally? . . . Hi. It's me. . . . I'm downstairs."

For a split second, I consider not answering it. I consider letting his voice empty out into nothingness and never seeing him again. But suddenly logic or fear—I don't know which—seizes me and I rush across the living room, bungling the phone as I pick it up. "Jack! Hi!"

"Good. You're there." There's a smile in his voice. "For a minute I thought you were standing me up."

"No. Of course not." I laugh nervously.

A siren drives by on Houston. I hear it through my window and over the phone.

He's so close.

"Do you want me to come up?"

"No. I'm ready. I'll be right down."

I slam down the phone. A nervousness grips me, so intense it sends sharp shoots of near pain up between my legs and into my abdomen and chest. I check my reflection in the mirror, bring the brush through my hair one last time. I had quite a debate over what I should wear tonight. The panties and bra were a particular dilemma for some reason. I started out with a white sports bra and black lace panties. The panties were too sexy for the bra so I switched to white cotton panties. But then that looked too plain, so I switched to a black bra and white panties, finally deciding on all black lace. As for my outfit, it was even worse. I went through my entire wardrobe. Runner-up ensembles are strewn around the apartment like guests passed out after a cocktail party. I eventually decided on a white Gap T-shirt, my old leather jacket, a long paisley-printed wraparound skirt I bought at a vintage store, and my Steve Maddens (because they're marginally less scuffed than my ancient Doc Martens). The look—I hope—is a hard-won cross between "trying too hard" and "Big deal, I go out with network presidents all the time."

When I get outside, the setting sun plays half-tricks with my eyes, melting the whole world into shifting globs of gold and black, like molten ore. But he's there, smoking a cigarette, leaning against a black car double-parked out front. As his expression comes into focus, I can see that he's smiling at me appreciatively. He comes toward me, holding out his hand.

"You look beautiful."

"Thanks. So do you. Well, handsome, I mean."

And he does, in the kind of hip Casual Friday look most men can't pull off. I take his hand and the energy throbbing deep within him transfers to me for a moment. Enveloping. Surging. He leads me to the gleaming black sports car—a Porsche—and opens the door for me. As I duck inside, I notice a nun in front of St. Francis. She's sweeping the steps with an old straw-bristle broom, her silver cross swinging back and forth. She looks up to watch us for a moment. I look away from her, embarrassed. I keep putting off making an appointment at the convent to talk to someone about my character. Every time I think about sitting alone with a nun, I feel an unpleasant rush. It's Sister Ruth. *God has a reason for everything, Sally. . . . The meek shall inherit the earth.*

I make another mental note to myself: Call St. Francis tomorrow.

The day after, at least.

Jack is walking around the front of the car. He notices the nun, too; he lingers outside the driver's side door to take another drag of his cigarette and meet her gaze, almost as if to challenge her. She averts her eyes and goes back to sweeping the steps.

He climbs in beside me. He smells clean and his hair is still damp, as if he's just had a shower. *Men—how can they get away with that?*

He turns to me, putting his arm over my seat. "Where to?"

"Doesn't matter," I say.

"Do you have a favorite place?"

"Not really."

"My choice then?"

"Yep."

"You like Italian?"

"Love it."

"Great." He flashes another grin and puts the car into gear. The engine growls and the car leaps forward, swinging around in a tight U-turn. We pull into traffic so quickly, it's as if we've been sucked there by a physical force.

One block goes by, then another. . . . He shifts gears roughly, slipping back and forth between lanes. Neither one of us is talking. He seems fine with it, but it's making me crazy. It feels as if the car is slowly filling up with lake water, and if somebody doesn't start talking soon, I'm going to drown.

Go on, Sal. Say something. Say something witty and cool.

I look around, shrugging my lips. "Nice car."

Nice car? Are you kidding? What a conversational pinnacle!

"Thanks," he says.

More silence. The lights of the city are a smear behind slightly tinted glass.

"You feeling better?" he asks. "You seemed a little upset yesterday."

I remember in a flash—Dara. *Unggh . . . unghhh . . .* "Yeah." I hide a little shiver. "I just had to visit a friend in the hospital, that's all."

"Ahh."

More driving. More silence. The red taillights spread around us, moving, swirling. *Think. Think.*

"Nice night, huh?" I hear myself say. *Come on. You can do better than that.* "I read somewhere we're supposed to have an Indian summer this year. Something about global warming."

"You know what they say about Indian summers, Sally?" His voice is low, throaty, another vibration in my chest beneath the rumbling of the car. "They say magical things can happen."

"Magical things? Really?" And I shatter my previous record for eloquence by saying, *"Neat."*

The car lurches to a stop in front of a large sandblasted warehouse deep in the heart of Tribeca. A male underwear-model type is opening a large stainless-steel door for a group of well-dressed customers. My eyes search the facade for a sign. Shit. No sign. It must be expensive. And then I see a small, stylized number above the door: 7. That seems familiar—and then it comes to me. *Sette!* We're going to *Sette?* I read a review of it a couple of weeks ago. Insiders (and people who read reviews about the places they eat) pronounce it *SEHT-tay,* like *seven* in Italian, and right now, it's the best restaurant in the city. That's no small feat, considering there are five hundred restaurants in this city that would be the best restaurant in the city if they were in any other city in the world.

I turn to him, clutching his arm. "Jack—we can't go to Sette."

"Why not? Don't you like it here?"

"Are you kidding? I've never even *been* here! But look at me!" I say, slapping my legs, my arms, my chest.

He's a little confused. "You look beautiful."

"No, Jack—I'm underdressed! I look like a bag lady! There are appetizers in there worth more than everything I'm wearing put—"

"Sally—" he laughs, taking one of my hands, which has been gesturing and flailing, and putting it gently in my lap. "You look *perfect.* You're going to be the most beautiful woman in there. Besides, you're going to be rich and famous someday." He gives a casual shrug. "You can wear whatever the fuck you want."

Two valets open our doors, letting in the star-pricked night. But I can't move. *You're going to be rich and famous someday.* I guess I don't have to tell you what it means that someone like Jack Weaver has said that to me. It's the sort of thing that—if you let it—could change your whole life.

THE sounds and smells of the restaurant descend upon me in a dizzying wave. The noise level is "high," as they say in the guidebooks, the lighting "low." The entrance is a narrow, dimly lit hallway; the walls are dark, rough-hewn, and glittering from within like the walls of an abandoned mine shaft. Hung at regular intervals along the way are

squares of Plexiglas, glowing in acid-bright shades. It's a strange combination of old and new, primitive and futuristic. At the end of the
hallway, a young woman is standing in silhouette; she slowly comes
into view.

"Hello, Mr. Weaver," she says. She's beautiful, very young,
Amerasian, with eyes that are—my goodness!—amber? That fake deep
gold contact color with dark flecks in them. But they seem natural on
her, not store-bought, and the smile that tilts her full, shiny lips is
unreadable, knowing, polite, demure, sexy, sweet, sly.

We follow the girl into the restaurant. She floats ahead of us,
smooth, graceful curves molded into a clingy dress. The main room
starts to emerge from the darkness at the end of the hall, glints of it at
first—a candle flicker, a table edge—and then, suddenly, the whole
room expands above and around us, a great Philippe Starck–designed
shrine. At the far end, a waterfall trickles down a slab of granite,
reflecting the dim lighting, which itself doesn't feel like anything I'm
used to seeing—not electric light or candlelight or even moonlight—
nothing so mundane. But something rare and slightly unsettling, like
the light of an eclipse. And the people gathered here have gathered as
they do to watch an eclipse, with a sense of excitement and occasion
and belonging. As we pass tables, the guests come into focus. Expensive suit jackets and purses are slung over the backs of chairs. Smiling,
animated mouths move over conversation or open up unpredictably
into a laugh until the sound of voices, the tinkling glasses, the music,
the laughter, all mesh together into one seamless roar, like the rush of
a nearby river—the Seine or the Thames, perhaps—a great famous
river, ensuring prosperity and privilege to all who come to settle on its
banks.

I hear a woman's voice ring out, "Jack!" I turn around to see—oh,
my God, is that, oh, my God, it is!—Courtney Cox! Courtney Fucking Cox is waving at us!

Jack leans into me. "Sorry. We're gonna have to say hi."

I nod numbly and let myself be guided over to her table. Her smile

is glorious, her eyes even bluer than a Tiffany box. When Jack introduces us, she shakes my hand warmly. I emit some gurgle of a sound
that I hope will pass for "Nice to meet you," because it's all I can manage in my nervousness, and while she and Jack are talking about something—I don't know what—I'm trying to decide whether or not I
should tell her what a big fan of hers I am, how pretty I think she is,
how great she was in the *Scream* movies, etc., etc., but it's too late
because suddenly we are moving again, following the girl with the
golden eyes, who has waited patiently, hovering just a few tables away.

"Oh, my God," I hiss. *"I can't believe what just happened. I can't believe
I just met Courtney Fucking Cox!"* Then worriedly: "Do you think I
should have said something to her? Maybe I should've told her I liked
her new hair."

"Sally," he says, putting his arm around me and giving me a reassuring squeeze, "relax! You were perfect."

The hostess leads us to what must be the best table in the house. I
try to stay out of the way as the waiters circle the table, filling water
glasses, unfurling napkins, straightening silverware. When they leave us
alone, Jack and I are just staring at each other. He smiles with that grin
that pleats one cheek. I stare back gape-eyed and tongue-tied, unable
to speak or look away. Finally I get the wherewithal to pluck up my
menu, a practical billboard of a thing that covers me from my head to
the tabletop. Thank *God*. I can hide behind it. "Mmmm, everything
looks so good. . . ."

A waiter emerges like an apparition from the darkness, his hands
first, then the rest of him. "May I get you something from the bar?" he
asks me.

"Uh—glass of house red, please," I stammer. And then I immediately regret it. I should have ordered some obscure, hip martini—a
cosmopolitan, at least.

"Would you prefer Amarone? Chianti? Or merlot?"

Oh, shit. Of course a place like this would have a thousand house
reds. "Uh . . . doesn't matter," I say, and then think it *should* matter

because if it doesn't matter I'm confirming for the waiter what he already probably suspects, and that is that I'm the least sophisticated customer to walk into his restaurant in a month. "Merlot," I blurt quickly, then recover with a smile.

Jack just nods to the waiter, who seems to understand this as "the usual" before disappearing back into the darkness with a bow. Jack gets comfortable in his seat, customizing his place setting, moving silver-ware, napkin, stretching his legs out into the aisle as if the table confines him. He catches me staring at him and I look away, embarrassed. I duck back behind the menu again. *Calm down, Sally . . . calm the fuck down. . . .*

"Oh, look, they have shark," I say.

"I hear it's good."

"Is shark red meat? Because I don't eat red meat."

"I think it's white."

"But it has a face. I try not to eat anything with a face. Well—sometimes I eat things with faces. Chicken and fish. But I try not to eat anything born alive."

"Sharks are born alive," he says.

"Oh. So much for the shark." I retreat behind the menu again and it looks like this:

Irgabuc Bqvt Greeb Sakad Tissed wutg Cubbabin abd Rausub Dressubg

"How's the show coming?" he asks.

I peek out from behind the bunker of my menu. "Great." Retreat. "I wonder what the soup is today."

"Because sometimes it's hard jumping in when everything's already up and running."

"Mmm. The agnolotti looks amazing."

"Sally, I can't see you," he says, pulling the menu down.

"Oh. Sorry."

"The show—are you enjoying it?"

"Sure. Absolutely. Except for this whole thing about the actress who got sick. I'm feeling kind of guilty about it." I wince a little.

"When I went to see her in the hospital, she started having another one of those fits. I think she bit her tongue again."

He look slightly stricken. "You saw *Dara* in the hospital?"

It's a bit unsettling he knows her name. "Uh . . . yeah. A bunch of people from the show were going up to see her. I thought I'd tag along. It seemed like the right thing to do at the time." I shrug helplessly. "Guilt gland strikes again."

"What do you mean?"

"You don't know me, Jack. I feel guilty about *everything.*" Then I give him my spiel about going to see a shrink about my guilt complex and then changing my mind because I felt guilty for wasting his time. It's a line I've used before and it never gets guffaws—but a little smile would be nice. He's just staring at me, deadpan.

"You're not feeling guilt, Sally."

"Excuse me?"

"You feel *emotions.* Anger. Joy. Jealousy. But guilt is not an emotion. It's entirely intellectual. You manufacture it. What you're really feeling is *fear.*"

"Fear?" I repeat dubiously.

"Yes, fear that because you've done something you think you shouldn't have, you'll be punished for it. Guilt is a way of camouflaging your self-interest. More than anything, it's a waste of time."

I stare at him, stunned. "No wonder you make such a good TV executive."

He grins. "Guilty as charged."

The waiter materializes, holding a bottle of red wine. "Excuse me. I'm sorry to interrupt. This is compliments of Mr. Fletcher." He nods to a table across the room.

Jack glances over; his expression deadens. "Damn."

I turn to see a very slim man with dark eyes, sunken cheeks, and thinning black hair. He waves to us eagerly. He's wearing a black turtleneck, which I think is odd on such a warm night, and a gray tweed suit.

"Who is he?" I ask as the waiter pours the wine.

"Marty Fletcher. He's from finance. Marty the Merlin, they call him, because he's so good with numbers. He's on the deal team for the Geostar thing."

Geostar thing? I am aware that he has just referred to one of the biggest media stories of the year as *"the Geostar thing."* Then it hits me again—*This is Jack Weaver . . . and I'm having dinner with him.*

Holy fuck.

"You want to do the honors?" he asks, motioning to the wine.

"No, no. You go ahead." If I tried to do the whole sniff/swirl thing, I'd probably spill it in my lap.

Jack takes a moment to taste the wine. He seems to be an expert at it, very natural and relaxed. He nods *fine* to the waiter, who fills my glass somewhere to the midway point. When he's finished, I practically pounce on it and take two good swallows.

There. That's better.

Jack lifts his glass to toast the man in the black turtleneck, who sits taller in his seat, grinning proudly. Jack leans toward me. "Now, pretend you're totally enthralled with me so he doesn't come over. He's a wiz with a balance sheet—but personally, I think he's a fucking weasel."

I glance back at the man in the turtleneck. He seems disappointed that he's lost Jack's attention. I feel kind of sorry for him. "Shouldn't you go over and thank him at least?"

"Why?"

"It seems like the right thing to do."

"You're really hung up on this, aren't you? Doing the 'right thing.' You went to the hospital because it was the 'right thing' to do. Now you want me to go over there because it's the 'right thing' to do. Don't you drive yourself crazy trying to do the right thing all the time?"

"It's not the worst of my problems, trust me," I say with a laugh.

The waiter steps up to the table again. "May I tell you the evening's specials?"

I lean back and politely listen to the waiter as he recites an increasingly tempting list of lamb and sea bass and sirloin tip. When the waiter is finished with the specials, he asks if we need more time. I've already decided on the two things that don't have faces: the pasta and an organic salad. Jack, naturally, has opted for a different route. He has a rare steak and the carpaccio to start.

Why don't they just wheel the cow right up to the table for him. . . .

"Let me get these out of your way," the waiter says. He picks up Jack's menu, then reaches for mine, but I grip the corner possessively. I was sort of hoping to keep it for the duration of the night. It was good cover. He looks at me questioningly, gives the menu a little tug. I finally have to surrender, watching the menu float away into the darkness, leaving me feeling vulnerable and exposed.

"I'm really fascinated by this," Jack is saying, still watching me. "Your desire to do the right thing. I'm not surprised. I got that feeling about you. But I just don't know how you decide what's right. Do you use the standard route? The Top Ten List or something?"

"Top Ten List?"

"With apologies to Letterman . . . 'Thou shalt not kill.' 'Thou shalt not steal . . .'"

I curl my lip at him. "Not necessarily. But the Commandments are a good place to start."

"So—stealing is a sin?"

"Yes."

"And lying?"

"Unless it's a little white lie to spare somebody's feelings."

"Committing adultery?"

That one catches me; I think of David. "Uh . . ."

"What about murder?"

"See—now that one's a gimme. Yes. Murder is always wrong."

"Absolutely wrong?"

"Absolutely."

"What about capital punishment?"

I make the sound of a buzzer. *"Beeggh . . . wrong."*

"And euthanasia?"

I consider it. "Well . . ."

"What about killing in self-defense?"

"Um . . ."

"So maybe murder isn't *always* wrong?"

I straighten my napkin, almost as if for something to do. "Can we talk about something else, please?"

"Why?"

"This is sort of weird dinner conversation for someone I just met."

"What do you want to talk about?"

"I don't know. Something more normal. Like our favorite movies."

"Why—because that would be the *right* thing to do?" He grins broadly.

I give him a sarcastic sneer. "I suppose a big network exec like you doesn't bother trying to do the right thing anymore?"

"Of course I do. But I make it easy on myself." He lets a beat pass. "I do what's right for *me.*"

I blurt-laugh, as if he's joking, but I can tell by the look on his face—confident, unfazed—that he's not. "You *always* do what's right for you?"

"Always."

"Even if it means someone else gets hurt?"

"People get hurt in life, Sally. That's not my problem."

I roll my eyes and make big air quotes. "How 'Machiavellian genius' of you," I say.

There's a beat. I don't know what he's going to do. He should be insulted. I just insulted him, didn't I? But he does the strangest thing. He starts to laugh. A low, amused laugh. "Don't believe everything you hear about me, Sally. I'm not nearly as bad as they say."

"I hope not," I murmur, half to myself.

The appetizers come and I'm grateful for the interruption. I start stabbing at my salad. I'm sure it's delicious, but right now it just feels like something cold and acidic I'm putting in my mouth.

"What about the others?" he asks, looking up from his plate.

"Others?"

"Taking the Lord's name in vain?"

"I said I didn't want to talk about this anymore."

"Or Thou shalt have no other gods before me . . . ?"

I'm about to respond when a pulse of light illuminates one half of his face. I look over to see a gigantic fireball hovering above a table of guests, their faces glowing like kids around a campfire. The fireball rises up to the ceiling, hangs there for a moment, then disappears, taking the light with it; a waiter sets a plate down on the table. It's a moment before I realize it's anything so prosaic as a flambé. I try to go back to my salad, but my hand is shaking.

"Will you excuse me?" I say, wiping my mouth. "I have to go to the rest room."

"Of course."

I stand up quickly and, as I do, my napkin drops from my lap to a heap on the floor. *Damn.* Not smooth. I pick it up, deliberate briefly where I should put it. Chair or table? Decide on the chair and turn away. I weave through the dark aisles created by tables and laughter and muted conversations. Oh, where the hell is the bathroom? There's a waiter. "Excuse me . . ." He smiles and points ahead of me. Good. At least I don't have to double back like some rat caught in a fucking maze—which is what I feel like.

The door is brushed stainless, cold and heavy beneath my hand; I push it open. The lighting is so dim, it takes a moment for my eyes to adjust. I see two women standing at the mirror fixing their lipstick; they both turn to look at me at the same time and I realize it's not two women, but just one, with long dark hair, and her reflection, staring back at me. I try to smile; she and her reflection go back to fixing their lipstick. I bat along the swinging doors for an open stall . . . find one . . . slip inside, lock the door. I sit down and put my face in my hands, letting out a big lungful of tense air. *Whooshhh. . . .* I make snapping and flapping noises with my clothes, bang the napkin disposal chute a couple of times so the woman with the lipstick thinks I've got something else to do in here besides sit around and fret and wish I were somewhere else. When I hear her leave, I slam the stall door with my palm. *Shit!* Am I ever blowing this. I can't believe how badly I'm fucking blowing this. Opportunity of a lifetime—dinner with a big, powerful TV exec and— Oh, what the hell did I do that for? Stand up in the middle of my salad like that. *Will you excuse me, please?* Like I'm Joan of Arc or something. Wait . . . why Joan of Arc? Oh, who cares? *Damn.* Gus is going to kill me.

Suddenly I hear a cough from the stall beside me. I am horrified that I'm not alone. I quickly pull out a few stray tissues, flush them down the toilet, open the stall door. My reflection in the mirror ahead of me materializes slowly, like a face floating up to the surface of a murky pond. I turn on the taps. Rinse my hands. Plop my bag on the counter, dig for my lip gloss.

Holy Christ . . . and what about *him?* Can you believe all that *'Guilt . . . is a waste of time.'* Hah. I should have known—absolutely no conscience whatsoever. Then I feel a twinge of regret—*Damn!* . . . I could name twenty actors who would shoot me in cold blood for this opportunity. Twenty? Try *all* of them. They'd all happily put me up against a wall without a blindfold for an audience with Jack Weaver. And *they'd* do the right thing—be charming, play the game. *Shit!* I find my lip gloss, applicator poised to . . . *Hey, wait a second.* There in the mirror, that murky-faced girl—her cheeks are flushed, her eyes are wide and shining . . . *Huh* . . . I look pretty good tonight.

Back at the table, I flop down, jam the napkin in my lap.

"Sally, I hope I didn't upset you. I really didn't mean—"

"You know," I interrupt, slamming my fork down, "I don't know why *I* have to feel like an idiot just because *I* try to be a good person."

"I'm sorry, I—"

"What's wrong with that?"

"Nothing. It's what I like about you."

I push my plate away, unfinished, grumbling to myself. *Oh, good—somebody topping off the wine. . . .* I take another big gulp. I look over at him, and he's watching me. Only *watching* seems like too innocent a word for what he's doing to me. His gaze is dark, almost oppressive, like a long, hot night in summertime, the kind you think will never end, the kind that makes you toss and turn, kick off the sheets, turn your pillow again and again, the kind that makes you pray for a breeze, for air conditioning, for the first relief of dawn—and yet, the kind of night, all winter long—in Wisconsin, at least—you long for, you pine over, you miss; the kind of night that makes the world seem so independent from you, as if there are great forces at work, operating on their own lush behalf, without any consideration for your comfort or ease.

"There's a nicer way of saying it, you know," he says softly. His voice interrupts the silence so perfectly, it's as if he's pried it open with his thoughts, eased it open and slipped in his words where they were meant to fit, as if the silence were filled with small dark cups to hold his words like chocolates.

"Saying what?"

"That I do what's right for me."

I refuse to look as interested in what he's going to say as I am.

"I listen to my heart."

I listen to my heart.

That catches me off guard. Such gentle words. Like the title of an early Beatles song. One of the ballads. The first five chords of a gentle little ditty that everybody hums all day after hearing it on the radio: "I Listen to My Heart." And it has moved me to hear him say these words. But I don't want him to know. So I pout playfully. "Awww, you're right. That *does* sound better. You should use *that* one on the girls." When I see the look on his face, I immediately regret the sarcasm. But I think he knows I didn't mean it.

"You should try it sometime," he says.

"Try what?"

"Listening to your heart."

"But I do! I listen to my heart all the time!"

He just smiles. I think he knows I didn't mean that either.

THE food comes in a flourish of waiters and staff and it is quite simply the most delicious meal I've ever had. I had no idea food could taste so good. That it could have character, resolution, depth. I have Agnolotti con Funghi. They say it's just ravioli filled with garlic and wild mushrooms, but that's sort of like saying the Sistine Chapel is just a church.

Surprisingly, we talk about everything except our favorite movies. I learn that his parents died in a car accident when he was nine. He moved in with an aunt and uncle in Boston, who enrolled him in private schools, Catholic and otherwise. Somehow—I don't know how—the story about my father's suicide comes out. I never tell people about what happened to my father. Whenever I've tried, they feel sorry for me or they're horrified or they look at me as if I might "do something to myself" someday, too. But Jack just listens. His eyes gleam in the candlelight. The story comes out, one detail at a time, and I measure how much I can tell him. *I saw police cars outside the house. . . . The ice cream truck was in the driveway. . . .* His brow knits sometimes in concern, but he never looks away. He never flinches. He absorbs all these horrid details about me—and it's okay with him. In fact, he seems to be closer to me because of it. It feels as if I have taken him inside of me. I feel his heat pressed against my heart.

The hours pass. Quickly or slowly, I'm not sure. I only know the restaurant starts to empty out around us. We linger, unrushed. We have grappa. And share dessert. We order espresso . . . then another. It's as if neither of us wants to leave. After a while, the conversation stops and we sit quietly, not saying anything, looking from the candle, which has burned down to a flickering pool of wax between us, to each other, then back again. At first, I feel embarrassed when he catches me staring at him and I have to look away. But then I don't look away anymore. I just stare back. We're not talking. We're not actually saying anything, but it seems that some dialogue, some communication, is taking place between us without either of us uttering a word. I feel the vibrations of his voice on my mind. He seems to be talking to me in some language I've always known but haven't heard since childhood.

I'm not sure when it started. I have a vague recollection that he took my hand when I was telling him about my father and then never let go, because suddenly I realize we are holding hands, maybe have been for quite some time. Our fingers entwine and gently explore, clasping, stroking, grazing. There just seemed to be too much space between us and we had to close it. It was a relief to close it. I know I shouldn't be holding hands with another man in public—what if someone were to tell David? But I can't help myself. Just holding hands with him feels like the most physically pleasurable thing that has ever happened to me. Like that place where our hands touch is the only thing in the world that makes sense right now. I feel a single phrase repeating itself in my head—*Something is happening to me . . . Something is happening to me . . .* I feel its fire grip around my heart, a tender, relentless squeezing . . . *Something is happening to me . . .*

WE drive home slowly. I don't want the night to end. I don't think he does, either. He finds a parking spot a couple of blocks from my place. We take each other's hands and beneath a sterling white moon walk slowly toward my place. The streetlights shine through the soft green lace of the sidewalk trees. Apartment windows are open on the warm night. Voices drift down. And the sounds of late-night TV—applause and laugh tracks and guns.

We hold hands and bat lazily against each other as we walk, putting one foot slowly in front of the next, making the finite number of sidewalk blocks between us and my apartment door last as long as possible. We're talking about casual things. Little snippets of conversation to keep the night moving along. He asks me how old I was when I knew I wanted to act and I tell about my *People* caption.

"*People* caption?"

"You know, those little captions they put underneath photographs in *People* magazine. 'Julia Roberts: Loves Her Dog.' 'Bruce Willis: Practices Tae Kwan Do.' "

He laughs.

"I guess I've known ever since I was a little girl I wanted to act. It was sixth grade. My class was putting on a production of *The Wizard of Oz.*"

"Wait a second. 'Sally Carpenter: Played Dorothy in First Grade.' " He nods his approval. "You're right. It *is* a *People* caption."

"I'm flattered you think I got the lead role. But the principal's daughter played Dorothy."

He shakes his head. "Nepotism in elementary school. It starts early in this business."

I laugh. "I didn't care. I didn't *want* to play Dorothy anyway. I wanted to play the Wicked Witch of the West. But everyone wanted me to be Glinda, the Good Witch of the North. Of course." I roll my eyes. "I begged my teacher to let me be the Wicked Witch, but she said I couldn't be mean enough. I was so upset. I don't know why . . ." My voice trails off for a moment and my pace slows. "Okay, I *do* know why. That was the same year my father died. It was really hard on my family. Everything changed so much. My mother nearly had a nervous breakdown. And my brother turned into a discipline case. Skipping school, getting into drugs. It made things even worse. Everyone was always taking me aside and telling me not to be more of a burden on my mom than everything already was. That I should try to be a 'good girl.' I think I was just sick of it. I wanted to be *bad* for a change."

He smiles as if he understands.

"Anyway, the night before the tryouts—we didn't call them auditions then—I went home and dug through an old trunk where my mom kept the Christmas decorations and stuff. There was a long black wig I had worn for Halloween one year—I went as Cher. I mussed the wig up and made myself a black hat out of construction paper and showed up the next day cackling and casting evil spells on people. The teacher laughed and let me have the part. I had *such* a riot playing that witch. Maybe the most fun I've ever had with a role. Probably because it was so far away from who I am. Or *was,* anyway." I sigh in resignation. "And now look at me . . . playing a nun."

"Is that far away from who you really are?"

I look at him cagily. "Probably farther away than my mother would like!" He laughs. But thinking about the *DUD* role has made me quiet. Another unpleasant jolt as I remember Dara in the hospital.

"What's wrong?"

It's amazing how he can tell when there's something bothering me. I find it hard to believe that only hours ago this man was a stranger to me—and now . . . now . . . I cannot *remember* what my life was like when I didn't know him. "Nothing—just a little retro-guilt about Dara. I'll get over it. Eventually."

"You should. It's not your fault what happened to her."

"I know . . ."

"There's something I should tell you, Sally. I'm not unacquainted with Dara."

"Not . . . unacquainted? What does that mean?" Then it occurs to me. "Wait a second! You're George Dubya, aren't you?"

He frowns in confusion.

"The guy she was seeing!"

"She told you she was seeing me?"

"She didn't mention *names*. But she did say it was some big shot who could give her anything she wanted. It's you, isn't it?"

He shakes his head, quite adamantly. "We were *not* seeing each other. Not for her lack of trying, of course."

"Oh? What happened?" I realize I'm on the very razor's edge between wanting to know everything and not wanting to know even this much.

"Um . . . I think 'stalking' might come close to describing it."

"You're kidding."

"I couldn't get away from her. She'd wait around for me after work. Show up at my favorite restaurants. She found out when my birthday was and gave me a tie in her favorite color . . ."

"Don't tell me—pink."

He smiles. "Good guess."

I laugh a little, like this isn't bothering me. But it is.

"So what happened between you two?" I ask. "Not that it's any of my business, of course."

"It's your business—if you want it to be." He smiles wryly. "But nothing happened. I just wasn't interested in her. Dara's like most people, Sally. She'd be willing to do anything to get ahead. I meet a hundred people like her every day. Producers, writers, other wannabes trying to get into the business. And they're all the same. After a while it gets boring." He looks at me meaningfully. "You start looking for someone different."

"Is that a compliment?"

"A big one."

"Compliment taken, then." Finally we can't avoid it. We're standing in front of my apartment building. The light from the entranceway illuminates only one side of his face. We link bodies. My arms around his neck. His around my waist. I don't want to admit how relieved I am that nothing happened between him and Dara. One thing—I don't feel so sorry for her anymore.

"I had a really good time tonight, Sally."

"Me too," I say.

"I hope I can see you again."

"Me too. . . . But there might be *one* little problem." I wince slightly. "Since we're coming clean here, I have a confession to make, too."

"You're seeing someone else," he says.

That unnerves me. "How do you know?"

"I know a lot of things about you, Sally."

I falter for a moment, uncertain how to feel about that.

He laughs softly. "I'm sorry. That didn't come out right, did it? I mean—I just assumed . . . I would have been surprised if you *weren't* involved with somebody."

"Oh." And that makes me feel better. At least marginally.

"But don't worry about it," he says. "I'm not afraid of a little competition. In case you hadn't noticed. Take your time. I'm in no rush. You've got to do what's right for you."

"Listen to my heart, right?"

"Right," he says softly. His face is half shadows, half light. He touches my chin and tilts it up gently. He looks from my mouth to my eyes and back again. He leans down tentatively, as if judging whether or not I will retreat from him. I don't. I feel him press me into him ever so slightly as he kisses me on the mouth. *Oh, my God. . . .* My heart turns over on itself. When he pulls away, I waver a little on my feet.

"Good night, Sally."

I stammer something that sounds like "G-night" and slip in through the door. He waits until I'm safely inside the building. Then he dissolves into the night.

SIXTEEN

The devil can cite Scripture for his purpose.

WILLIAM SHAKESPEARE

Gus is in the dressing room, staring at me speechlessly. Her round, orange-lipped mouth hangs open. The only sound in the room, other than the beating of my own heart, is the vague tinkling of her earrings swaying to and fro against her neck.

"You went out to dinner with him?" she says, in a croaky, incredulous voice. I nod excitedly. "He took you to—to Sette?" I nod again. "Whew!" She flops back in her chair, tugging lightly at her bodice as if to cool herself. "Was it like a date?"

I shrug that I'm not sure.

"Well, what happened?"

"Nothing. Really. We talked."

"About what?"

"All kinds of things."

"Like what?"

"Like, I don't know."

"Like *what,* Sal?"

"Like all kinds of things. The difference between right and wrong. You know—our philosophies on life."

"Aw, Sal," she groans. "Couldn't you have talked about something *normal?* Like your favorite movies or something?" She shakes her head, brooding for a moment or two. "Did you talk about your career at least?"

"Kind of. I told him how I got started."

"No, no, no, your *career* career." Gus means the part where she gets 15 percent, which doesn't include my Wicked Witch of the West role.

"Well, he *did* say he thought I was gonna be rich and famous someday."

Gus whoops triumphantly, punching the air. "I knew it, Sal!" she says. "I knew your ship would come in! This is just like a fairy tale! Prince Charming sweeps young girl off her feet! Makes all her dreams come true!"

"Gee, Gus. So glad to see you're keeping up on your women's studies. How far are you now? The fifties?"

"Oh, relax, Sally. That's not what I mean. I'd take a bullet for Gloria Steinem too. It's just that when it comes to guys like Jack Weaver, I can't help myself. This tide of estrogen just sweeps over me—I start drifting . . . floating . . . fantasizing . . ." She sighs dreamily. "Before you know it, I'm calling my doctor and canceling my hormone replacement therapy."

I laugh.

She leans forward, a sly smile on her face. "So—did he kiss you good night?"

I nod dazedly.

"Ohmigod . . . Was it hot and heavy? Or short and sweet?"

I think about it. "Short—and heavy!" We both buckle forward with laughter.

"Who was short and heavy?" Raine asks, coming into the dressing room in a red evening gown, her hair piled special-occasion high.

"Sally had a hot date last night," Gus says.

I shake my head at Gus, not wanting anyone on set to know. What if David finds out?

"Oh, what's the big deal?" Gus says. "It's going to come out in your *E! True Hollywood Story* anyway." She turns to Raine, who is already at the counter fixing her first martini of the day. "Sally had a hot date last night."

"Who's the lucky guy, Sal?"

"Jack Weaver," I answer quietly.

She stops in midpour.

Gus pumps her eyebrows. "Pretty impressive, huh? They went to Sette."

Raine doesn't even turn around. "How . . . great," she says uncomfortably. "Does anyone else want a drink?"

"Isn't it a little early for martinis?" Gus asks.

"Sorry. You want champagne instead?"

Gus, clearly disappointed Raine isn't going to join the hen party, turns to me. "Are you gonna see him again or what?"

"We didn't plan anything." Then: "Raine—is something wrong?"

"Not at all," she says too brightly. "It's just this damn gown. It's giving me a rash. How the hell can a two-hour cocktail party take three days to shoot?"

Gus says, "Are you gonna call him?"

"I don't know. Should I?"

"You don't want to look too desperate. But you don't want to look too *cool*. You didn't have the foresight to leave behind a glass slipper, did you?"

"No such luck."

"Damn. Fairy tales were so much easier before they invented phones."

There's a knock on the door. I get up to answer it. A man in a gray uniform is standing on the other side holding a long white box. My name is on the card. Gus screeches excitedly. She's takes the box even before I can and starts yanking at the tissue paper. "Look at them, Sal!" she says. "There must be two dozen! And no thorns!"

I open the card. I can't help but smile when I read it: *To the sweetest Wicked Witch of the West . . . Love, Jack.*

At the end of the day everyone gives me a slap on the back, congratulating me on my first full week on the show. The crew wraps and disperses for the weekend. In the dressing room, Raine is finally sliding out of the evening gown. "Good riddance," she says. She starts getting dressed, pulling on slim dark jeans and a pale silk blouse.

I move to the counter and adjust my flowers (Raine lent me one of her numerous vases for them). The fragrance fills my senses, heady and lush.

"Raine, can I ask you something?"

"If it has anything to do with borrowing my Manolos, forget it."

I laugh softly. Shake my head.

"What is it?"

" . . . Why don't you like Jack?"

She falters but doesn't look at me. "Who says I didn't?"

"Just a feeling I get."

"Because I didn't hit the roof when you got roses? Sorry, honey. Unlike your agent, I save high gear for my own love life."

"If it's because of Dara, he told me about her."

She turns to face me, frowning. "What about her?"

"That she sort of . . . had a crush on him."

She shrugs and goes back to getting dressed. "I knew she was interested in someone, but if it was him, she knew better than to talk to me about it. I don't believe in mixing business with pleasure, Sally. It's like using too much vermouth. It ruins everything you started with. Especially when it comes to guys like Jack Weaver."

I laugh uncomfortably. " 'Guys like Jack Weaver'? What's that supposed to mean?"

She regards me for a moment, a serious look on her face. "I know it's exciting, Sal. Sitting close to the fire like this. But the guy destroys at least one career before most people are finished brushing their teeth in the morning. Just be careful, that's all. And I mean more than safe sex." She winks. "Now, you better take those home with you." She motions to the flowers. "If you leave them here, they'll die over the weekend. Damned roses. Don't even last as long as a decent manicure."

I climb the stairs to my apartment; the flowers seem so heavy in the crystal vase. I'm trying to shake off Raine's warning about Jack. I shouldn't let it bother me. I know a lot of people feel that way about him; it's because of his power, his reputation. But he's really . . . very charming. Very sweet.

Then why don't I completely trust him either?

When I open the door, David leans out of the kitchen, a slice of bologna flapping out of his mouth. "Hey," he says with a smile.

"Hey . . ." I try to cover my disappointment that he's there. I kind of wanted to be alone for a while.

"I'm making a sandwich. Want one?"

"I'm not hungry."

"Your loss," he says. He finishes up and walks into the living room, carrying his sandwich on a plate. "Who got you those?" he asks, motioning to the flowers.

"Uh . . . the cast got them for me. For my first week."

"Nice. They didn't ask us to chip in."

"I guess the show paid for them or something. They must do that for all the new kids on the block."

"I don't recall getting flowers after *my* first week," he says with a grin. "They must just do that for the *stars.*" There's a playful sarcasm to his voice. He kisses me on the cheek, flops onto the futon, and turns on the TV. The room fills with the beeps and burps of suppertime newscasts, game shows, and commercials as he zaps through the channels.

I take a low, steadying breath and go into the kitchen, setting the roses on the table. They blush splendidly in the setting sun. At the very last second, I glimpse the white gift card tucked in among the leaves. I slip it out and slide it into the back pocket of my jeans. I walk back into the living room, trying to act natural. David has alighted on a *Seinfeld* repeat, the one where George won't give up the perfect parking spot. As I pass the futon, he looks up from his sandwich and smiles at me. I smile back. *Act normal . . . act normal. . . .* I go to the bathroom to pee, wash my hands, collect myself.

I hear him saying something to me from the living room. I turn off the taps. "Pardon?"

"I asked where you were last night."

"Nowhere," I say. I come to stand in the doorway, drying my hands.

"I tried calling. There was no answer."

My heart tenses. Piano wire round a spool. "Oh, yeah, right." My voice is innocent, casual. "I just went out to grab something to eat."

"Didn't you get my messages?" Then he looks at the answering machine. The red light is flashing. "Of course you didn't. You didn't check your machine." He leans over and presses PLAY. I feel a little surge of resentment, like he's searching through my purse or opening my mail. But I don't stop him.

The machine engages. *"Hey, Sal. It's me."* David's voice. *"Call me when you get in."*

Click. Beep.

"Sal? Hey. Me again. You there?" Beat. *"Someone picked up my shift tonight. I'm gonna go—"*

Suddenly, in a panic, I leap across the room.

"What's wrong with you?" he asks, trying to fend me off as I climb over him, reaching for the machine.

"Why don't we go out for dinner?"

"I thought you said you weren't hungry."

"I changed my mind." My shins bang against David. He grimaces. Suddenly another voice fills the room, this one much deeper than David's.

"Sally? . . . Hi. It's me. . . . I'm downstairs."

I freeze. Staring at the machine. David turns slowly and watches the little rotating eyes of the tape. I am breathless. Hearing Jack's voice has suddenly sucked me back in time to that inconceivable point in my life when I didn't know him. There is mechanical fumbling on the tape and then my voice comes on, excited, nervous.

"Jack! Hi!"

"Good. You're there. For a minute I thought you were standing me up."

"No. Of course not."

"Do you want me to—" I reach over and finally hit STOP. I make a mental note to get voice mail and ditch this old thing.

David's gaze turns slowly from the machine to me. "Who the hell was that?"

I look away, unable to answer.

"Sally . . . ?"

"Jack Weaver," I say in a little voice.

He widens his eyes. "The *president?*"

I nod my head.

"What's he doing calling *here?*"

It takes me a moment, but I finally say, "We . . . kind of went out last night."

He puts down his plate, watching me warily. "You . . . *what?*"

"We went for dinner—well, not really dinner, just for something to eat."

"So you lied to me?"

"I didn't *lie* . . ."

"You said you stayed in."

"I *told* you I went out to grab something to eat."

"Sally—of *course* it's a lie. You didn't tell me with *who.*" He picks up his plate and stomps into the kitchen. I follow after him, my tone beseeching.

"I was *going* to tell you . . ."

He scrapes crumbs into the garbage, slams the plate into the sink. "Yeah, right."

"I was! *Please* don't be mad."

"I'm not mad. I just don't see why you have to fucking *lie* to me." He grabs a can of beer from the fridge and stomps back into the living room. I follow him.

"It was nothing, David. Really. Just dinner."

"Fine. Good. No problem." He flops back onto the sofa, popping open his beer can. He slurps loudly, hacking through the channels like a soldier through dense bush. *Click, hiss, whirr, zip, shhhhh* . . . "What the hell were the two of you doing going out for dinner anyway?"

I shrug innocently. "I bumped into him at the studio and—"

"Then why was he picking you up here?"

"Well . . . I—I—got all mucked up in makeup and I had to come home and change." The lies! I can't believe the lies! I deal them like Blackjack cards: *Hit me, hit me . . . stick . . .*

He narrows his eyes on me. "So—where'd you go?"

I shrug innocently. "Nowhere special."

"Where'd—you—go?" he repeats, little beats between each word.

"To Sette . . ."

"Sette?" he squeals. "The place that wouldn't even *hire* me?"

Shit. I forgot David applied for a job there last summer. They didn't even call him back. It was worse than an audition. "It wasn't a big deal, David! Trust me!"

"Yeah, right! What happened?"

"Nothing happened!"

"Nothing?"

"It was totally and completely p-professional!" Then I think of something to throw him off the trail. "I had an MCS," I tell him.

"Oh, yeah? Who?"

"Courtney Cox."

He takes the bait. "You're kidding? Courtney Cox was there?"

"Yeah. She was so gorgeous. And *so* nice."

"You . . . *met* her?"

Oh, oh. The plan backfired. It's like I'm bragging or something. He actually looks hurt.

"She *seemed* nice. From a distance, I mean." I slide closer to him on the sofa. "Please don't be mad, David. It was nothing. *Really.*"

"You don't like him, do you?"

"Who, *Jack?*" I laugh in a dry, lilting way. "Are you kidding? He's not even my type! We're just . . . friends. You know—casual . . . professional . . . acquaintance . . . type . . ." He's watching me dubiously, witnessing me dig myself farther and farther into the ground. ". . . friends," I finish, with a smile.

He narrows his eyes on me. "You sure he didn't try anything?"

I *tsk* loudly, emphasizing the ridiculousness of his statement with a little flap of my hand. But even as I'm doing that I'm thinking about our kiss; half of his face lit by the light from my apartment door. "I told you, it was completely and utterly . . . professional."

"So you said." He's watching me closely. Intensely. I don't look away. I just hold his gaze. I try to remember a documentary I saw on TLC about micromovements in the human face. People can tell if you're lying by how you move your eyes. Is it up and to the left? Or down and to the right? *Damnit.* I don't remember. Lucky for me, he caves in first.

"Sorry, hon," he says. "I don't mean to be such a bastard. I trust you. It's just that . . . I guess I'm a bit jealous. Things are so shitty at work and they still won't give me any lines and that guy—you know, he's . . ." He lets out a small, hurt laugh. "He's just got so much going for him and I don't want you falling for him or anything."

I scrunch up my nose. "That's *not* going to happen."

"Better not," he says, playfully warning, then his attention goes back to the TV. He's landed on the Cartoon Network and *Looney Tunes* is on. "I love this one," he says, pointing to the screen.

"Me too."

It's the one where Wile E. Coyote is trying to steal sheep from under the nose of the shaggy sheepdog. They're pals on lunch break and when they punch in on the time clock each day—*"Morning, Ralph. . . ." "Hey, Sam"*—but sworn enemies during their shifts. After a moment David turns to me: "Bet he drives a Porsche, right?"

I nod.

"Figures," he says with a derisive laugh.

I can tell it bothers him; I can tell it *all* bothers him. He has to swallow a large lump in his throat, trying to camouflage it with a sip of beer. I feel heartsick. I snuggle closer to him, settling into the crook beneath his arm. *How can I be so horrible?*

We both watch as the coyote slinks around the flock, feeling for the plumpest sheep to take back to his cave. David starts running his finger along my neck; I feel a rake of chills run up my back, not entirely pleasant, but not unpleasant either. Then he pulls out his ponytail, shaking his long hair free.

Oh, oh. David always takes his ponytail out when he wants to have sex. He thinks his hair is so irresistible, it's equivalent to foreplay.

It's not.

He moves toward me, enclosing me in the bracket of his arms. He kisses me softly at first. *Peck. Peck.* And I kiss him back. But then his whole mouth finds mine and he becomes more passionate. There is a sort of feigned confidence in his kiss. I try to kiss him back, but we bump noses. I pretend not to notice, gently rearranging my position. His hands start roaming. I don't want to do this, really I don't. But I'm going to. Do you know what a guilt fuck is? It's something a woman does to ease her conscience when she's feeling guilty for doing something she shouldn't have done, say—oh, I don't know—going out for dinner with another man? Sex. Woman's eternal currency in the everlasting battle of the sexes. Such a versatile commodity, valuable in even the most depressed economic conditions, always in high demand, completely nonelastic, eagerly lapped up by men whose appetite for it strikes them deaf, dumb, and blind to even the most blatantly inequitable fiscal transaction involving it. From domestic deceit to international espionage, men will take the bum end of any deal as long as it means getting laid.

I reach for him with a determination that is not so much passion as it is will. I can't even begin to feel remotely aroused. I feel like we're two big elbows banging into everything. We both pull my bra up over my breasts, not taking it off completely. He begins running his tongue over my nipples, which, I must admit, feels okay. I stroke my hands over his hair. His mouth goes down my belly. He starts to undo my jeans.

But suddenly, suddenly it's not him. In my mind, it's Jack. It's Jack Weaver's head lowering on my abdomen. His full mouth laying kisses along my skin. His hands sliding my jeans off, his tongue moving over my skin.

"Oh, God . . ." I moan out loud. I drag David up to my lips and begin kissing him wildly. But it's not David I'm kissing. It's Jack. I rub myself against him. Fumble desperately at the buckle of his belt.

"God, Sal, take it easy!" David is laughing, flattered.

I push him down and crawl on top of him, slipping a condom on him and sliding him inside of me. In moments, in seconds, I am coming and David is coming along with me, making all the familiar noises I don't want to hear. I ram and ram and ram myself on top of him, and then when it's over, I collapse off of him, breathless.

"Christ, what got into you?" Still laughing, he pulls the condom off the end of his prick and grabs a tissue, wrapping it up. Breathless, I pull my bra down over my chest. My heart still hammers. *Wow.*

We both turn to face the TV again. David snickers as the coyote slips into a sheep suit. I reluctantly let the last image of Jack Weaver fade from my mind.

SEVENTEEN

Speak of the devil and he is bound to appear.

PROVERB

SATURDAY afternoon the streets outside the Backburner are filled with people scouring the flea markets and lingering over latte. I'm sitting on the stool behind the counter, my head in my hands, my eyes watching a small black spider crawling with intent along a plank of the wooden floor. A few customers come in, jingling the bell above the door. But they don't stay long. The inside of the Backburner is a cool, dank place, a place for spiders and other things that don't like the sun. I sigh forlornly. I look at my watch again. *Only 1:20?*

The jingle of the bell over the door snaps me alert. The spider picks up its pace, racing toward the shadows and under a shelf. A dark form moves into my periphery. It's a man, judging from the heavy footsteps. I turn slowly. I see a pair of well-worn Adidas at first. Then his jeans. Then a white T-shirt. He takes off his sunglasses.

It's him.

I nearly topple off my stool. Jesus. My first instinct is to be happy to see him; yet I'm also a little weirded out that he tracked me down like this.

"Hi, there," he says with a cocky half-smile. "Hope I'm not inter-rupting."

"Of course not." I straighten the stool, recover myself. "How did you know where I worked?"

"You told me."

"Did I?" I try to remember. "I told you I worked in a bookstore. I don't think I told you the *name.*"

"You must've. Otherwise this is a pretty good guess." He looks around the place, nodding as if impressed. "So this is where Sally Carpenter worked before she got rich and famous. Very convincing. Possibly another *People* caption."

I look down, trying to regain my composure. "A close second, anyway."

"Distant second," he says with his smile. He pockets his shades. His dark hair is tousled. There's a warm tinge to his cheekbones, as if he's been in the sun. I am aware that I can't quite remember the last time I saw him. Yesterday? The day before? An eon ago? Since I met him, something has happened to the way time passes; one moment, it stretches like taffy, the next it shatters like glass. I feel my reserve about his showing up at work begin to melt in his presence. I must have told him the name of the shop. I *must* have, that's all—we talked about everything.

Didn't we?

He leans forward onto the counter, emphasizing the breadth of his shoulders. "I was going to call you last night," he says. "But I didn't want to look too desperate."

"Me neither." I laugh softly. "The flowers were lovely, by the way."

We're interrupted by banging from the back room and the sound of paper being torn. It's the fifth sketch Jeremy's ripped up today.

"What the bloody . . . fucking . . . hell! Fuck! Damnit! Fucking . . . fuck!" The dingy curtain puffs open and Jeremy emerges in his grayed undershirt and baggy brown pants, his shoulders permanently hunched forward from sitting at his easel too long.

"I can't work!" he rails, holding his skull. "It's all this sunshine! I thought summer was over!" He stomps to the front of the store, behind the counter. I slip out of his way a bit. "That's it, Sally. Close up shop. Let's go get drunk." He starts digging through the drawer for his keys to lock up. Then he senses Jack standing there. He smiles, bearing yellowed teeth and discolored, receded gums. "I'm sorry, good sir, but as you can see, we're closed for business." He motions to the door. "If you don't mind."

But Jack doesn't move; he's still leaning on the counter. Jeremy looks from me to Jack, then back again. Jeremy may not be the world's most astute businessman, but he intuits that Jack is not just another soft porn customer.

"Jeremy," I begin nervously, "this is Jack Weaver. Jack Weaver—this is my boss *and* artistic genius—Jeremy Lambert." They shake hands. "Jack's from UBN, Jeremy. He's the *president*," I add, hoping stupidly for a little decorum.

"The president?" Jeremy sneers. "What an *honor*. It isn't often we mere mortals get the opportunity to meet someone personally responsible for the decline of Western civilization."

Jack laughs at that. A surprising, relaxed laugh. But he's straightened up now, to his full height.

"Don't mind Jeremy, Jack. He doesn't like television. He thinks it's shrinking the prefrontal cortex."

"Ahhh." Jack nods, as if it's all coming together for him.

"So tell me, Mr. Weaver," Jeremy says, leaning his bony hip against the counter, "what does it feel like to be in a dying industry?"

Jack shrugs and looks around the shop as if to say: *I'm in the dying industry?*

"Well, you are, you know. With all those Japanese conglomerates taking over. I'm all for it myself. The Japanese are responsible for some of the highest artistic and cultural achievements in human history. If they so much as breathe in the general direction of American television, they should improve it considerably." He snickers in self-satisfaction.

"I hate to disappoint you, Jeremy," Jack says, "but your information is a little out of date."

"Oh?" Jeremy is uncertain, offended his insult didn't hit the mark.

"The Japanese are out of the picture. They bailed out so fast, you couldn't book a flight back to Tokyo for five years. That's the great thing about TV, Jeremy"—he gingerly opens the cover of a musty *Time* magazine on the counter, one entirely devoted to coverage of the assassination attempt against Reagan—"you're guaranteed never to run across old news."

Jeremy, whose congenital pallor has flushed pink with indignation, turns to me: "Never mind the drink, Sally. It feels like a cloud has passed over the sun." He throws Jack one last contemptuous glare and stomps to his back room, letting the curtain flap decisively closed behind him.

Jack grins. "Hope I didn't get you in trouble."

"Don't worry. He doesn't expect much from TV types. At least you didn't let him down."

He laughs a little, and then we're just staring at each other; it seems like a moment that is suspended, at once full of tension yet perfect and still. When he speaks, it is as if I have drifted safely back to earth.

"Are we going to see each other again?" he asks.

"Yes—I mean—if you want to."

"How about tomorrow night?"

I feel a rush of adrenaline.

"I'd understand if you're busy. It's short notice. But I've got this premiere to go to. I usually hate that stuff, but it would be fun—no, it would be *amazing*—if you'd come. It's the opening of that new flick . . ." He snaps his fingers. "What is it? That new Cruise movie."

I manage to camouflage my reaction. He's talking about the biggest gala screening of the season. Everyone on set has been trying to get invitations all week.

But I can't go. David and I are supposed to see a mutual friend of ours in a play. We've been planning it for weeks. *Say no, Sally. Say no.*

"Sure, Jack. Sounds like fun."

He smiles, leaning his weight forward onto the counter so that our lips are only a few inches apart. "Thanks," he whispers, then he kisses me softly. He walks backward toward the door, hands in his pockets, a sly smile on his face. "Maybe we'll talk about movies this time." The bell jingles above him and the bright sunlight melts him away.

I pat my chest, trying to make my heart slow down.

I go back to work, pricing some used Harlequins—all those kissing couples, all those swarthy men. . . . *Whew.*

"I get it." I hear Jeremy's voice. He's standing in the doorway at the back of the shop. "It's all making sense to me now."

"What is?"

"I see what's going on. Why you're getting all this work all of a sudden. You're sleeping with the boss."

"I am *not!"* I snap.

"Did he get you the part on the soap opera, Sally?"

"So what if he did? It's the way the business works."

"I'm just concerned about you, that's all. He might expect something in return   *if* you know what I mean."

"Jeremy, you're being a sexist pig."

"People don't do things for other people for no reason at all, Sally. They always want something in return. Don't be so naïve. It went out with the Impressionists." He turns on a worn heel and disappears back into his room.

For the rest of my shift, my spirits are dampened. The sun moves to the other side of the sky and the street outside stays in cool shadow for the afternoon. I lock up, calling good-bye to Jeremy, who ignores me. I try to dismiss his warnings as silly, but on some level I can't entirely ignore them. I don't completely trust Jack Weaver, either—and I don't know why.

I should probably call him and cancel. Just tell him something came up at the last minute. Maybe I could end this all before it goes any further. I don't even have anything to wear, really.

It's the color that catches my eye—a shade of blue that I've seen on the cover of every fashion magazine on the stands. It's a lovely slip dress on a mannequin in the window of a shop I've never dared go into because I couldn't afford so much as a belt. But that color . . . Maybe I'll just see how much it is. I watch my hand open the brass handle of the door. I watch my shoes move across bleached wood floors. A pretty shop girl smiles at me. I ask about the dress in the window. She says it would look amazing on me. I'm still trying to talk myself out of it as I move into a white fitting room and pull the curtain closed. There is one silver hook on the white wall and a three-way mirror. I slip out of my jeans and into the dress; it falls over me like rainwater, stopping to rest in all the right places. I'm surprised it fits so well. I turn this way and that, smoothing the dress against my skin. My nipples go hard beneath the thin silk. I feel my cheeks begin to burn with daring. I look at the space beneath the curtain; I hear the shop girl's voice; she's speaking to another woman. In the cubicle next to me someone else is trying something on, sliding clothes on and off her body; somewhere else someone is crinkling shopping bags. I lean against the wall, my head only inches from the silver hook, and lift the hem of the dress. My hand slides up between my legs. I am shocked by how wet I am—how wet I am just thinking about him.

Jack.

I remember the sound of his voice.

Jack . . .

The way his hand felt on my back . . .

Faster . . .

I hear the shop girl's voice outside: "You okay in there?"

"I'm . . . fine . . ." I breathe.

There is the hollow click of high heels on wood floor. Another voice but it fades into the background.

I feel my breath heat up, my chest swelling, my skin turning hot beneath the dress . . . *Jack* . . . and then suddenly the world is flashing red around me. The floor and walls spin; I have to bend over to stop myself from falling. I take a second to catch my breath, swallowing big mouthfuls of calming air. The colors around me are fading from red to orange to shades of gray, then white again, and I am once again standing in the cubicle by myself. I scramble out of the dress quickly, smiling in spite of myself, ashamed but half amused, too.

The nerve—the fucking nerve.

I put my street clothes back on and move quickly to the counter, averting my eyes and taking out my credit card. Even if I *don't* go to the premiere, I need a new dress, don't I? The only decent one I have is Hazel's knockoff and I probably won't wear that one again.

"You know," says the shop girl, ringing up the dress, "those shoes would look perfect with this." She points to a shelf behind her; several pairs of strappy black sandals are arranged spare and elegant as line drawings. I think about it and then laugh as I surrender to trying on . . . maybe just a pair.

Twenty minutes later, I reemerge onto the street, swinging two shopping bags from a store I'd never even had the nerve to walk into before.

Oh, what the hell? I'll go to the premiere. I don't know what Jeremy's worried about. It's Jack's power, I guess—everyone's so suspicious of it. Even I was at first. Maybe still am. But it's not like he's *evil* or anything. He's one of the most amazing people I've ever met. Smart. Funny. Utterly charming. And he just makes me feel so—I don't know—special. Damnit, I hate admitting it to myself. I know I shouldn't be thinking that way. I missed the bra burning by a few years, but I still get the point. You're not supposed to depend on anyone—especially a man—for your self-esteem. But I still can't *help* it. Jack Weaver could have any actress in the country. How can I not feel at least a little flattered that he's chosen me?

EIGHTEEN

*. . . [T]he devil took [Jesus] to a very high mountain
and showed him all the kingdoms of the world. . . .*

MATTHEW 4:8

"GOD, you sound awful," David says over the phone.

I fake-cough again.

"What do you think it is?"

"I don't know," I say, working my voice in its very scratchiest octave. "The flu maybe?" Another cough. All this while I'm dashing around my apartment, brushing my hair, shoving my makeup into my evening bag. I run past the window to make sure that I wasn't imagining it before. Nope. A black limousine is waiting for me. The back window is open and Jack's arm leans on the frame, his fingers casually rapping a beat on the roof.

"Maybe you shouldn't be alone," David says. "Let me come over. I'll bring chicken soup and lots of TLC."

"Oh, no! Don't do that!" But I've been too emphatic; I take it back a notch, coughing again. "I mean, maybe I'm contagious. I wouldn't want you to catch anything." I've got the phone shouldered against my ear, trying to put on my new sandals. I bounce around on one foot trying to clasp the ankle strap.

"Are you sure you don't want me to—"

"I'll be fine, David. Just tell everyone I'm sorry, okay?"

"I will. You just get some rest." He tells me he loves me, I tell him I love him back, he pecks me a kiss, warning me to take my echinacea and vitamin C.

Finally we hang up.

I lean on the phone for a moment and growl out loud. God, what a bitch I am! I'm going to rot in hell for this! I've got to come clean—tell David what's going on with Jack.

But I'm not even sure what *is* going on with Jack, only that whatever it is, it fills me with the same kind of fearful anticipation as the prospect of spending the whole night in my new three-inch heels.

FIFTY-FOURTH Street outside the Ziegfeld Theater is dense with limousines, onlookers, and photographers when we pull up in front. A team of handlers open our limo door and corral Jack and me onto the red carpet. I see Sarah Jessica Parker and Matthew Broderick. George Clooney. *My God!* Gwyneth herself! Everyone moves at an unhurried pace up the red carpet, tilting this way and that for the photographers.

"Take your time," Jack whispers to me.

"What for? Nobody knows me."

"They *will.*"

THE movie is a typical dick flick, with lots of stunts and witty one-liners, but I still can't really pay attention to it. I'm too busy stealing glances at the back of Tom Cruise's head three rows down or Drew Barrymore's profile four seats across.

When the movie's over, we all slide back into our limousines and go to the Rainbow Room for the after party. White-jacketed waiters swerve through the crowd serving champagne and canapés. The celebrities, S.J., Gwyneth, Tom, and the others, can only be seen through small chinks in the crowds that surround them. It seems as if their fame created a kind of gravitational force within them and that they attract more people the way the largest planets in the galaxy attract more moons.

UBN has two tables in the corner; Hazel Grippe comes over and gives me a big hug, as if we're long-lost friends. Sabrina Calliope-Clark is there, and when Jack introduces me she air-kisses me, seeming to have forgotten all about snubbing me in the makeup trailer. Jack reminds Griff Hughes, the executive producer of *Precinct,* the one with the thick glasses, that I played Candace in the bank robbery episode, and Griff tells me I was "terrif," and I think, Yeah, right—as if fluttering my eyelashes and screaming for my life makes me Meryl Streep. It's because I'm with Jack, of course; that's the reason everyone is being so nice to me, and for brief, glittering moments, I don't even care. But sometime around midnight, just when it seems I can't be having a better time, I feel the gravitational pull of my pessimism. Jack seems to sense it. He holds out his hand and we leave the room, stepping into a long marble hallway. We walk slowly, my new heels echoing softly. Behind us, the sounds of the party are muffled, haunting and glamorous.

"You okay?" he asks.

I shrug but don't answer.

"I can tell something's bothering you, Sally."

"I don't know," I begin uncertainly, "I guess I'm just waiting for Allen Funt to jump out and say, *'Smile!'* "

He laughs but seems a little confused.

"This isn't my life, Jack! This *can't* be my life. I don't go to Tom Cruise premieres. I don't have executive producers telling me I'm 'terrif.' I'm a Bad Luck Schleprock. Even this dress! It's not a knockoff so it *can't* be my dress! Meaning this *can't* be my life!"

"It is *now,*" he says.

"Yeah—now that I've met *you,*" I grumble.

"Is *that* what's bothering you?" He laughs. "That you think *I'm* responsible for all this? No way, Sally. You're a talented actor. You were going to get all this on your own. But if I'm in a position to speed it up, why shouldn't I? It's my job."

I feel a pang of bitterness at that. Is that what I am? Part of his *job?* We reach the end of the hallway. I lean against the window ledge, tracing the veins of marble with my fingertip. Outside, the lights of the city gleam, and below us, traffic glides steadily, silently.

He pushes a strand of my hair off my face. "Sally, why don't you trust me?"

"I just don't understand why you're being so *nice* to me," I begin. "Even Jeremy thinks it's strange. He says I should be careful because people don't do nice things for each other unless they expect something in return."

"Does he say that?" He smiles sadly. "He can't be a very good friend, then."

And that makes me falter for a moment—the truth of it.

"Oh, wait a second!" he says with a snap of his fingers. *"I know what this is about. It's back to that 'owing' thing again. You think if I help you with your career, you'll have to—"* He shoves me gently against the marble ledge and whispers the word *fuck* into my ear; it sounds vulgar and sacred and immediately makes me wet; but I slap him anyway—*Jack!*—and struggle in his arms. He laughs and pins me harder, and I feel the fight go out of me. "Well, Sally—I'd be lying if I told you I didn't want to . . . *make love* . . . to you. You're one of the most amazing women I've ever met. But that's not what this is about."

"What's it about, then?"

"I told you. I want to help you. I *can* help you. So why shouldn't I? You didn't become an actress to price used paperbacks for the rest of your life, did you?"

I give him a playful shove. "I *like* my job."

"But don't you like this too?" He motions behind him, indicating the party, the people, the whole night.

"It's not *bad,*" I say playfully.

"What, then. What do you really want . . . if not this?"

I think about it, blurt: "World peace!"

He laughs softly. "Sorry. Can't help you with that one."

I snap my fingers as if we're out of luck. He presses me against the wall again. He watches my mouth. "I'm serious, Sally. You can't get what you want out of life unless you admit what it is. So . . . what is it? What would make you happy?"

I try to sidestep the question, pulling away from him, but he only holds me more tightly.

He asks it again. "What would make you happy, Sally—what do you want?"

In the moments that follow I remember all the years growing up with movie posters on my walls and constantly rotating film clippings on my bulletin board. I think of all the nights I spent in the bathtub pretending I was answering David Letterman's questions about my latest movie while the bathwater went cold around me. I remember all the hours I spent in front of the mirror wishing my lips were fuller, like Uma Thurman's, my nose cuter, like Meg Ryan's, my legs longer, like Cameron Diaz's. All the nights I went to sleep dreaming of my white Mediterranean mansion in Beverly Hills, the one with the Louis XIV chandelier in the foyer and one whole closet just for shoes. I remember those moments like I am living them again, have never stopped living them. I look up at him.

"I want to be rich and famous," I tell him in a small, deadly voice.

He smiles. "You see? That wasn't so hard."

"You really have the power to do that?"

"No," he says, touching the skin beneath my throat. "*You* really have that power."

I take an unsteady breath. "Sure doesn't feel like it."

"All you have to do," he says, "is choose."

"Choose?"

"Yes. You have to *choose* to take what you want from life, Sally. Once you do that, everything else takes care of itself."

"It can't be that easy."

"It *is*. You'll see." And he kisses me softly along the neck.

★ ★ ★

We ride home in the limousine leaning against each other, holding hands. Sometimes I look at him and wonder, Who is this man? This man who seems, to me at least, to have his hands on the levers of the world—this man who doesn't seem to have the nature of giving, but who wants to give to me. I want to believe him. Really I do. That I'm going to be happy, that my life is going to work out the way I want. But his logic is like a magnet to me, more like a magnet than anything else I have ever encountered, because even as part of me is irresistibly drawn to him, a part of me is forced away.

I can't believe he is standing behind me as I slide the key into the lock on my apartment door. I open the door and feel the intimacy of my world open to him. He waits on the threshold until I nod and then he follows me into the darkness. I watch him move slowly from room to room then turn and smile at me, as if he's learned something new about me. I watch him standing there, looking at me. His eyes are like pathways, like doors leading me deeply away from myself. I go to him in the darkness. Our mouths begin to search each other out. Gently at first. Tentatively. Then with more assurance. We lie down on the bed. Kissing. Beginning to explore each other's bodies. Fingers touching here. Moving there. Sliding. Stroking. The first moan escapes up into the ceiling. Mine. Sharp and sweet. Then his. A low, painful growl. He never goes too fast. Or too slow. Everywhere he touches me, it seems I have yearned to feel his hands my entire life.

I don't know how long we kiss. Each hour that passes, I feel him struggling more and more against his own desire . . . until his round shoulders begin to tremble. And his teeth begin to clench. I've never felt this place . . . this ecstatic darkness . . . red-edged, piercing, and sweet. *Oh, my God* . . . He could do anything he wants to me right now. I've never wanted a man more than I want him. There is nothing I would stop him from doing. Not tearing off my skin. Not slowly peeling me down to my heart—nothing. *Do it, Jack . . . do it . . . fuck me. . . .*

But suddenly—at four, five, in the morning? I don't know—he sits up, growling in frustration.

"What's wrong . . . ?"

He lets out a low laugh. "Nothing's wrong . . . absolutely nothing. But I don't know what I'll do to you if I stay here much longer."

"Stay," I whisper. "I won't tell anyone how easy you are."

He lets out a low, frustrated growl, but shakes his head. "Not yet . . . it's too soon."

"Tease," I tell him, rolling onto my side, flattered. I watch as he moves through the darkness getting dressed. He comes to the edge of the bed and sits down, tucking the blanket up around my neck. He leans forward. Kisses me sweetly, so sweetly, on the lips. "Good night, my princess. Sleep well. . . ."

Though half-closed eyes I watch him go to the door. He is nothing more than a silhouette, great cliffs of darkness against the rest of the world. The door closes. I am asleep before his footsteps have completely receded.

NINETEEN

Always the same, they never scent the devil,
even when he has them by the nape of the neck.

JOHANN WOLFGANG VON GOETHE

"So you guys want the usual?" the waiter with the tattoo on his arm asks. He puts down a glass of cheap red wine in front of me and a sixteen-ounce mug of beer for David.

"Yep," David says without consulting me

Not that I mind. I like the usual.

Usually.

I can't believe I'm here for pizza night. David popped by my dressing room this afternoon. His hair was freshly smoothed back. He smelled like his favorite cologne. "Are we still on for tonight?" he asked me. There was such a sad, hopeful smile on his face, I couldn't say no—because I canceled pizza night last week (I told him I had some scenes Raine was helping me with). I've only seen David outside of work a few times since I started seeing Jack and it's been almost three weeks. "Of course we're on for tonight," I told him, not wanting him to get suspicious. I had to wait for him to leave the dressing room before calling Jack to tell him I'd be late.

David is sitting across the table from me, catching me up on all his news. They hired a new pretend waiter, a hunky Latino guy who's getting more face time than anyone else; he's thinking of running a marathon in the spring; someone stiffed him on a two-hundred-dollar tab at work the other night. I follow along earnestly, laughing when I should, nodding when I should, chewing my pizza and drinking my wine, and the whole time I'm thinking of Jack.

I can't help it. I try to force myself to stop thinking of him, but even then it's only partially successful because my mind automatically starts taking inventory. David's voice isn't as deep as Jack's; his hands aren't as big; he's got bad table manners; his hair needs a trim; he slouches; he should work out more. These are not things I *want* to think—I give myself a mental slap every time one of them occurs to me—but they just happen. When I finally get them under control, my mind starts wandering again, this time to the food: how the pizza is almost inedible compared with the gustatory revelation I had last night at Vong. How the wine tastes like vinegar next to what Jack and I have when we go out.

And then something brings my train of thought to a screeching halt. It's The Question.

"So, Sal—were you out with Jack Weaver the other night?"

I stop, swallow a thick wad of crust. "Why?"

"Someone told me you were at some kind of club opening with him." He's picking at his pizza. His hands are shaking a little.

Come on, Sally. Tell him. Here's your chance to come clean.

God knows I've tried telling David about Jack a hundred times over the last few weeks. During lunch in the commissary or down on the street having a cigarette. *David, we have to talk. You're one of the sweetest people I know and I really don't want to hurt you . . . but, David, I've met someone. . . . If you knew him, you'd understand. . . . He's charming and funny and smart and sensitive and not nearly as bad as everyone says. And he makes me so happy. I've never been so happy in my life. David . . . God help me . . . God help me . . . I think I'm falling in love.*

David is watching me, a slightly fearful look on his face. I don't know why I can't just *tell* him. The idea of hurting him, of saying something that I *know* will hurt him, is almost impossible for me, like trying to force myself to stick my hand in an open flame.

The same thing happened when Benny Ecclestone asked me to my senior prom. He had come up to my locker after school, red-faced and nervous. Benny Ecclestone was a loser. Bad skin. Bad hair. Bad breath. I didn't want to go with him, of course, and quickly shuffled through a list of excuses. I could tell him I already had a date (though I didn't) or that I was baby-sitting that night. But even as I was staring at Benny Ecclestone's bad complexion, I was thinking of the plastic Jesus. He still sat on his shelf in the kitchen watching me eat breakfast every morning—a little worse for wear, maybe, the grease settling in the folds of his plastic robe. But his teachings were as unchanged as they had been for two thousand years.

Do unto others, Sally . . .

I felt the resigned weight of my conscience. Saying no to someone just because he had bad acne was wrong. So I went with Benny Ecclestone to the prom. It wasn't a total loss. We left early and I was home in time to watch the season finale of *X-Files*.

But that's what's happening right now, isn't it? The plastic Jesus may be a thousand miles away, and I may be eating greasy pizza instead of my regular morning Froot Loops, but he still has his eye on me. He still wants me to do the right thing. But what *is* the right thing? If I tell David the truth, it'll hurt his feelings. Which is wrong. But if I lie to spare his feelings, that's also *technically* wrong.

Finally I decide on what I think is the lesser of two evils and say, "It's just work stuff, David. A bunch of people were there. I told you—Jack and I are just friends."

He watches me closely. "You sure?"

"Absolutely." I smile innocently, taking a sip of wine. He seems to consider it for a moment, then goes back to his pizza. He believes me. Or maybe he just *wants* to believe me.

I wonder if the plastic Jesus would be appeased?

The waiter comes up to the table and points to the last two wedges of pizza. "You guys gonna finish that?"

"Wrap it up," David says. "We'll take it home."

We'll take it home?

He reaches for his wallet. "There's a Monty Python special on Comedy Central tonight, Sal," he says. His voice trails off.

I panic mildly. I know David doesn't have cable. But he's not really asking to come over to watch Python, is he? He's asking if he can spend the night.

"Um . . . I'm really tired, David." I cover my mouth as I yawn. "Can I tape it for you?"

He smiles, kind of sadly, and says "Sure." We split the tab.

LATER that night I lie alone in bed, staring at the ceiling. I listen for the growl of his car through the open window. When I hear it, my heart speeds up. The engine cuts, the door slams, the phone rings twice. I lean over and buzz him up without saying a word. I've left the door unlocked for him and he lets himself in. He gets undressed and slides into bed with me, all shadows and heat.

"I'm going to tell him, Jack, I promise. . . . It'll be over soon. . . ."

He quiets me, putting his finger on my lips. *"Shhhh . . ."*

In a moment none of it matters. I've already begun to surrender to him—to his mouth, his hands. In the last few weeks I have had more sexual pleasure with him than I've ever had before. We've gotten positively tantric on each other.

Yet we have not yet made love. Officially, I mean.

This is not like me, to wait so long. He says it's different for him, too. He wants to draw it out . . . to enjoy it. I do too. But that doesn't mean it's not driving me absolutely crazy. That night we come close . . . so close.

"Do it, Jack . . . do it . . ." I hear a voice say. It's my voice. I know it is. But I've never heard this voice before. It seems to come from someone buried deep inside of me. Someone unafraid of what she wants.

He lowers his mouth to mine. "Not yet, Sally."

"Please. I need to feel you inside of me."

"You're not ready."

I laugh weakly and rub against him. "I've never been *more* ready."

He smiles and lets out a low laugh. "Not that. . . ."

"What then?"

"Do you know what it means to let go of your heart . . . your soul . . . to give them to someone else?"

"Yes . . . yes . . ."

He laughs, low in his chest. "Not yet . . ."

I grab a hunk of his hair and pull it back until his lips are bared over his teeth. His eyes gleam darkly, with a prick of light.

"Who are you?" I whisper.

But he doesn't answer me.

TWENTY

He who has no mind to trade with the devil,
should be so wise as to keep away from his shop.

ROBERT SOUTH

Jack's loft takes up one whole floor of an old building in the meat-packing district. I don't know what kind of factory it used to be, but it was used for something, because the wide-planked wood floors are original, and no matter how many coats of acrylic are on it, the wood still dips softly beneath your feet. In the right light those hollows create ripples that make the whole apartment, and everything in it, seem as if it's floating on the surface of a shallow lake. There are sixteen windows overlooking the Hudson, all with their original glass, which warps the view of New Jersey across the river and the streets below. The walls are white, the furniture is mostly midcentury and spare. Unstudied Masculine, I call it, because even as one corner of the apartment looks ready to be photographed for *Architectural Digest,* the other is stacked with empty cardboard boxes; even as a Danish floor lamp gleams next to a Charles Eames chair, there is something—jeans or newspapers or takeout containers—cluttering something else. It is like Jack. I am familiar with it. I spend a lot of time with it. But I can't quite figure it out.

Sometimes, after I've spent the night, I like to wake up early and watch him sleep. He likes to sleep in when he can, which seems unusual for the kind of person I thought he was. I expected him to be up before the sun, hitting his treadmill, checking with his stockbroker about the closing of the Nikkei, like some postmillennium Gordon Gekko from *Wall Street*. Instead he sleeps, beneath white sheets, his browned shoulders round, his eyes closed, his breathing even and peaceful. He seems so relaxed. Like a teenager who doesn't care if he's late for summer school. Life is effortless for him.

As it has become effortless for me when I am with him.

It has been twenty-seven days since we've been together. I have counted. Twenty-seven blissful days on the calendar. I have never been so happy in my life. Even so, there is something inside of me—an ache—that is always there. Is it fear? Fear that I will lose him? Is it sadness? Because I have spent so many years of my life without him? Or is it just the way happiness feels—kind of bittersweet and unbearable—because it is a condition that is so unfamiliar to me?

"I think I know why we're here," Gus says, elbowing me.

But I'm too stunned to really pay attention. I can't believe we've just walked into Lee Roswell's office. It can't be the same room where I did the read-through for Meridien's part. It's so much smaller than I remember. And there aren't as many plaques on the wall as I thought. And that view that I thought was so spectacular is just an average gridwork of windows in the insurance building across the alley.

Has everything changed that much?

"Don't ask too many questions," Gus is saying, "but I pulled in a few chips and got a copy of a focus group they did on you last week." She opens her tattered briefcase and slips out a sheaf of papers.

"They did a focus group on *me?*"

She shoves the papers over to me. "Guess what. You have an AF of ninety-two!"

"AF?"

"Appeal Factor, Sally," she says, giving me an admonishing shove. "I think ninety-two's the highest one at the network. Mind you, John Monroe's up three points since the rehab."

I'm flipping through the pages, trying to make heads or tails out of the figures and percentages, the pie charts and the graphs pertaining to Meridien's character. "But isn't it expensive to do a focus group?"

"Of course it is."

"Why would they do one just on *me?*"

But she's not listening. "Look at this! Look at the write-ins. They loved you! And see how much they liked your hair! And your *teeth!* Whoa! Your teeth are off the chart!"

"My teeth?" I open my mouth, fingering my bicuspids with renewed curiosity.

"Your teeth scored higher than Susan Lucci's teeth. And no one's *ever* scored higher than—"

There are a few shouts from the hall. We're getting used to this sound. Lee and Ruben arguing. They're always fighting. The divorce was redundant, it seems. Finally Lee comes in alone. She sits down across from us, a little breathless. "Fuck Ruben. Can men get PMS or what?" She opens a manila file in front of her and puts on her tortoiseshell glasses. She looks at me. "Sally, you look different. Are you doing Pilates?"

"Uh . . . no."

"She's in love," Gus says.

Lee smiles wryly, as if she understands, but won't pry. She knows about Jack, doesn't she? Maybe everyone does.

Lee says, "We've been having some very encouraging overnights, Sally. Ratings have been going up for three consecutive weeks. Nine percent the first week, eleven percent the second, and thirteen percent the third—"

"Fourteen percent," Gus corrects.

"Oh, yes. You're right. Fourteen." She proceeds with more caution. "At any rate, that's one of the most dramatic ratings increases we've ever seen on the show." She adds, "Without a wedding, of course."

"So you're telling me," Gus begins, "that my client is responsible for one of the biggest ratings increases in the history of daytime TV—without a wedding?"

"I'm not saying that Sally *alone* is responsible—"

"That's what it looks like to me."

"Any number of factors could be contrib—"

"Don't try to snow me, Roswell." Gus flaps her focus group material onto the table. "I know that Sally has an AF of ninety-two, so feel free to cut the crap anytime."

Lee looks at the report. Her smile falters a notch or two. She perseveres with a soft laugh. "As a matter of fact, a focus group *was* done on Sally."

"Isn't that unusual?" I ask. "I mean, why would you guys do a focus group on me?"

Lee shrugs, as if she didn't really think about it.

"Whose decision was it?" I press.

"Marketing arranges focus groups. Or is it Sales?" She thinks about it a moment, then flaps her hand in the air. "The bean counters anyway. They get their orders from higher up the line. We just get the results."

Higher up the line?

"Now, we know Sally's temp contract is up next week. So what we'd like to discuss is the possibility of renewing her option."

"For how long?" Gus asks.

"The season, at least."

I stifle a surprised gasp.

"For how much?" Gus asks. "Because if you think you're getting her for scale again, you can forget it." Gus reaches in her briefcase and retrieves my old contract, most of which has been highlighted, crossed out, or annotated; a fresh, yellow legal pad; her pirated focus group report; and a copy of the most recent SAG agreement, the last of which she slams on the table with an impressive thump.

I take that as my cue. Gus hates me being around for the money talk; she thinks I'll cave too easily. "I really should get going, guys. I have to be in Makeup."

"I'll walk you out, Sal," Gus says, tucking her hand under my elbow and propelling me into the hall. She closes the door behind her. "Can you believe that? I'm going to have to hose her down. Hey, how *is* Prince Charming, by the way?"

That makes me bristle. "What do you mean, 'by the way'?"

She shrugs as if she's confused.

"You think this is all because of *him,* don't you? You think Jack had the focus group done, don't you?"

She scrunches up her nose. "Even if he did, who cares? It was the *viewers* who liked you, Sally. Man, you're awfully touchy—for someone with an AF of ninety-two." She shimmies her hand in the air as if indicating my name up in lights. "Now, it's time to make us both several percentage points richer." She shoos me away and slips back into Lee's office.

I wander down the hallway, fighting a little surge of resentment. A focus group on *me?* A temp character? Four weeks after I started the show?

In the dressing room, Raine, wearing a silky kimono, is rifling through heaps of clothing, scattering nylons and lacy things here and there. "Have you seen my cobra belt?" she asks.

I shake my head.

"Damn it." She keeps searching.

"Raine, how long were you here before they did a focus group on you?"

She's distracted. "I don't know. . . . I think they had one done after my first Best Villainess nomination." She puts her hands on her hips. "Shit. Maybe I left it in Wardrobe." She hurries out of the room, her silk robe billowing behind her.

I sit down and try to picture twenty-five people sitting in a room talking about me. *My* voice? *My* hair? *My* smile? I pick up the phone and dial Jack's number. His assistant puts me through right away.

"Darling," he says in his softest, sexiest voice. "What a—"

"Jack, did you have a focus group ordered on me?"

"Yes," he says, "why?"

Damn. I almost wish he hadn't told me the truth. Now I have to deal with it. "I told you I don't want you doing any favors for me, Jack."

"Favors?" he laughs. "Have you seen the overnights? They've been amazing. And the only thing that had changed about the show in the last couple of weeks was you. So yeah, I wanted to find out for sure. But I arranged *eight* focus groups this month and there's probably gonna be more with sweeps coming up. So it's not a favor. I'm just—"

"Doing your job," I finish for him, my voice sarcastic.

"That's right. What's wrong with that? Besides, if you don't believe *me* when I say you're a good actor, maybe you'll believe them."

I hesitate, reluctant to accept a compliment from him. "I just don't want special treatment, Jack. You know that."

"I'm sorry. I thought it would make you happy . . ." There's a beat. "I guess this means we're not on for dinner tonight."

"I have an early call," I tell him, then hang up almost without saying good-bye. I immediately dial another number, one I jotted down weeks ago on my notes about Meridien. If all these things are happening to me—focus groups, raises, renewed options—it's going to be because I'm serious about my job. Not because of Jack.

TWENTY-ONE

Wherever God erects a house of prayer,
the Devil always builds a chapel there;
And 'twill be found, upon examination,
The latter has the largest congregation.

DANIEL DEFOE

THE Sisters of the Order of St. Francis de Sales Convent is a plain, unassuming building three stories high, with pale brick and institutional windows. You might not even notice it at first, surrounded as it is by the whimsical shops and lively cafés of SoHo, but it sits there stoically, its doors tightly closed, its street-level windows sealed shut, as if a little caulking and some dead bolts were all one needed to hold back the colorful tide of godlessness awash in the streets outside.

I nervously approach the front door. The heavy brass knocker is tarnished black except for one bright gold spot near the bottom; I lift it and drop it twice. I squint against a sudden gust of wind.

I glance over my shoulder; Jack's car is parked in a funnel of light shining from a street lamp across the street. The driver's-side window is down. He's on his cell phone, talking to someone from the network. Snippets of his voice carry over to me, but I can't make out everything he's saying. He's waiting for me and then we're going for dinner. He told me if I wasn't back in an hour, he was coming in to get me. He said he didn't want to lose me to a house full of nuns.

I don't know—maybe I shouldn't be so angry with him about the focus group. At least they liked me.

My teeth anyway.

I move to lift the knocker once again, but the door opens. A shapeless dark form stands in the doorway. It is a moment before my eyes adjust and I make out a small, pale face almost lost amid the folds of a black habit.

"Yes?" says a woman's elderly voice; she seems protective, uncertain, as if I'm a door-to-door salesperson with something nobody wants.

"I'm Sally Carpenter. I have an appointment with the Mother Superior."

"Of course. Please come in." She backs slowly out of the way.

I step up into the dim, stale-smelling vestibule. She closes the door, chinking the lock into place. She turns and gives me a small smile. From a candle flickering on a nearby credenza, I get a better look at her. She's frail-looking and quite old, but her skin is almost lineless, as if she's rarely disturbed by extremes of emotion, either happiness or grief.

"The Mother Superior will be a little late," she says softly. "This way, please."

I nod a thank-you and follow her down a dark hallway. As we walk, I hit a chilly spot, then a warm spot, then a chilly spot again, as if radiators and drafts were in an eternal fight for domain of the place.

"It's so nice that you're here," she says. "We don't often get young women interested in the order."

I smile politely. Glimpse a small chapel on my right. Then I realize what she means. "Oh, you think I'm joining? Are you kidding? *Me?* Join a convent?" And then I catch myself. "I'm sorry. I didn't mean it like that. It's just that, no, I'm not here to join. I'm doing some research for a character. I play a nun on TV."

Her smile fades and she looks away. I think I've disappointed her. We begin to climb the curving staircase. The stone walls are recessed with urns and religious statuary. The marble steps are sunken slightly from years of use. She leads me to a dim hallway on the third floor. Most of the office doors are closed, but one is open, casting a bridge of white light into the hall.

The office is of medium size, with a wooden desk and a few mismatched chairs. On the floor is a large red rug woven with an exotic South American motif; a small IKEA lamp casts a disk of light across a cluttered desk. There is a single window behind the desk with an institutional-looking metal frame and no curtains or blinds. But a bright-red begonia sitting in a foil plate on the window ledge makes the place seem homey and quaint. The only way I know it's the office of a nun is that there is a portrait of the Pope and a wooden crucifix on the wall. I can only guess that the enormous black book lying open on the desk is the Bible; its onionskin pages curve gracefully to either side like the wingspan of a fallen gray goose.

"You can wait here," the nuns says. "The Mother Superior shouldn't be long." She lowers her eyes and backs out of the room.

I take a seat across from the desk and put my hands in my lap. I use the time to get a better look at the room. Besides the picture of the Pope and a few portraits of less familiar-looking men in robes, I notice several photos hung at regular intervals along the walls. One of the most prominently displayed is of a nun with plump cheeks and wiry gray hair bending to kiss Mother Theresa's hand. In another one the same nun is standing with Rudy Giuliani, the two of them smiling as if caught at a party in the Sunday Styles section of the *Times*. There's a plaque beneath the photograph from the City of New York: TO SISTER MARGARET RIPLEY FOR HER CONTRIBUTIONS TO SAMARITAN HOUSE. There are also several photographs of her as a much younger woman, in light blouses and dirndl skirts, her smile natural, her hair more brown than gray. In one of them she stands on the main street of an arid village with dusty, thatch-roofed huts in the background. She is surrounded by dark-skinned children dressed in white uniforms. They all seem to be giggling happily, straining for something she holds above her head. A toy? A book? Another photograph makes me smile: It's a publicity still from the set of *The Nun's Story* with Audrey Hepburn sitting in a director's chair, elegantly smoking a cigarette.

I jump when I feel something brush against my legs. I look down to see a black cat with a white patch on its head rubbing against me. It mews lightly.

"Hi, there, little fella . . ." I bend and scratch its head; it purrs and presses its neck affectionately into my hand.

I hear her voice before I see her. "Sorry sorry sorry I'm late," she says, rushing into the room, bringing with her a great draft of disturbed air. She wears an oversize indigo shirt, beige chinos that are casually rolled up past her ankles, and on her feet, of all things, are Birkenstocks. She's out of breath and leans forward onto the back of her chair, fanning herself. "Don't mind me. The doctor says it's hot flashes. I say it's Indian summer and rush hour. Sally, right?" She reaches forward and shakes my hand. Her skin is warm and rough, a working hand. "I'm Margaret. Sorry for making you wait. Traffic was the pits."

I frown. I don't remember traffic being bad at all tonight.

She draws her hand through her frizzy hair. "Whew! Give me a moment here . . ." She hurries behind the desk and cranks open the window a bit. The begonia nods its head a little as the breeze catches it. The pages of the Bible shuffle softly, then lay flat again.

"Oh, hello, there, Wimple," she says as the black cat rubs against her leg. "You met our mascot, I see." She bends to stroke his back. "I hope you don't mind if I change while we're talking. I have vespers in half an hour."

"Vespers?"

"Evening prayer service," she says. "Please make yourself at home. I'll just be a minute." She opens a door on the right side of the room, turns on a light, and disappears from view. Through the crack around the hinges, I see it's a walk-in closet of sorts. She starts to get undressed and I look away, embarrassed. I dig for my yellow legal pad and write "Vespers" on the top line.

"It's for a soap opera, you said on the phone?" she says. I hear the shush of fabric and the snap of elastic against skin.

"A daytime drama. Yes."

"And you play a nun?"

"Not a nun, exactly, but someone who's going to become a nun. She hasn't"—I search for the word—"graduated or flown up yet—or whatever it is you do."

She leans out of the closet; I see the straps of her brassiere. "She hasn't taken her vows?"

"Right."

"That means she's a 'novice.' " She ducks back into the closet.

"Novice," I write on my yellow legal pad. Wimple rubs himself one more time on my leg, then hops easily onto the cushion of a chair in the corner to get comfortable. The window behind the desk squeaks slightly on its old hinges as the wind outside picks up; I feel the cooling breeze on my cheeks.

"Tell me what sorts of things you need to know," she asks, her voice muffled as if she's pulling something over her head.

"Everything, I guess. I'd really like to shadow you one day, see the kinds of things nuns really do."

"I'm at Samaritan House most of the week. It's a day-care center in the Bronx. We work with single moms and underprivileged kids. Have you heard of it?"

I glance at the plaque on the wall. "Of course," I lie.

"There!" She comes out of the closet in full attire. The habit is long but comfortable-looking, the light cotton shifting easily as she walks. The veil is simple—there aren't ornate folds. It looks not much heavier than a long black cotton bandana tied neatly around her head. As she moves behind her desk, I see her chapped heels and her Birkenstocks beneath the hem of the robe.

"Other sisters have different vocations," she says, sitting down. "Some teach. Some volunteer. Some work with the homeless. Basically our job is to make the Lord's unbounding mercy and love visible in everyday life." She shrugs as if this were not an extraordinary task. I feel myself shrivel. Clearly, being an actress in a soap opera wouldn't be considered much of a vocation in here.

"This character you play," she says, "I hope it's not one of those typical ones where all we do is go around and scare small children and hit them with switches."

I laugh uncomfortably. "Not quite." But I'm thinking of Sister Ruth: *God has a reason for everything. . . . Remember—the meek shall inherit the earth.*

"So, tell me about her," the nun says, "this character you play."

I explain Meridien's situation—that she doesn't know whether or not she should join the convent as she'd planned or reunite with her long-lost parents, the wealthy jet-setters and most popular couple with women twenty-five to thirty-four. When I'm finished, she curls her nose.

"Yuck. Who writes that bunk, anyway?"

I laugh. "No kidding."

"Doesn't sound like your character is in much of a dilemma to me. At least, not for someone with a true calling. If she's truly bound to God, she would join the convent, of course. Regardless of what else was offered to her."

Behind her, the wind seems to be picking up—a low, distant moan. The little red begonia nods its head again, the tinfoil plate scratching the window ledge as it shifts.

"I'm not saying some of us didn't have our doubts," she says. "Of course we did. We're human. But you see, these are the true tests of our faith, Sally. To have all the splendor of the world in front of us and still choose God. The Lord said, 'I have set before you blessing and cursing. Therefore, choose life that thou may live.' "

I start writing that. I only get as far as *cursing* when she starts to talk again. She leans forward, clasping her hands on the desk. "Are you a religious person, Sally?"

It seems like an odd question, but maybe it's not. In a place like this.

"I don't know. Just average, I guess."

"Average?"

"I mean, there has to be *something*, right?"

She smiles a little sadly. "It must be hard getting through life just believing in *something*."

"Oh, don't get me wrong. It's not that I *don't* believe. I do. I guess. I think I was more religious when I was a little girl. I used to pray every night and go to church with my mom sometimes. She had this statue of Jesus in the kitchen and I used to take it down and play with it!" The nun giggles along with me. "My mother caught me one time and it got her so mad . . ." My smile fades. My voice trails off.

"Sally?" she asks softly.

I'm staring at the Bible on her desk.

"Sally?"

"But then my father died," I tell her, still staring at the book.

"What happened?" she asks in a sympathetic voice.

"It was an accident," I say. That's what I usually tell people; it's easier on everyone. "But I just got scared, you know. Of what was going to happen next." The pages on the Bible shuffle softly in the light breeze. "I guess I thought God was punishing me."

She dips her chin back skeptically. "Punishing you? For what?"

I swallow, remembering Tommy Bishop on his bike. My dad's ice cream truck parked in the driveway. That splash of red on the window. But I don't answer. I can't answer.

I am suddenly aware of a low, melodic sound carrying through the halls. "Evening hymns," the Mother Superior explains. She closes her eyes as if to appreciate a Mozart concerto. I listen, too, turning my ear to the open doorway. The women's voices are light, feminine, and yet strangely haunting, too, filtered as they are by the marble stairwell, the long hall.

"I'm sorry to hear about your father, Sally," the Mother Superior says after a while. "Life is hard. So full of suffering. But there has always been suffering and there always will be. That's why we're here, after all. To suffer."

"We . . . are?"

"Eternal happiness is the gift we receive for enduring the suffering of earth. It purifies our soul for entrance into heaven. Remember what the Lord said: 'Happy are you who weep now, you will laugh. How terrible for you who are rich now, for you will go hungry.' "

I start writing that *Happy are you who weep now*, but then stop. "So—what does that mean?" I let out an uncomfortable laugh. "That it's a sin to be happy or something?"

"I guess that depends on what you're doing to be happy," she says with a wink. "Remember, *'Blessed is the man who endureth temptation, for—'* "

The *bang* is loud enough to make me jump in my chair. I twist around to see the door behind me blown shut in the wind. Wimple is up on all fours on his chair, back arched, ears flat against his head. His sharp white teeth are bared as he hisses at the window, which itself rocks back and forth on its hinges.

"Drat!" the Mother Superior says, scowling. "This happens *all* the time." She stands up to close the window, holding her black robe out of the way. Her hip knocks the begonia pot and it falls off the ledge, hitting the floor with a dull thunk. It rolls in a half circle toward me, spilling soil all the way.

"I'll get it," I tell her, springing from the chair. I bend down and begin to scoop the soil into my palm.

"I *have* to get this fixed," she's saying, her voice tight with effort as she leans against the window ledge, reaching for the handle. Her veil flaps behind her. Papers and dead leaves fly around the room in mad little eddies. The pages of the Bible skitter back and forth.

I'm still on my knees, feeling the moist dark earth on my hands. My head fills with the smell of it, musky and sweet. I hear the window squeaking open wider, almost taunting the nun, staying just out of her grasp. She reaches out for it . . . *farther* . . . *farther* . . . When I see her Birkenstocks come off the floor, I leap up, screaming.

"Got it!" she exclaims with a hoot of victory, settling back down on her feet and pulling the window closed.

The whole room seems to heave outward with the wind trapped inside, then deadens as the latch is secured. She claps her hands as if finishing a long task. "Now—where were we?"

I catch my breath. I thought for sure she was going to fall out. "You were saying something about being blessed for enduring temptation," I tell her.

"Ah, yes. *'Blessed is the man who endureth temptation; for when he is tried, he will receive the . . .'* " Her voice trails off for a moment. She is staring down at the street. Unmoving. Unblinking. The light from a nearby street lamp illuminates her features unevenly.

I scribble furiously on my yellow legal pad. " . . . 'endureth temptation for when he is tried . . .' " I look up. She still stares down at the street. "Sister?"

After a moment she seems to remember where she is. When she turns to me, she seems older, worried. "Sally, maybe we should cut this short tonight. I think I would like to join the others in evening prayers." She gives me an uncertain smile.

"Of course." I start getting my things together.

"Please call me . . . call me anytime. We can meet again." She gives me a distracted smile; her voice stops, but her lips keep moving, as if she's half talking to me and half praying to herself. "If you don't mind, could you show yourself out?"

"Yes . . . of course."

She moves past me into the hall, her black habit rustling. Wimple, who has been waiting against the door, scurries out with her. I watch after them both, feeling suddenly alone.

I'm still holding the begonia; it leans over at an odd angle in its loosened soil. I move behind the desk to put it back on the ledge. At the window, I hesitate. Down on the street, in the circle of light cast from the street lamp, is Jack's black car, waiting for me. I feel a slight shiver. When I turn to leave the room, I see the pages of the Bible flutter one last time, even though the window is closed.

TWENTY-TWO

The devil tempts us not—'tis we tempt him,
reckoning his skill with opportunity.

GEORGE ELIOT

I gulp back two glasses of wine at Balthazar. Underneath my nails there are still small crescents of soil from the begonia, even though I scrubbed my hands twice in the rest room downstairs. The sound of people laughing and talking and eating seems removed from me, as if it's happening in another room.

I poke distastefully at my food. "Nothing like visiting a convent to make you feel like you're wasting your life," I tell him.

He looks up. Smiles. I watch him for a moment. The way he uses his utensils deftly, like two small weapons in his hands. "Jack—I know this is going to sound strange, but the nun asked me something when I was in there and I thought . . . well . . . I don't know this about you."

"What is it?"

I let a beat pass. "Do you believe in God?"

He frowns at me slightly. Picks up his wine. Sips slowly.

"I'm just curious." I try to shrug as if it's not important, but I'm hanging on his answer. *It seems like something I should know about you,*

you whom I've let into my life, my world, my soul, so completely, without ques-
tion—you who has changed almost everything about my life. It's strange that
you know so much about me and yet all I know about you is "Machiavellian
genius" . . . "meteoric rise."

"Yes, I believe in God," he says. His voice is hollow.

"Really?" I laugh softly. "I'm a little surprised."

"Why?"

"I just never took you for the God-fearing type."

He shrugs casually. "Who said anything about *fear?*"

The server comes to the table. "Will either of you be having
dessert or coffee?"

"Do you have ice cream?" I ask. "Not tartuffo or sherbet. Just normal ice cream? Chocolate or vanilla or something?"

"Vermont Maple. Or White Peach."

"I'll have the maple."

After the waiter leaves, Jack is staring at me. "I thought you said
eating ice cream depressed you."

"I eat it sometimes. It's like watching *The Way We Were.* I know I'm
gonna cry, but I still do it."

The waiter drops off my dessert and an espresso for Jack. I shove
the edge of the spoon into the ice cream. Collect a small mound, put
it in my mouth, turning it on my tongue, eating it the same way I did
when I was a little girl. It's cold. Sweet. It makes me think of my dad.
Of the freezers full of free ice cream we used to get, of summer vaca-
tions and trips to the beach, before it all happened.

It.

"Don't let her make you feel guilty, Sally," Jack is saying. "We can't
all devote our lives to saving the world."

"It's not that, Jack."

"What then?"

"Never mind. Just drop it." The bowl is still warm from the
kitchen and the ice cream is already starting to melt into a little pool in
the bottom. I feel slightly sickened, but I eat anyway.

"Why do you let other people's problems bother you so much, Sally?"

"You don't understand, Jack."

"What don't I understand?"

"Nothing . . . forget it. . . ."

"Sally . . ." He reaches forward. He gently takes my wrist, as if to get my attention. "What's *wrong?*"

"It's just something I said in there. I told the nun about my father—and I wish I hadn't. I wish I hadn't said anything." And suddenly, stupidly, I'm crying. *Shit.* I drop the spoon with a loud *clink.* My eyes fill with tears. "It's my fault." I tell him.

"What's your fault?"

"Everything!" I'm so embarrassed for crying in public. I rub my eyes. He takes my hand. "Let's go," he says.

On the cool dark street outside we walk slowly. My throat is hurting as I begin to tell him about that perfect night in late June. Summer vacation had just started and the sun dropped slowly, catching most of the neighborhood kids out after dark. We had all taken to the streets that night to play ball hockey or hide-and-seek or sneak cigarettes. I had turned ten that year. Tina Calleri was fifteen. She lived next door to us and used to baby-sit me sometimes. On certain days she even seemed willing to tolerate my company when she wasn't getting paid. She didn't have a lot of girlfriends, but she always seemed to be surrounded by an orbit of boys. She was an "early bloomer," as my mother called it, with hips and breasts and nipples that you could see through her bikini top when she took sun in her backyard. She wore black eyeliner inside the bottom of her lid. My mother said it made her look "hard." I thought she just looked drop-dead cool. Tina was the one who had explained to me the mysteries of the "minstral cycle" in the all-pink guest bathroom of her parents' house, showing me how much blood was on a tissue after just one wipe.

"It doesn't hurt?" I asked her.

"Nah," she said, "except for the cramps. And they go away. I wish I could start using tampons, but my mother said I'd lose my virginity if I did. That's a laugh."

This was Tina Calleri. She knew about menstrual cycles, tampons, and virginity. She also knew about boys. She had been expelled from the Catholic high school for getting caught with her pants down in the backseat of a college boy's car in the school parking lot. It had been after hours and Tina thought the place was empty, but Sister Ruth had been skulking around the grounds. She pulled Tina out of the car and gave her a good whipping right then and there with her goose-head cane (if Tina is to be believed). The boy drove off in a squeal of tires. Tina complained that it was against the law to hit students anymore and she threatened to press charges. But I could tell that even Tina Calleri was afraid of Sister Ruth. Tina quietly enrolled in a different high school and nothing else came of it—except that Sister's Ruth's reputation grew—and I started my own campaign to convince my mom to let me go to a public high school, too.

That night Tina said some guys were coming to "spot her some stuff." That's how she said it. I didn't know what she meant, but I didn't tell her that. Her parents were away for the evening: her dad on a business trip, her mother working the graveyard shift. She waited at the end of her driveway, sitting on the curb, smoking a Vantage Light, which she offered to me. I glanced over my shoulder to make sure no one was watching. Everyone seemed busy playing hide-and-seek. Tommy Bishop was pumping his little bicycle up the street. I took the cigarette and puffed on it lightly, holding the smoke in my mouth before exhaling it into the night. I watched Tina rub dust off her black shoes, the ones with the pointy toes and laces up the front. She called them her Madonna boots. She wore them everywhere.

"Hey!" I heard a strange voice from down the block. Two boys—men, really, as far as I was concerned—were making their way toward us, their denim jackets open, their running shoes scraping on the road.

Tina stood up and brushed the dust off the seat of her Levi's. "Hey," she said. Her voice seemed an octave lower. "You got it?"

"Right here," one of them said, tapping his crotch. She gave him a shove but didn't seem offended.

One of the boys pulled out a small sandwich bag from his denim jacket. It was filled with green flakes. I knew the green flakes were marijuana. I'd seen them in a school presentation about saying no to drugs.

"Who's she?" One of them motioned to me. I felt my cheeks burning.

"She's cool."

Tina Calleri actually thought I was *cool*?

"Are you going to try some?" she asked me.

I thought about it, but quickly shook my head. Cigarettes were one thing. But *marijuana?* I was too young. Wasn't I? And yet too old to play hide-and-seek with the other kids on the street.

"I hope you don't expect me to take any without trying it," she said. "I don't want any oregano from you guys." They laughed and said they had some rolled. She turned to me. "Stand guard, Sally," she said. "Make sure no one comes." The three of them disappeared behind the lilac bush in Tina's front yard.

I knew I shouldn't stand guard. I knew I was supposed to run and tell a grown-up someone I knew had offered me dope. But something as powerful as hunger pangs made me want to stay. I heard the match ignite. I tried to see what was happening, peering through the lilac leaves. I could only make out the orange ember of the joint as it was passed around and the rivets of their jeans as they stood in a small circle. I smelled the raw, sweet smoke and wondered if I could get high by breathing it. I strained to hear what they were saying, but I only caught the occasional word and tight laughter, as if they were trying to hold their breath and talk at the same time.

I didn't really hear Tommy come up behind me. "Did you see how fast I can ride, Sally?" He was so proud of the fact his training wheels were off.

"Shhh, Tommy . . . shhhh . . ." I flapped my hand at him, not even looking.

"I'm fast!"

"All right, show me," I told him, turning only briefly. "Ride to the end of the street and back again ten times, and then we'll see how fast you are."

Tommy was off. The sound of his wheels faded and I listened more closely to Tina and the boys. I heard one of them say, *"You do it"* and Tina laugh suggestively. I leaned nearer to the lilac bush. My heart felt like one big fist squeezing down on itself. I thought I would faint from the excitement of it. I don't remember seeing the wash of my father's headlights spill onto the street; I don't remember hearing anything until Tina came running through the bush, the boys scattering the other way. "What happened?" she asked.

I saw my dad's ice cream truck stopped on a strange angle in the middle of the street. "Holy fuck," she said. "Somebody got run over!" She grabbed my arm to pull me after her, but I slipped out of her grasp easily. She didn't seem to care, dismissing me quickly and racing off toward the scene.

People came from everywhere. The bungalows on the street simply poured people. You'd never know they could hold that many people, spilling them like a canister of sugar tipped over on the counter. I saw my mother. Weaving in a panic through the crowd. I'd never heard her scream before. I wonder why it sounded so familiar. Then the sirens started, so loud it was worse than walking down the stairs during a fire drill at school. I saw Tina Calleri trying to get as close as she could, and the other kids who had been playing on the street. The only person I couldn't find was Tommy.

I backed up farther into the lilac bush and crouched down. I heard the branches breaking. The twigs scratched my bare hands and cheeks. I remember the sound of screaming and voices, running feet and a grown-up throwing up onto the sidewalk not far away from me.

I stayed there hidden.

"Ride to the end of the street, Tommy . . ."

Police cars came, their lights flashing, turning the lush green trees and the vinyl siding of the bungalows shades of red. Then ambulances and white vans from the local news stations. I don't know how long I was there when the first police car finally pulled away with a man in the backseat, a man with graying hair. I knew it was my father, swaying slightly as the cruiser turned the corner. Then the ambulance left the scene, slowly and without a siren. There were still voices and cries, but they got quieter as people went back into their houses and the screen doors slammed. My mother stayed on the street, calling my name, and then, when her voice got hoarse, my brother took over. *"Sally! Sally!"* But I stayed hidden. For hours. Until long after I had to pee. I just stayed there, listening to the sound of crickets chirping and my brother calling my name.

I don't know what time it was when I finally got home. My mother and brother were at the kitchen table waiting for me. She clutched her rosary beads in her hands. Her face as white and old-looking as my grandmother's.

"Something terrible has happened," she said. I listened as she shared the news; I pretended I didn't know. Pretended I hadn't seen anything. I didn't tell them about Tina Calleri and the boys and how I had been the one who made Tommy drive in front of my father's truck. I went to my bedroom and got down on my knees and put my hands together and prayed. The only prayers I knew at the time were "Now I Lay Me Down to Sleep" and the Lord's Prayer. I said them both so many times that it made me dizzy. I prayed for God to forgive me for being such a bad girl.

In the morning I wanted to wake up feeling excited about summer vacation, listening to the birds sing, and looking forward to going to the mall with my friends, the way summer mornings were supposed to be, the way they had always been. I wanted to hear my mother and father bickering; I wanted to hear my brother complaining that he wasn't going to "eat that shit" for breakfast. But all I heard was the phone ringing, again and again. And my mother crying.

My mother knocked on my door once and opened it. Her eyes were red. "Get dressed, Sally," she said. "We're going to church."

"I'm not going to church!" I heard my brother yell behind her. "Just because he ruined his life doesn't mean I have to ruin mine!"

I put on pink stretchy shorts and a white tank top, a normal summer outfit, and my mother told me to change into something decent. She went into the bottom drawer of autumn clothes and pulled out navy pants and a brown blouse and got my black Mary Janes from the back of the closet, the ones I had worn to a cousin's wedding the summer before. They were snug on me, pinching my toes. When we left the house, my mother took my hand very tightly and led me out into the blinding sun of the front yard.

There were several cars parked on the street, as if someone was having a barbecue or a birthday party. But when the people in the cars saw us, the doors popped open and they rushed toward us with microphones and cameras. My mother said "No comment" to them and I was impressed because it sounded like the other grown-ups on TV.

It was the beginning of a strange world to me, a world of half-fame and humiliation, where all the secrets of the family, and the neighborhood—the drinking and the divorces and the unpainted eaves—seemed to be highlighted in the glare of the local news. I learned the word *privacy* that summer. And *invasion*.

When I finally got up the nerve to go to Tina Calleri's house a few days later, her mother answered the door and didn't smile at me as she usually did. She said Tina wasn't home. Yet I saw Tina's Madonna boots on the mat beside the door. In that moment, I understood why my friends hadn't called to see how I was or ask me if I wanted to go to the mall. The accident had changed not just my dad's life, but mine, too. It had separated me from the way things used to be. Things weren't "normal" anymore. I nodded to Mrs. Calleri and turned away. It hurt a little bit, but not having friends seemed the least of my problems. I was too busy making amends to hang around with anyone, anyway. Washing the dishes without being asked. Vacuuming the whole house. Putting Ken and Barbie away and promising never to let them have sex again. I knew, eventually, God would forgive me for what happened to Tommy. Because God was All-Merciful and that meant He would forgive anything.

But then my father died.

I don't remember much about the few days after his death. It seemed to be a blur of relatives visiting and phone calls and rushing. My father didn't want a church service, but my mother felt she had to do *"something"* for fear he would burn in hell for what he'd done to himself. She and my grandmother arranged a small visitation at Cooper's, a nondenominational funeral home across town. Cooper's was a busy place that night and six other people were "resting." Outside our room, the smallest in the place, was one of those black signs with the removable white plastic letters like the ones they use in cheap burger restaurants. The sign had my father's name on it—WILLIAM "BILL" CARPENTER—and nothing more. The room was set up like a chapel, with rows of brown vinyl chairs on either side, separated by one short aisle at the end of which was my father's coffin—closed, for obvious reasons, though I didn't like to think why. Except for the sign at the entrance, the only indication you were even at my father's funeral was the big photograph on the stand next to the coffin, the one of him in the backyard. Enlargement technology not being what it is today, the picture was slightly grainy, but everyone who saw it agreed how happy my dad looked in it. With the green lawn behind him and that big smile on his face, he could have been a successful businessman on a golf course somewhere and not a soon-to-be suicide truck driver getting drunk on Schlitz in his own backyard, which was, unfortunately, the case.

I was sad that night—but I wasn't *just* sad. I was also scared. I knew all these arrangements, all this work, all the crying, was because of *me*. The grown-ups didn't know yet, but God knew, and I was afraid someone else would find out, too. I thought the best way to avoid detection was to be quiet and behave myself. So in my new navy dress from JCPenney (my mother said children should never wear black), I sat in the end chair of the very front row and didn't move for most of the night. My brother skulked along the edges of the room, looking uncomfortable in a suit and tie, his long hair greased back. We didn't talk to each other much that night; it seemed there was nothing to say.

The people who came to pay their respects were divided into two distinct groups: guys from the bar who sat on one side of the room, staring at the coffin, shaking their heads and looking like they just had the wind knocked out of them by a Green Bay Packer, and on the other side of the room, the ladies from my mother's church. They all wore dark dresses and seemed to have a magic supply of crumpled tissues in their pockets or up their sleeves. When they arrived, they would first go to the coffin, kneel, and say a prayer; then they would gravitate toward my mother, embracing her, kissing her cheeks, handing her fresh tissues. When they saw me or my brother, their faces would crease with worry. They'd give my brother a pat on the head and tell him to be brave, he was man of the house now, then they'd bend down even with my height. They'd smile sadly and say things that stunned me. They said things like:

"It's not our place to question, Sally."

And "The Lord works in mysterious ways."

And "God has a reason for everything."

So it was true, then. My worst fear had come true. God was the one who had taken my father away. He was still punishing me for the night Tommy Bishop died.

But why did God do it? He knew how sorry I was. He saw what a good girl I was being. He was *supposed* to forgive people, wasn't he? Isn't that what "all-merciful" meant?

It was so confusing for me that I just couldn't stay in that room anymore. I slid off my chair and told my mother I had to go to the bathroom. I wandered into the main foyer. It smelled like freshly cleaned carpets and flowers. I found the ladies' room; the white stalls were empty. There were two sinks. One of them had a leaky faucet, and the water dripping against the porcelain made a dark yellow stain like the ones on the bottom of my father's ashtrays.

I just leaned against the counter and stared into the sink. Watched the little drop of water appear, grow, become round and heavy, fall, disappear, and begin again.

I was still stunned. How had I missed it all these years? This cruel side of God? This mean side of him that just didn't fit in with everything else we knew about him? Why did they tell us he would forgive anything if it wasn't true? I became aware of a growing pressure, as if someone were blowing up a balloon inside my ribs and wouldn't stop blowing until I burst. I don't know why I started doing it, but I pulled out a brown paper towel from the dispenser and put it in the drain of the sink. Then I turned on the leaky faucet and watched a white shaft of water spill down onto the paper towel. Then I pulled out another one, crumpling it and putting it on top of the first. Then another. Then another. All the while, letting the water run. The paper melted into a thick brown wad and the sink began to fill up. My heart was pounding with excitement as the water filled to the rim and began spilling across the counter and onto the floor, splashing my black shoes.

It was only a few minutes before an old woman in a dark dress came in to use the rest room and saw me standing there amid the flood from the overflowing sink. She ran to get help. My mother dashed in, along with a few of the other church ladies. They all clucked and cooed around me. One of them cleaned the drain. Others mopped up the counter.

My mother didn't seem angry, just frustrated and maybe a little embarrassed in front of her friends. "Why did you do this, Sally?" she asked me.

I looked at her and said simply: "Because I'm mad at God."

The other church ladies gasped and my mother looked at me as if I had just said the word *fuck*.

She didn't waste any time. The next morning she put me back into my navy dress and dragged me down the driveway. She was taking me to confession, she said. I had to ask God for forgiveness.

It terrified me. *I* had to ask God for forgiveness? After what he had done to me? To us? To our family? *I* still had to ask for forgiveness?

When we got to church, my mother crossed herself at the basin of holy water. I did, too, imitating her and not quite sure if I was doing it properly. The church was almost empty, a few people dotted here and there. My mother took my hand roughly and walked me to the side of the church. I had never been to confession before; my father thought it was "bunk" and every time my mother brought it up, there was a fight. I think the only reason he had allowed me to receive First Communion was because my mom had gone out and spent sixty dollars on the white dress. But a regular weekly confession for a child was morbid, in his opinion. I could tell already that things were going to be different without him.

My mother pulled open the curtain of one of the confessionals and shoved me into the chair. I had always been afraid of the confessionals; they seemed like little haunted houses to me, all wooden and spooky. "You say, Bless me, Father, for I have sinned," my mother said. "Tell him it's your first confession and then tell him what you did." She closed the curtain and I was alone on the leather stool, my feet not touching the floor.

A small door slid open and there was a man on the other side of a screen, like someone selling tickets at a theater.

I tried to talk. "B-bless me, Father, for I have . . ." But I forgot the rest.

"My child? Don't be afraid to tell me your sins. Whatever you did, the Lord will forgive you."

I wanted to believe that. Really I did. I wanted to believe that God

would forgive me for what I had done that summer, but so far everything I had ever heard about God had been a lie. There was a pain in
my throat worse than when I had my tonsils taken out and then I
started to cry. I cried so loud that the priest slid the screen closed
again. I covered my face, sobbing.

Suddenly the curtain beside me flung open. I expected it to be my
mother or even the priest, but instead something big enough to block
the whole door was standing there, shapeless, towering, and dressed
entirely in black. The distinguishing feature closest to my eye level—
besides a large silver cross—was the handle of a wooden cane with a
goose head. It was Sister Ruth. I was petrified. I had only ever seen
her from a distance, chasing kids from the street corner where they
smoked cigarettes or shaking her cane at stray dogs that had the mis-
fortune of wandering onto the church steps.

"What is going *on* in here?" she said, clipping her words sharply.
Her voice was rough, like the sound of gravel scraping beneath your
shoes. I was too nervous to respond to her, just staring at the cane. The
shiny neck of the goose protruded slightly from her hand; her clenched
fingers did not quite cover one amber eye, which stared out at me.

When I didn't answer, she bent down level with my gaze. She had
a large jaw and a broad, thin mouth with stiff white bristles above the
top lip. Her eyes had an even worse intensity than the glare of the
goose head—dark gray like puddle water but without a gleam. Her
breath smelled like old-lady things. Hard peppermint candies. Moth-
balls. Coleslaw.

I shivered, but couldn't speak. My mother squeezed up behind her
(I imagined she had been using the time for her own confession). She
had an embarrassed look on her face, trying to peak around the great
folds of the sister's habit.

"I'm so sorry, Sister Ruth," she said. She grabbed my hand and
dragged me out of the confessional. "What is *wrong* with you?" She
shook me roughly, glancing at Sister Ruth as if for approval of her
harsh punishment of me.

I still couldn't speak, staring at that cane, thinking of Tina Calleri and the beating she took.

"She's just a child," Sister Ruth said, standing at her full height again. "What could she have done that's bothering her so much?"

"She committed blasphemy last night," my mother said.

Blasphemy? Was that what it was called? Was that what I had done?

"What did she say?" she asked, as if I wasn't there.

"She said she's mad at God—" my mother began, but Sister Ruth cut her off before she could explain about my father's death.

"Mad at God?" she repeated. Her fist clenched hard around the handle of the cane. I stared at the amber eye, sure I was going to take a whipping with it. I suppose that's why it shocked me so much when all she did was shake her gnarled finger in my face. "God has a reason for everything, Sally," she told me. "It's not our place to question. Remember, the meek shall inherit the earth."

Then she turned around and hobbled away, her habit dragging unevenly on the ground with each step.

That made me stop crying. I had never heard the word *meek* before. My mother was kneeling down beside me, drying my eyes with a Kleenex that smelled like her hand cream.

"What does *meek* mean?" I asked her.

"It means you have to be a good girl," she said.

And that made sense to me. So *that's* why God hadn't forgiven me for Tommy Bishop yet. I hadn't been a good-enough girl. When I went home that night, the first thing I did was get down beside my bed and pray.

Then I cleaned my closet.

Then vacuumed my room.

When school started, I didn't squirm in my seat or eat sunflower seeds and spit them on the floor. I did my homework. I helped erase the blackboards. I got gold stars on all my work.

The only respite seemed to come when they announced the

school play that year would be *The Wizard of Oz*. I got to be the Wicked Witch of the West. And for those few hours every day as we practiced, and when I went home to rehearse alone in my bedroom, I could be evil, I could be mean—I didn't have to be a good girl. I wasn't really "me" then. I was somebody else. And God didn't care.

WE'RE at his place when I finish telling the story. Lying in his bed. My eyes sting a little from fighting tears. It's dark. Everything in the room—and our faces—are planes of shadow and blue light from the window.

"Poor Sally," he says. "I can't believe you've never told anyone . . ."

I laugh slightly, embarrassed by my own weakness. I feel so exposed. As if I've rebroken an old bone.

"Is that why you always try to do the right thing . . . because you thought God was punishing you?"

"I don't know," I tell him. I can't help it, a few tears shake loose, sliding down my cheek toward the pillow. "Maybe . . ."

"But that doesn't make any sense—what happened to a little boy on his bike." He kisses my neck, my face, my shoulders. "Or your father—how can it be your fault how much your father had to drink that night? It's not your fault, Sally . . ."

Not your fault . . .

And that opens something in me, just for a moment, like a valve that lets in fresh air, but it closes again quickly.

"Poor Sally. You make everything so hard on yourself. You've got to stop taking responsibility for everything bad that happens—it's not your fault . . . not your fault . . ."

I just stare at him, blinking slowly, dazed and aching inside.

Not your fault . . .
You're a good person . . .
You've got to stop blaming yourself . . .
You deserve to be happy . . .
Just let it go . . .

Trust me . . .

I love you.

And that makes me stop.

It's the first time he's said it. *"I love you."* I watch him, electrified and still, to make sure I haven't misheard. His eyes are gleaming in the darkness.

"I've never loved anyone before," he whispers. His voice is weak. He lowers his face, burying it in my neck. *"Never . . ."*

I take a breath, a shallow one that cools my throat. "I love you, too," I say.

I happens that night. In a square of moonlight the exact shape and size of his bed. Me on my back, Jack over me, our hearts matching beats. He kisses my neck and my mouth, whispers words against my skin, words that slip like water down to the deepest, driest parts of me.

"Are you ready?"

"Yes . . ."

The room fills with our whispers and moans. "Are you mine, Sally?"

"Yes," I say, delirious, dazed, "yes . . ."

"Are you ready to be with me, forever?"

"Yes . . ."

"Your heart . . ."

"Yes . . ."

"Your soul . . ."

"Yes . . ."

"Forever?"

"I'm yours, Jack . . . I'm yours . . ."

"Thank you," he whispers. "And I am yours. . . ."

A strange clarity seems to overtake him then. He rises up on his hands, his teeth bared slightly, his shoulders rounded. There is the moment of absolute suspense. And then, with a gasp of pain and pleasure, he is inside me. It is done. We stop for a moment, stare at each other, absorbing what has happened. It's as if we have to acclimatize ourselves to some new atmosphere, like learning we can breathe underwater. He moves slowly at first. Softly. But then we start kissing and the momentum starts and it soon feels like a dam splitting open. *I love you . . . IloveyouIloveyou. No one will ever love you more. . . .*

TWENTY-THREE

For what shall it profit a man,
if he shall gain the whole world, and lose his own soul.

MARK 8:36

I wake up early the next morning, watching day break over the river. I think about last night. About making love to him for the first time. I feel reborn. Drained. Quietly ecstatic. *Oh, God . . . I love him so much.* I feel that something essential in me has been ruptured and that the hard cement core of me has broken and tumbled out. Pieces of me lie around the room in great, violent chunks. Every breath I take disturbs them, and they fall away from me, like fragments of the past, leaving healthy, quivering pink flesh beneath.

And then it's there, through the bliss, like a slash in my consciousness.

Tommy Bishop.

The ice cream truck.

Sister Ruth.

An instant passes where my automatic reaction to that summer overtakes me, the tangle of anger and fear, but like a whip that doesn't quite hit its mark, the sensation is stunted, perhaps partially replaced, by words I've always wanted to hear:

Not your fault.

I feel relieved but strangely disappointed, too. It's as if I have just finished a long journey and only now that I'm done has someone shown me a map. I see a million better routes I could have taken, but at least I got here.

He slowly begins to move, to rouse; his dark eyes open, then close again, and he smiles. "You're here."

"Ta-dah."

His voice is weak, groggy. "Did that really happen last night?"

"I think so."

He lets out a long breath of amazement. His voice is a whisper, barely audible. "I love you, Sally."

"I love you, too."

"No, you don't understand. . . . I *love* you."

"I *know* . . ."

"But that's never happened before. It's usually over by now. I usually lose interest or move on."

I give him a slap. "Cad."

He laughs softly. "That's not what I mean. I just don't understand what's happening to me. I didn't even think it was possible."

I blow on my fingernails and polish them on my shoulder. "Another one bites the dust."

He gives me a puzzled smile. He strokes my hair, looking from my lips to my eyes and back again. "You don't understand," he says. "I'm in *love*. Me." Then he laughs softly to himself and shakes his head. "What a *rush* . . ."

TWENTY-FOUR

I can resist everything except temptation.

OSCAR WILDE

I'M humming to myself, thrilled and blissful, as I push my orange plastic tray along the rails of the commissary. It's lunch break. I can't stop smiling. Can't stop thinking about him. Sometimes I have to close my eyes to endure the rush of excitement that runs through me when I think how happy he makes me.

"Hey," a voice behind me says. There's something jarringly familiar about it.

Shit!

A drama teacher once told me that it requires seventeen muscles in the human face to form a smile—I'm aware of every single one of them right now. "Hey, David."

"Long time no see." He grabs a carton of milk, puts it on his tray. *Ker-plunk.*

"Yeah. I guess." With trembling hands, I pick through the sandwiches. His shoulder brushes against me as he reaches for a tuna on whole wheat and I feel a vague repulsion.

"I haven't talked to you in a while," he says.

"Oh, you know. I've been busy."

"I bet." He lets out a soft, sarcastic laugh.

We're at the cash register now. "Allow me." He takes out his wallet and pays. He motions to the extras' tables. "Feel like sitting with the riffraff?" he asks.

I laugh, shrugging it off as a joke. We walk single file across the room, David ahead of me. I see Raine sitting at one of the sunny tables by the window. Her expression brightens when she sees me and she quickly pulls out an empty chair so that I'll join her. I shake my head subtly, motioning to David. She widens her eyes in understanding and pushes the chair back in.

At the table beneath the air ducts, David and I unwrap our sandwiches. "You look good," he says.

"Thanks. You too."

"Bullshit."

"Well . . . maybe you've lost a little weight."

"That's what happens when you get fired from a network gig," he says.

I stop. Swallow a mouthful of food. "Are you serious? You got fired?" He nods, trying to look brave, but I can tell how upset he is. "Did they say *why?*"

"My hair was attracting too much attention on camera."

"Did you tell them you'd cut it?"

"For a fucking background gig? Are you nuts?"

"Sorry. Of course not." I try to think of something to say, something to lift his spirits. "Don't worry, David. You'll get something else. You didn't even like the job. Remember, Danny Aiello didn't—"

"Get his big break till he was forty. Yeah. I know. Just another eleven years of hell. Yippee." He pops open his carton of milk. "You wanna know what I think?"

"What?" I'm picking at my sandwich, having completely lost my appetite.

"I think that friend of yours had it done."

I try to sound innocent: "What friend?"

He rolls his eyes, as if I know who he means. And I do. "You think I'm stupid, Sal? You don't think I know what's going on? I think he wants to get me out of the way so he can get to you."

I shake my head. "No way. He'd never do that. He's not like that. He's really a great person."

He gives a sarcastic laugh. *"You're* the only person who seems to think so. Everyone else knows what a conniving prick he is." He lets a beat pass. "Did he tell you he's fucking Sabrina Clark?"

I feel the bottom drop out of my heart, but I don't respond.

"I went for a run in Central Park the other day and I *saw* them go into the Plaza together. Saw them with my own eyes. Or maybe he's just 'friends' with her, too?"

I try eating my sandwich again, trying to be cool. But all I can picture is the two of them going into the Plaza—*Fuck*—the Plaza!

"Sal—I can't believe what you're doing. The guy's just using you, like he uses everybody. If you don't get out of this soon, you're going to—" Suddenly he drops his milk and jumps back from the table so quickly the chair topples over behind him.

"What is it?"

He's staring in horror at the overturned carton. White liquid seeps from the spout, spilling across the table. We watch for several seconds and then something dark and shifting emerges slowly from the spout. I cover my mouth because it feels like I'm going to throw up. My skin tightens with chills. It's a large insect of some kind—a spider or a cockroach. It scurries quickly out of the milk and under the edge of the table. We stand there for a moment, breathless.

"Jesus Christ," David says. "I want my fucking money back."

I march down the gray carpeted corridor of the executive floor. Muffled voices conduct phone conversations from behind closed doors. Pictures of the network's biggest stars smile down on me like the benevolent gods of a futuristic church.

I can't believe he's fucking Sabrina. *Shit!* I knew it . . . I knew I couldn't trust him.

Then another concern, almost an afterthought: *And he had David fired, too!*

Wait a second, Sally. You don't know either of those things for sure. . . .

At the end of the hall is Jack's secretary's office. She's always so happy to see me, it's as if being nice to me were part of her job. She is a woman in her mid-fifties with neat salt-and-pepper hair and a penchant for cardigans. A vase of fresh flowers adorns the corner of her desk and there are pictures of her grandchildren on the window ledge. The nameplate on her desk reads: AGNES MCGREGOR. There is a man with thinning black hair leaning over her desk.

"Sally!" She beams, when she sees me, completely ignoring her guest.

The man turns. He looks vaguely familiar. He has sunken brown eyes and olive skin. He's wearing a dark blue turtleneck and tweed jacket. Then I remember: the guy who sent us the wine at Sette. He gives me a distracted smile but seems preoccupied with his appointment book.

"Is he busy?" I ask, motioning to Jack's door.

"He'll see *you*," Agnes says, winking as if I'm the only person in the world he *would* see. "Go on in." She turns back to the man in the turtleneck. "How's tomorrow at ten thirty?"

I approach a set of adjoining double doors. Through a glass panel on one side I see Jack on the phone, standing at the window. His suit jacket is off. The sleeves of his white shirt are rolled up. I hear the timbre of his voice gently penetrating the walls. I knock loudly. He smiles when he sees me and waves me in.

Jack's office never fails to impress. It seems as if he could keep an eye on the whole world from up here. The back wall is floor-to-ceiling windows with a view of the park. The furniture is mostly chrome and black leather. The left wall is covered with a built-in shelving unit that holds at least a dozen video monitors, each tuned to a different feed: talk shows, commercials, celebrities, politicians, wars. The first time I came in here, I searched his desk playfully and told him I was just looking for his THE ONE WHO DIES WITH THE MOST TOYS WINS plaque. He smiled and said that would be for people who played with toys.

Jack hangs up the phone and comes around the desk to kiss me, but I pull away. "Did you have David fired?" I ask crossly.

He looks upward, as if trying to remember. *"David . . . David . . . ?"*

"You *know* who David is, Jack."

He smiles. "You're right. How could I forget *David?*" He moves back behind his desk.

"He got fired this week and he thinks you had something to do with it. Did you?"

"People have to blame their trouble on somebody. I'll take the rap if it makes you feel better."

"I don't want you to take the 'rap.' I want you to tell me the truth."

"Would you care?"

"Of course I'd care."

He watches me for a moment, then leans forward, grabbing a baseball from a silver holder on the corner of his desk. It was a gift from Steinbrenner when UBN got the rights to the Yankee games. It's autographed by some famous team from about fifty years ago. He bounces it gently on his desk; it makes a soft thudding noise when it hits the leather blotter.

Thock . . . thock . . . thock.

"So, he thinks I had him fired, huh?" he asks. "What did you say he was? Just an extra or something?"

Just an extra?

"Yeah."

"Well, there you go."

"What?"

"Sally, I wouldn't even know who to *talk* to to have someone like that fired."

Thock . . . thock . . . thock.

I feel myself waver a bit. "So you didn't do it?"

He sighs, a little hopelessly, rolls his eyes as if to say *"Of course not."* But he doesn't actually answer.

Thock . . . thock . . . thock.

Do I believe him? I don't know. I drop into the chair. My throat feels like it's strangling with the effort of holding back my next question. But I ask it anyway. "Jack, is anything going on between you and Sabrina Calliope-Clark?"

He frowns in confusion.

Thock . . . thock . . . thock.

"What were you doing going into the Plaza with her the other day?"

He stops the ball in midbounce. A frown settles over his features. He replaces the ball gently in its holder. He stands up and comes to sit in front of me on the edge of the desk. He's in slight silhouette because of the window behind him. He picks up a red binder. On the cover is a logo of a sun eclipsing a small globe. It's the press package for the Geostar deal. "You know what's going on with all this, right?"

I nod.

He flips through a few tabbed sections and opens the binder in front of me. I see a full-color photograph of Sabrina standing backstage at a television studio. Her arms crossed, her well-turned ankle shown to its best advantage on the first rung of a tall ladder. *"Reality Blues,"* it reads, "with host Sabrina Calliope-Clark."

"If the deal goes through, I want Sabrina to host a show on the new network," he says. "A reality cop show. It's a good fit and the shareholders love her. That's why we were at the Plaza. Phil Nesbitt wanted to meet her, so we had lunch at the Palm Court."

I feel myself wither inside. Sir Phillip Nesbitt is the titled Brit who is selling his satellite company to devote more of his time to his real passion—raising polo ponies. "Oh. . . ." I say in a small voice.

Jack shakes his head and drops the binder back onto the desk. "But

I knew this was going to start happening sooner or later. It was only a matter of time."

I stare at him uncertainly.

"I've always been a target, Sally. People want to see me fail. They'll do anything they can. They might even try to come between us now that they know we're together. So you might start hearing some things."

"What kinds of things?"

"You name it. You'll hear that I'm the worst motherfucker who ever walked the face of the earth. That I'm a liar. A coward. A cheat. You'll hear that I ax-murdered my own family when I was a kid. That I'm quitting the business—going to Disney or Microsoft . . . or"—he smiles—"Tibet. Maybe you'll hear that I'm into bondage. Or that I'm gay. Or that I'd crawl over my dying grandmother to close a deal—"

That one makes me hitch—David says that about him.

"And of course you'll hear that I'm fucking *this* actress or *that* model behind your back." He smiles. "The point is you're going to hear a lot of things about me. And some of them will be true—I *am* a prick, when I need to be. But some of them won't be. And you've got to know how to tell the difference."

"But how will I know?"

He takes a thoughtful breath and reaches for my hands, putting them in his lap. "Do you remember one time you said that it must be hard for me to know who to trust? And I told you how important loyalty was to me?"

I nod.

"That's what this is about. We have to know that we can trust each other—no matter what."

"Of *course* we can trust each other, Jack."

"Don't answer so quickly. I'm not talking about two people coming together for as long as it's convenient for them. I'm talking about total and absolute loyalty, Sally."

The way he looks at me, the tone of his voice, unnerve me. "Jack, you're scaring me. What are you asking me to do?"

"I don't know how you want to put it. I just have to know you're on my side. It's very important to me."

I pull my hands away. "But what about me? How do I know I can trust *you?*"

He falters slightly. "Because I love you. And I would never do anything to hurt you. Not as long as you live." He watches me with a sad, gentle smile. "Think about it, Sally. Because I need you on my side now more than ever." He taps the Geostar binder with his finger. "Especially with this going on." He stands up and moves behind the desk. "Marty Fletcher says we have some comers."

"Comers?"

"Somebody else interested in Geostar. I don't know who, but it's pushing the price up. Could be CBS. Or maybe Turner. If they're running around crunching numbers, there's nothing I can do about that. What I've got to concentrate on is the 'Handshake Factor.' That's why Phil went out to lunch with Sabrina. That's why he and his wife have been to just about every Broadway show in town. And that's why he's going to be a guest in our VIP box at the opening game of the World Series tomorrow night. I want him wearing a Yankee cap and drunk on Budweiser by the third inning. The next day, if we're a few million off, it's not going to make a difference. Phil is still going to want to be in business with me." He smiles rakishly and picks up the baseball again. "It's my trade secret, Sally. I give people what *they* want, and they give me what *I* want. Everyone's happy that way."

Thock . . . thock . . . thock.

THAT night I don't see him. I tell him I have too many lines to memorize. It hurts me to lie to him, but I have to be alone. I stay home with the lights off and smoke cigarettes.

The phone rings three times, but I don't answer it.

There's an evening mass at St. Francis, and when latecomers straggle in, the sound of hymns rise up from the street. Every candle in the building must be lit because the stained-glass window glows like the door on a giant wood-burning stove.

What's wrong with me? Why don't I trust him completely? I love him more than I've ever loved anyone else in my life. What's holding me back? Sometimes when I'm with him lately, no matter what we're doing or where we are, this little shiver passes over me, like a ripple in the surface of my consciousness, something that I can't quite place. It's as if I have sensed something moving in my periphery, but when I turn to see what it is, it's not there.

I sit up and put my cigarette out. Distractedly, I go to the window. I hear the scrape of footsteps and see a nun hurrying down the sidewalk. I think of Sister Ruth again—how I rarely saw her after that day in the confessional. She died of a heart attack a few years later; rumor had it that at the Catholic high school they cheered.

When the nun on the street gets closer, I can tell it's the Mother Superior. The lightness of her footsteps. The plumpness of her face. "Sister Margaret!" I call through the open window. But she doesn't hear me. She disappears into the church. The sound of hymns rise up, then fall away as the doors drop closed behind her.

TWENTY-FIVE

From all evil and mischief; from sin,
from the crafts and assaults of the devil . . .
Good Lord, deliver us.

PRAYER BOOK

Gus's office is mayhem. Paint-spattered drop cloths cover just
about everything. Ladders are everywhere. A large hole has been
smashed through the right wall into the vacant office next door. She's
giving somebody with a paintbrush orders as I try to make my way
into the room, stepping around buckets and boards.

Gus motions with a bangle-bedecked arm. "Come on in, Sal!" She
comes around her desk and grabs a short dark-skinned man in white
painter's overalls. "Carlos, Carlos, this is her! This is the nun!"

Carlos looks at me, smiles, brown eyes shining politely.

"Here, Sally, sign this," Gus says, poking one of my old head shots
under my nose. We keep meaning to get new ones done. I wince
when I see the photograph. That tense smile. The gray gathering of
makeup where my frown lines are. Or should I say *used* to be? Because
they're not as bad anymore. I guess it's true. Frown muscles do atrophy
from lack of use.

"It's for his wife," Gus says to me. "She's a big fan of the show."

I quickly scratch my signature across the photo. It was weird sign-
ing my autograph at first, but I'm used to it now. People wait outside
the building and ask for it or they write me fan letters wanting a picture of me. They tell me their problems, their favorite colors, how
much they like my hair or my eyes—or my teeth. A lot of them write
to *"Dear Meridien."* Raine says I'll get used to it.

Gus puts her arm around Carlos. "There you go, Carlos. Tell your
wife to write to the show and say how much she loves Sally. You know,
write?" Gus mimes writing a letter. Carlos just nods, smiles politely
again, and goes back to his work in the other room.

"Well? Whaddayathink?" Gus asks, motioning at the mess. Where
the walls are finished, I can see that they are going to be soft gray with
sections of glass block. "I'm thinking of putting a koi pond over there.
It's good for ch'i. You like it?"

"It looks . . . wonderful, Gus."

"Good. 'Cause your commission is going to pay for it! Now, siddown. Lots to discuss." She yanks a new tan leather briefcase onto the
desk. She blows a bit of plaster dust off it. "Hermès" is all she says, pro-
nouncing it "Hermies."

"Hey, did you hear Dara Dempsey left town?" she asks.

I feel a catch in my breath. I haven't thought of Dara in weeks.
"Really?"

"Yeah. Friend of mine saw her and said her roots were *this* long."
She motions with her thumb and forefinger. "She's got a bit of lisp,
too. Her tongue didn't heal properly. Anyway, apparently she's going
home. Back to Minneapolis to become—"

"—a teacher," I finish for her.

"Yeah . . ."

I sigh sadly. She always wanted to be a teacher. I try to picture
Dara Dempsey—my onetime archnemesis—standing at the front of a
classroom in her hometown teaching algebra or English. *God . . . everything has changed so much. . . .*

"You got some auditions coming up," she says. "One's for an ad campaign. One's for a theater thing. You'll turn that down. It's nothing great. But the commercial looks good. I've also got an appointment booked somewhere for a new head shot. The sooner we get rid of that one, the better." She looks to the wall of photos beside her and shivers, as if creeped out. "The real news is that Griff Hughes called. He wants to take us to dinner tomorrow." A few beats pass. "Sal—didn't you hear me? I said Griffin Hughes called. He and the head writer want to take us to dinner. You know what that means?"

"What?"

"You might be the love interest."

"Love interest?"

"They've been looking for a love interest for Hogan for years. I heard they tested the assembly cut for the bank robbery episode and everything was fine until you died. I don't want to jump the gun, but why else would they take us to dinner? You might be the one."

I watch her, the news slowly sinking in. "You mean, a prime-time gig—for *me?*"

She slaps the desk. *"There* you go! I knew it would come to you sooner or later!"

"Jesus . . ."

"How are you for tomorrow?"

"Not tomorrow. I've got to go to the baseball game."

"I thought you hated baseball."

"Jack wants to take Phillip Nesbitt. It's about this Geostar thing."

She raises her eyebrows, impressed. I'm now referring to the biggest media takeover of the year as "the Geostar thing." *Things have changed a lot indeed.*

"So I'll make it for another night. No biggie." She starts riffling through her date book.

"You really think they want me, Gus?" I ask nervously.

"Hey, hey, hey. Let's not get too excited. You know what they say: When something seems too good to be true, it probably is."

Leave it to Gus. She always could hit the nail on the head. That's what's been bothering me so much lately. Things seem too good to be true.

TWENTY-SIX

The Devil watches all opportunities. . . .
WILLIAM CONGREVE

THE streets of the Bronx leading into Yankee Stadium are dense with cars and baseball fans. We make our way through the crowd slowly, our arms around each other. He's wearing a bunchy stadium jacket, faded jeans, and a vintage Yankees ball cap. The brim of the cap brushes his hair forward onto his forehead, making him look almost boyish—nothing like the network president who's really here to try to close the biggest media deal of the year. The deadline for bids on Geostar is noon tomorrow. By then Jack will be responsible for creating one of the largest communications conglomerates in the world—or a rival company will be even more powerful than it already was.

Jack squeezes his arm a little more tightly around my shoulder. "The second you stop having fun, we're gone. I promise."

"I'm already having fun," I tell him, and it's not a complete lie. It's almost impossible to resist the energy of the crowd. It seems that there's nothing brighter, nothing more alive, nothing more exciting on the whole planet than the glowing, almost volcanic mouth of Yankee Stadium.

Inside the building we pass a battalion of ushers who stream us farther and farther away from the foam-finger-carrying, face-paint-wearing masses to more sedate corridors. I notice the crowd starts to change, gradually at first. Better haircuts. Better shoes. Until it looks more like a matinee at the Met than a baseball game. We get to a long, quiet corridor that extends in such a perfect curve around the bowl of the stadium that I can't see the end of it, that it feels there *is* no end. On one side of the hall are framed photographs of Yankees players, the occasional plant. On the other side, doors with gleaming plaques on them:

MATTEL.

BUDWEISER.

WALT DISNEY CO.

We stop at double doors with a sign that reads UBN in polished brass letters.

The door opens onto a room full of oak antiques, Persian carpets, and brass lamps. It looks as if one whole wall of the place has been blown off by a Category 4 hurricane, because the room is vertiginously open on one side to the expanse of the green field. Thousands upon thousands of microscopic fans squirm in their seats, whole lives reduced to dots of red, green, and blue like the tiny pixels on a TV screen.

There are about twenty people milling about the room, drinking champagne and nibbling canapés. Two waitresses in the obligatory black skirts and white blouses weave through the crowd balancing trays over their heads.

"Jack!" A man in his fifties notices us and waves. He extricates himself from a cluster of men and women in suits and walks over, smiling. I know it's Sir Phillip from all the press. His gray hair is wavy and collar length and his mustache is well trimmed. He's wearing an open-necked button-down shirt, a navy blazer, and crisp chinos, everything looking casual Savile Row.

"Jack, this is extraordinary," he says. *Ex-troh-dinree!*

Jack smiles, puts his arms around me. "Phil, this is Sally Carpenter."

He shakes my hand. "The soap star!" he says. *Soap stah.*

I'm surprised he recognizes me, but then he goes on to explain he took a tour of the studio that day and saw me on set.

I nod in comprehension, flattered.

Jack leans into me, his voice low. "I should make the rounds. Shake some babies. Kiss some hands. Wanna come?"

"Knock yourself out," I say, grinning.

"Enough excitement for one day, huh?" He smiles. "Back in two minutes." He follows Sir Phil into the crowd.

A voice from behind me says, "Would you like some champagne?"

I turn and see a waitress with dark hair offering her tray of champagne flutes. She seems older than I originally thought, the lines materializing around her eyes as she holds her smile. I nod "Thank you" and take a glass.

She narrows her eyes on me. "Sally?"

I smile uncertainly.

"Lorna," she says, pointing to herself. "Lorna Callaghan? We were in Scene Work together."

I now remember her from an acting class I took last year. "Oh, Lorna! Hi! How *are* you?" And then I feel painfully embarrassed. She's serving drinks at a baseball game. *How well could she be?* I quickly sputter: "Wow! You look great!"

She self-consciously shifts her tray over a stain on her blouse. "I *don't*. But *you* do!" Then her eyes widen. "I saw you on *DUD* the other day! Congratulations! What a great gig!" But there's a slight pull in her tone. Like she really doesn't mean it. Like what she really means is "I hate you, you bitch. I hope you get some debilitating disease and give someone else a chance."

Like Dara Dempsey.

"Wait a second—" She points a finger at me. "Didn't I just see you come in with Jack Weaver?"

I nod. She's quiet a millimoment, as if trying to process this information, trying to comprehend a universe in such total upheaval that

Sally Carpenter could not only have a network gig but be dating an *über*-exec. But her faculties seem unable to deal with the magnitude of this task and she gives up with a little shrug. "Well, it's good seeing you again," she says uncertainly. She hands me a cocktail napkin and backs away with a polite bow. "If you need anything, you know where to find me."

I watch after her as she swerves off through the crowd, wiping down tables and serving champagne. She only smiles when she knows she's being watched. I could tell she was an actress from a mile away. There's a look actors get when they've been around for a while, a hesitation that comes into their smiles, an uncertainty in their manner as they begin to realize the only thing separating determination from desperation is a couple more years. I know. I used to be that way myself.

I feel someone hug me from behind. "All done. Now let's go where the real fans are."

I smile and drain my champagne.

WE make our way down through the stadium toward the field-level seats. We stop and get beer and hot pretzels. Jack buys me a baseball cap and pats it on my head and laughs and tells me *"Now* you look like a real sports fan." I flip the cap backwards and make a funny ape face and say, "No, *now* I look like a real sports fan." He laughs and picks me up and spins me around and I tell him this must be our romantic development montage. He looks at me with curiosity. I tell him this is the part of the movie where you see just how much the starring couple is in love; we begin to move in slow motion, pretending to run to each other as if across a meadow of daisies. We hug and kiss, all in slow motion, and I ask him what's the sound track and he says, "Let's Spend the Night Together," and I laugh and say that we don't need the R rating. Then the music fades and real time resumes, we put our arms around each other and make our way toward our seats, happy and still in love, even if we're not moving in slow motion anymore.

★ ★ ★

I may not be a baseball fan, but I know good seats when I see them. We're in the fourth row, right between home plate and first base. The section is full of celebrities. Billy Crystal is two seats down from me. Robert De Niro just three rows up. Rosie O'Donnell is across the aisle. Jack doesn't seem impressed. It's all part of his life.

My life, too, I guess. Now.

As the game starts, I'm surprised by how much fun Jack seems to be having. Clapping and cheering and yelling at the pitcher. I even find myself starting to get into it after a while, jumping to my feet and punching the air. *"Hey, battah, battah, battah!"* And *"You call that safe?"*

Sometime in the fourth inning, I have to pee. "Bathroom break," I tell him. I stand up. His leg is on the seat in front of me and I nudge against him to get past. He puts his other leg behind me, trapping me for a minute, with a sexy, almost threatening smile on his face. "Gotcha," he says. But then he laughs and lets me go by.

I'm a little drunk from the beer, and dizzy on an oxygen overdose from all the yelling, when I get into the main corridor of the stadium. The place isn't as busy as it was before the game, but there are still a few people lined up at food counters or watching the closed-circuit feed from stand-up bars. I follow signs to the women's rest room and am peeved to see that, even with the game on, there's a lineup.

Damn.

I take my place in line. Wait. Shuffle. Wait. Shuffle.

It's the turtleneck I notice first. I don't know why. It's such a warm night and no one's wearing turtlenecks. Then I recognize the rest of him. The sunken dark eyes. The thinning hair. It's the guy from Jack's Geostar team. He's on his cell, gesticulating wildly and trying to keep his voice down. His olive complexion is reddened with emotion. He paces back and forth. When he turns, his gaze alights on me. I think about smiling and waving. *Hey, it's me. We saw each other in Jack's office the other day.* But after a moment he looks away again. I guess he didn't recognize me with my baseball cap on, and something about his demeanor says I shouldn't disturb him. I shuffle forward again, this time close enough to hear him say,

". . . How can I fuckin' relax? I've never done this before. . . ." He paces back and forth, raking his hand over his balding head. *"Noon tomorrow. If not, I'm fucked—totally fucked."*

I feel a momentary twinge of worry. I know the deadline for Jack's deal is noon. I hope everything's okay. But then the line shuffles out of earshot through the bathroom door.

"DID something happen?" I ask Jack, when I get back to the seats.

"Yeah," he grumbles. "They stole third base."

"No, with the Geostar deal."

He stares at me curiously.

"I just saw that guy from finance—the one who sent us the wine that time?"

"Marty Fletcher?"

"I just saw him having a fit into his cell phone. He looked upset. And he mentioned something about the deadline tomorrow."

"How interesting . . ." he says, even as he's reaching for his cell. "Fuckin' weasel."

AFTER the game, we're stuck in traffic, horns honking, cars moving mere inches at a time. "Screw this," Jack says, screeching around in a U-turn and making a break for an alley lined with Dumpsters and crates. We emerge onto a smaller street, lush with sidewalk trees and closed produce markets. He pulls up in front of a small, dark brick restaurant with a big Italian flag. "Wanna try it?" he asks.

"You bet."

The place is corny—red-checked tablecloths, Chianti bottle candleholders, Dean Martin music—but the spaghetti and meatballs are delicious and the house wine is great. His cell phone rings several times throughout the meal. Sometimes he just listens, sometimes he laughs, sometimes he uses a low, threatening tone. What he is able to find out at this time of night is that a suspiciously high number of UBN and Geostar shares had been traded just before the end of the day.

"You think Marty Fletcher is involved?" I ask him.

"That's what I'm going to find out."

"What happens if he is?"

"His head's gonna roll," he says, then chuckles to himself.

I'm not sure how it makes me feel. All this deal making. All this backstabbing. It's all so . . . so . . . *television*. But Jack loves it. It's all part of the game to him. It's unnerving to be so close to someone who enjoys power so much. Unnerving, but thrilling as well, like standing outside the chain-link fence of an electrical plant looking in. You read the sign next to your head—DANGER! DANGER! KEEP OUT!—but what you really want to do is scramble over that fence and run with your arms open toward all that power. You want to feel the electricity in your teeth, in your hair, on your skin; you want to taste it on your tongue. I'm surprised by how turned on by it I am. I want to fuck him tonight. I *have* to fuck him tonight. I have to find some kind of relief for my own complicity. My own desire. I can feel the liquid heat between my legs. I can't wait to get to my apartment . . .

WHICH is why I'm heartsick when we pull up in front of my building and I look up to see the pulsing blue-white glow of the TV in my window on the third floor. I groan out loud. "David's here."

He lets out an incredulous laugh. And then: *"Fuck!"* He bangs the steering wheel. The solid car reverberates.

"I'm sorry, Jack . . ."

He just shakes his head. He runs his tongue along the back of his teeth. "The end to a perfect day," he says.

"I'll talk to him tonight, Jack. I promise."

Shhhh. His finger gently touches my lips. Then his hand cups the back of my head and he pulls us gently together. He kisses me softly at first, tenderly, but then I sense a shift in his breathing—it becomes heavier, more hoarse—his kisses deeper. I feel my own breath heating up, my skin turning warm beneath my clothes, and then suddenly, God, his hand is sliding down the front of my jeans and I don't stop him, only squirm beneath him, and I know he wants David to see. In my dazed periphery, I try to watch my living room window, the blue flicker of the TV, but my vision begins to blur, the windows turn silvery around me, my eyes fall closed and soon I am coming—*How can he do that how can he do that*—I don't stop him from making me come, there in front of the building, when all David has to do is walk to the window to see.

When it's over—when my heart has stopped pounding so hard that I can hear the silence between the beats—I turn to him and his eyes are closed and he is licking his fingers, savoring them as the car fills with the smell of me. "Thank you," he whispers. I am dazed. I cannot speak. He waits until I get inside the vestibule before he tears away in a screech.

When I get upstairs, I stop outside my apartment and straighten my clothes, take a few breaths. I unlock the door. David is centered in the blue wash from the TV, his stockinged feet up on the trunk.

"Where were you?" he asks. He's trying to seem casual, but his voice has an edge to it and there's a slackness about his features, as if he's trying to hide his true emotions. Being an actor, he can make a pretty good stab at it, but I know him too well.

"I asked where *were* you, Sal?"

I still don't answer. I am painfully aware of the evidence of my infidelity. The whisker burn. The flushed cheeks. But what he sees is the baseball cap.

"You were at the *baseball* game?" he asks with an incredulous note in his voice. "Sally, what the hell were you doing at a baseball game? You hate baseball."

"I don't *hate* baseball," I tell him, tossing the cap into the corner. "*Hate*'s kind of a strong word for organized sports."

"Oh. I see. You'll go with *him*. But you won't go with me."

I don't say anything. He watches me. Waiting for me to tell him I went with Gus or Raine. Waiting to hear it was a "work thing." But I don't say anything.

He turns back to the TV. "I can't believe you even *talk* to him when you know he had me fired."

"He didn't have you fired," I say tiredly.

"How do you know?"

"I asked him."

"And you believe him?"

I don't respond.

He stares at me awhile longer. "So—did you fuck him yet?"

"David—"

Then: "What am I? Stupid? What else have you been doing with him every night? Of course you fucked him." He stands up, shaking his head. "That's it. I've had it—enough of this shit."

In minor shock I watch him walk past me, bending down at the door to tie on his running shoes.

"It's not fair to me, Sal. You can't expect me to just stand around and take it."

"I know, David. I'm sorry—really I am. . . ."

And then he says them—the words I've been dreading to say myself: "It's over, Sal."

I can't believe the relief. He broke off with me first. It's like a plunge in lake water.

"So you call him tomorrow and tell him you're not seeing him anymore."

The world turns end over end. *"Wh-what?"*

"I want you to tell him you're not going to see him anymore."

I feel myself swoon.

"Sal—you know I love you, don't you?" He puts his hands on my shoulders, stares at my eyes.

I nod.

"And you love me, too, right?"

I can't respond.

"Right?"

"Of course I love you," I say, "but—"

"Then that's all that matters. That we love each other. That's the important thing. Now—you know I don't ask you for much, but I'm asking you for this. I want you to call him tomorrow and tell him you're not going to see him anymore. We can't throw away everything we have together for some guy who's just going to end up hurting you. Sally, you can't honestly care for him. You're just infatuated or something. But it's going to pass. What *we* have is real." He motions between us. "So, you call him tomorrow and you tell him it's over. If he has a problem with that, he can talk to *me.*" He thumbs his chest lightly. "Now—I need some time to cool down. I'm gonna go for a run."

I nod but don't say anything. I know David likes to run at night and I need time to think. The door closes and he's gone.

It's 2:12 when the phone rings. *2:12, 2:12, 2:12* flashing on the dig ital clock by my head. I grope across the darkness for the phone.

"Hullo?" I say in a croaky voice.

It's a woman on the phone. I'm confused at first. I have to tell her to repeat herself. She says she's calling from St. Vincent's Hospital. David is there. He's been in an accident.

An accident?

It's amazing the way bad news hits you. You could be doing any-thing. Mopping the floor. Watching TV. Fast asleep. Bad news just hits you. And you have to start all over again.

TWENTY-SEVEN

Through envy of the devil came death into the world.

BOOK OF THE WISDOM OF SOLOMON 2:24

THE emergency waiting room of St. Vincent's is chaotic with the major and minor tragedies of life. Bloody limbs. Torn skin. Frightened eyes.

I approach the admissions desk nervously. I explain to a toffee-skinned woman what happened and she consults her chart for David's name. Scribbled next to it, in the space that reads EMERGENCY CON-TACT, is my phone number. The woman who called said David gave it to them before he lost consciousness. I guess I should be honored to be his emergency contact—instead I just feel sick. The receptionist tells me I have to go to another section of the hospital. When she sees how confused I look, a small nurse with strawberry blond hair sighs tiredly and says, "I'll take her." The nurse walks quickly, swinging her arm for momentum as I fall into line behind her. Her foam-soled shoes make soft squeaking noises on the floor ahead of me. Somehow, amid the chaos and the crying, all I can hear are the nurse's shoes. A gentle *shkuk, shkuk, shkuk* as she walks. She escorts me through two sets of doors, leaving me in a stale-smelling hallway. She gives me directions, pointing with her finger, then turns efficiently on her rubber-soled heels in search of a more worthy emergency. *Shkuk, shkuk, shkuk.*

I go to the ninth floor as instructed. This is the old part of the hospital, a place that reminds me of iron lungs and wartime amputations and women dying in childbirth. The lights in the corridor are turned down low, like a suburban home after midnight. As I walk, I see the glint of chrome. Smell the pierce of antiseptic. But it's there. Underfoot. Leaking in through the walls. Seeping up through the floors. Like a bloodstain that won't come out in the laundry. Death. Running like a sore through the surface of our illusions. Ruining everything.

At the nurse's station I check in with a woman with dark, glassy eyes.

"Is he going to be okay?" I ask nervously.

"He'll live," she says, and it seems like such a marginal achievement, like we should all be capable of more heroic acts in the hospital's Great War Against Death.

I find him in a double room. A small nightlight is on, illuminating the table between two beds. An old man, who barely makes an impression under the sheets, turns his head on the pillow to look at me. Large liquid eyes regard me for a moment, then resume their nocturnal vigil of the ceiling.

David is sleeping. No, not sleeping. *"Unconscious,"* they said.

They told me over the phone it looks like a hit-and-run.

The ultimate victimization.

Hit-and-run.

Like words to a rap song.

Hit 'n' run.

He's got a broken leg. A gash in his head that took nine stitches. Multiple contusions. *Contusions.* I didn't know what that meant. I went to look it up in Meridien's Bible/dictionary before I left the apartment. Suddenly horrified that I'd waste time in such an emergency, I closed the book at *contrition.*

I approach his bed uncertainly. His face looks strangely relaxed. Not in repose, necessarily, but slack. His eyes are slightly open in an unseeing way. His mouth is held ajar on one side by a thin white tube, freezing his lips in a waxen half grimace. An intravenous unit beside the bed delivers a clear substance into or out of his arm—I don't know which. His head is wrapped in white gauze bandages, his long brown hair sticks out stringily beneath. A small patch on the right side of his head is shadowed slightly darker as the blood oozes rebelliously toward the surface.

I touch his hand. Cool. Bony. He seems so small next to . . .

Jack.

A pang of guilt. I flop into the chair beside the bed. I can't believe that just a couple of hours ago I was at a baseball game. The bright colors and the cheering of the crowd come at me in a wave that quickly collapses in upon itself. Right now Yankee Stadium couldn't be farther away from St. Vincent's Hospital, not if one of them were set upon a barge and sailed off into the night.

My eyes take in the spare details of the room. White walls. Gleaming instruments. A polished wooden crucifix above the bed. Jesus upon the cross. INRI it reads on a small scroll. I don't know what that means exactly, but I have some vague recollection that it's been shamefully misinterpreted down through the ages. I often wonder why that doesn't bother people more, why it doesn't make them rush out in great droves to biblical scholars demanding to know what other mistakes have been made.

Poor Jesus. He looks so miserable up there on that little cross. So different from the plastic Jesus who watched me every morning. His head hangs down, his mouth droops open, his ribs show. For a brief moment, the crown of thorns looks like a bandage, and with his long hair and half-closed eyes, I am horrified how much like an accident victim he looks. And maybe he is. The biggest hit 'n' run victim of all time.

I find myself beginning to pray. "Please, God," I whisper, hands clasped nervously in front of me, thumbs not knowing what to do. *"Please,* God," I say again. But I don't know how to finish. I don't know what I'm praying for.

"Please, God, let *him* be all right"? Or "Please, God, let *me* be all right"?

Because the truth is, I resent David's timing. And God can't be too happy about that.

And then, in a flash, an impulse in my brain that I'm not prepared for, that I can't control—I remember Jack's car pulling away from the building in a screech of tires.

What if he did this to David?

Sally . . . don't be crazy.

No, really. Think about it. He knew David was at my place. He was mad—the way he screeched away like that. What if he waited for David to leave—followed him in his black car . . . and just when the street was empty, stepped on the gas and . . .

Come on, Sally! Jack isn't capable of something like this.

But then I feel something hollow opening in me then, like a rip in the surface of a vital organ. I don't know exactly how it happens. Not at first. It's not like it's a *thought* that materializes fully formed in my consciousness. It ekes in slowly. It trickles in, drop by drop, squeezes in, slippery limb by slippery limb, like a thin impresario slithering out from behind a closed curtain to stand on a dark stage, calmly waiting for the jittery spotlight to find him. Not so much a thought as an intuition. Dark and silent and running deep.

Jack is the Devil!

What?

Jack is the Devil!

Sally, don't be—don't be—an idiot. Jack's not the— How can he be the—

But my thoughts don't go anywhere after that. And a stillness follows. A horrible suspended moment of nothingness during which it feels like I've had my last thought—*should* have had my last thought—

because when a brain goes this far, when it spins out of control like this, there's nothing left to do with it but take it back to where you got it and demand a full refund, because how the hell are you supposed to work with *this* one? This cruddy, malfunctioning, bloody blob of a thing that—let's be honest—hasn't worked properly since the day you got it. Not once. And you know all about cheap foreign labor and economies of scale but, hey, how much shoddy workmanship is one person expected to handle in her lifetime? Especially when it comes to something so important as a *brain?* I'm sorry, I'm sorry, but I demand a refund—or an exchange, at least—because I just can't go on with this one. Not the one I have. It's too . . . it's too . . .

Dangerous.

But there it is again.

Jack is the Devil.

Oh, God! Stop it! *That's crazy!* How could I possibly *think* that?

I try to push the thought away.

But it won't go away.

Jack is the Devil.

Stop it!

Jack is the Devil . . .

You're crazy!

Jack is the—

STOP! That's impossible!

But what about all the luck you've been having lately?

What about it?

The soap opera gig? The appeal factor?

So—so what?

Doesn't it seem a little peculiar to you?

Are you telling me it's easier for me to believe that my boyfriend is the Devil than I just happened to land a couple of gigs? Do I think I'm *that* bad an actor?

And what about Dara with her tongue bit off?

Tropical brain disease . . . tropical brain disease. . . .

And what about how happy you've been—and now this? David in a hit-and-run?

Oh, why, why at this time of night, with David lying unconscious in a hospital bed, with poor Dara back in Minneapolis getting her teaching degree, why does it seem so possible that Jack is the—

Then I remember what he told me: *I want to help you be happy, Sally. What would it take to make you happy?*

I know it sounds crazy. I know it does. But when crazy things start to happen, people start to think crazy things. It's the only logical thing to do. And there it is. Elegant. Black. And deadly.

Jack is the Devil.

I have had that thought. And I will never be able to unthink it again.

TWENTY-EIGHT

It is easier to raise the Devil than to lay him.

PROVERB

I wake up with a start early the next morning, forgetting for an instant I'm at the hospital, until I see a small, pale nurse replacing the empty bag beside David's bed. I rub my eyes against the light of the rising sun. I straighten in the chair, feeling every muscle pull open like an old elastic band. There's a bad taste in my mouth.

"How's he doing?" I ask in a croaky voice.

"He'll be fine," she says, and I wonder if that's an improvement on "He'll live." She leaves the room in a flurry of instruments and a different brand of foam-soled shoes. *Shkick. Shkick. Shkick.*

I'm surprised to see that the old man in the other bed is gone. The mattress has been stripped down. Hospitals are such strange places. Some people vanish without a trace; others look like they're going to stay rooted to the same spot forever. Like David here, who hasn't moved a muscle all night.

It's not the first thought in my head—that must be a good sign. But it comes to me in a rush of fresh panic, like waking up with a hangover and suddenly remembering something stupid you did after getting too drunk at a party.

Jack is the . . .

I don't even want to finish the thought.

But I don't have to. Because it's already inside of me, leering away.

It really seems crazy now, though, doesn't it? Ha-ha. In the morning, with the sun rising and the sounds of traffic from outside? *Doesn't it seem crazy?*

Sure it does, Sally . . . *sure* it does . . . crazy . . .

I leave David a note telling him I had to show up for my call, but that I'll be back. I move out into the hall, craving a coffee, a cigarette. Anything. I make my way through alert clumps of nurses and doctors, who gather here and there discussing dying patients, the baseball game, and what to do for lunch with the same chilling degree of disinterest.

WHEN I step out onto the street, the smell of exhaust is welcome after the night's lungful of chemicals. I try to hail a cab, but all the ones going uptown are hired. I start to walk. I pass an electronics store. The window is full of television sets tuned to a morning news program. The UBN logo appears over the anchor's shoulder. The anchor's mouth is moving. But I can't hear anything through the glass. Then the news cuts to another story, an earthquake in India that appears to have leveled a whole village. I turn away from the window, aware that my interest has waned.

Happy are you who weep now . . .

I bump into someone by mistake and let out a mumbled, "Excuse me."

"No problem," says the voice. Then I gasp when I see who it is.

Satan is staring down at me.

Okay, well, not Satan *himself,* but someone dressed up as Satan, in a plastic mask and a red cape, wearing a yellow sandwich board that reads: SAMMY'S ELECTRONICS: THE BEST DEALS IN TOWN.

"Sorry," he says, his voice muffled by the mask. "Didn't mean to scare ya." He hands me a flyer that lists Sammy's Halloween specials. I forgot it was so close to Halloween.

"Prices slashed on a wide selection of TVs, DVDs & Stereos!" it reads.

"Satan" must take my hesitation as a sign of interest in his sale. "Make us an offer," he says through the little breathe hole in his lips. I look at him. Young eyes blink behind the red plastic mask.

"No thanks," I say, handing the flyer back.

"Your loss," he says with a shrug, and I feel him watch me as I walk away.

O*H, what the fuck am I doing? What the fuck am I doing?*

I hurry down the long white corridor of the basement parking level at UBN. Light bulbs, shining within wire baskets, cast long, shadowy grids along the floors and walls. I hear the distant drone of the furnace room, a low, unbroken hum, and something drumming at regular intervals, like the beat of a great metallic heart. I follow the red EXIT signs toward the parking garage. I smell fuel and stale exhaust even before I open the door.

The parking level is lit with the unnatural gloaming of yellow sodium vapor lights. It feels dead and subterranean, a place that hasn't seen sunlight since the concrete was poured. Jack's car is parked in its spot not far from the elevators, gleaming and lethal-looking.

This can't be the same car . . . the same car where only last night . . . I remember him sliding his hand down my jeans, making me cry out. *It can't be.*

I crouch down and begin slinking along the driver's side of the car, squinting and scrutinizing the shiny black paint. I slowly make my way down the length of it, careful not to touch it in case I set off the alarm. I freeze when I see the headlights of another car pull down the ramp and grumble slowly into the garage. I duck down. A burgundy Camry drives by. I wait until it passes before I resume my search. I'm at the front bumper now, squinting at the paint. There's not a scratch. Not a smudge. I can see my own distorted reflection in it. Maybe it's been polished. I check for fibers, wax marks. Anything. But even the head-lights are—

"Sally?"

I straighten, my heart pounding. I see a woman with a cardigan draped over her shoulders standing outside the Camry parked a few spaces away. It's Agnes, Jack's secretary, some newspapers clamped under one arm and a Styrofoam cup of coffee in her free hand.

"Hi, Agnes." I wave casually.

"Are you looking for Jack?" Her voice echoes slightly, making her sound suspicious.

"Uh, not really. . . . I was just checking for something I thought I left in the car last night." I give her a nervous smile. "But I guess it's not here."

"I'm sure he's in. We could call him and ask him to come down if you—"

"No, no. I'll get it later." I walk over to her and join her on her way to the elevators. Our shoes click and scrape on the asphalt.

"You look a little tired, dear," she says.

"Didn't sleep well."

"Don't blame you." She puffs out her cheeks and widens her eyes as if dreading something. "I can't imagine what kind of a mess is wait-ing for me up there today."

"Why? What happened?"

"Didn't you hear?" She takes a copy of the *Wall Street Journal* out from underneath her arm. The headline reads: UBN WITHDRAWS GEOSTAR OFFER PENDING INVESTIGATION.

DETAILS come in pieces and chunks throughout the morning, some of it gossip, some of it from business reports. Less than twenty-four hours before the proposed takeover of Geostar, Marty Fletcher, the chief auditor for UBN, and a member of his team began selling their sizeable holdings of both UBN and Geostar shares. As of closing bell yesterday, Marty was $450,000 richer, having cashed in when the prices were at their peak in anticipation of a successful deal. The Justice Department and the Securities and Exchange Commission have been called in, investigating allegations of insider trading and fraud. When I see an image on the local news of Marty being escorted from the building and led to a government car by two men in suits and dark glasses, I feel a twinge of guilt. After all, I'm the one who started all this when I overheard him at the baseball game.

But my sense of responsibility is minuscule compared to the relief I feel. See? Jack's *not* the Devil. He *couldn't* be. I know how much he wanted this deal to go through. I know how much work he put into it. If he was really the Devil, there's no way he'd let a fuckin' weasel like Marty Fletcher screw it up for him.

LATER, in the dressing room, while Raine and I are debating whether or not to go out for lunch, my cell phone rings. It's Jack. "Just want to let you know," he says, "that this is biggest day of my career so far—and all I can think about is you."

I smile, then try to make myself sound convincing when I say, "I'm so sorry about this mess, Jack."

"Sorry?" he laughs. "What for? Marty fucked up, but Phil still wants to sell. And after this fiasco, if anyone *was* interested, they're backing off. Meaning, when trading resumes tomorrow, I'll get the whole company for about the price of the tape stock." He laughs. "Let's go out and celebrate tonight. I'll take you wherever you want. It's the least I can do, since you saved me several hundred million bucks."

I rub my head. Try to think. *So the deal didn't fall through . . . it's working out better than ever . . .* Then there it is again . . . the thought I'm trying to unthink . . .

Jack is the—

STOP!

"Sal? Where do you feel like going?"

I manage to respond. "I'm sorry, Jack. I can't see you tonight. I have to visit a sick friend in the hospital." I wait for his reaction. Wait for him to let his culpability slip. But all he says is, "That's too bad. I know how much you hate hospitals." I laugh weakly in spite of myself. He tells me he loves me and hangs up. The dial tone sounds as long and lonely as a country road.

THE hopeless smell of the hospital assaults me when I get there. I scurry through the halls, trying to find David's room.

So what—so what if the price of Geostar went down to less than half what Jack was prepared to pay for it? So what if it looks like Jack is going to be the head of an international news empire with divisions in every major city in the world?

And so what if my sort-of-ex-boyfriend is lying in a hospital bed practically dead from a hit-and-run?

So what?

That doesn't mean anything . . . nothing at all.

Not a scratch . . . not a smudge. . . .

David is sitting up in bed when I get there. He's watching a small portable TV suspended from the ceiling. A rerun of *Happy Days* is on.

"Hey, hon." He smiles; his voice cracks. The large blue "contusions" around his eyes make him look like one of those circus clowns painted to look sad. His casted leg is elevated slightly on a pillow, his toes poking out, purplish and tender-looking.

I approach the bed. "How are you feeling?"

"Been better," he says with a weak laugh, then winces, as if it hurts him to laugh. And maybe it does.

I notice that the other bed is no longer empty. A man in his fifties with a beer belly and a thick neck is reading *Car and Driver* and chewing a toothpick. He gives me a bored glance, then goes back to his magazine.

"Does it hurt anywhere?" I ask David.

"Everywhere." Another wince-laugh.

"Well, just thank God you're okay." But somehow it seems like entirely the wrong thing to say.

A heavyset nurse walks in the door behind me, wheeling a silver cart. Her name tag reads: M. MARTINEZ-BAILEY, R.N. "Time to change your dressing," she announces, with the easy cheer of someone accustomed to dealing with people whose confidence in the ways things are has been forever shaken by random tragedy.

I smile uncertainly at her, getting out of her way. I slip to the other side of the bed. "So—do you remember what happened yet?" I ask David.

"It's still kinda foggy. . . ."

The nurse picks up a small pair of silver scissors, which flash in the light. She takes the first nip of the bandages and replaces the scissors with a delicate tinkle.

"I've been trying to think. . . . I know I stopped to stretch out my hamstrings on the steps of the church . . ."

I feel myself tense, sitting forward.

"The streets were really quiet. I guess everyone was uptown at the baseball game." He tries to look at me, to see whether or not I'm suitably moved by the situation, but the nurse hooks him around the chin and makes him face straight ahead again. She unwinds the bandage slowly. Every foot or so contains a widened patch of discolored blood from the gash. "I remember passing Bleecker—at least, I think it was Bleecker—I'm not sure." His eyes are fixed unseeingly ahead of him. His voice is faraway. "The street was quiet. . . . It was such a nice night. . . . There was this kind of mist hanging in the air and I could see the park up ahead—I was going to cut through it. I glanced back, just to make sure no one was coming, but there was nothing, not for blocks. I got about halfway across the street, and then all of a sudden I heard something . . . this roar. . . . I turned, but before I could see anything, *wham!* Something hit me from behind—I went flying. And I mean flying, Sal. Twenty or thirty feet. I saw the pavement and the buildings whizzing by me and I remember thinking, 'Okay, this is it . . . this is how I'm going to die. . . .' Man, it was weird, thinking you know how you're gonna die. . . ." He shivers, remembering. "The next thing I know"—he looks around the room with fearful wonder—"I'm waking up here."

I'm trembling. "And nobody saw anything?"

"Nope."

Not a scratch. Not a smudge.

"Well, what do the police think?"

"They don't know."

"Do they think they're going to find the guy?" Then I add quickly, "Or girl—who did it?"

"Who knows? They're not even sure it's a hit-and-run. They think maybe I tripped over a loose manhole cover or something. But come on. A manhole cover? As if a manhole cover could do *that* to *me.* I *know* somebody hit me, Sal," he says with certainty. "And if I ever catch the bastard who did it . . ." He clenches his fist and punches his other hand, but the blow makes him cringe. He shakes his hand out a couple of times and looks at me hopelessly. I am reminded of the futility of vengeance in the hands of those who need it most.

The bandage is almost off now. I can see the color of his hair through the loose weave of the cotton. The yards of gauze lie on the tray next to the nurse like moist, molted snake's skin.

"You a little queasy, are you, dear?" the nurse asks with a smile.

But I can't talk. I'm just staring at a long, crooked pink wound on the right side of David's head; stitches are pulled through it, raising it into a pinkish ridge, like a mountain range on a topographical map. But it's not really the hideous scar that has stunned me. It's what's surrounding it.

Nothing.

Absolutely nothing.

But a long, crooked patch of bald skin that they've had to shave into his head to take the stitches. It hacks up from his hairline toward his crown. The roots of the surrounding hairs bristle up like tiny tree trunks on the edge of a clear-cut forest.

"What is it, Sal?"

I try to say, "Nothing," but my voice is small.

He knows something is wrong. His hand goes up to his head. He starts batting around. A look of horror comes into his eyes as he realizes there is bare skin where there shouldn't be bare skin.

"Get me a mirror," he says, and I fumble for my compact, handing it to him. He tilts it this way and that, eyes wide with disbelief. When the full force of what's happened to him sinks in, he lets out the kind of horrible, bloodcurdling scream that gives hospitals a bad name.

The guy in the next bed looks up from his magazine and says, "Who the hell *died?*"

Iᴛ's dark when I leave the hospital; the sky is navy, unbroken by stars or moon. I walk home past the Backburner; I don't have to, but I do. The ʙᴀᴄᴋ ɪɴ 5 ᴍɪɴᴜᴛᴇs sign is up. There is no light coming from the room at the back of the store. I check the street to make sure no one is watching as I dig through my purse looking for a key I haven't used in ages.

Ages?

You could count the number of days it's been since I spent every afternoon in this place, wiping charcoal prints off the shelves and waiting for the phone to ring. It's been less than the length of a summer holiday, not much longer than Lent.

I unlock the door and the bell tinkling above me seems louder in the darkness, since I'm not supposed to be here. The place smells the same way I remember it. Charcoal. Dust. Mildewy books. The floorboards squeak beneath my weight as I move past the register. The till is open, indicating Jeremy has cashed out for the night.

I turn on a shelf lamp against the far wall. It illuminates a small clearing of light, like the corona around a star in an otherwise black sky. I begin searching the shelves. I'm looking for a copy of the Bible.

No use consulting Meridien's OED unless all I want is a *definition* of *Devil,* which, incidentally, I looked up today. It was there, right after *deviation* and *device: "devil, n. 1. The Devil, supreme spirit of evil, tempter of mankind, enemy of God, Satan. 2. Heathen god; evil spirit; superhuman malignant being. 3. Wicked or cruel person; mischievously energetic, clever, knavish person. . . ."* The definitions devolved into "devil-dodger, devil-fish, devil-may-care," none of which made me feel any better.

Jeremy has a copy of the Tibetan Book of the Dead, the Koran, the Talmud, and several copies of the I Ching. But no Bible. There *is* a Children's Bible; it has a bright yellow jacket and a picture of Noah's Ark on the front. I flip through the pages and see Moses coming down from the mountain; Adam and Eve in the Garden of Eden, the snake harmless and goofy-looking. Like a G-rated comic book, the gratuitous violence has been edited out. I continue tracing the spines of the books, moving farther and farther from the orbit of light. I'm in Literature now, searching for Milton, Marlowe, Goethe. . . .

I grab an armful of books and crouch down in the shadows, cracking the aged spine of *Faust.* Chills tighten the skin on my arms when I read that Mephistopheles disguises himself as a black dog as he weaves his way into Faust's life, offering to grant Faust his earthly desires in exchange for his soul. I remember the dog who followed me home from the store.

"What are you doing here?"

Even a familiar voice in a familiar environment can scare the shit out of you when you think you're alone. It's Jeremy, a bony shadow looming above me on the very fringes of the light.

"I—I—I thought I'd come in and clean up," I offer hopefully.

He observes the floor around me, strewn as it is with books. "Don't do me any favors."

"Sorry," I say, standing up. "I guess I was just lonely. I wanted to come by and see the place."

"I guess selling your soul's not everything it's cracked up to be?"

I feel a rush of anger. "What's *that* supposed to mean?"

He throws his hands up. "Calm down," he says. "I just knew that working on a soap opera would eventually leave you craving greater artistic sustenance."

I try to rein in my indignity—and my fear. "Anyway, the lights were off. I didn't know anyone was here."

"I forgot the deposit bag," he says. He motions with a canvas bag. "I came in the back way. You were obviously too wrapped up in your . . . cleaning . . . to hear me." He bends down and picks up a copy of the Children's Bible.

"It's research," I tell him, grabbing the book back. "For my character."

"I see."

"You don't have any grown-up ones, do you?"

"Not at the moment. People probably think it's bad luck to give them away. Are you staying? I've got an inspiration. We can have a drink."

I nod, grateful. A drink would be good. I follow him to his back room, where he turns on an old brass floor lamp; the orgy of sketched lovers on the walls around us seem momentarily distressed by the light, then immediately go back to their fucking and kissing.

He retrieves a bottle of screw-top port and sits down in front of his easel, flipping to a fresh page. I pour two dirty tumblers of wine.

"I know this is going to sound stupid, Jeremy," I begin. "But I have to ask you something."

He grumbles a syllable of some kind, starting to draw a figure, a few simple lines that I know will begin to materialize into faces, bodies, lives.

"Do you believe in the Devil?" I ask.

His gaze shifts over to me. There is a look of mild annoyance on his face. As both a tortured artist and official genius, Jeremy has been through too much existential angst in his forty-odd years to actually be titillated by a sophomoric question like "Do you believe in the Devil?"

"Are we really having this conversation?" he asks.

"Yes."

He sighs boredly. "Sally, the Devil is a metaphor. Every story needs a bad guy. And in this one, he's it. Just a small part of a very flawed little fairy tale a handful of old coots jotted down a few thousand years ago as a way of ensuring their names were remembered forever." He turns to me. "Not unlike *your* chosen profession, really. Minus the royalty checks." He puts down his charcoal nub and picks up another.

"So you don't believe the Devil exists, then?"

"I don't believe *any* of it, Sally. Virgin births? Rising from the dead? Please. If anyone tried writing that today—what is it you people say?—it would never get out of development." He rubs softly to smudge the lines of a face. "We're accidents of biology, Sally. A little carbon. Some chlorophyll. A dash of O_2. God, the Devil, Adam and Eve—they're all just characters in a story we had to make up, because if we really faced the fact that we're just sitting on a piece of pointless rock spinning in the middle of an endless void, and there's absolutely no reason for any of it at *all,* we'd go insane or kill each other within a generation and that would be the end of us." He shrugs and goes back to his sketch.

I smack my lips blandly. "Gee, thanks, Jeremy." There's a note of sarcasm in my voice. "I feel better already."

I lie awake in bed for hours that night, watching the changing shadows in my room. I try to tell myself over and over again that Jeremy is right. There's no such thing as the Devil. I'm a sophisticated, twenty-first-century woman. I've just met a guy, that's all. The kind of guy the glossy covers of *Cosmopolitan* have been promising us is out there for years. The Perfect Guy. Prince Charming. Mr. Right. Even though most of us suspect this guy doesn't actually exist, that he's just a myth to make us keep buying more magazines, there's a part of us that secretly hopes we'll bump into him someday. And now, as hard as it is to fathom, I have met him. The Perfect Guy. Naturally I'm a little skeptical. It has nothing to do with religion or superstition . . . or the Devil. Because there's no such thing as the Devil.

No such thing as the Devil.

Nosuchthingasthedevilnosuchthingasthedevilnosuchthingasthedevil.

But no matter how many times I say it, I still can't relax enough to fall asleep. It feels like I'm seven years old again, listening to the house creak and settle, trying to convince myself the bogeyman is not under my bed. I wasn't very good at it then, either.

TWENTY-NINE

The Devil never seems so busy as where the saints are.

ELIZABETH RUNDLE

"SALLY, please, calm down." It's the Mother Superior's voice over my cell phone; she chuckles, as if nothing could be cause for such panic.

But she doesn't know.

"I just . . . just have to see you again," I tell her.

I hear the flipping of pages. "How's next week. We could meet at the—"

Next week? "Can't it be sooner than that?"

More flipping. "I don't think so. . . ."

I'm pacing back and forth in an all-white photography studio in Chelsea where Gus and I are having my new head shots done. White tissues are tucked in my collar to keep the makeup off my blouse. The studio is cool with air-conditioning; each white wall reflects an even, almost heavenly light. This is a high-end place. The photographer has actually done layouts for *Vogue* and *Vanity Fair*. There are pictures of Kate Moss and Heather Graham on the wall. Reese Witherspoon. Matt Damon. Christy Turlington in an elegant yoga pose. It's not anything like the overpacked back-of-a-garage studio in Queens where I had my head shots done when I first came to New York. Of course, nothing is like it was when I first came to New York.

"I'm afraid I don't have anything this week," she says. "Is there something I can help you with over the phone?" I glance across the studio. I see Gus by the craft services table, talking to one of the photographer's assistants.

"Yes . . . maybe there is something." I take a big swallow. "I need to know everything you can tell me about . . . the Devil."

A beat passes. I hear her breathing. I wonder if, like Sister Ruth, she knows that I've done something wrong. "Why?"

I consider what to say next.

Mercifully she lets me off the hook. "Is it more research for your character?"

"Yes—more research. The writers are trying to work a whole temptation angle into the plot." Then I roll my eyes. *Not a very good lie.*

"Well, you know the Devil was one of God's archangels, right? His name was Lucifer."

I dig for my yellow legal pad and my pen. At the top of the page are the words *vespers . . . novice . . . Happy are you who weep now . . . Blessed is the one . . .*

"Yes . . . yes . . ." I write that down. *Lucifer.*

"It meant light bearer. But he became envious of God's power and was cast out of heaven."

"Right, right . . ." I'm jotting as she speaks. I feel my heart beginning to slow down. A simple brawl. Some jealous friends. How conveniently the human mind translates the unknowable. "So . . . how would we know if we'd met the Devil?"

"I suppose you'd just sense it."

"But what if you wanted to be *sure?* What about that whole '666' thing? Is that true?" *Because Jack has a perfect view of that sign on Fifth Avenue from his office—the one with all the sixes—and it's starting to creep me out.*

"The Book of Revelation *does* say six hundred three score and six is the 'mark of the Beast.' "

"Does it have to be a birthmark on his head? Like in *The Omen?* Or could it be a sign—a neon sign on a building?"

"I don't think we should take those things too literally, Sally," she says with a laugh.

And I wonder which one she means not to take literally. Horror movies. Or the Bible.

"So, what would he look like?" I ask her. "How could we know for sure it was him?"

"It's hard to say. He's taken many forms. Serpent . . . dragon . . ."

"But could he make himself look like a man?"

"Of course." Her voice is starting to sound suspicious. "They say he possessed Judas to betray Jesus."

"So you're telling me," I squeal-whisper, starting to pace, "that the Devil could look like *anything?* Anything he wants? How fair is *that?* Isn't that like stacking the deck against us? How are we supposed to resist temptation if we're not even sure who the Devil *is?*"

"Sally, are you okay? Is something wrong?"

Gus slinks up to me. She motions to the phone in a nosy *Who's that?* kind of way.

I cover the receiver. "Research," I whisper.

"Make it fast. They're ready for you." She shuffles away.

"I'm sorry," I say into the phone. "I have to go. But could you tell me just one more thing? When I met you the other day, you said something about 'Blessed are those who avoid temptation' or something."

"Yes. James 1:12. *'Blessed is the man who endureth temptation: for when he is tried, he shall receive the crown of life. . . .' "*

"That means if a man resists temptation—a woman, too, I guess"—I'm a little annoyed I have to specify—"that person will go to heaven, right?"

"That's right."

"And if not?"

"Then he or she goes the other way."

I let out an uneasy sigh. "That's what I thought. Okay, thanks." We make plans to see each other next week. I hang up the phone and try to compose myself.

I make my way to the center of the studio, where a tall, brushed-stainless stool is set up. The makeup artist comes over with her powder brush. "You're shining again," she says admonishingly.

Your sweat glands would be working overtime, too, if you thought you were in love with the Devil.

"What's wrong with *you?*" Gus asks me.

"Nothing. I'm fine." I take the tissues out of my collar, stare at the gleaming, myopic eye of the lens.

"Ready, Sally?" the photographer asks. She's a woman with clipped bleached-blond hair and expensive jeans. She has one camera set up on a tripod in front of me and two around her neck. I nod. She asks me to tilt my chin up . . . down . . . to the left . . . right . . . "Nice," she says. There is no flash; the lighting in the studio is bright enough. The small sound of the shutter opening and closing is lulling, like the slightly uneven tick of an old clock.

With the camera trained on me, and nothing to do but tilt my chin and smile or not smile on command, my mind wanders to my mission: I have to resist temptation.

I have to leave Jack.

I feel a hot sting in my chest at the thought of living without him.

But what if he's *not* the Devil? I mean, it's all pretty ridiculous, isn't it? I don't want to turn the only man I've ever loved out of my life just in *case* he's the Devil. Even a murder suspect is innocent until proven guilty. The problem is, how to be sure? It's not going to be easy for me. I'm notoriously indecisive. In high school, when we studied Hamlet's tragic flaw—indecision—I was, like, *Yeah, and? What's the problem?* I have trouble making up my mind about everything. I can spend half an hour at the MAC counter rubbing my lips raw trying to decide between two shades of red lipstick you'd otherwise need a spectrometer to differentiate. And I *still* wonder if I would break down and wear fur if I could afford it. But these are annoying uncertainties I've been able to live with.

Whether or not I'm in love with the Devil? That's something I want to know for sure.

I get a speed visit in with David. We watch a hidden camera exposé on Fox and the last half of an A&E *Biography* on Robin Williams. I keep glancing at my watch, waiting for visiting hours to be over. David doesn't seem to notice.

I rush home in a cab. I have a quick shower to get the smell of the hospital off my skin. When I hear Jack buzz up from downstairs, I run down to meet him. I get in the car and immediately feign a yawn. "I'm kind of tired tonight," I tell him. "Why don't we cancel the reservations and go to your place. We could rent a movie and order something in."

He smiles. "Sounds great."

As he drives, I sneak glances at him. *He can't be the Devil.* I mean, look at him. He's so gorgeous. The Devil wouldn't look like that!

How would the Devil look, then?

The Mother Superior said he could take any form he wanted. You think he's going to come up out of the pit of hell in a red cape? With horns and a forked tail? You think he's going to elbow you in the ribs and say, "Hey, let's make a deal," like some sort of cosmic Monty Hall? Of course not. We've known for thousands of years what making a deal with the Devil would cost us—burning forever in the fires of hell—and since cowardice is the only trait that runs deeper than greed in human nature, the Devil knows he'd never win that game. His dilemma, then, is how to make us override our fear of hell, how to trick us into surrendering our souls. There could be no telekinesis, no levitating beds, no speaking in tongues. The Devil would have to seem—at first, at least—like a mortal, someone we could trust implicitly, someone who could implicate himself into our lives so completely that we *almost* couldn't picture life without him. Almost. And then it would start happening, one compromise at a time, one principle at a time, the slow, steady bartering away of our souls.

WE go to the Blockbuster on Broadway. It smells like freshly made popcorn. Title by title, DVD by DVD, I lead him farther and farther away from the New Releases aisle and into the shadowy labyrinth of older movies in the center of the store. Finally we're in the Horror section. The shelves are crammed with images of monsters and murderers. I remember reading once that the Devil owes everything to Milton, but I'm afraid Milton had nothing on Tinseltown.

I find what I'm looking for. A copy of *Rosemary's Baby.* "How about this?" I ask him, holding it up. "It's a classic." I watch him carefully for his reaction. If he *is* the Devil, this might be a little tricky to try. He takes the DVD case, turns it over in his hands, reads the back, shrugs.

"Sure. If you feel like it."

"Or this?" I've now got a copy of *The Exorcist.* Carefully watching, watching.

He gives another shrug. "If you want."

"What about this one?" I pluck *The Devil's Advocate* off the shelf.

He squints at it—seems to consider it—then shakes his head. "Nah."

Hmmmm . . . Is that a sign that he's Lucifer? That he doesn't like *The Devil's Advocate?* Maybe he just doesn't like Keanu Reeves? I sigh and shelve the disk. Eventually we end up in another aisle altogether, agreeing on a Ben Stiller comedy.

THAT night I lie stiffly beneath the sheets, waiting for him to fall asleep. When he's breathing peacefully and hasn't moved for several minutes, I slip out of bed. I tiptoe to his closet. Close the door. Turn on the light. I don't know what I'm looking for. Do I think he's just going to keep his black mass robes tucked away next to the Armani and Hugo Boss? I sift through a few shelves, feeling unforgivably silly. I turn off the light and creep into the living room. The streetlights from below cast long dark shadows against the walls.

This is ridiculous, Sally . . . just go back to bed. . . .

I riffle through his bookshelf. Looking for—what? Satanic scriptures? I only find the usual assortment of business bestsellers, trade magazines, and, naturally, *The Art of War.*

Nuts.

Mind you, I do remember him putting the Rolling Stones on the CD player once. I think he likes that song "Sympathy for the Devil." . . .

So? So do you!

I go into the kitchen, rummaging through the cupboards. Maybe there's a sacrificial dagger hanging around. I open the fridge. In addition to the leftover Thai takeout containers, a bottle of champagne, and a few veggies, there is a single red apple sitting on the middle shelf.

An apple.

Christ.

I slam the fridge closed.

So say he *was* the Devil—which he's probably not, let's face it, because that's ludicrous—did *you* do anything to summon him? *Think . . . think . . . what happened when you met him . . . when he came into your life. . . .* Were there any clues? I remember getting lost in the halls of UBN after Hazel cut me off in the audition . . . slumping down by the half-dead rubbertree plant. I remember my little plea to God, the Buddha, and *everyone* to help me get the part. I remember saying I'd do "anything" for it.

Anything?

It *can't* be that easy to summon the Devil! It *can't* be! There's no way!

And even if it is, why would the Devil choose *me? Me,* of all people? I'm not anything special. I'm not even religious. Not *that* religious, anyway. But maybe the Devil doesn't look for religious people.

Maybe, like the coyote in that *Looney Tunes* cartoon, he just slips around the edges of the herd . . .

Morning, Ralph.

Hey, Sam.

. . . and nabs whoever he can get.

Or maybe it's not that personal. Maybe it's just like that old Chris de Burgh song about God and the Devil playing cards for people's souls. Is that what it boils down to? A couple of guys sitting around, smoking cigars, and bartering with people's *lives?*

Damnit. I knew I should've paid more attention in church.

I try to shake it off, sneaking back into the bedroom. I slide quietly into bed. His face is turned away from me. His breathing is even and relaxed. I feel a sting of—I can't help it—love, absolute love for him, as I lean across and hover just above his head. I see his slightly wavy hair in the moonlight. I shift a lock of it with my fingertips. Another.

Oh, Christ. I'm looking for a birthmark, aren't I?

This is stupid. I'm not in some cheap seventies horror flick. This is real life. Even if it hasn't felt like "real life" (in other words, boring, pathetic, depressing) since I met him.

I roll back to my side of the bed. These are all just coincidences, Sally. Just coincidences. There's no such thing as the Devil.

And then I remember him saying to me: *"You can be happy, Sally . . . all you have to do is choose."*

THIRTY

I see the devil's hook, and yet cannot help nibbling at his bait.

MOSES ADAMS

DAVID and I hobble down a long, busy corridor of St. Vincent's Hospital. He's clumsy on his new crutches, thunking his cast softly on the ground beneath him. He wears a pale green hospital gown tied over striped Joe Boxer shorts. We shuffle into the cafeteria. The tables are scattered with nurses, visitors, and patients whose IVs are pushed up to the table beside them.

I have the soup du jour. I'm not sure what kind it is because there's a mysterious layer of congealed scum on top of it, but there are carrots involved. David selects a hot turkey sandwich with fries and a piece of apple pie.

We find a table and sit down together. He talks about how his leg is getting itchy under the cast, how the hospital food doesn't suck as badly as he thought, how tonight will be the longest night he's spent here because he's getting out tomorrow. Throughout the conversation there are awkward silences of the type David and I never used to have. At least *I* find them awkward. Because every time one of them starts, it feels as if what we really should be talking about is suspended in the air between us like a hospital curtain.

Did you honor my last request before I became the victim of a hit-and-run? Did you tell Jack Weaver you wouldn't see him anymore?

But he doesn't ask that. He just eats his hot turkey sandwich and chitchats. He thinks I've already talked to Jack, I bet. That he trusts me makes me feel worse than anything.

"I was looking for you," says a voice from across the cafeteria. We turn to see M. MARTINEZ-BAILEY, R.N., heading over to us. "Time to change your bandage," she tells him.

"I'm eating," he whines, motioning to his plate.

She shrugs indifferently. "Those are bad for you, you know," she says, pointing to David's fries. She picks one up and shoves it between her teeth in two even pieces, chewing.

"Help yourself," he says with a grin.

"Don't mind if I do."

"Whose food are you gonna steal when I get out tomorrow?"

"I got more where you came from." She turns to me. "I saw you on TV yesterday. It's not my show, but I wanted to see you. You were pretty good."

"Thanks." I smile.

"I wanted to be an actress, too. Just didn't get around. Your mother must be so proud."

"You don't know my mother," I mumble. Since I haven't heard from her in a few weeks, I guess Father Silvio allayed her fears about my portraying a nun on TV.

The nurse glances at her watch. "You got five minutes. Then I'll see you back at the room." She holds out a finger to me. "You should come, too."

"Why?"

"To watch me change the bandage. It needs changing twice a day or it'll get infected."

I still don't understand.

David puts down his fork, winces a little. "I hope you don't mind, Sal. They told me I'm not going to be able to get around much until I get my walking cast on. They asked if there was somewhere I could stay. I kinda thought of your place. I mean, I had nowhere else to go."

He holds up his hands. "If you can't do it, it's fine. I'm sure I can fend for myself."

"You can barely *walk,"* the nurse says.

"I'll be doing the hundred-yard dash in no time."

She *pshaws* him. "Nobody's askin' you to look after yourself." She turns to me. "Men. They think they can get on without us."

I try to smile. Swallow. Blink. But I don't say anything. The nurse cocks her head, sensing my reticence. She crosses her arms, glaring at me with increasing disapproval as the seconds drag out. This is a woman who earns her living caring for sick strangers—that the possibility existed that someone wouldn't take her injured boyfriend into her own home and nurse him back to health is beyond her comprehension. I glance at David. He's munching his hot turkey, his crutches leaning against the table beside him. The nurse has now grit her teeth and is practically leaning over me.

It comes out in a single breath. *"Ofcourseyoucanstaywithme,David, noproblem."*

Nurse Martinez-Bailey smiles, satisfied with my level of sacrifice. "See you back at the room," she says, then turns on her foam heal and saunters away.

"Thanks, Sal," David says. "You're a sweetie. Just think"—he leans into me, whispering—"we can play doctor."

I try to smile. But I'm as close to tears without openly bawling as I've ever been before in my life.

Oh, Christ. What a pushover I am. Waves of desperate, helpless rage wash over me as I stomp through the halls of UBN toward my dressing room. *Sure you can stay with me, David. Sure. No problem.*

But what choice do I have? Poor David. I've *got* to.

Maybe I'm doing some kind of penance or something. After all, *shouldn't* I be trying to do something to repent for the fact I've sold my soul to the Devil? *Come on, Sally! Jack is not the Devil.* And even if he is—it's not like you *already* sold your soul, is it?

What about the first time we made love?

Are you ready, Sally . . . are you mine?

Forever?

There's no way. It couldn't have happened then. There must be
some kind of qualifier. God can't take anything I say under the influ-
ence of carnal bliss seriously, the same way they don't let drunk people
get married at City Hall.

What about that meeting in his office? *Whose side are you on, Sally?*

But you didn't actually tell him you'd be on his side then, did you?

Then my heart stops. I see him.

Him.

Walking down the hall toward me. There's a grin on his face.

Nosuchthingasthedevilnosuchthingasthedevil.

He collects me in his arms and leads me into the dressing room,
making sure Raine's not there. He locks the door and kisses me. I feel
everything inside of me collapse—my bones, my muscles, everything
that holds me up.

"I'm away from you for a few hours," he says, "and I miss you so
much . . ."

He pushes me against the door. He kisses me harder. My mind
begins to vaporize. I can't help myself. I'm like an addict, a junkie in a
rush. I rub against the hardness of him. I push up my skirt. He finds
the edge of my panties, slides them down my thighs. Together we fumble with his belt. In a moment, it is happening; he slides into me, causing a quick, sharp slice of pain—then dark relief. We wait a moment,
not moving, like two people dying of thirst, just letting the water soak
our mouths. Then it begins. The door shakes in its frame behind me. I
have to bite my lip so I don't cry out. My eyes seal closed and I am
soon in the red-edged darkness. The whole wall behind me seems to
bend. I am deaf with the sound of breathing and moaning and bliss.

IloveyouIloveyouIloveyou.

This can't be happening. This *can't* be happening. Not the Devil.
Just a man. Just a wonderful, perfect man.

When I come, I hear my voice echo against the walls; he covers my mouth with his and we ride through it together. When the world is in focus again, I hear him whispering against my neck.

"I love you, Sally. . . . I love you so much."

And that makes me feel better. See? He *can't* be the Devil. The Devil couldn't be in love with anyone.

I tense again when I remember him telling me he'd never been in love before. That this had never happened to him. *Never.*

Oh, God.

A light, high-pitched ringing fills the room. It's my cell phone. I'm almost grateful for something to do. I dig for it in my purse.

"Hey—what're you wearing tonight?" It's Gus.

"Tonight?" I clutch my head, not understanding.

"The Precinct *thing, Sal. Don't tell me you forgot."*

"No, of course, I didn't," I lie. But I'm dumbfounded. I *did* forget. A year ago, even a few months ago, during my time of pricing used paperbacks at the bookstore and getting cut off in auditions, the idea that I would ever be having dinner with the executive producer of a prime-time hit to discuss the possibility of joining their cast next season would have been too much to hope for. The fact that I could *forget* such a meeting, which I have done, would have been completely beyond belief.

"Be casual," she says, *"but not too casual. And don't be late! Honmura An, remember. Eight o'clock. Cheapskates. Should take us to Nobu instead."* She hangs up.

"Sal?" It's Jack's voice; he's staring at me, doing up the buttons on his shirt. "You okay?"

"Yeah . . . fine." I try to smile.

I look at his mouth, trying to focus on what he's saying. He tells me he has good news and bad news. "The bad news is—I've got to go to L.A. tomorrow. It's about the Geostar thing. I'll be gone for a few days."

"Oh, no. . . ." I react with a genuine dip of disappointment—I know how much I'll miss him. But almost immediately my mind begins to calculate. *This could work.* I can move David into my apartment, look after him for a few days, then maybe by the time Jack is back . . .

He's still talking. "The good news is"—he lets a beat pass—"I want you to come with me."

What?

"You can fly out after studio on Friday—we'll spend the weekend together . . ."

I want to be excited, but I'm not. I feel my spirits sink. No, not just sink. They wrench away from me, violently ripping me in half and pulling me down, where I will come to rest, like the *Titanic,* in two irretrievable pieces on the ocean floor.

". . . we'll drive up the coast on Sunday. Maybe stay somewhere on the beach . . ." He stops when he sees the look on my face. "Sal—what's wrong?"

A sharp ache in my throat almost prevents me from speaking. "I'm sorry—I can't go, Jack."

"How come?" He seems curious; maybe a little hurt.

I consider telling him that I have too many pages to memorize or some other lie, I'm so good at them. But I don't.

"Sal?" His voice is soft, questioning.

"That sick friend I told you about?" I begin guiltily.

He nods.

"It's not a friend—it's David."

A beat passes. He waits for further explanation.

"He was in an accident the other night, Jack," I begin. "The night of the baseball game. . . . It was a hit-and-run." I try to see what effect the news has on him. *Did you do it, Jack? Did you do it? Just tell me! Were you parked there . . . waiting for him? . . . Did you follow him . . . just tell me the truth. . . .*

I'd forgive you. . . .

And it surprises me to think that—would I really forgive him?

"Poor guy," he says. "He's really had a string of bad luck lately. But why does that mean you can't come? It's not as if you have to—" He stops. His expression drops. "You have to look *after* him?"

"He's got nowhere else to go, Jack!"

"Aw, *Sal*—" He starts pacing the room.

I follow after him, pleading. "But you should see him! He's in such bad shape! He can't get around! He can't cook for himself! He's got this big cast on! And this gash in his head . . . and if the bandage doesn't get changed twice a—"

He holds up his hands. "Please, spare me the details. I'd rather not picture you nursing your ex-boyfriend back to health." He stops. "Wait a second—he's not an *ex*, is he?"

I look away guiltily.

There are a few moments of silence. He sighs in resignation. "All right, Sally. If that's what you want . . ."

"Oh, it's not what I *want*, Jack. You think I *want* to do this? Of course not! I wish more than anything I could go to L.A. with you!"

"Then why don't you?"

Oh, his logic. His precise and painful logic.

"I just . . . can't, Jack. Not when David's like this. I wouldn't feel good about it. It just wouldn't be . . ." I hesitate, but there is no other way to say it. "It just wouldn't be right."

And I know what he's thinking: *Right for whom?*

THIRTY-ONE

The devil was sick, the devil a monk would be;
the devil was well, the devil a monk he'd be.

PETER ANTHONY MOTTEUX

HONMURA *An* is crowded for a midweek night, the din of voices
and laughter echoing off exposed brick; the small fountain burbles
merrily in the center of the room. Across the table from Gus and me
are two of the most influential creative types in prime-time television:
the executive producer of *Precinct,* Griffin Hughes, with his sloped
shoulders and thick-lensed glasses, and the show's head writer, Marcy
Kornfeldt, her glossy curls clipped up in a barrette. The two of them
are effortlessly sipping expensive sake from the kind of wooden boxes
that always make me drool. They have been talking all evening about
how poorly the assembly cut of the bank robbery episode tested after
Candace dies. They're considering reediting so Candace lives. They
also say that they've been looking for the past three seasons for a
potential love interest for John Monroe's character, Hogan. Such a
move would also do much to divert attention away from John's failing
rehab program.

"We didn't know exactly who we were looking for," Griff says.

"Only that we'd know her when we saw her," says Marcy.

"She had to be pretty."

"But not *too* pretty," Marcy adds, "because we didn't want her alienating the women."

"She had to be smart."

"But not *too* smart, because we didn't want her alienating the men."

The conversation winds around like this, like a giant, slippery soba noodle, and the whole time Gus just lets them talk, casually slurping her soup (she bypassed the chopsticks and went straight for the spoon). She's implementing our plan to play hard to get. But even as she's wearing her poker face, she excitedly knees me under the table every time a new detail comes up.

All *I* can think about is my dilemma. Two people from a top-rated show have taken me and my agent out for dinner to discuss the possibility of my joining their cast. I should be thrilled. But I'm petrified. I remember Jack asking what would make me happy the night of the premiere. And I remember telling him I wanted to be rich and famous.

Is that what this is? A prime-time gig as part of the payment for my soul?

Finally, over green tea ice cream, Gus clears her throat and asks if she can be frank. When a person as painfully frank as Gus Koniklouris has to ask to be frank, it's usually not a good sign.

"We really like the noises you guys are making," she begins. "But are you saying you think Sally's right for the part of Hogan's girl-friend?"

There's a pause. The other two look at each other, then back at me. They smile and nod. "We think so."

"I don't know if you noticed," Gus says, "but Sally already has a job."

"We know," Marcy says, "but it's on a *soap* opera."

"I *like* the soap," I interject.

Gus smiles with approval. "Exactly. Daytime drama is great training ground. Sally can afford to wait for the right vehicle and we just don't know if this is it. She's not leaving a regular-paying gig just to be some cop's fling for a couple of months—that's for sure."

"We couldn't agree more," says Griff. "That's why we'd like to send you guys a deal memo next week."

"Deal memos are nice," Gus says, "but they're kind of like being asked to shack up when what you really want to do is get married." There's a brief laugh-track chuckle from the other two. I press on:

"Seriously. I really like the soap. I'm perfectly happy there."

"That's good, Sal." Gus pats my hand. She wants me to back off now.

"It doesn't matter to me about a prime-time role . . ."

And that does it. They all turn to stare at me with such horror that for a moment it seems as if I've belched out loud.

"Would you excuse us for a second," Gus says. "Sally—I think I have something in my eye. Could you come to the rest room with me and check it."

"I don't see any—"

She grabs my wrist. "Thanks," she says, clenching her teeth.

THERE is only one women's bathroom at the back of the restaurant, and when we slip in together, we attract some curious stares from the servers tallying tabs at the station. Gus smiles at them and locks the door.

"What the *hell* are you doing?" she demands. "I said let's play hard to get. I didn't say let's commit professional suicide."

I groan out loud. I lower the toilet lid and flop down. "I just don't feel good about it, that's all," I tell her.

"Why not?"

I wonder what I should say. *Because I think my lover is the Devil and he's trying to buy my soul with a network gig?* "I don't know, Gus. . . . It's just a feeling I have. I'm scared."

"No kidding you're scared! You wouldn't be *normal* if you weren't a little scared." She's digging for her tube of orange lipstick. "But I always knew things were gonna work out for you, Sal. Ever since you walked into my office, I knew you were going to be a star."

I *tsk* loudly at her. "Gus, don't bullshit me. You only started returning my phone calls two months ago."

She widens her eyes, indignant. "That's my M.O.! Every agent uses it. The last thing you need is a star client with a swelled head!"

"It's because of Jack and you *know* it. That's why you started being so nice to me. *None* of this would be happening if it weren't for Jack." I motion to the door, indicating Griff and Marcy.

"Sal—would you have a little confidence in yourself? This is getting pathetic. I'm not going to say that it's *hurting* your situation that you're dating one of the most powerful men in the business. Griff has more pilots out there than Delta. He needs a guy like Jack Weaver on his side. But that doesn't mean you don't deserve it, Sal. This is a prime-time gig we're talking about. Everything you ever dreamed of is waiting for you out there. Everything you've worked so hard for. *Please* don't fuck this up."

"Tell them I want to think about it, Gus."

"Sally . . ."

"I'm serious."

She watches me worriedly for a moment, but finally finds her game face. "Sure, Sal. That was our plan from the start, remember? Play hard to get." She fixes her lipstick. "Just hurry up in here. I want you to finish your ice cream. You're turning into a bone rack."

She leaves me alone in the rest room. I stare at the closed door. I think of her words. *"Everything you ever dreamed of is waiting for you out there."* She's right. I feel like telling her, *"That's the problem."*

On the sidewalk after dinner everyone air-kisses good-bye. Griff and Marcy make me *insist* that I won't say no until I see their offer. Gus gives me one last look of concern before they all head off to their respective taxis. I decide to walk. Jack's coming to pick me up. It's our last night together before he leaves for L.A. and I need some time to think.

I walk slowly down Prince, past the mannequins in the shop windows, the laughing people in other restaurants. Horns honk. I hear a siren in the distance. Usually that sound makes me feel a twinge of compassion, but not tonight. I'm in the middle of my own emergency right now.

What if Gus is right? What if I *am* just being insecure because everything is happening so fast? Until a few weeks ago, I was spending my free time flipping through night school course guidelines. Isn't it understandable that I'd be a little paranoid about all this good luck?

I hear the wail of another siren, this one closer. Traffic pulls over to let an ambulance pass. For the first time I notice a flashing red knot of emergency vehicles a few blocks away. Fear creeps through me. As I get closer to the commotion, the sidewalk becomes dense with onlookers. I shoulder my way through the crowd, which separates for me easily, people interpreting my intensity as some personal attachment to the scene.

And maybe it is. Because everyone is standing in front of the convent.

I am out of breath by the time I make it to the front of the crowd. The arm of a brawny police officer bounces me back so hard that he knocks what's left of the wind out of me. But I pay no attention. I am too struck by the sight on the street. In the middle of the tangle of reporters and paramedics and onlookers is a small clearing where no one seems to want to step. There is a white shape on the sidewalk. It's a moment before I realize it's not a street person asleep under an old sheet, but a body, lying in an awkward position, knees pointing one way, arms the other. Beneath one end of the sheet, bare feet protrude, the heels rough and chapped. From the other wiry tufts of gray hair flutter in the wind.

No.

My gaze slowly lifts to scan the facade of the building, up to the third floor, where a metal window is bobbing back and forth in the wind.

I feel the first convulsion deep inside of me. I don't know whether I'm going to cry or scream.

The crowd jostles slightly and a slight-boned man with dark hair squeezes through, saying, "Excuse me . . . excuse me . . ." in a soft voice. He moves toward the clearing around the body; the police officers close in to hold him back until they see his white collar. Then they back away. The priest nods in gratitude and moves toward the shape, kneeling down beside it. He sets a leather case on the sidewalk beside him.

Several older women in the crowd cross themselves quickly. There is the clatter of rosary beads. It's the nuns, standing on the sidewalk, staring down at the lump beneath the sheet. They look so stricken, so frozen with fear. Amid the jaded reporters, the police officers and the trendy clubgoers, they almost seem like a distinct species let out of their pen.

The priest crosses himself, then grabs the edge of the pale sheet, pulling it back to reveal the Mother Superior's dead face. The crowd utters a subdued gasp. Several people push up behind me to get a better look. My heart starts to beat very slowly, very hard.

Beat . . . beat . . . beat . . .

I don't want to look at her, but I can't look away. Her eyes are open, staring toward the dark sky. Her frizzy gray hair flutters in the wind, her plump cheeks are grayed and still, slackened on her face. There is a stream of blood coming out of her nose, a second larger one oozing out of the corner of her mouth, both of them seeping slowly, coming to meet in a puddle of red on the sidewalk. The priest leans toward her. The first thing he does is close her eyes, using his thumb and forefinger to do so. I am surprised by how firmly he must press her sockets to do it, one eye, then the other, not quite in sync. It's nothing like the gentle sweep of an open hand that is enough to close the eyes of actors playing dead in movies. He retrieves a Bible and a rosary from his case. He crosses himself and begins to read. His voice is low and only disconnected words carry toward me.

". . . I am . . . resurrection and the . . ."

". . . blessed be . . . name . . . the Lord. . . ."

Somebody behind me mutters something to a friend; someone else shushes them, as if they're being rude in a theater.

A rustle of wind flaps the Mother Superior's sheet, giving her the momentary appearance of kicking it off and starting to rise, perhaps to better hear what the priest is saying to her. But she does not rise; she lies still, and like the rest of us, doesn't hear what the priest is saying.

When it seems like someone at the back of the crowd is going to yell, "Speak up!" because the tension of his soft voice is too much, the priest finally finishes. He kisses his fingertips, gently runs his thumb on the woman's forehead. He pulls the sheet up and once again the woman is just a form on the sidewalk. I finally feel the release of a tear, cooling my eyes.

The police officers close in quickly. The paramedics position a stretcher on the sidewalk next to the body. They kneel down, silently synchronize counts—*one, two, three*—and heave the corpse onto the gurney. The body responds with surprising looseness as it is jostled. The stretcher is carried to the waiting ambulance and slid into the back. Onlookers respond with a mixture of disappointment and relief as the doors close with a dull *cluh-thump*. The ambulance drives away, siren quiet. The crowd begins to break up, whispers turn to murmurs, turn to voices, and, somewhere in the distance, to laughter as we all move on with our lives.

I sit on the church steps in the darkness waiting for Jack. There is a sharp ache in my chest. *What other proof do you need, Sally? You were supposed to see her next week. . . . Of course the Devil would stop you from seeing her . . . she would have helped you do what's right. . . .*

But her window blows open in the wind. She almost fell out when I was there. . . . It *could* have been an accident. . . .

Another accident?

The black Porsche pulls up, the engine growling. The passenger-side window hums down. I see his shadow inside the car. Detect the glint of his smile. "Need a ride?" he asks, playfully suggestive.

It is several moments before I have the strength to force myself to stand up and get inside.

THIRTY-TWO

When devils will their blackest sins put on,
they do suggest at first with heavenly shows . . .

WILLIAM SHAKESPEARE

JACK'S apartment is chilly the next morning. My bare feet are cold on the wood floor. I hold one of his robes tightly around me, clicking through the channels on the big plasma-screen TV in his living room. I left him sleeping in the bedroom. I've got the volume turned down low so I don't wake him.

Diane Sawyer interviewing Hillary Clinton.

I quickly change the channel.

A gardening show.

An infomercial about a juicer.

There. The local news. The word "Live" appears on the screen. I see the familiar pale brickwork of the convent. A lovely African-American reporter is standing outside it. The collar of her beige trench coat is turned up. "*. . . Sister Margaret Ripley was a respected member of the Order of St. Francis,*" she is saying, "*and a prominent member of the community . . .*"

The image cuts to a photograph of Sister Margaret, the one of her standing with Giuliani.

". . . spent six years operating a mission in Guatemala . . ."

Another still shot of the photograph of her in the dusty village surrounded by smiling children.

The screen cuts back to the reporter standing outside the convent. In the absence of the body, the camera zooms in on the blotch of reddish brown on the sidewalk; it's protected by a wide boundary of yellow police tape, beyond which pedestrians stop and stare, like tourists clustered around the Mona Lisa at the Louvre.

"The incident appears to have been an accident, but the police have not ruled out foul play."

Foul play?

". . . One thing is certain—the children at Samaritan House who looked forward to Sister Margaret's visits every day will miss her terribly."

There is a shot of a bright playroom full of children's furniture and colorful toys. The camera closes in on a young boy with curly dark hair, his finger in his mouth. He looks at the microphone jabbed toward his face. *"I'll miss her. But my mom told me she's in heaven now."*

The scene cuts back to the reporter, standing outside the convent. *"Debra Wilson, live for NY4 News . . ."*

"Oh, God." I start pacing the room, running my hands through my hair. This is crazy. He wouldn't actually *kill* someone. . . . Is that what I'm thinking? That he'd actually go into the convent and push an old nun out a window?

"Hey." I hear his voice from behind me. I turn to see him standing in the doorway, bare-chested, in a pair of drawstring pajama bottoms.

"I'm just watching the news," I tell him. "It's freaking me out, Jack. I was going to *see* her next week."

"I know, Sal. But you'll find another nun to help you with your research."

I stare at him, stunned. "That's not the *point.*"

He seems to catch himself. "You're right. I'm sorry." He walks over and puts his arms around my waist. "I didn't mean it that way. I just don't want you to make this any harder on yourself than it already is." He kisses me lightly, then moves into the kitchen. "You want to go out for breakfast?"

"I'm not hungry," I say, following him into the other room.

He shrugs and says he'll wait until the plane. He takes out a carton of O.J. Pours himself a glass.

I try to keep my voice light when I say, "Where did you say you were last night?"

"Working."

"At the office?"

"Yeah. Why?"

"No reason."

He puts the orange juice back in the fridge. Closes the door.

I let a beat pass. "Jack, I'm thinking about calling the police."

There's a strained beat of silence. *"Why?"*

"They're not sure how she died. They don't know if it was an accident or foul play. Maybe I could tell them that her window flew open when I was there. It might help them find the truth."

He lets out a dry laugh at the word *truth*. *"Truth?* What *is* the truth? Were you there when it happened?"

"No, but . . ."

"Do you know for sure she fell out the window?"

"No . . ."

"Or if she was pushed?"

I stammer a little.

"Then how can you help them? It's just going to be a waste of time. You'll have to go down to the station. Answer a bunch of questions. And what if *they* get to you?" He motions to the TV, indicating the reporters. "Is this the kind of publicity you need at this stage in your career?"

I feel a quiver of uncertainty. I remember my mother taking me roughly by the hand and leading me down the driveway. *No comment no comment.* I'm ashamed of my own reticence. Maybe this is how the

Devil does it. Maybe he whittles down your conscience one self-interest at a time.

He gives a fatalistic shrug. "Do what you want—just be prepared, that's all." His tone brightens suddenly. "Now, I've got to finish packing. But while I'm doing that . . ." He walks to the console table and returns with a slim red envelope. He slides it across the counter to me. It's a first-class ticket to Los Angeles leaving late Friday afternoon.

I make a little whimpering noise. "Jack—I told you I can't go."

"I just want you to think about it. This could be a great opportunity for you. If you're going anywhere in this business, you're going to end up in L.A. at some point. The sooner you get a feel for the place, the better. I could even set up a few meetings at some studios for you."

That one, I admit, plucks grudgingly at my interest, as does the fact he's staying at the Four Seasons. But I shake my head. "I don't think so, Jack. Not this time."

He gives a sad, closed-lipped smile, as if to say I can't blame him for trying.

I stare after him as he leaves the room. *Damnit.* Is this really happening to me? One minute, he's the most incredible man I've ever met. The next, he's the Devil, promising me every worldly desire in exchange for my soul. It's like I'm looking at one of those optical illusions you used to see in high school art classes. One minute a drawing looks like a beautiful woman with her face turned away, the next, it's an ugly hag with a hooked nose and a hood over her head. It's as if he's both things at the same time—only this time it's not as easy as writing *optical illusion* in your notebook and moving on.

The crash is so loud it makes me jump. A shattering sound, like a rack of dishes falling in a department store. I run toward the direction of the crash and find him in the bathroom. The mirror above the sink in front of him is broken, lying in gleaming shards on the floor. His hand is bleeding into the sink. I can see his ribs heaving. Every muscle in his arms and chest shakes.

"I just don't understand, Sally," he says, not looking at me. "I don't understand what's happening to me . . ."

I do. You're the fucking Devil. And you're falling in love.

WE pull up across from my building; he takes the Porsche out of gear. There is a small knick on his hand; it stopped bleeding even before I could get a Band-Aid out for him. I don't know why his outburst didn't frighten me more. I guess there's one thing he promised me that I believe no matter what: *that he'd never hurt me—not as long as I live.*

"I'm sorry," he says; his voice is weak. He hooks his forearms over the steering wheel, lowering his head. "I guess it's getting to me more than I thought. This David thing. I know I told you to take your time, but I didn't know how I would feel about you." When he looks at me, he's never seemed so vulnerable—he's never seemed so *real*—before. "Now, I just love you so much . . ."

"I love you, too," I whisper.

And, *God help me,* I mean it.

He looks down at the airline ticket in my lap; the folder is slightly rumpled from my playing with it so much. "Please think about it," he says. "If you're not going to do it for me, do it for yourself. Really listen to your heart. And if you do that and can still tell me that you want to stay with David, I'll accept it. I won't *like* it, but I'll accept it. Because I know you'll be doing what makes you happy." He leans over and kisses me, slow and sweet. When our lips part, I feel the first inch of three thousand miles begin to separate us.

I get out of the car. He rolls his window down. There's a cocky smile on his face. "Remember, if you change your mind—bring your sunblock. It's supposed to be eighty-five and sunny all weekend."

The car pulls away with a playful screech. I watch after him. *Damnit, he doesn't make this easy for me, does he?*

Inside the vestibule, I see that my mail slot is full. I haven't checked it in days. I'm just so distracted. I find a few bills. Some useless flyers. I'm still holding the plane ticket. I rip it once . . . twice . . . and again so I can't change my mind. I toss it into the recycling bin along with a Kmart circular. Then I stomp upstairs to clean my apartment. David gets out of the hospital today.

THIRTY-THREE

How agrees the devil and thee about thy soul?

WILLIAM SHAKESPEARE

"*OKAY, everyone,*" the director says over the intercom. "*Scene six. Meridien in the garden. Places.*"

I move to my mark. I can't see much beyond the bright lights shining in my face. The darkness beyond the circle of light glints with eyeglasses, watches, ladders. I suppress a yawn. Last night was David's first night at my place. He and his cast kept me up half the night thunking around on the futon.

"*VTR 22 ready with playback.*"

"*You ready, Sal?*"

I nod blindly. I feel the lights on my skin. The black dress absorbs the heat, holding it like a handprint.

"*Quiet on the set.*"

"*Quiet, people.*"

"*Roll tape.*"

"*Rolling.*"

"*In three, two— Wait a second. Stop tape.*" A beat goes by. "*Sally?*"

I turn in the direction of the voice.

The first AD steps out of the shadows. "Sal, you're not supposed to be crying in this scene."

I look at him in confusion. "Was I crying?" Just then large tears break from my eyes and spill down my cheeks. "Oh, sorry," I say. I wipe my tears with my fingers, surprised.

The AD yells tiredly: *"Makeup!"*

A woman emerges from the darkness, with a sponge and some powder. She dabs at my moistened cheeks. "You're all set, Demi," she jokes, then disappears again.

"From the top of eight," says the director over the intercom. *"Roll tape."*

"Rolling."

"In three, two . . ."

I manage to get through the scene without any more tears; when the director yells *"Cut!"* I rush through the darkness of the studio into the white hall, down the white hall, and into my dressing room. Raine is there, touching up her nail polish. She sees the look on my face.

"Oh, oh. You look like you need a martini."

I shake my head, sniffle a bit, slide some of her lingerie off one of the chairs, and flop down. She knows about my dilemma—at least, the made-for-TV version of it. I didn't tell her *everything.* As far as she's concerned, I'm in the middle of a love triangle. Which isn't a *complete* lie.

"Raine . . . I have a strange question."

"Shoot." She's blowing on her nails.

"I know you're going to think this sounds crazy, but . . . do you think you could resist temptation?"

She curls her lip. "Honey—you're talking to the wrong girl. I went into Barneys yesterday for a pair of stockings and came out with earrings, two bottles of perfume, and some Jimmy Choo slingbacks."

I smile weakly. "I'm not talking about a shoe sale . . . or a piece of chocolate cake . . . or another martini at lunch. I'm talking about *real* temptation. The kind you read about in the Bible."

"Sally, you're not taking any of those little green pills the boys in editing are handing out, are you? Because it's a little early to start with the addiction thing."

"It's not drugs Raine! I'm talking about *life.* I'm talking about good and evil and God and the Devil and what if . . . just what if all this"—I motion around me—"really does make sense and there *is* a reason for things and it really *does* matter if we do what's right?"

She narrows her eyes on me. "I know what's going on here. You're overidentifying with your character. It happens to a lot of actors. You should've tried living with me when I first took this gig. I was acting like such a bitch, my husband—at the *time*—was on PMS red alert for a year. Same thing is happening to you. You're playing a nun, so it's bringing out your martyr complex."

"I *don't* have a martyr complex."

She arches an eyebrow skeptically. "Yeah, right. But don't take it personally. A lot of women have one. How can we help it? When our most long-standing role model is an all-suffering, all-sorrowful virgin?"

I shrug. She has a point.

"You want my advice, Sally?"

"Of course," I say.

"There are three rules I live by." She counts on her fingers, expertly fanning her wet nails away from each other. "One, never let a good accountant go. Two, never eat more than four hundred calories at one sitting. And three—and this is the most important one." She lets a long, dramatic beat pass. Being a soap actress, she knows all about long, dramatic beats. "Listen to your heart," she says with all the wisdom in the world. When she sees my reaction, her expression turns deadpan. "What the hell are you laughing for?"

THIRTY-FOUR

Watch and pray, that ye enter not into temptation:
the spirit indeed is willing, but the flesh is weak.

MATTHEW 26:41

DAVID is sitting amid his outcropping of pillows on the futon when I open the door. I'm out of breath from climbing three flights with groceries.

"Hey, Florence," he says. As in Nightingale. It's my new nickname.

"Sorry I'm late. I had to go to two places."

He smiles. "Did you get it?"

I reach in one of the bags and try to bring a triumphant smile to my face. It's a copy of *Rambo: First Blood, Part 2*. He's going through the whole roster of eighties action flicks—Stallone, Schwarzenegger, Willis before he expanded his repertoire. He says ridiculous macho role models are even funnier when he can't so much as answer the phone.

I go to the VCR and insert the new tape. I hit PLAY and try to adjust the white flecks and horizontal hash of bad tracking. David gets comfortable on the futon, a big grin on his face. I sort through the groceries, hand him a couple of the things he wanted me to pick up—Doritos and some plain M&M's. Everything else I carry into the kitchen, stopping on the way to pick up what I can of the stray garbage piling up around him: dirty glasses, candy wrappers, empty soda cans. In the kitchen, I put the food away. Then I pile the dirty dishes into the sink. I turn on the water. Squeeze out a little soap.

This is the right thing to do, Sal, I'm telling myself, as I sink my arms elbow deep in the sudsy water. *You feel good about this. Really you do.*

I scrape at a congealed ketchup stain on a plate from the scrambled eggs I made him for breakfast.

There's a muffled voice from the living room. I turn the water off. "Yeah?"

"Hate to bug ya, but when you're finished in there, it's time to change my bandage."

Oh, shit. Seems my Florence Nightingale title is in jeopardy here. "Be right there."

"Don't worry—it can wait till you're done."

"I don't want it to get infected." I dry my hands, gather the gauze and ointment, and join him in the living room.

On TV, Sly Stallone is flexing a muscle the existence of which I'm only peripherally aware from a poster I saw in a doctor's office once. I look down at David's head. The bandage has soaked through with the now familiar mix of brownish, pinkish green from the combination of ointment and dried blood. I remember how quickly the cut on Jack's hand started to heal. Gingerly, I pull at the edge of the gauze and it gives easily on the skin of David's scalp, revealing the raw-looking wound beneath. His hair is growing in a little, looking like tiny pepper flakes sprinkled around the pink gash. I dab a little salve onto my clean finger and pat gently.

On TV, Rambo is reloading his gun.

David says, "You think it looks like Florida or Italy?"

"What?"

"The bald spot. Is it shaped like Florida or Italy?"

"I don't know."

"I thought Italy at first. But it's too thick at the bottom. What do you think?"

I study it. Cock my head on an angle. "Florida, I think."

"Shit. Italy's skinnier." He reaches for his bag of M&M's. "Uh-oh."

"What?"

"These are peanut."

"They *are?*" He shows me the yellow bag. I stare at it in shock. "I thought for *sure* they were plain."

"You trying to do me in or what?" He grins.

"Yeah, right," I say, giving a light laugh. But I don't know how I got peanut. I know David is allergic—not deathly allergic like some people, who can't even get on an airplane because the people sitting next to them are munching on peanut snacks, but bad enough that if he ate *whole* peanuts, I'd be digging for the emergency EpiPen in the bottom of his knapsack. "I'll go back. I'll get you plain."

"Don't worry." He tosses the bag on the table. "You can get them tomorrow."

And that word—*tomorrow*—is like the roof caving in.

Because tomorrow is Saturday. Long, lonely Saturday cooped up in the apartment with him— not even the excuse of going to the studio.

Then Sunday.

I won't even be able to talk to Jack. I remember his voice.

"It's going to be eighty-five and sunny all weekend."

I sigh inwardly.

"Blessed is the one who endureth temptation. . . ."

"There." I pat the fresh bandage lightly on his head. "All better."

"Thanks, Flo." He leans forward. I automatically fluff the pillow behind his back.

I go into the kitchen to finish the dishes. The steam rises up from the sink. I work slowly. I'm in no hurry to get back into bed with David. At least we haven't had to have sex yet. This must be a record for a nongeriatric couple. Every free hour in bed together for almost three consecutive days and no action. Last night he tried. I'm not sure what time it was, but he scooched over to me and began kissing my neck. I brought a soft snore to my throat and pretended I was asleep.

When I'm finished washing the dishes, I pour myself a big glass of wine and go back into the living room. I very carefully crawl onto the futon, trying not to disturb his cast. It means I have to lie on the outside quarter of the bed. That's the way I'm sleeping, too—or at least *trying* to sleep.

On TV, it's turned into a real squibfest. Explosions. Machine guns.

But I'm not really paying attention. I'm thinking of Jack. Then again, I'm *always* thinking of Jack. I'm aware that I couldn't stop thinking of him even if I *wanted* to, the same way I couldn't suffocate myself by holding my breath.

David shifts his cast a bit and I have to adjust my position to see the screen. *How am I going to lie here for the next ninety minutes watching Sly tear up the jungle?*

I'll go insane. I know I will.

"You know what, David?" I say, sitting up. "I feel really bad about those M&M's. I'm going to get you plain."

"Sal, I said you don't have to . . ."

"Really—no trouble. I need the air anyway."

W HEN I get down to the street, the sky is the color of bruises. I look guiltily at the church. Mother Margaret's funeral is on Sunday. There's going to be a full mass; several cardinals are attending and some people from the Vatican. I know I should go—pay my respects. But I'm afraid the minute I walked in the door, she'd sit bolt upright in her coffin and point at me: *"That's the Devil's whore! Don't let her in!"*

The store smells sweetly of candy bars, fresh tobacco, spilled Tide. I wander gloomily to the snack aisle, carefully scrutinizing the colorful wrappings. I pick up a bag of M&M's, check to make sure I get plain instead of peanut this time, then drag my feet, like a sulking child, to the cash register. There's an old woman ahead of me buying dandruff shampoo with a plastic change purse full of pennies. She clicks them out onto the counter with trembling fingers. I'm actually grateful for the delay. I'm in no hurry to get back to my patient.

On the dusty window ledge behind the cash, along with the cigarettes, the Elvis busts, and a cardboard skeleton that says HAPPY HAL-
LOWEEN, are a few plastic religious trinkets with gold skin, flowing
robes, and rubies for eyes. I see these statues every time I come in here,
but I'm not positive what religion they represent and I'm afraid it
would be rude of me to ask. I wonder if those gold-faced gods tell
their worshipers things like "Happy are you who weep now" and
"Blessed is the one who endureth temptation." I've skimmed enough
Eastern religion books on slow days at the Backburner to know that
they probably do.

But could you imagine if that's not true?

Think about it. What if all the things we learn about good and
evil, God and the Devil, suffering and sacrifice, just don't apply anymore? What if it all just started as a way to make sure we didn't club
each other to death for that extra piece of mastodon meat? What if it
doesn't help to turn the other cheek? What if the meek *don't* inherit the
earth? I remember Sister Ruth again. Oh, how I absorbed that particular lesson. It became my bumper sticker. It may have been the first
time I heard the word, but eventually it started to make sense to me.
Meek. It sounded like the noises mice made. *Eek* and *squeak.* I thought
if I wanted God to love me more, I had to be more like a mouse. Small
and shoulderless and running away when the lights came on. It's
almost as if I started to see my life as the physical space around me.
Every year I tried to take up less and less room. But still, it did not
seem that God loved me more.

So what would happen if I wasn't so timid all the time? What if I
just straightened up and stretched out my arms into the forbidden territory around me? Would God be angry at me? Would he strike me
dead? What if nothing happened? What if Jack is right? What if you *can*
just take what you want? What if happiness on earth really *is* possible?

I feel a shiver.

I don't know what's worse. That I'm wrong about him now. Or
that I've been wrong about everything else before him.

I am jerked out of my thoughts by the cashier, who coughs in a bored kind of way. I didn't notice that the old lady has already tottered away with her dandruff shampoo.

"You ready or what?"

"Oh, sorry." I put the M&M's on the counter with a jumbly click. The cashier picks up the candies and begins ringing them through. "Wait a second!" I grab the M&M's out of his hand and stare at them in disbelief. *Shit!* They're peanut! I can't believe it. They're peanut!

A dull panic goes through me. Am I losing my mind?

"Are you gettin' those or what?"

"They're the wrong kind. I need . . . plain."

"So get plain." He shrugs. *Out on a day pass or what?*

I spin around and head back into the aisles, wandering blindly. I return with my purchase, putting it on the counter quickly, afraid someone will hack my arm off when they see what I've done. The cashier looks down at the counter.

"So you're gettin' this now?" he asks.

"Yes."

"Are you sure 'bout that?"

I think about it. I nod, almost panic-stricken. He shakes his head and lets out a big sigh, then rings in my bottle of Coppertone.

On my way back to the apartment, I dial Jack's cell. He answers. The sound of his voice—just the sound of his voice—makes me feel better, as if I'm lying down to sleep after a month of insomnia.

"Jack—I'm coming to L.A."

I can almost hear him smiling. "You've made me the happiest man in the world."

"But it doesn't *mean* anything," I tell him. "It doesn't mean that . . . that I've decided anything."

"About David you mean?"

"No, no, about . . ." I sigh desperately. I want to ask him. *Shouldn't*

I ask him? Isn't that the safe thing to do? *Are you the Devil, Jack? Just tell me. Let me off the hook. Make this easy for me.*

But what if he said he was—what would I do then? What would I truly do?

"I just need a break," I tell him weakly. "But I'm buying my own ticket!"

DAVID is lying on the sofa when I get back to the apartment. He's munching on Doritos. His pillows are freshly fluffed, his bandage white and clean. I hear myself say, "David, we have to talk."

"Sure, Sal. But can we do it later. I love this part."

"David—it's really important."

"Sal?" A little whimper. He points to the TV, silently complaining. I look at the screen to see Sly Stallone, his face smeared with grime, wincing with effort, trying to tie up some wounds.

I throw up my hands in a gesture of futility. "Don't say I didn't try."

I go to the closet. I rummage through it, throwing my navy blue duffel bag out into the middle of the room. I grab for a few more things, tossing them out behind me. My bathing suit. My makeup case. *Clunk! Thunk! Kerplunk!* They all land in the middle of the floor. When I emerge from the closet, I see David leaning up on his elbow, holding the bottle of suntan lotion, checking the bottom of the other-wise empty paper bag.

"Where are my M&M's?"

"I'm sorry. I didn't get them." I stand up quickly and go to my dresser. There is a kind of momentum in my heart, as if a piston were working there that would never get started again if I stopped it.

"Were they out?"

"No. I just didn't have enough money." I fold up my T-shirts, tucking them into the corners of the duffel bag.

"So you got *sun*tan lotion instead?"

"Yes."

It's then he realizes what's happening. "Sal—why are you pack-ing?"

"Because I'm going away for a few days." I count out four pairs of panties—my *best* panties—and set them aside.

"O-kay," he says, in the tone people use when they're humoring lunatics. "I'll bite. Where are you going?"

"To L.A." I pivot on my shoes, hurry into the bathroom, collect my shampoo. Conditioner. Deodorant.

I hear him mumble something, but I can't quite make it out. I return to the living room with an armful of plastic bottles.

"What is it?" he asks. "Is it like a gig or something? Did Gus call while you were at the store?"

I stop in my tracks. *Oh, Christ.* I stare at him for a moment, actu-ally consider saying, Yes, David, that's what it is. A gig. But instead I shake my head.

"What, then?"

I look from his cast to his bandage to the yellowish bruises around his eyes. A million excuses occur to me in the next minute—a million of them—and each and every one of them would do. Instead I take a deep breath and reach out into the forbidden territory around me: "I'm going with Jack."

He lets out a skeptical laugh. "Ex-*kewz* me? I thought I told you to stop seeing him."

"I *can't.*"

"Why not?"

I take another deep breath. Steady myself. "Because I'm in love with him, David . . ."

Whoooshhhh! There. I said it.

I brace myself for God's inevitable fury. I look up, half expecting the heavens to crack open and God to reach down and strike me dead. But the heavens are quiet. All I can hear is the tinny *rat-tat* of tiny machine guns on TV. I feel my shoulders relax. *Wow . . .* So the world doesn't self-destruct when you take what you want from life—at least, not immediately.

He looks around the room in disbelief, as if checking for hidden cameras. "You can't be serious."

"I'm sorry, David—really I am. *Please* don't make this any harder for me."

"Harder for *you?*" he squeals. "Hah! Harder for *you?* That's a joke! Look at me here! Look at the shape I'm in! I just lost my job. I was hit by a goddamn car, fercrissakes! I have a broken leg! Bruises everywhere! A fuckin' bald spot on my head in the shape of *Florida!*" He delivers the last injury as if it were clearly the worst. "And now you're telling me that you're in love with that snake and you're going out to California to *be* with him?!"

"David! Don't *say* it like that! You make it sound so awful!"

"Well, it *is* awful, Sal! Jeezus! It *is!*"

I feel myself weaken. I look down guiltily and realize I'm twisting—*shit*—I'm twisting a black lace thong in my hands. I quickly shove it behind my back.

"What is it about this guy, anyway, Sal? Is it his money? Is that it?"

"*No!*"

"Then what is it?" He's sitting up now, his cast angled off the side of the bed. "It's because he gets you work, isn't it?"

"He *doesn't* get me work! I get those parts on my own!"

He tilts his head on an angle, his voice skeptical. "Come on, Sal. He comes onto the scene and all of sudden your career starts taking off? It's a little coincidental, don't you think?"

I run my hand through my hair. I think he knows he's getting to me. He comes in for the kill.

"That's what people think, you know," he says. "That you're fucking him to get work. Everyone's talking about it."

I feel the sting of an old, stale fear, but I bite it back. "I don't give a *shit* what people think, okay?" I start packing again. "I can't waste my whole life worrying about that."

He laughs at that. "Since when do *you* not care what people think?"

I don't answer. Still shoving, folding, zipping. I hear him standing up, thunking over to me on his good leg.

"What the hell's gotten into you, Sal? Ever since you met this guy you've changed completely."

"So? Maybe I *wanted* to change."

He lets out an angry squeal. *"Want* to change? Why would you *want* to change? You're a great person!" He stops himself. "Correction. You *were* a great person. Now I hardly even recognize you. I mean, *look* at you. Running off to be with him just because he asks you to. Letting him make all your decisions for you."

I stand up then and face him. *"He* didn't make this decision for me, okay? *I* made this decision. It might be the first decision I've made for myself in a very long time. And you know what? It feels pretty damn good."

He flaps his hand at me. "Well, good for you. I'm glad you get your rocks off hurting other people."

That one shocks me. "David, don't say that! I didn't want to hurt you! Hurting you is the *last* thing I wanted to do!"

"Bullshit. If it was the *last* thing you wanted to do, you wouldn't be doing it." He bounces around on his good leg another moment, searching for his crutches. They're in the corner. He hops toward them, but knocks his cast on the trunk. *"Ow!"*

I rush over to help, but he pushes me away.

"Don't touch me! I don't need your help! I don't *want* your help!"

He seethes in silence for a moment, then, trying to sound masculine, he says, "Just—just hand me my crutches."

I fetch his crutches and he snaps them angrily out of my grasp, tucking them under his arms. He thunks across the room, fumbles with the door a moment. He seems to remember something. He digs in his pocket and drops something on the table beside the door. It's his copy of the key.

He turns around and snarls at me: "I hope you both *rot* in hell!" he says. He tries to slam the door behind him, but the door thonks on the rubber tip of one of his crutches. He grits his teeth, gets the crutch out of the way. He glares at me one last time and gives it an acceptable slam. I hear him hobbling down the hall on his crutches.

On TV, Sly Stallone runs in to save the day.

THIRTY-FIVE

Few men have the virtue to withstand the highest bidder.

GEORGE WASHINGTON

The next day, two hours before my flight is supposed to take off, a storm moves in over the city. Weighty gray clouds snap with lightning and rumble with thunder.

That can't be a good omen.

I stand downstairs in the vestibule of my building in a new black DKNY suit, holding my duffel bag and an armload of scripts Gus wants me to read. I stare trepidatiously from the gray and roiling sky to the slippery, wet streets below. I see an old woman hobbling down the sidewalk, carrying a black umbrella. She makes her way up the steps of the church, shakes out her umbrella, and with some effort opens the great wooden doors and disappears inside. I stare at the doors. The wooden archways to another world.

I don't know what makes me leave the comfort of my apartment building. I don't know what makes me step outside. It's a sudden desire—maybe even a *need*—to be inside that church. I feel the plucking chill of the rain on my hands and cheeks. I tent the scripts over my hair and climb the steps to the church. For the first time since I moved here, I put my hand on the great wooden handle and open the door. It's not as heavy as it looks, floating open easily on well-oiled hinges. I step inside and the familiar smell of wood benches and candle wax wash over me. I close my eyes for a moment and I am not in New York, but tugging on my mother's hand as she brings me to confession for the first time.

I go to the basin of holy water and cross myself. It's been so long, but I haven't forgotten. I walk down the aisle slowly. There are a few people scattered along the pews at random intervals, heads bent. Nobody turns to look at me. The woman with the umbrella is up ahead, her head lowered in prayer. I feel the great peak of the church open up around me. Graceful arching beams reach toward the ceiling. The Stations of the Cross are carved in bronze along the walls. Above the organ behind me is the round stained-glass window, even more beautiful from the inside than it is from the outside.

I take a seat near the back. The pew makes a muted, cracking noise as I sit down. I try to set my duffel bag on the seat beside me, but it slips off, thunking on the floor. I leave it there, not wanting to attract more attention. I stare at the altar and, above it, the enormous wooden crucifix, Jesus on the cross. His head lowered. His ribs showing.

I bring my hands together and close my eyes. I hesitate for a moment, uncertain how to carry on, uncertain how to make my plea acceptable to God.

Dear God . . . I know I don't pray to you very often, except when I'm on an audition, and I can't imagine how stupid you must think I am to start pray-ing to you now. But the truth is, I need a little help. I guess I don't have to tell you what's happening to me. If it is happening—you probably already know. And you probably know how confused I am. I remember hearing that you're not supposed to ask for signs from God, but I thought, in this case, keeping in mind the extent of my dilemma, you might make an exception. So if you could just give me a sign—just any kind of sign—that the man I'm in love with is really the Devil . . . I hesitate, wondering if I should have used his name inside a church. *I'll leave him. I promise. Because more than anything—maybe even more than being happy—I want to do the right thing.*

Amen.

I open my eyes and look around for any indication that God was listening. Somebody in a confessional coughs. But that's about it.

THE silver-haired limo driver is waiting for me, peeking in the doors of my apartment building. He seems confused when he sees me coming from the church. He holds the back door open for me. I tell him we have to make one stop before the airport and I slip into the false black comfort of the limousine.

THE colorful shops and boutiques of the Village seem morose in the downpour. They look so moody, in fact, that it has the effect of making the Backburner look more cheerful by comparison.

It's been a few weeks since I've been here. I've had to cancel out on Jeremy the last few weekend shifts.

To be with Jack.

I open the door and the bell jingles in a sad, familiar way. The smell of dust and must and charcoal permeate my senses. But the shop seems different; it's like visiting your old grade school and looking at all the tiny desks and half-height water fountains and wondering if you were ever really that *small.*

The curtain at the back of the store puffs a little as Jeremy reluctantly emerges in response to the bell. When he sees me, he freezes in his tracks. He betrays a small, stained smile. "Is it Saturday already?"

"Jeremy . . . I have to talk to you."

He leans against the doorjamb, watching me expectantly. *This oughta be good,* he seems to say.

"I'm sorry, but I don't think I'm going to be able to make it into work anymore," I begin uncertainly. He doesn't react. "It's just that things are so busy at the studio and there might be this new part coming up on *Precinct* and I just don't know when I'm going to have time off, so I just wanted you to know so that you can hire somebody else full-time."

"And, of course, there's the matter of the network president," he says.

I lower my eyes. He walks to the cash register, opening it with a familiar clang. "Would you like your final week's pay in cash or check?"

"Jeremy—"

He sifts through the bills. "It'll have to be check. I don't have enough cash."

"That's not why I'm here."

"Then why *are* you here?"

"I told you, to give you my notice. And . . . to say good-bye, I guess. I mean, I hope we can still be friends."

He shrugs nonchalantly. "Of course we can be friends, Sally. I sincerely hope things work out for you. But somehow . . . I doubt it."

I stare at him in confusion.

"Think about it," he says. "If there were really happy endings, why would people in your business get so rich making sequels?" He gives me a dry, stain-toothed smile, then trots to the back of the shop.

"*THANK you for your patience, ladies and gentleman,*" the pilot says. A tense hush takes over the plane. I peer outside the cabin window. The rain beats down on the tarmac. Gray clouds obscure the distant skyline. We've been waiting half an hour to take off.

Half an hour is a long time when you're contemplating the fate of your soul.

There's a high-pitched whining sound and the plane begins to taxi along the runway. I grip the armrests of my seat tightly. I hate flying at the best of times, let alone during a storm. I look around at the other passengers. Is there anything about these people that would lead me to believe that I'm destined to die with them? Does anyone look like he might suffer from air rage? Do any of them seem to harbor anti-American ideals? But no. They just seem like average people, reading their newspapers, clicking away at their laptops.

The engines squeal. Speed picks up. I feel myself pressed against the seat as the engines strain to break the wet bonds of earth. When the tires finally do leave the surface of the runway, the wings dip treacherously to one side. Someone at the back gasps loudly. The plane rights itself and heads up through the storm. We move higher . . . higher . . . waiting for clear sky . . . But the gray clouds thunder resistance and the rain pelts against the windows in horizontal slashes, straight and silvery, like knife blades. The plane bucks and swerves. The flight attendants don't get up. The seat belt light bings and bings, reminding us to stay seated. A baby starts to cry somewhere, which makes me more afraid than anything, because I remember reading that babies, like animals, have some sixth sense, some premonition of doom.

The people around me have put down their newspapers and closed their computers. Some are looking nervously out the windows. Still others have pressed their heads against the headrests with their eyes closed. I can see some of their lips moving.

They're praying. So do I.

Our Father who art in heaven, hallowed be thy name . . .

It's amazing how I remember the words, even though I haven't recited the Lord's Prayer in years. It's like turning on the radio, hearing "Girls Just Wanna Have Fun" for the first time in a decade and being able to sing along.

. . . and forgive us our trespasses as we forgive those who . . .

And then it comes to me. This is it! This is my sign from God! The sign that I shouldn't be with Jack. God's not going to save me. He's going to kill me, and this is how he's going to do it. In a plane crash! Oh, how can I be such a hypocrite? Asking God not to lead me into temptation when I don't have the guts to do it myself?

But then something happens. The plane suddenly lifts from the storm and steadies itself. I look out the window. Blue sky and pristine sunlight are on all sides, for as far as I can see. A few people cheer out loud. I hear the welcoming *bing!* of the seat belt light going off. And I am safe.

For now.

THIRTY-SIX

Better to reign in hell, than to serve in heav'n.

JOHN MILTON

I get off at LAX legless and jittery. I'm afraid that the narrow escape on the plane was just luck, God toying with me, a stay of execution. I make my way through the airport, my knees shaking beneath me.

Nosuchthingasthedevil . . . nosuchthingasthedevil . . .

I see an uneven, smiling line of chauffeurs in black caps by the exit. A little man, shorter than me by a head, with a near toothless grin, parched skin, and dark sunglasses, holds a white sign that reads:

SALLY CARPEN-

ter

I approach him and smile tentatively. He seems friendly enough, though I can't see his eyes behind the sunglasses, which are too big for his face.

"Mr. Weaver sent me, miss. He apologizes, but he was held up."

"Of course." I relinquish my bag to him, though he seems less capable of managing it than I am.

I follow him out through the automatic doors. A gust of California air wafts at me, unexpectedly and unnaturally hot, as if created not by the sun but by a furnace or fire. The driver holds the door of a black limo open for me. I duck inside. It smells of Jack's cologne. His brand of cigarettes. I endure the near Pavlovian reaction I have to him: a wave of love—and a knot of fear.

The driver turns around to face me, wrinkles coiling in his neck. "Mr. Weaver asked me to call him the moment you arrived." He motions to a satinwood compartment in front of me. I open it. It's a car phone. As the driver pulls onto the gray gridwork of freeways surrounding the airport, I pick up the phone.

"You came," he says. I can hear the smile in his voice. And the relief.

I try to sound cheerful. "You bet!"

"I'm glad I got a chance to talk to you before you heard . . ."

"Heard what?"

I feel apprehensive. I see a few trade papers lying on the seat beside me. By the time I read the headline, Jack is already telling me: He's being appointed president and CEO of the newly formed parent company, *United Geostar Media*.

"Congratulations, Jack," I say, trying to sound happy for him. He tells me he'll see me soon. I hang up the phone. A headline in *Daily Variety* reads: WEAVER SET TO HEAD NEW CONGLOM. I scan the details, all the while trying to calm myself down.

This doesn't mean anything. He got promoted. That's all. He's a smart guy. He deserved it. This is business . . . just business . . . mergers happen everywhere . . . all the time.

It's *not* some sinister plot to take over the world!

Then I see a small article in the very bottom corner of page 4: AUDITOR FACES PRISON ON FRAUD CHARGES.

It's about Martin Fletcher. The New York Attorney General's office filed criminal charges against him. His sentencing is in two weeks: He's facing ten years in prison.

Jesus . . .

I hear a loud bang from outside the car. I look up to see we're not on the freeways anymore but in a dilapidated neighborhood full of boarded-up shops and run-down buildings. Everything looks stale and sunbaked, the way furniture and curtains look when they fade from sitting in front of a window for too long. We're stopped at a red light. A crowd of shabbily dressed pedestrians is crossing in front of us. One of them, a young man in a T-shirt with the sleeves cut off, is leaning over the hood of the car, glaring menacingly at the driver.

"You almost hit me!" he yells, his voice muffled.

"Did not, you little shit," snarls the driver, taking his right hand off the steering wheel and reaching deftly for the glove compartment. When he opens it, I see a gun.

Oh, my God . . .

The man bangs the hood of the car again. Other people with him are trying to peer in the tinted windows. In a flash, I suddenly know: *This* is how God's going to do it! This is how he's going to punish me! He's going to have me pulled from a car and torn limb from limb on the sidewalk by a mob of disenfranchised Angelinos.

The light changes and the car leaps forward. I look back to see the crowd closing in a frustrated wave behind us. The driver's wrinkled hand shuts the compartment and relaxes back on the steering wheel. I heave a sigh of relief. Then, as quickly and totally as an edit in a film, the street splits into a grand boulevard and the scene around me changes. The run-down businesses are replaced by high stone walls over which I can see the tops of lush palm trees and the tiled roofs of Spanish colonial mansions. The rusted trucks and low-riding sedans are replaced by gleaming sports cars and limousines. I stare around in wonder. If there were a single place on earth that represented the contrast between heaven and hell more clearly, and if it were possible to cross from one place to the other in a car, I am almost certain that it would happen on La Cienega Boulevard at a sign that reads: WELCOME TO BEVERLY HILLS.

★ ★ ★

THE sun is almost down now, chased away by the encroaching wave of ink from the east. But the sunset is beautiful. I remember reading that it's the smog in L.A. that makes the sunsets so spectacular. An irony that should bother us more than it does.

We pass Melrose and Rodeo Drive, all the places I expected Jack to be. The driver takes me up to the Hollywood hills, dusty, sepia toned, deserted. I'm thinking *Chinatown* . . . *Mulholland Drive* . . . *CHiPs* repeats.

At a chain-link fence, the driver stops the car and gets out, coming around to open my door. A sweet-smelling haze rushes in. I make my way through the gate of the fence, past a sign that says NO TRESPASSING, where a security guard in uniform watches me but doesn't stop me. I step over a mound full of yellowed grasses, down a rough incline.

"Hi, there." It's Jack's voice. He steps out of the shadows. I run to him and throw my arms around his neck. He kisses me and I let myself fall into the darkness behind my closed eyes. I want to stay here for ever, with my eyes closed; I don't want to open them. I don't want this to be happening.

And yet I don't want it to stop.

He laughs, extricating himself. "This way," he says, taking my hand and leading me down the grassy hill.

I don't understand what it is at first; it's too large to absorb, certainly too large to read, the white letters big as drive-in screens. I see a blanket spread out on the ground; a bottle of champagne is chilling in a silver bucket. Ahead of me, spread out in a flickering grid that makes the stars look mundane by comparison, is a view I've been dreaming about ever since my dad used to let me stay up late to watch Johnny Carson with him. I know where I am now. Standing in front of the Hollywood sign.

"I thought this was the perfect place to celebrate," he says, as we kneel down on the blanket. I watch him open the champagne. I briefly remember a night so long ago—a lifetime at least—David opening a bottle of wine in my kitchen. "The best champagne money can buy," he laughed. "My money, anyway."

"How would you feel about moving out here, Sally," he says, handing me my glass. "We could get married . . . buy a big house in the Hills. . . . You'd be near all the studios. I could work from here, too. You said you wanted to be rich and famous. *This* is the place to do it."

I feel a twinge of nervousness, remembering my dilemma. "But what if I'm happy just the way things are, Jack? What if I don't need anything more?"

He smiles at me over the rim of his glass. "What if I *do?*"

THIRTY-SEVEN

Set a beggar on horseback and he'll ride to the Devil.

PROVERB

I've heard Julia Roberts say in an interview that the most comfortable beds in the world are at the Four Seasons. She's right. But she forgot to say how beautiful the antique repro furniture was, all upholstered in the shades of an expensive beach house. Or that they put a fresh flower on your room service tray. Or that the white terry robes are soft as silk against your skin.

I sigh happily and pour myself a cup of coffee; I curl up on a pink velvet chair and survey the suite. The floor leading to the bedroom is strewn with clothes—Jack's black suit, my lace thong—and beyond the double doors I see the king-size bed, empty except for artfully rumpled sheets (Jack had to leave early for a meeting). It felt so good to be with him again last night, to feel his hands, his body, his mouth. I forgot how he seems to resuscitate everything about me. I forgot how he makes me feel alive.

As I'm blissfully sipping my coffee, I hear a knock at the door. "Yes?"

"Sally? It's Lenora Feldman. Jack told you I'd be coming over?"

"Oh, yes. Just a sec." I rush through the suite, picking up our discarded clothes and tossing them into the bedroom.

I tie the robe around me more tightly and answer the door. A small-boned woman in a baby-blue skirt suit is smiling up at me. She gives me the kind of handshake you could use to screw bolts into Boeings. "Great to meet you. These are for you." She hands me several garment bags from Saks. She sees the look of confusion in my eyes. "Jack didn't tell you?"

"Well, he said somebody from the network was dropping something off, but he didn't say what."

"*This* is it," she explains. "They're holding a reception for Jack tonight. He said he wasn't sure you brought anything to wear, so he had me bring these over for you to try on."

"I can't take these . . ." I tell her uncertainly.

"He *told* me you wouldn't accept them. But you've got to pick at least *one*. The reception is black tie. He said to tell you he remembered your first date . . . and that you'd know what he meant." She gives a confused shrug.

I remember sitting outside Sette complaining that I looked like a bag lady. I can't help but smile. I let her in.

Forty-five minutes later, I've tried on five different gowns and three different pairs of shoes in every possible combination and permutation. I put them on in the bedroom and come out and model them for Lenora, who oohs and aahs, sitting on the couch eating strawberries and sipping morning glories we ordered up.

"I can't decide which one," I complain happily.

"I like the Stella McCartney. But the Marc Jacobs looks great, too."

We both stare at each other helplessly. "Looks like I have to try them on again!"

When I've finally made up my mind, I have a new strappy, silvery, bias-cut Dolce & Gabbana and my first authentic pair of Manolos. At the door Lenora air-kisses me and tells me she'll see me tonight.

I walk back into the suite, delirious and relaxed. I feel a minor panic when I notice a beautifully wrapped box on the end table. Lenora must have forgotten it—but then I see the card:

So you're never late, it reads. *Love, Jack.*

I untie the ribbon and open the box. It's a new Gucci watch. I smile. I hold it up next to my knockoff. There's no comparison. The real one gleams like a string of gold coins.

Shit.

This is so *Pretty Woman*—Julia would be proud.

I planned to take a few hours' sun this morning, so I change into my bathing suit—which seems so shabby, so old-lifey compared with everything else—and slip on a hotel robe. I head to the pool deck, and as I emerge into the sunshine, I have to shade my eyes. Sunlight glances off the rippling surface of the water. The deck is arranged with white lounge chairs and airy cabanas; red frangipani trees and lush bougainvillea vines filter the view of the hills beyond. A young blond man in a short-sleeved white uniform is standing behind a shaded kiosk.

"Hi, can I get you something?"

"Uh . . ."

"Mineral water? Coffee? Juice?"

"Mineral water, please."

"Still or sparkling?"

"Uh . . . sparkling."

He smiles and disappears through a set of glass doors off the deck.

I find a chaise and table on the far side of the pool. I slide off the robe, take off my new Gucci, slipping it into the pocket. I breathe deeply and stride two steps, diving into the pool. The water engulfs me, crashing and bubbling around my ears. I soar underneath it, feeling it rush along my body. I emerge into the sunlight, stroking back my hair. I paddle to the side of the pool, gently lift myself out of the water, move across the deck to my table. The pool boy has left clean towels, a glass of sparkling mineral water, copies of *Vogue, Elle,* some trades, and the *Times* in the perfect semicircle of shade created by the umbrella.

Is this really my life?

I find the bottle of suntan lotion I bought back in New York. It's a little grimy from being on the convenience store shelf too long, the cap and shoulders of the bottle covered in the same immobile dust that settled on the Elvis bust and the golden Eastern gods. I rub the lotion on my arms and legs, then lean back and close my eyes. The white lounge chair squeaks lightly beneath my weight. The backs of my eyelids turn scarlet, then black.

I feel a sweet ache in my chest. I let the sensation fill me until it feels like I'm weightless and spun, and that the slightest breeze could carry me away. I'm so happy right now. I don't think I've ever been so happy in my life. *He* makes me happy. And even if he *is* the Devil—which he probably isn't—it's not like he's truly evil, is it? So he stole the *Friends* spin-offs. So he's a little ruthless in the boardroom. So what? It's not as if that's any real threat to religion, is it? Or God himself? Besides, we love each other. God *is* love, they say. And Jesus taught us to love our neighbors as we love ourselves. Before I met Jack, I didn't even know what love was, and now I do. How could that be wrong?

Of course, is that love—is any love—worth the price of your soul?

A quiver of uncertainty passes through me. The only cloud in the sky gravitates toward the sun. A chill wind pulls up the hairs on my arm and I see gooseflesh coat my body in the sudden shade. When the sun finally does come back, I try to relax again, but I can't. I put the robe back on and pad across the deck into the hotel.

Nosuchthingasthedevilnosuchthingasthedevilnosuchthingasthedevil.

THIRTY-EIGHT

. . . [A]nd they have no rest day or night
who worship the beast and his image. . . .

REVELATION 14:11

THAT night UBN holds a reception in Jack's honor at the Bel Air. Producers, actors, people from the trades are there. Courtney Cox and Jennifer Aniston show up. John Monroe and Sabrina Calliope-Clark fly in from New York. They move through the room, followed by their little orbit of people moons.

By the end of the night I'm feeling a little drunk from all the champagne and dizzy from meeting so many new people. I've even gotten a few offers from producers who want to send me their scripts. Around eleven o'clock Lenora, looking a little tipsy herself, holding a wineglass covered with fingerprints, leans over to us to tell us there's a huge Halloween party at a new club called Shallow.

Halloween. I almost forgot it was Halloween. It's always been my favorite holiday. Not that that should surprise you. All actors love Halloween. Gives us a chance to be somebody else.

A bunch of us pile into limousines. The streets are chaotic, a whirling mass of clowns and ghosts and vampires. Cops on horseback shout orders into the crowd. It takes us a while, but we finally pull up in front of the club. The neon sign glows against a black sky that stretches quietly above us like an unblinking eye. A long line of witches and ghouls wait outside. A transvestite dressed up as the bride of Frankenstein opens the car door for me and takes my hand. "Welcome," he says in his deep, modulated voice.

We all make our way to the front of the queue. Our names are on the guest list and we are quickly let into the club by the thick-necked bouncers. Inside the doors, a pair of jokers in clashing neon satin with white plastic masks of the expressions of tragedy and comedy wave us through.

Entering the club is like trying to push into a world of perpetual storm, the pounding music, the pulsing lights, the bodies pressed so tightly together they provide the resistance of densely planted trees. On tall platforms around the room, beautiful young women in glittering bikinis and barely clad men whose bodies have been shaved clean writhe and dance to the music, swinging their hair. I look up at Jack for his reaction; he observes it all coolly.

"Wild" is all he says.

Someone dressed up as a witch, with an incredibly convincing prosthetic nose and green warty skin, walks up to me, tapping me with her broom. She holds out a Styrofoam cauldron. I see an assortment of empty eyeholes staring up at me. They're masks—plastic eye masks. She motions for me to take one and I do—a silver one for me, a black one for Jack. He smiles at me, amused by the unexpected gift. We slip on our masks and are suddenly hidden, like everyone else.

A tall drag queen dressed as Hedwig carries a tray of drinks by us. He smiles a wide, toothy grin and hands us each a white plastic glass filled with a purplish liquid. The last pebbles of dry ice or seltzer beads skim around the surface, kicking up foam. I just shake my head and take a sip. Then another.

Jack and I try to talk, but the music is too loud, so we just laugh and watch the raucous throng of monsters, movie stars, and ghosts. People come over, but I don't recognize many of them in their costumes and gruesome makeup. The noise level doesn't seem to bother them as much. Or Jack. Everyone carries on close conversations, laughing rowdily at jokes I can't hear as if they're used to this atmosphere, acclimatized to it, Romans in Rome.

I have another drink.

The dancers on the platforms above us take on a more sinister tone as a deep red-orange light show is projected against the walls, making them—and everyone else in the room—seem as if they're on fire. The music is relentless. Driving. So loud I feel it pounding against my chest. Everyone is moving, dancing, pressing against each other through the crowd. Their eyes are drunk and greedy, hungrily taking in the diversions. Two of the girls on the platforms take off their tops. One of the men has strapped on an enormous fake penis. The girls tend to it worshipfully, this fake yardstick of a cock.

I have another drink, a green one, staring at it curiously. My mind feels like its digitizing. I shake my head to clear it. Take another sip.

There's a beautiful woman dressed up as a vampire dancing not far from me. A model. A porn star? She has to be, with that body. Men are all around her, touching her, urging her on.

"Whoops!" I nearly spill my drink as someone squeezes by me.

"Sorry, honey!" says Alice in Wonderland. She toasts my glass and throws her head back, laughing.

I steady myself on my feet. Adjust my mask, which has slipped slightly. Look around the room again, with my slightly blurry eyes, my loosened brain. Lenora swerves up to me, a plastic kitty mask pushed up on her forehead, making a messy lump of her bangs. Her bright eyes are hooded and drunk. "I *lahhvv* that man," she yell-says, pointing to Jack. "You hang on to him. He's a *gawwwdddd!*"

I look over my shoulder and see Jack standing a few feet away, deep in conversation with Charlie Chaplin.

"I know!" I scream, but can't hear my voice, only feel my vocal chords curling up in themselves, and it tickles.

She grabs my hand and drags me onto the dance floor. We work ourselves a little clearing in the bodies so we can dance. I move. Writhe. Laugh. Jack is by the bar watching me.

Suddenly I am almost knocked off my feet. Something pushes roughly past my calves and I look down to see a goat—a real goat—skittering through the crowd. It dodges this way and that, confused by the music and the crowd. I think I hear its distant, plaintiff *baaaahaaaa* and the bell around its neck is swinging. The poor thing. Buckling one way, then the other, as he tries to find his way through the thicket of legs. No one else seems to notice him—they just dance and move. Drunkenly, I bend over, hoping it will run into my arms. But it sees an escape route through someone's legs. I barely manage to touch it as it grazes me, darting through the crowd and disappearing into the blackness. I turn around, trying to find Jack, but I don't see him.

The Devil is standing in his place.

The. Devil. Is. Standing. In. His. Place.

There is a crystalline wash of blue, green, and purple behind him, from the lights and the wall of bottles behind the bar. He has grayish, discolored flesh; his whole body seems moist, covered in some substance, thicker than sweat, that reflects the fiery lights. He has a tight, exaggerated musculature that heaves awkwardly with each breath, as if he's breathing backwards. His hips and buttocks are narrow, pushed forward. A stump of a tail protrudes. His face has not so much features as ugly, misshapen bumps where features should be. I cannot make out his sunken black eyes in the shadows of an exaggerated brow. From the skull above his forehead, two thick, rounded gray bones protrude dully. One of his satyr-like legs is propped up on the rail beneath the bar. Almost as if he can sense me staring at him, he turns and looks at me. He looks right *at* me. He raises his glass in a toast. A great wave of dizziness comes over me. I feel the music pulling me down. *Where's Jack? Where's Jack?* My eyes search the crowd. I see Charlie Chaplin, but where's Jack?

I turn back and the Devil isn't at the bar anymore. He's walking toward me with an awkward gait. Legs that bend too much with each step. Breathless, I push through a maze of bodies, looking back over my shoulder to make sure he's not following me. But he is. Pursuing easily through the crowd. My heart pounds. My breathing is painful. I want to scream. Still he follows. I keep running. Pushing people out of my way. Alice in Wonderland. A vampire. A nun. Then Alice again. I am going in circles . . . in circles . . . the laughter . . . the lights. The goat runs past my legs, *baaaa-aaa,* and I scream, backing right into the solid body of someone standing behind me. I twist, horrified. But it's Jack. His mouth moves, but I can't hear him. Not for the music pounding. I feel my knees weaken. I feel Jack lift me into his arms. I see Charlie Chaplin watching me before the world goes black.

THIRTY-NINE

Satan, so call him now, his former name
Is heard no more in Heaven. . . .

JOHN MILTON

I wake in a freezing gasp of panic. It is a moment before the walls and
ceiling make sense. Then I remember last night—*the Devil following me*
through the crowd. Bile rushes up in my throat. I kick free of the covers
and run to the bathroom. I bend over the toilet, gagging. I'm nauseous, but I can't throw up. Groaning, I sit back on my bare haunches.

It was someone in a costume . . . it had to be! It's the only thing that
makes sense.

I move weakly to the sink. Rinse my mouth. My face. When I step
back into the bedroom, I see Jack sleeping, his face turned away from
me. The curtains are closed against the morning sun. I bend to grab
my robe from the floor and see something glinting in the partially
open drawer of the nightstand. The gilt-edged pages of a book. I feel a
flutter of hope. The Gideon Bible. I slide the book out quietly, making
sure Jack doesn't hear. I tuck it into the folds of my robe and hurry out
of the room, closing the door.

I curl up on the silk sofa in the sitting room and hold the book in
my lap. It's white fake-grained leatherette. I run my hands over the

gold embossing: Holy Bible. It feels good beneath my fingers, calming. I open it and the spine cracks loudly, as if it's never been used. And maybe it hasn't. Unlike Meridien's Bible, there are not hundreds of definitions, one after the other, but millions of reassuring gray words, all joined together into one cohesive whole. I start flipping through the frail pages. *". . . In the beginning there was the Word . . . and the word was God . . ." ". . . peace of God which passeth all understanding . . ." ". . . and something like a great mountain burning with fire was thrown into the sea, and a third of the sea became blood . . ."*

So many gray words . . .

Too many . . .

I feel a shadow creep over the book.

"Interesting reading material," his voice says.

I close the book, hold it against my chest. "Just doing some research for Meridien," I say lightly. He remains standing behind me, his shadow unmoving. I twist around, give him a smile that I hope passes for natural.

"You feeling better?" he asks.

"Yes . . ."

"I was so worried about you last night. You were really tripping. I wonder if someone put something in your drink."

"You never know," I tell him, still gripping the Bible. "You never know in L.A."

THAT afternoon we drive up the coast in a silver-gray convertible Jag. You can rent those here. You can rent anything here. The mountains, the ocean, the birds.

We pull off a dusty side road onto a long drive. It leads to an enormous old mansion set back amid lush grapevines. Jack tells me it's his favorite vineyard. He wants to bring several cases of wine back to New York. The man and woman who greet us at the door are dignified and well dressed. They seem delighted to see Jack. They have thick accents I can't quite place and sometimes it seems to me Jack is speaking to them in another language. An old man with white whiskers, stooped shoulders, and long white hair emerges from the grounds and takes us down many hallways until we come to a large wooden door reinforced with rusted bolts. He opens the door and leads us down a stone stairwell into the damp, cool cellar. It smells of must and dirt and fermentation. The only light comes from small lanterns on the walls. The old gentleman leaves us alone in a low-ceilinged room lined with wine bottles. There is a small fire burning in an ancient fieldstone fireplace. A table and two chairs. An old rug on the mossy stone floor in front of the hearth.

Jack pours me a glass of wine from a dusty wine bottle. Just an inch. Then another. And another. We sit there for a very long time. Speaking. Not speaking. Jack opening wine bottles. Throwing craggy logs on the small fire.

It seems natural when he takes my hand and leads me to the rug. It seems natural that we are suddenly making love in this place. When he falls into me. And I fall around him. I smell the must of the cellar . . . the thickness of wine—it fills my senses. The darkness . . . the fire . . . the perpetual night. I am taken away by him. By the idea of him. Somewhere we stop being two people, flesh and bones and blood, and become something else. Energy. Fire. Sin itself.

"*Sally,*" he whispers in my ear as he makes love to me. "*You're mine, aren't you?*"

I don't answer. I'm breathless. Weak. Gone from myself.

"*I knew it when I met you. . . . No matter who has had your body, there was part of you that was completely untouched. Your soul. No one has had you there. No one but me. . . .*"

And I know it's true. I am helpless to stop it. I am pulled to him as if by a force, like a wave moving toward a fault in the ocean. I fear what has happened. But there is no hope.

I have fallen in love with the Devil.

And he has fallen in love with me.

FORTY

*. . . I should renounce the devil and all his works,
the pomps and vanity of this wicked world,
and all the sinful lusts of the flesh. . . .*

THE BOOK OF COMMON PRAYER

AFTER we get back to New York, we start talking about weddings.
And children.
And a place in Beverly Hills.

I find myself making excuses for my behavior. I comfort myself by
saying it's not as if I did anything *deliberately* wrong, is it? I didn't set
out to sin. I didn't summon the Devil from the depths of hell with
potions or incantations or Wiccan rituals I read about from the Occult
section of Jeremy's store. I wasn't looking to sell my soul in exchange
for a network gig and a new Dolce & Gabbana gown. So big deal. I
fell in love. It was all so innocent. It was all so pure. Couldn't God forgive me? Just this one little time? Besides, we had a deal, right? If God
ever gave me my sign that Jack was truly evil, I would do the right
thing. I would leave him. But until that happens, the situation is out of
my hands. I even start to notice the scope of my dilemma shrinking
somewhat, getting smaller every day. I have gotten used to being in
love with the Devil, the same way I have gotten used to eating in fancy
restaurants and wearing expensive clothes. . . .

FORTY-ONE

. . . I beheld Satan as lightning fall from heaven.

LUKE 10:18

THE director's voice bellows over the speakers of the *DUD* studio: "And that's a wrap!"

The studio erupts with cheers. People come up to hug me around the neck. I feel tears coming to my eyes. They're throwing me a good-bye party. It's my last day on set. I got the part on *Precinct*. Instead of Candace being killed off after the bank robbery, she recovers, and she and Hogan strike up a relationship that, as far as Gus was able to negotiate, will last at least two seasons.

The writers of *DUD* have had to work overtime wrapping up Meridien's storyline. Fate decided it for us all: Meridien will join the convent, never to be heard from again. We shot the last few teary scenes this morning.

"We're going to miss you *so* much, Sally!" Lee Roswell croons, holding a champagne flute. "Is there nothing we can do to tempt you to stay?"

I shrug apologetically. "Talk to the boss."

Gus just grins. "No way."

"Well, I'm telling you, Sally," she says, "if you ever need anything, you just call Ruben or me. I mean it."

Ruben is tipsy, too, leaning on his ex-wife. "Thass' right, Sal . . . if you ever need *hany*-thing, you just call. . . ."

"After all," Lee says, "Meridien's not dead. The writers can always reprise her." Then she laughs. "Hell, even if she *is* dead, they can reprise her!"

"Don't be stupid," Raine pouts. "She's going turn into a prime-time snob and forget she ever knew us."

"No way!" I insist.

"Enough with the blubbering, Sally," Gus whispers to me. "We gotta go."

"But what about the party?"

"We'll be back in a minute." She grabs my elbow and drags me toward the studio doors, past the craft services tables set with finger foods and champagne.

Gus ushers me into the hall. We've been holed up in the studio all morning and the white walls are so bright, I have to squint against the light.

"Gus, I can't miss my own party!" I complain, being propelled along.

"You're not going to miss the party. But I'm not going to feel comfortable until the ink's dry on that contract."

We go to the 21st floor. The normally hectic *Precinct* production offices look eerily evacuated. We walk slowly down the hall. As we pass offices and cubicles, we notice clusters of people gathered silently around television sets, their expressions stricken, their voices hushed and worried. That's never a good sign. I feel a growing sense of trepidation.

"What happened?" I ask warily.

"I don't know," Gus says.

Griff's office is a large, spacious one at the end of the hall, decorated with overstuffed leather furniture and Emmy Awards. The room is normally off-limits to all but the highest-ranking production staff, but today dozens of people are clogged in and around its doors, everyone watching a large-screen TV. Griff is sitting in a purple armchair, his back to us, facing the television. Marcy sees us and waves us in quietly.

"What's going on?" Gus whispers.

"Didn't you hear?" Marcy asks.

Gus shakes her head. "We've been in studio all morning."

"A guy killed himself last night. *In* the building."

I react with a wince. Gus feigns concern, but her eyes are scanning the room for the all-important contract, which is sitting squarely in the middle of Griff's desk. I can tell she doesn't like the look of it over there all by itself.

My attention goes to the TV, where a stone-faced anchor is reading the breaking news: "*. . . was found dead of a self-inflicted gunshot wound this morning in his Manhattan office. The .45 caliber gun was purchased at a midtown gun shop two days ago. . . .*"

"Uh, Marcy," Gus asks in a canny whisper, "can we get this thing signed? Sally's got to get back to the show."

"In a second, Gus."

Suddenly I stop hearing the voices. My eyes widen as I see a photograph of the suicide victim. He may not be wearing a turtleneck, but I recognize the olive skin, the thinning black hair. It's the fuckin' weasel!

"*. . . assistant director of finance, Martin Fletcher . . .*"

I gasp, covering my mouth.

"Do you know him?" Marcy whispers.

"I-I've got to go," I say, stumbling back through the crowd.

"Sal?" Gus complains worriedly, motioning to the contract.

"I'll be back," I stammer. I spin around and dash out of the office into the quiet hall.

THE normally sedate corridors of the senior management floor are swarming with men and women talking on cell phones, running down hallways, disappearing behind closed doors. I hurry to Agnes's office. Several people are gathered around her desk. She looks up, her face scored with worry. She motions that I can go into Jack's office.

I hurry into the room, but he's not there. Beyond the window, it's a gray day, the mist hanging like cobwebs between the trees of Central Park. The wall of monitors flickers in a ghastly kaleidoscope. Game shows. Car commercials. I rush to a television with a talking head and a graphic of UBN. I turn up the volume.

"... as a legal consultant at the ABC affiliate in Chicago. From there he moved to ..."

Then another one. "...faced possible imprisonment for his participation in the recent ..."

And another one. "... discovered on the premises this morning by a cleaning lady ..."

Until it's all a mash of sound.

I begin to pace the office.

There it is. Three red sixes hovering in the misty skyline.

I hear a sudden cacophony from the hall. I turn to see Agnes stand at attention. I see Jack pursued by a pack of PR people. He seems pre-occupied, but a relieved smile comes to his face when he sees me. I feel a surge of hopefulness. He comes into the office and closes the door on the others. We move to each other and hold each other for a moment.

"It's him, isn't it?" I ask.

He nods weakly. He seems exhausted. He releases me and walks slowly behind his desk. The televisions drone in the background. "... implicated in the Geostar fraud ..."

"... findings of the SEC committee are still confidential, but Martin Fletcher was ..."

"This is awful, Jack. Does anyone know why he did it? Did he leave a note or anything?"

"Worse than that." He taps the edge of a black cassette on his desk.

I shake my head, not understanding.

"He put it on tape, Sally."

The floor seems to roll beneath me. "What?"

"He let himself into his old office . . . he set up a camera. . . . He put it *all* on tape . . ."

"My God . . ." I put my hand on my chest. Feel the thud of my heart.

His intercom buzzes. *"I've got the* Times *on the line."*

"Tell them I'll have a statement in twenty minutes."

I stare at the screens. "Jack . . . this is *terrible."*

"I know," he says tiredly. "A real nightmare."

There's a soft knock on the door behind me. A young woman in a beige suit slips in. "Excuse me." She walks across the office, putting a document on Jack's desk. "We checked with Legal," she says. "They said CNN wants to air it, but—get this—he did it on UBN property. The rights automatically revert to us."

That makes Jack shake his head, laugh slightly. "Thanks."

She turns around and tiptoes back out the door.

A reporter on TV continues: *". . . won't confirm whether Mr. Fletcher was released because of any implication in the Geostar fraud . . ."*

The intercom buzzes again: *"Jack . . . Phillip Nesbitt's on the line."*

"I should take this, Sally," he tells me. He picks up the phone. He stands up and turns around to face the park. I watch the TV again.

". . . the thirty-eight-year-old Fletcher is alleged to have brought video equipment with . . ."

". . . Who knows?" Jack's voice. "Security was told not to let him in. . . . Yeah. . . ."

". . . SEC investigation which found Mr. Fletcher guilty of . . ."

Then I hear the strangest thing. Jack's laugh. A hard burst of genuine laughter. "Maybe you had the right idea getting out when you did. Can I join you?" Another chuckle. "Okay, Phil. . . . Thanks for calling." He hangs up the phone. He takes his jacket off, slings it over the back of his chair. For a moment—just a moment—the three red sixes from the skyline are superimposed on the back of his white shirt in the reflection on the glass. But then he bends to sign a document and it's gone.

I feel a flutter of uncertainty. "Jack . . . you . . . don't seem very upset by this."

"Are you kidding? I told you, it's a nightmare. A fucking PR nightmare."

I let out a small, shocked laugh. "It's a little more than *that,* don't you think?"

There's another buzz from the intercom. In a fatalistic tone Agnes's voice says: *"Drama just fielded its first call. Some guys from the West Coast. You want to talk to them?"*

"Tell them if there's going to be a movie—it's going to be in-house."

The intercom clicks off.

I stare at him, confused. "Jack, I can't believe it. . . . A man is dead . . . and you're talking about a movie of the week?"

"They're called docudramas now, Sally. MOW is too eighties." He turns to his computer.

Surges of cool disbelief sift through me. I don't hear my voice, not really, when I say, "I want to see the tape, Jack."

He glances at me. "No, you don't, Sally. Trust me."

"Let me *see* it," I repeat through clenched teeth.

He turns his chair to face me. "You really wanna see it? Why don't you go over to CNN. Or NBC. Everyone's got a copy of it. The cleaning lady who found him this morning turned the tape over to the news desk. An associate producer got hold of it. She fed it out on satellite."

"*Shit.* . . . You fired her, I hope."

He regards me levelly. "No . . . I promoted her."

I feel a force in my chest, like a punch. "Jack . . . give me the tape."

He watches me for a moment, then shakes his head. He leans forward, handing me a black cassette with a simple bar-code label. I snatch the tape, moving to the wall of images. I insert it into the VCR stacked in with the other components. I press PLAY. The largest monitor in the very center of the bank of flickering screens, the one Jack uses for assembly cuts and demo tapes, goes dark while the rest of the images continue to swirl around it. Trembling, I back up, sit down on the black leather sofa. My mouth is dry. The screen crackles into a blue-white wash of video hash, then bursts to life with a bright panel of color bars. The office fills with the annoying hum of "tone."

"Color bars?" I ask. "He put down color bars?"

"The police have the original. I made the guys pull a dub for me."

Pull a dub? As if this was just another screening copy of a pilot. Horrified, I picture a small team of techies working in dark, window-less edit suites, drinking coffee, eating sandwiches, putting down color bars by rote. I'm trembling. I fast-forward through the prescribed minute until the screen slides into a different shot. I see a small office. There is a wooden desk cleared of clutter. It is not quite centered in the frame. The single chair is empty, angled as if someone got up and didn't push it back under the desk. A lamp on a credenza in the back-ground is half out of frame; it provides the only light in the room, making everything look shadowy, slightly sepia-toned. There is one window to the left of the screen, but it is black. The city is reduced to a series of disconnected dots of light behind the glass. I swallow a hurt-ing lump in my throat. I hear muffled banging on the camera mic. The shot shakes as someone squares it more cleanly on the chair. A hand comes in. An elbow. There's the sound of glass clinking clumsily.

A man's voice. Kind of in the distance. *". . . fuck is it . . . ?"* Words drop out as he talks. You catch a couple of mumbles, but nothing else.

The camera shudders around a bit as Marty stumbles into frame. He moves clumsily across the office. He seems drunk. He sits down in the chair. It squeaks beneath his weight. He's slightly off-center. Too far over to the left. He's wearing a turtleneck and a dark leather bomber jacket with the zipper open. His hair looks greasy. He is gaunt, unshaven. His skin looks slightly jaundiced in the bad lighting of the office.

I hear people murmuring behind me. I turn around to see a small group gathered there, everyone watching the tape. I turn back to the screen. Marty is still in his chair. He's staring at a half-full tumbler of amber liquid in his hand. Something else in the other hand, but it's hard to tell what it is. The lighting is too low. Parts of his face, his eyes, his mouth, warp into sloppy black shadows as his head turns back and forth. He stares at his glass. Swirls the liquid around for a moment. Then he looks up at the camera. Cocks his head. Wavers slightly. His eyes are sunken, blurring black into his face. He squints at the lens as if confused. Then he stands up and walks toward the camera. The jacket obscures the picture as he stands in front of the lens. The sound of the movement bangs on the camera mic. The angle of the shot changes slightly. He walks back to the chair, thumps clumsily down. He looks at the camera again. Satisfied that he's centered, he lets out a sad sigh. He sips his drink. Finally he addresses the camera. His voice is small, set back from the camera mic, but clear. He gives a crooked smile and a wave:

"Hi, everyone out there in . . . *teevee land . . .*" he says. And it's then you can see what's in his other hand. A gun. A gun that's so large it makes his hand look small by comparison.

"Marty the Merlin here, folks . . ." His head teeters on his neck. He takes another slurp of his drink. ". . . I got a pitch for ya. I know how you guys like those . . . *pitches. . . .*" He lets out a sneer which warps his mouth.

"He looks awful," somebody behind me says.

"He didn't white-balance," someone else says.

I turn to look at Jack. He's sitting behind the desk, watching the screen. His gaze shifts to me for a moment. His expression is blank.

"It's got everything you're lookin' for—money . . . violence. . . . Shit, no sex." A wavering beat. "No sex." He regards the lens for a moment, then his face breaks into an amused grin. "Maybe you could bring someone in to punch up the script." He chuckles harshly at that, pleased with himself. But the laughter fades quickly and the corners of his mouth curve down and suddenly a hoarse sob bursts out of him, almost like a bark. And then another one. Marty's head lolls forward. His shoulders slump and he sits there for a moment, sobbing messily.

I'm thinking of my dad. I'm coming home from the grocery store. There are police cars outside the house. . . .

A string of shiny saliva drips from Marty's mouth, gleaming whitely against the black turtleneck. He wipes it away with the back of his hand. The gun hand. He suddenly seems to see the gun—as if for the first time. He stops crying. He stares at the gun, as if trying to understand how it got there. His gaze slowly lifts back to the camera. He regards us bitterly.

"I guess I should cut to the chase—that's what you say, right? Cut to the chase. . . ." A sick determination seems to come over him. "This is a real tearjerker, folks. There's no happy ending. . . . But the reviews are in, and so far it's two thumbs"—he sucks a breath and lifts the gun to his head, a bent loop of black against the white wall of his office ending in his temple. He's staring straight at the camera—*"down."*

Pow!

It happened so fast!

He couldn't have even thought about it!

There's a really clumsy jerk, a disgusting *jerk* of a movement. Worse than watching JFK get bonked in the backseat of the convertible. I hear everybody behind me wince.

The wall explodes black behind him.

I watch Marty Fletcher twitch for a minute. Get limper in the chair. The chair squeaks. Turns slightly. Stills.

The top right curve of his head is gone. It's gone. His head is clumped square. Somebody says he looks like Gumby, but nobody laughs.

My heart is beating so fast, a wash of sound in my head. I feel the skin on my forehead, my cheeks, turn hot. I am trembling inwardly. I have to grip the leather of the sofa.

The ice cream truck in the driveway . . .

My eyes fill with tears. I want to stop the tape. Stop it. Tell everyone to leave. But I am mesmerized. I am watching. I can't help myself.

The chair squeaks again.

"Oh, my God . . ." somebody says.

Marty starts to move.

Jesus Christ!

He's not dead! Marty's not dead!

He comes to. Awkwardly. Squares his eyes on the camera. His mouth is open in a weird shape. Something you couldn't do if you had your whole brain. His eyes spin up in his head. They turn almost all white. The camera really picks it up. He says something . . . *what?* It *sounds* like "Fuck."

He must have figured out he's not dead.

But it could just be blood in his mouth or his lungs.

The gun hits the chrome of the chair, making a messy metallic clunk as he tries to lift it again.

Jesus Christ, his arm's like rubber. He can't control it.

That gun looks so heavy. It shakes as he brings it to his head. It rests against his ear. Pokes into the hole above it. Sort of. The eyes roll. They glow, bleeding white into his face.

There! He said it again!

"Fuck?"

"No way. He can't talk! Half his brain's gone."

"Shhhhh!!"

The gun rolls across the front of his face. Along his cheek. The barrel drags a line of black red on his skin. The gun finds his mouth. The metal hits his teeth.

What a sound. Like ice cubes in a glass. Then . . .

Pow!

More black on the wall.

He slumps forward. Then the tension goes from his body. Marty Fletcher fills to time. Unmoving. Bleeding. Dead.

In the fresh silence the sounds of the city swell up in the background.

Two car horns. And a siren.

But it's going the wrong way.

"Shit," somebody says behind me. *"So much for my bagel."*

I hear Agnes *tsk* crossly.

I'm sitting on the sofa. Limp, exhausted, aching everywhere. I hear Jack's voice, but I'm not sure what he said, only that everyone files out of the office in response to it. I feel his shadow approach me from behind. "Are you okay?"

I shake my head. I just shake my head. The movement almost feels good—more solid than the room, which seems to warp and twist.

"Told you you shouldn't have watched it," he says. He takes the remote from my hand, turns the machine off. The screen goes mercifully black.

I look up at him, trembling. "You know why he did this, don't you, Jack?"

"The guy was obviously whacked, Sally. He must've—"

"He did it because of *us.*"

He puts his hands on my shoulders to massage them. "Sally, don't think that. We—"

"Don't touch me!" I say, pushing him away. I stand up. "Just don't touch me right now. Not while I'm try to . . . deal with this. . . ." *Deal with this . . . trying to deal with this . . .*

The sound of the intercom fills the office. *"Jack? Martin Fletcher's wife is on the phone."*

"Oh, Christ," he says softly. He takes a deep breath. Sits back down at the desk. "Okay, Agnes, put her through." As he picks up the phone, his whole demeanor seems to change. He hunches forward visibly. Lines appear on his face where they weren't before. "Mrs. Fletcher?" There's a compassionate tweak in his voice. "Yes . . . yes . . . I'm terribly sorry for your loss . . ."

Waves of rage, fear, nausea, roll through me.

". . . talented man, Mrs. Fletcher . . ."

God, I'm shaking . . . shaking so badly.

" . . . yes . . . a tragedy . . ."

Thock . . . thock . . . thock . . .

What is that *sound?*

". . . some kind of compensation . . . in your time of need . . ."

Thock . . . thock . . . thock . . .

Jack has picked up the autographed baseball. He's bouncing it gently on his desk. *Thock . . . thock . . . thock . . .*

Oh, my God.

Pow! Black against the wall.

I bury my head in my hands. Feel myself trying to sink into the immense responsibility of this horror. The next thing I'm aware of is the sound of his voice speaking into the intercom. "Agnes, clear me for the funeral." Then, as an afterthought: "And send some flowers." Whatever emotion had settled in over his features is gone.

I stare at him in horror. "This doesn't bother you at all, does it?" I ask him. "A man killed himself because of us and it doesn't bother you at all. . . ."

"How is it because of us?"

"I'm not saying we went in there and held the gun to his head. But somehow, along the chain of events, it's *our* fault he's dead. You think he would've killed himself if he wasn't facing ten years in prison?"

"You know how I feel about disloyalty. The guy was fucking cheating me."

"He didn't deserve to *die* for that!"

"Maybe not." His voice is calm. "But I'm not the one who made that decision."

I stare at him in disbelief. And then I realize: *This is it, isn't it? This is my sign. . . . God is giving me my sign. . . . A man is dead . . . and he doesn't care. . . . God is letting me know . . . God is telling me . . . this is something truly evil. . . .*

Jack approaches me slowly, a more compassionate look on his face. "Sally . . . I know this is bothering you. Even more because of what happened to your dad . . ."

"It's not my dad!" But I feel something touch me. Quick, slightly electric, like the wick of a nerve exposed. His voice continues, sickeningly lucid.

"You always try to take responsibility for things you didn't do—you *know* that."

"Don't say that."

"It's true."

"Stop it!" I cover my ears.

"Why else would you be so upset?"

"Because a man is *dead!*"

"We didn't even know him, Sally—what difference does it make?"

Then I feel something bolster me, a way out . . . a way it could still work. "Just say you're sorry, Jack. . . ."

"What?"

"Just say you're sorry. . . . It's important to me."

"Why should I be sorry? If you want to believe this guy killed himself because of us, go ahead. I can't stop you. But I'm not like you, Sally. I don't go around looking for reasons to feel like shit."

"You bastard!" I hiss.

He crosses his arms, leans against the desk, watches me evenly. "All right—what if the worst it true? What if he *did* kill himself because I fired him? And what if I'm not going to ruin the rest of my life because of it? What then?"

I feel tears burn my cheeks. "I wouldn't want to think that. I wouldn't want to think you're so cruel."

"Yeah? Well, you knew what you were getting into when you met me."

"You're right. I did. I knew all along." And then a cold, brilliant clarity moves over me—desperate and chilling. His voice continues—he moves closer to me.

"Sally, do you remember I told you once that the only thing I wanted from you was to know you were on my side? What did you think I meant when I asked you that?"

I don't answer. Seconds pound by like drumbeats.

"It means I had to trust you. No matter what. And I've got to trust you now, because I've got the whole world out there against me." He motions to the windows. "So what's it gonna be, Sally? Whose side are you on?"

My sign . . . my chance to do what's right . . .

"Sally?"

I try to fix my gaze on him. Try to see through the warp of tears.

"Whose side are you on?" he repeats.

I back away from him, trying to think . . . *think.* . . . I feel the tension between us drop like a rope.

"I can't do it, Jack," I say.

He watches me. I've never seen that look on his face. Disbelief. Anger. Disgust. I have to look away. There is a moment of nothingness, of absolute deadness, and then I hear a great clattering sound. I look up just in time to see what was on his desk—the papers, the videotapes, the baseball—fly across the room in a perfect arc, and him finishing the swing of his arm. He grabs his coat and storms past me with enough speed that the air around him makes me feel as if he's touched me.

"Bastard!" I yell at him.

But the door has already slammed.

A large crowd is waiting outside UBN when I finally stumble my way out into the cool, gray afternoon. Satellite trucks. Reporters. Arms, microphones, cameras jammed up in my face.

"Did you know Mr. Fletcher?"

"Have you seen the tape?"

I remember my mother, the practiced effortlessness of pushing through a small band of reporters waiting in a second-class neighborhood in the summer sun. *No comment. No comment.*

My apartment is quiet when I open the door—so quiet it threatens to split my eardrums. I stumble across the room, willing my feet to move in front of each other, betrayed by them when they tangle and trip me up. I fall against the kitchen counter. Turn on the taps. Rinse my face. My mouth.

Above me, the cupboard door wheezes open with a squeak. I slam it shut. It bounces open. I slam it again. *Slam! SLAM! BASH! KABANG!* The wood starts to make splintering noises.

"*FUCKING BASTARD!*" I yell. I let out a few feverish breaths. *What more evidence do I need?* Of course he's the Devil! Of course he is! He doesn't even *care!* Poor Marty . . . dead because of . . . because of . . . I try to conjure up feelings for him, poor headless Marty, but I can't. It horrifies me, but I can't even remember his face.

What if Jack's right . . . what if it is about my dad?

No! No! Don't listen to him, Sally! Haven't you listened enough? God is giving you a chance. A chance to do what is right. Aren't you going to take it?

Suddenly there is a sound in the apartment. The dullness is broken by the metallic ring of the phone. The first ring dies off into an echo. Even as it fades, I feel the hope in me swell. I scramble to my feet and race toward it. God, God, let it be him! Let it be him! We'll forget all about it and . . .

But I don't get to the phone before the machine picks it up and I hear Gus's voice fill the apartment. I stop in my tracks. "Jesus Christ, Sally, where the hell are you?" Her voice is raspy, breathless, angry. "Everyone at the party was so worried! And the contract! Griff was pretty pissed off. You can't just keep people like that waiting for you." She breathes in frustration. "Look, c-call me. Just call me. As soon as you get in."

The machine clicks once, hisses, and is silent. Leaving me in the rushing stillness. I am aware of the great wave of loss pouring over me. How I wanted it to be him . . . even now.

Forgive me, God. . . . Forgive me, God. . . .

I start to pace the room. Back and forth. Back and forth.

Please, God, please forgive me. . . .

Thank you for being so merciful. . . .

Thank you for giving me this sign. . . .

Thank you for showing me how truly evil he was before it was . . . too late. Before I went any further. Before marriage. Children. The house on the hill. There's a moment of horrible inertia, a moment of nothingness where I actually feel the finality of life without him. Then it all flies away from me, like a lace curtain taken by the wind. The tears start to come. They come up through the hollow channels of me like water forced through cracks in the earth. I fall to the floor. Just drop forward helplessly. I knew all along, didn't I?

I knew it was too good to be true.

FORTY-TWO

Through me is the way to the sorrowful city. . . .
Through me is the way to join the lost people. . . .

INSCRIPTION AT THE ENTRANCE TO HELL—
DANTE'S INFERNO

MORNING comes. The color of bones. Gray, brittle, lifeless. The phone rings. It's Gus. Again.

"Where are you, for crissakes? You can't just disappear like that, Sal. Griff's pretty pissed off. Call me!"

And again.

"I can't keep covering for ya, Sal. Come on! We're on the line here!"

Next time her voice is desperate, incredulous.

"Sal? What the hell's goin' on? . . . Did you and Jack get in a fight? Is that what's going—"

I pull out the phone cord with a violent jerk. It gives me a bitter and short-lived surge of power. I fall back down onto the bed and stare at the ceiling. I lie there for hours. I don't know exactly how long. I have a vague awareness that the sun is slowly, slowly moving its white body overhead, sliding down the other side of the sky and finally disappearing behind the leer of the horizon.

I don't eat. I don't bathe. I just cry. And when I can't cry anymore,

I scream. And when I can't scream anymore, I feel pieces of myself fall away into a haunted, hollow sleep.

THE days pass. One into the other. I stumble around the apartment. Ignore buzzing from the intercom downstairs. Eat what there is in the house. Crackers. Cereal from the box. Stale peanut M&M's.

I cry constantly. I've invented a whole new language of tears. An articulate new way to express myself through my sobs. A sentimental, quiet mewling in the morning. A heart-wrenching, lung-collapsing howl at night.

I can't stop thinking about him. I am chained to my thoughts of him like a dog to a post. No matter how much I pull at them, no matter how much I fight them, eventually I tire myself out and return to them, defeated and drained. God . . . I loved him so much. . . . Still do. . . . So much. I try to make myself stop loving him. But it's not easy. Like pulling off my own skin. Not impossible. Just excruciatingly painful. And very, very slow.

I don't know how many days pass when I finally decide it's time to venture out into the world. Gus is not answering her phone and her voice-mail box is full. I should at least try to see her. Tell her that I'm all right.

Well, not all right. But alive, at least.

I comb my hair, which seems two shades darker. I lean close to the mirror. Finger my forehead. My frown lines have come back.

I stumble out into the light of a gray November day. I am struck by how fast everything seems to be moving—the people, the cars. It's as if I've woken up in a foreign country, where I only know enough words to get by but have no hope of making a friend.

THE smell of fresh paint still permeates the fifth floor of Gus's office building. I hesitate as I approach her door. Her mail slot is overflowing with back issues of trade magazines and envelopes, some of them littering the floor outside her door. I knock, but there's no answer. It seems like she hasn't been here in days.

I've only been to Gus's apartment once, to pick up an audition piece when she first became my agent. I check a phone book to confirm the address and take a cab to Murray Hill. She lives in a well-kept old brownstone with wrought-iron railings and a bright red door. I buzz her apartment several times before a grumble from the small silver speaker responds.

"Gus? It's me."

The door reluctantly clicks open.

When I get upstairs to her apartment, she squints at me from the shadows. She's holding an ice pack to her head and wearing a turquoise robe and matching satin slippers. "I have a migraine," she tells me.

"For three days?"

"That's what happens when my star client fucks up the best deal I've ever made." She gives me a disgusted snort and I follow her into the living room.

I remember her apartment as being very pretty, full of overstuffed chenille furniture, framed photographs, and healthy plants, but everything is so dim, I can barely see the shape of the windows. There are no lamps on. The heavy drapes are drawn.

She flops onto the sofa. For my benefit she turns on a small ceramic lamp; a kerchief is thrown over the shade, so the light cast is soft. The whole place smells like cinnamon potpourri. On the coffee table in front of her is my contract from *Precinct*. It's crumpled and torn on one edge, as if she's tried to rip it in half but didn't have the strength to finish.

"Have you talked to Jack?" she asks me. It seems like the first time she's focused on me.

I shake my head.

"Are you guys going to get back together?"

I don't answer.

"I'm worried about you, Sal. You two were made for each other—he's your good luck charm. Your Prince Charming." She swings her arm in the air. "Your knight in shining—"

I interrupt her. "It's over, Gus. I can't go back with him."

"Why not?"

"I can't explain it. I just can't." We sit quietly for a moment. I pick up the contract, flipping through it. "So much for putting a koi pond in the office, I guess."

"Ah, who cares?" she says. "They smell anyway."

I leave Gus's apartment angry. I don't *need* him. I just loved him. It doesn't mean I can't go on with my life. Maybe not easily, maybe not happily, but I can do it.

When I get home, the first thing I do is call Lee Roswell. I expect her to get back to me right away, thrilled to hear from her lost starlet with an AF of 92. But she doesn't return my call. I call again the next day. Twice.

Finally, tired of being hounded, the assistant puts me through to Ruben, who answers with the irritated tone of someone who's been interrupted.

"Ruben? It's Sally Carpenter." My voice is tentative.

"Yeah?" An unreadable syllable.

"Well, I . . . I just wanted to apologize for what happened last week. Missing the party and everything."

"Uh-huh . . ."

"Just some . . . some stuff went down and I couldn't make it back to the set. I'm *really* sorry about that."

"Uh-huh . . ."

"I, uh, I just want you to know that the *Precinct* thing fell through." A beat passes. "Ruben? Are you there?"

"Mm."

"The *Precinct* thing fell through and I'm available." More silence. Unbearable beats of it. "It's just that Lee told me if I was ever free again that maybe we could talk. About reprising the character or working on something else or—"

Ruben interrupts me. "Uh, thanks, Sally. . . . I'm right in the middle of something here."

"Will you keep me in mind if anything comes—"

But the phone goes dead in my hand. I stare at the receiver a minute, feeling the chilling precision of being amputated from my dreams. The network gig. The Appeal Factor. All of it, gone. Isn't it amazing how well the penance fits the crime?

FORTY-THREE

The devil knoweth his own and is a particularly bad paymaster.
FRANCIS MARION CRAWFORD

Maybe it's my sudden lack of professional prospects that makes me go back or maybe it's just loneliness, but on a dark night just after Thanksgiving, the one holiday that seems even more removed from me this year than it usually is, I find myself trudging outside to see Jeremy. I have to talk to *someone*. I've considered calling David, but when I actually think about talking to him, I realize it's not him I want to talk to, it's Jack. My next best option is Jeremy, my sad stand-in for a best friend.

Not surprisingly, the Backburner is the only store on the block not decorated for the coming holidays. Amid the bright cheer of the rest of the street, it looks something like a missing tooth in an otherwise perfect smile. I push the door open and the bell jingles pitifully above my head. I am shocked, and a little resentful, to see a young girl counting the float behind the cash. She's one of those lazy half-Goth girls with white makeup and the right amount of facial piercings but not enough ambition to spike her hair.

"Uh . . . can I help you?" she asks.

I look around the place, feeling like an interloper, as if I've just knocked on a stranger's door and told them I grew up here. . . . *Do you think I could just see my old room?*

"Is Jeremy around?"

"He's in the back," she says, then goes back to her counting.

I head toward the back. Rustle the curtain a few times. He pushes it open. I see him sitting in front of his vanilla-colored sketch pad. "Don't tell me. Your Prince Charming turned into a frog."

"Worse," I say.

WE trek down the street to Pab's and slide into our favorite booth. I tell him what happened to Marty Fletcher and how Jack reacted, searching for someone who will agree with me, someone who will confirm the fact that this was unforgivably callous.

Jeremy doesn't disappoint. "I'm not surprised. I knew he was like that. He didn't have me fooled. I knew something like this would happen sooner or later."

I silently slug back another harsh swallow of wine.

"Aaggh! Look at you. You're upset, aren't you? You're actually *sad* about losing him. You're such a dreamer. That's your problem. You don't know what life is all about. But *I* do. I know what it all comes down to, Sally. To piss. To shit. To rotting worms in the ground. Because people like *that*"—he points nowhere in particular, but I know he's talking about Jack—"people like *that* get all the luck. They get all the money. All the breaks. And why? Because they only care about themselves. They're the ones who get ahead in the world. And the rest of us? The ones who have compassion and integrity? Life does nothing but crap all over us. Now I ask you, what kind of life is that? It's hell on earth is what it is. Hell on earth."

I don't say anything. But I couldn't agree more.

Finally I get up the nerve. "Jeremy? I was wondering if you needed a little help in the store. I'm running short of cash and it doesn't look like I have anything coming up."

"Say no more," he says. "Of course you can come back. You can start tomorrow."

"What about the Goth chick?"

"She doesn't know Hemingway from Harold Robbins. Fuck her." He pours another glass of wine for me, a big one. I drink it quickly. The world is beginning to blur.

I stare across the table at my friend, the genius, and suddenly, more than anything, I miss having a best girlfriend. Someone I could have told the whole story to. I decide to take a chance.

"Jeremy, you're gonna think this is crazy," I begin in a quavering voice. *You're gonna think this is crazy.*

And then it comes out. All of it. And so do the tears. And a few pathetic laughs. *"The Devil . . . can you believe that? . . . You had to be there, Jeremy . . . you had to see everything. . . . Dara in her hospital bed . . . and David, poor David . . . the hit 'n' run. . . ."* It goes on. *"The Mother Superior. . . . The fears. . . . The gigs. . . . The money."* Everything. It comes out in one breathless rush, and when I'm finished there are six of my mashed cigarette butts in the ashtray between us, I don't know how many of his, and at least two pitchers of wine have come and gone. After I finish, he is quiet for a long time. Then he turns to me and starts to laugh.

"Jeremy," I snap, "it's not *funny.*"

"I'm sorry, I'm sorry." He coughs a few times, then manages to compose himself. "Is that why you were asking about the Devil that night in the shop?" I nod. "This is all making sense now. You're speaking metaphorically, of course. You don't *really* think he's the Devil."

"That's the *point!* Yes, I do!"

He considers it a moment, still trying not to laugh. "How fascinating. It's not all of us who get the opportunity to meet the Devil firsthand. I'm curious. What's he like? Is he a good guy or a bad guy?"

"He's *bad,* of course. He's the *Devil.*"

He chuckles again and shakes his head. "Sally, I'm not sure you even know what the Devil is. I'm sorry to baffle you, but there was a whole train of thought I spared you that night because I didn't want to confuse you and your thirty-frames-a-minute mind. Are you familiar with the Book of Job?"

"Sort of," I say, remembering sermons from church about a man named Job—a stupid name, I thought—who was being tested by God. All kinds of horrible things were happening to him. Something about cattle and goats. And even his children, I think. God was always doing things to people's children back then.

"In that story the Devil is an obedient servant of God's. It's the Devil's idea to test Job's faith. God and the Devil are in cahoots, really." He raises his eyebrows in an almost vaudevillian gesture. "The Devil existed to test us, to obstruct us, but he was basically just a sidekick. Then, of course, we could get into the pagans and the splits within and between the Jews and the Christians, not to mention everyone else who's come along since then." He twirls his hand in the air as if to hurry up the plot in a boring story. "We'd follow him up through Milton and Marlowe and the rest of the gang, all the way to a young girl with a penchant for projectile vomiting and levitating beds. And you know where it would get us?" He lets a beat pass. "Exactly where we started. With a really good *yarn*. A story, Sally. Fiction."

I groan helplessly. "That's what *I* thought, at first."

"This man of yours—tell me he's selfish. Tell me he's heartless. Tell me he runs a television network and I will give you *bastard* or *prick*. But"—he raps my skull for emphasis—"there is—no—such—thing as the Devil. He's a figment of our imagination. Nothing more than an excuse—and a lame one at that—for all the meanness and cruelty we do to each other. He no more exists than the Loch Ness monster or the bogeyman. If there is a Devil, let him stroll in the bar right now and strike me dead for renouncing him!" He raises his finger theatrically, his voice loud enough to attract attention from the other tables. "If the Devil exists, let him come up from the bowels of hell to possess me! Get me to speak in tongues! Tempt me to sell my soul! Come, Satan! If you're there!" He widens his eyes theatrically, staring at the door with feigned anticipation. A few of the winos turn drunkenly in our direction, but the Devil does not show his face.

He sighs scornfully, stubbing out his cigarette. "So much for your Satan. You watch too many movies, Sally. Go home and read a book for a change—but not the Bible. That'll only make it worse." He grabs his coat and stands up. On the way out of the bar, he gives one last skeptical chuckle. "The Devil—how ridiculous."

I stay in the half-light of the table. Finish smoking my cigarette. Drinking my wine.

No such thing as the Devil.

I want to believe him. But I don't.

FORTY-FOUR

. . . [T]here was given me a thorn in the flesh,
the messenger of Satan to buffet me. . . .

2 CORINTHIANS 12:7

I pass all the familiar shops on my way to work the next morning. *I can't believe this,* I grumble to myself, depressed. *I'm actually going back to the bookstore.* As if none of it ever happened.

But as I approach the Backburner, my steps slow. I see the black dog sitting across the street, watching a slight commotion outside the store. There are two police cars parked out front. Uniformed officers traipsing in and out the door. I barely watch for traffic as I race across the street. When I get to the stoop, a burly police officer puts up his hand. "Step away, please, miss."

I point to the store. "But I work here. . . ."

He nods in comprehension. He leaves me out front and turns into the store. I look across the street again, only to see the black dog break into a run and disappear.

A woman in a brown pantsuit and a beige coat approaches me from inside the store. "Sally Carpenter? My name is Detective Joanne Mankewicz."

"What happened?" I ask her, a slow panic starting.

She excuses the policeman and guides me into the shop, where officers and plainclothesmen trample here and there. There are black smudges everywhere, but not just charcoal—fingerprint powder.

"Has there been a robbery?"

She shakes her head sadly, sits me down on the stool in front of the counter. "I'm afraid I have some bad news for you, Miss Carpenter."

And then she tells me that Jeremy is dead.

"Mr. Lambert is dead."

I shake my head in disbelief.

She nods soberly. As she speaks, I have to look at her mouth, follow what she's saying like a lip reader because I can't make sense of it any other way. "I'm sorry—his body was found last night in an alley off Delancey . . ."

Oh, my God . . .

"There is no such thing as the Devil. If there is a Devil, let him stroll in . . . right now . . . and strike me dead . . . !"

Dead? He can't be dead!

"He no more exists than the Loch Ness monster or the bogeyman. . . ."

She pulls a notebook from inside her jacket. "Are you okay to answer some questions?"

I shake my head. Then nod it. Then shake it again.

"I will give you bastard . . . but . . . the Devil"—and that sorry laugh— *"a story, Sally. Fiction."*

The detective's voice breaks in through my thoughts. "How long have you known Mr. Lambert?"

"About two years," I stammer.

Her pen hisses along her pad. "And when is the last time you saw him?"

"Last night. . . . Listen"—I clutch her sleeve—"please . . . could you tell me what happened?"

She hesitates, as if appraising how much I can handle, then decides I pass the test. Barely. "His body was discovered at approximately 2:15 this morning a few blocks from his apartment. Robbery doesn't appear to be the motive. He was found with a safety-deposit bag containing two hundred dollars cash. We won't know for sure until they conduct an autopsy, but it appears he was attacked—by one or more persons—and struck repeatedly with a blunt instrument of some kind. Most likely a pipe. Or a baseball bat."

I feel a cold repellent rush. I think of Jeremy, of his fragile skull. The deep hollows in his temples. And the unstoppable ringing strength of a baseball bat. *God, not a baseball bat.*

Thock . . . thock . . . thock . . .

All of a sudden, a little sob breaks out through my throat. It shocks me with its force. I cover my mouth and stare at her with surprise, as if betrayed by my own body. She gives me a sad smile, permission to cry. She reaches in her pocket for a small, half-used package of Kleenex. I stare at the package and wonder how many other tragedies this unassuming little package has observed. She just lets me cry, handing me a fresh tissue when I need it. *This is a three-tissue case.* When she thinks I'm sufficiently collected, she continues in a gentle voice.

"As far as you know, was Mr. Lambert involved in any dealings other than this bookstore?"

"He was an artist."

"I mean any drugs? Weapons? Other illicit activities?"

I shake my head.

"Did he have any known enemies?"

"I don't think so. . . ." *But I'm thinking of Jack.*

"Was Mr. Lambert a homosexual, miss?"

I am struck by the question, how senseless it seems. "Why would you ask that?"

"We're trying to determine if this was a hate-motivated crime," she explains.

I stare at her, dumbfounded. "Obviously, it *was.* Don't you think?"

She gives a philosophical shrug. *Ahhh, civilians.* She pockets her notebook. "Thank you for your help," she says. "There's one other thing we'd like to ask you. There's no next of kin and we haven't been able to find any of Mr. Lambert's dental records. Nor do we have fingerprints on file." She lets a beat pass. "What I'm trying to say is we have no means of identifying the body."

A wave of vertigo runs through me when I understand what she's saying. I nod weakly. I stand up and she supports me as we hobble out onto the street.

At the Medical Examiner's Office, the morgue attendant, a short, squat woman in a white lab coat, leads us down a stale green hallway. Her name is Lil.

"Haven't seen you in a while," she says to Detective Mankewicz. "How've you been?" She's unlocking the frosted glass door of a small room. She's got a cute, compressed little voice, like a cartoon character's. It seems unsuitable for a job like this.

"Not bad. You?"

"Same old," answers Lil.

My mind is racing as the morgue attendant opens the door of a small room with a couple of vinyl chairs and a television on a rolling metal stand.

Would Jack really do this because of what Jeremy said? Is that possible?

Why couldn't Jeremy just believe me? Why couldn't he have just listened?

Lil turns on the fluorescent lights. "We try to avoid this at all costs," she's saying. "It takes so much out of people. But sometimes you don't have a choice. It's a necessary evil." I realize she's talking to me. She motions for me to take a seat. The detective sits beside me. She puts her stranger's hand on my knee and taps it reassuringly.

"I should warn you, the body's not in very good shape," says Lil, leaning an arm on the TV. "It can't be cleaned until the pathologist sees it." I nod that I understand. She turns on the TV. The screen flickers to life. I'm confused. I look from the screen to Mankewicz to Lil and back again.

I'm here to identify a body. A *body*. Why are we watching TV? I should be taken down a long white corridor into a large room with a wall of stainless-steel crypts. They should open one of the drawers and pull out a long mound lying inside a dark plastic bag. They should unzip the bag and I should look down to see the body—the physical form—of my dead friend, lying there helplessly. I should see him and swoon over in a faint, falling forward onto his chest, pounding on him with my fists, begging him not to leave me here, not to leave me all alone. It would be dramatic. It might even make me feel better. But I don't get any of that. What I get is a television set and an image of Jeremy—a medium close-up of him, to be specific—in the center of the screen. He's lying on a pale, gleaming slab. His face looks bruised and discolored. A bluish sheet is pulled up around his shoulders. In fact, everything about him is a soft, monstrous shade of pale blue from the cold glare of the fluorescent lights.

Lil sees my wordless confusion.

"This is the way it's done nowadays," she explains, pointing to the monitor. "We don't actually bring people into the morgue anymore. They just do that on TV."

I look to the detective, who nods sagely as if "They just do that on TV" was the universal explanation for all the shortcomings of life.

I look back at the screen. Feel continuous rolls of horror and fear. Jeremy's face is full of shadows, which I slowly start to recognize as bruises and blood. His short, thin hair lies down in dark patches against his skull, where the blood has dried in swirls. The details, one by one, separate from the visual tricks of badly lit video and become the signs of a violent death.

"Are you ready?" Lil asks, in her sweetly compressed voice. I nod. "Do you recognize this person, Ms. Carpenter?"

I swallow the first threat of bile. "Yes."

"Could you tell us who it is, please?"

"Jeremy."

"Full name, please."

"Jeremy Lambert."

"How do you know that?"

A sob comes out of me. I manage to say: "He was my friend."

"Thank you," Lil says. She turns off the TV. Jeremy disappears into a staticky burst of electrons.

Detective Mankewicz pats my knee again, as if to say: *Good job.* She helps me to my feet and we leave the sterile room together. As we walk down the hall, I am thinking, *Forgive them, Jeremy. Forgive them for putting you on TV.*

FORTY-FIVE

Hell hath no limits nor is circumscrib'd in one self place,
where we are is Hell, and where Hell is,
there must we ever be.

CHRISTOPHER MARLOWE

Long, dark shadows stretch across the floor of my apartment when I unlock the door. The first thing I do is turn on the TV—for company. Then I go to the window to let in some air. *Why is it already so dark?* But then I remember—it's almost winter. It's been so warm lately, a person could forget that the sun sets early, that the night is long.

I drop two newspapers on the floor. I bought them on the way home. SWARMING SUSPECTS SOUGHT IN DEATH OF LOCAL ARTIST read the *Times*. DEADLY TREK HOME was the headline in the *Post*. Jeremy's name is only mentioned once and after that he is referred to only as "the victim."

I get undressed and climb into bed, feeling tired and alone. I fall asleep with the television on, as I often do lately. Only it's not really sleep, but more of a semiconscious condition that—to me, at least—doesn't feel that much different from how I spend most of my time. In this state of mind, I can often apprehend sounds—car horns and voices from the street, theme songs and laugh tracks from old sitcoms on TV. But what wakes me up this time is a long, low growl—the deep, shuddering growl in the back of a big dog's throat. I half open my eyes, perceiving the world through only a narrow slit. The curtain on the window is billowing. I hear the growl in the big dog's throat again and realize it's thunder. Rain pelts the windows. I sit up, wondering why the storm didn't wake me sooner. I notice the TV screen is black, but I don't remember turning it off. I reach over and flick the switch on the bedside lamp. It clicks uselessly back and forth. I feel a slight sense of alarm, as I always do when the power goes out. There are certain things in life you come to depend on—that there will be light when you need it is one of them.

I stand up to close the window, squinting against a sheet of lightning that flashes white outside. I lean my weight on the frame, force the window down farther into the sash even as another clap of thunder makes the floor beneath my feet vibrate.

Worriedly, I look up at the sky. The clouds are not as dark as the night beyond them; they are charcoal gray and moving swiftly, a herd of buffalo stampeding across a plain, all heads and shoulders rushing in the same direction, seeking refuge from the storm. I look down at the street. The heavily falling rain stipples the pavement, snakes along the gutters, tinnily hits the hoods of parked cars. The lightning flickers again, bleaching the street brighter than day, then plunges it into blackness, darker than it was before.

Blackandwhiteblackandwhiteblackandwhite.

I must admit, it makes me catch my breath when I see her. A nun, standing on the steps of St. Francis, looking nervously up at the sky, trying to stay dry. I hadn't noticed her before. I watch her for a moment; her body seems so still, though her black habit snaps and pulls in the wind around her. And then, in a flicker of lightning, I see it's not a nun. It's a man, in a long, billowing black coat.

It's Jack. And he's looking up at me.

Trembling, I steady myself against the ledge of the window. I have to. It feels like I might fall out.

Or jump.

God, no.

He knows I've discovered him; he knows I've seen. He takes two easy strides off the steps and crosses toward the building, his coat flowing behind him. My heart thrums nervously as he disappears beneath the lip of the brick. Panicked, I turn away from the window. *I won't let him up. That's all.*

But there is no buzz from the intercom downstairs. The electricity is off. The next thing I hear is his soft, expectant knock on the door.

It's not me who moves toward the door and unlocks it.

It's not me who says, "Come in."

It's not me. It can't be me. I'm a good person—I want to do what's right.

He stands on the threshold. His hair is wet. Silver drops of water slip down his cheekbones, off his jaw. The hollows of his face seem slightly more pronounced than I remember them being.

I back away from the door. He steps into the apartment, takes off his coat, and shakes out the rain. "I'm sorry it's so late," he says, his voice deep, familiar.

"What are you doing here?" I ask weakly, holding myself.

"I read about Jeremy. I wanted to see if you're okay."

"You *read* about Jeremy? Or you *knew* about Jeremy?"

He stares at me evenly, but doesn't answer my question. He lays his coat across a chair. "Are you all right?" he asks.

"I'm fine," I tell him. "I *will* be fine."

"They said in the newspaper it might be a group of kids."

"That's what they *said.*"

He shakes his head. "Jeremy always thought the world was a shitty place. It must have been a relief to find out how right he was."

And for some reason that makes me angry. "You shouldn't have come," I tell him. "You can leave now."

"I don't want to, Sally," he says. He moves toward me, taking my arms in his hands. His voice is the softest part of the storm, the gentler aspect of the rumbling outside. "Not without you. I want us to be together." And then he says it: "I love you," and there is such honesty in his voice, it seems he has not expressed an emotion, but uttered an absolute truth.

I feel something collapse inside of me. Perhaps the first level of the bones that hold me up.

"You said we'd be together forever."

"I know what I said."

"You told me you were mine."

"I know what I told you."

His face—like the room, like the world—morphs back and forth, one moment familiar, one moment unfamiliar, in the uncanny flashes of the storm.

"Jack, don't do this to me," I plead with him. "Don't make me do this again. I can't. I'm not strong enough." I try to pull away. But he holds me harder. I stop fighting. I let my head fall back. *What more can I do?* The desire is too great.

Suddenly I feel a crash of thunder so violent, it shifts the floor beneath my feet, as if for a moment we were not on solid ground. I look to the flickering window. I hear shouts from outside. I pull myself away from his arms and hurry across the room. The lightning plays tricks with my eyes, each step toward the window seeming disconnected from the last. I lean against the ledge, looking down at the slick street. The stained-glass window of the church looks different, with a concentrated glow pulsing slowly near the bottom. Then I hear something—a clean, sweet note beneath the roar. A siren. Getting closer. I watch flashing red lights illuminate the end of the street, brightening the buildings as they approach. And then I smell smoke.

Oh, my God!

The church has been struck by lightning. The church is going to burn tonight.

My sign, after all.

In the next flash of lightning I see his reflection on the glass in front of me. The dark hollow sockets of his eyes. The cut of his jaw. He is standing right behind me. I turn quickly, sliding against the wall, away from him.

"I know who you are, Jack," I say.

He holds out his hand. "We have to go, Sally."

I shake my head. *No.* I push myself off the wall to run in the direction of the door, but he grabs my arm. I'm shocked by the force of it. I yank hard, using all my weight to pull away from him, so hard that I fall backward. I scramble to my knees, crawling across the floor away from him, but I feel his hand clamp down around my ankle, dragging me back.

"Come with me, Sally!"

"Please, God, please! Help me! Please!"

Frantically, I kick and scream. I grab for table legs, chairs, anything to save myself. *God, don't make me do it.* I feel him pulling me back. I reach outward—my hand grabs the cord on the lamp and it crashes to the floor not far from me. I grasp the leg of the bed, I clutch the sheets. My hand slides beneath the mattress. I feel the cool handle of the butcher knife. I yank it out and twist quickly to face him.

His grip on my ankle loosens. He sits back on his heels, staring at the knife. I wish I could see the blade flashing in the light, but it's just a dark shadow in my hand. I grip it fiercely.

"Don't make me do it, Jack," I tell him.

He just watches me. We both stand slowly, matching move for move as if we don't trust each other. There is smoke coming in the window now. It makes me cough. I raise the knife, shaking with fear. I can't quite see his features in the darkness. I think he broadens his chest, as if to challenge me. My grip on the knife tightens. I want to end it. Finally. I want it to be over. My whole arm tenses with the strength it will need. Yet I can't will myself to lunge at him. Because I can't bear the idea that he will live through it.

And I can't bear the idea that he will fall.

My arm drops to the side of my body. My fingers open. The knife tumbles uselessly to the floor. I watch him for a moment, breathless, panicked, so much in love.

"Let me go, Jack," I say.

Just let me go.

I see the swell of his cheekbone as he smiles slightly and gives the slightest nod good-bye.

I turn toward the door. The smoke is thick now, moving in a gray canopy toward the ceiling. My eyes water. I'm not sure what is shadow, what is real. I feel through the grayness. My foot catches on something—the cord of the lamp—and the walls and ceiling are suddenly turning over each other. When I hit the floor, I feel an intense blow on the side of my head. I roll over, breathless. My gaze drifts to the ceiling, the gray smoke, the red wash of the emergency lights from the street. Then I feel the tug of a cold, inky darkness.

FORTY-SIX

The devil, depend on it,
can sometimes do a very gentlemanly thing.
ROBERT LOUIS STEVENSON

I'M not sure where I am when I apprehend the sound of a voice. *A voice?* Pleasant but meaningless, like a pigeon cooing on a nearby window ledge. I try to open my eyes, but the light feels like boiling water pouring into my head. My eyelids flutter to protect me until slowly, slowly, I can see a woman hovering over me. She is wearing white.

"How are you feeling, dear?" she asks.

I try to shift my head on the pillow. I see a pale gray curtain. The glint of instruments. And then I smell it: antiseptic thrown over something foul. I drop my head to the pillow again. I feel a part of my mind slowly inflating with memory. I remember the crack of lightning.

"Is the church okay?" I ask in a weak voice. "Did it burn down?"

She frowns at me. "No, dear. Not the church. Your building."

I blink at her incomprehensibly.

"There was a fire in your building last night. The paramedics brought you here."

My building? I remember the smoke—the sirens—and Jack's voice.

"Come with me, Sally." But the light on the stained-glass window of St. Francis. *Was it a reflection of my own building?*

I begin to tremble. *"Jack . . ."*

"You just lie still now," she urges. "You need to rest."

I hear the shuffling of feet, a man's voice. I look up . . . wanting . . . praying . . . for it to be him. But it's a stranger's face. He's wearing a stethoscope around his neck. He and the nurse mutter to each other.

"She's delirious. She should rest."

Jack . . . my darling.

I close my eyes and I'm in the darkness again.

I dream. I know it must be a dream. Real life is not so vivid and it can't be a movie; no director would have the nerve to make everything so colorful and bright. Jack and I are standing at the end of a long aisle strewn with flowers. Stained-glass windows on either side of us let in prisms of light. A man in a purple robe is reading from a large gilt-edged book. Behind us is a congregation of people in blue suits and yellow dresses . . . my mother is in the front row, smiling. My father is there, too, a red rose pinned in his lapel. Everything is so bright.

The next time I wake up, the face hovering over me is familiar. It's Gus.

"Sal? You okay?"

I clear my throat a few times, try to push myself up on my elbow. She helps me, propping pillows behind me, taking some of my weight. My eyes ascertain details more clearly. The gray curtain. A vinyl chair beside me with Gus's coat slung over it, her purse on the floor next to a stack of magazines, as if she's been waiting for a while. She tells me she saw a news report, recognized my building, and came as soon as she could.

"Where's Jack?" I ask weakly.

"I don't know, Sal. Was he with you?"

I think about that. The repercussions of it. The way I lifted the knife. I shake my head. *No.*

"Well, hello there," says a nurse, pulling aside the gray curtain. "We were hoping you'd join the real world soon. How're you feeling?"

I give her a weak shrug. "Okay." She wheels a food tray to the side of the bed. The smell makes my stomach turn. "When can I go home?" I ask her.

"There isn't much left to go home to, Sal," Gus says. "You're gonna have to crash with me for a while. Your place is a wreck. You should see it. It's a miracle you got out alive."

Really? I thought miracles were supposed to feel a lot better than this.

"It doesn't matter about the building," the nurse says, jotting down something on my chart. "What's important is that you and the baby are going to be okay."

There have been times in my life when I've been watching a video and something so confusing happens that I have to stop the tape, rewind, and watch the scene again. This is the first time that's ever happened in real life.

The—what—is going to be okay?

Gus looks at me with a big grin. The nurse, too, is smiling.

I shake my head as if to clear it. Clutch the sheets beside me. "I'm . . . I'm . . ."

"Yes," says the nurse, giving a wink, before disappearing behind the curtain and leaving us alone.

"I'm . . ."

Gus is nodding.

"I'm—*pregnant?*"

"That's right, Sal! Congratulations!"

I push the food tray away and throw the covers off. "Where's the bathroom?"

She points to the other side of the curtain. "Got a little morning sickness?"

"If that's what you want to call it."

I lift my legs off the bed to the floor. Pinpricks of heat rush to my feet. I don't seem to have the strength to carry my own weight. I feel along the curtain to find an opening into a wide aisle full of other gray curtains, some open to reveal empty beds. Others are closed and behind them I hear murmuring, sniffling, coughing. I see the sign for the bathroom and make my way toward it.

Pregnant?

I can't be pregnant. I can't be. It's impossible.

Okay, it *is* possible. This happens between men and women all the time. What I mean is that it *shouldn't* be happening. I don't *want* it to happen.

Do I?

I close the bathroom door behind me. It's a small, white, sterile room. I lean against the sink, feeling a wave of nausea come and go.

I can't have it, of course. I know it's Jack's baby. What if there's something *wrong* with it? Oh, my God. What if it has *claws* or something . . . or a tail? What if, like Mia Farrow, I end up eating raw meat every day? Getting all my hair chopped off? What if, when it's born, everyone in the delivery room screams?

Of course—and I feel a slight release in my tension—what if it's normal? What if it's perfect and healthy and sweet? And what if it's a part of him I can love forever?

Damn. Just once I'd like him to leave me with a dilemma that was easy.

When I hobble back to the hospital bed, Gus is on her cell. She puts her finger to her lips. *"Shhh . . . I'm trying to get the number for Kelly Ripa's OB-GYN,"* she whispers to me.

I climb up on the bed.

In an impatient huff Gus says into the phone, "Yes, I'm still holding." She tosses me a copy of a pastel-colored paperback. "Catch up on your reading," she says.

I look at the title. *What to Expect When You're Expecting.*

I groan. "Gus . . ."

"What?"

"I'm not having it." I put the book down.

"Don't be daft. Plenty of women have babies on their own. Wake up and smell the coffee—decaf, mind you. No caffeine during the first trimester."

"I just can't," I tell her.

"Why *not?*"

"What if something's *wrong* with it?"

She flaps a hand at me. "All expectant mothers worry about that. It's perfectly normal. But with you as a mom and him as a dad—what could possibly go wrong?"

Don't ask.

A few minutes later, a man from the FDNY comes to ask me some routine questions about the fire. There were some concerns about fire code violations in the building. He has sandy hair, broad shoulders, and a thick Brooklyn accent. He has a glow of confidence and heroism about him. Gus sits through our interview, fanning herself when he's not looking.

"We're trying to determine if there were any code violations," he explains. "What can you tell us? Did any alarms go off?"

"I'm sorry . . . I don't remember much. . . . I don't even know how I got here."

He's jotting things down as I talk. "What about the gentleman who died? Did you know him?"

That makes me freeze. "Someone died?"

"A male Caucasian."

The tears immediately move to my eyes.

"Joseph Kellock from the second floor—the fire started in his apartment."

In a flash that is part remorse, part relief, I remember the old man who raised pigeons on the roof.

"When the power went off," the fire marshal says, "he lit a candle.

He put it on the windowsill and then fell asleep. The curtain caught fire. Happens all the time. There wasn't much hope for him in that place."

In a fractured voice, in a fractured state of mind, I answer the rest of his questions about smoke detectors and proper signage in the halls. He gives me information about dealing with insurance problems, reclaiming important documents, and salvaging my belongings.

I think about that. Sifting through the rubble of my old things. Finding the brass photo frame of my family. Grabbing my old clothes. The portable black-and-white TV. I shake my head. I don't want any of it. I want to start over.

That sounds like a good idea.

I just don't know how to do it.

ALTHOUGH I feel fine to be released, Gus insists on my staying in another night to make sure the baby is okay. She even agrees to pay for it. A nurse shows me a blank calendar, asking me when my last period was, trying to determine my due date. I wish I could pinpoint the night it happened. The moment it happened. *September . . . October . . . November . . .*

I'm not sure what time it is when I wake up and see the curtain pulled aside and two figures standing in the dim light at the foot of my bed. I know it's nighttime. The rush-hour traffic noises have faded, but the sounds of ambulances coming and going has increased. Not that I really notice them. Sirens are part of reality here. Like birds in summertime—you only hear them when you try.

"Sally Carpenter?" the figure whispers.

"Yes . . . ?"

She closes the curtain and walks to the side of my bed. A man remains standing at the foot of the bed; he's holding something bulky under his arm.

"Ms. Carpenter, my name is Debra Wilson," she says to me, shaking my hand. She seems very familiar to me, a beautiful, polished-looking black woman wearing a beige trench coat. "I'm a reporter with NY4."

And then I remember seeing her on TV.

"How are you feeling?" she asks me, digging into her tote bag. Without waiting for an answer, she says, "My cameraman and I were at the scene last night." She motions to the man at the foot of the bed. He has a short, dark beard and reddish cheeks. "Is it okay if I ask you a few questions about it?" I nod that would be fine, yet I feel myself tense, my breath turn shallow in my chest. The man smoothly hoists his camera onto his shoulder, changing the shape of his silhouette. The sun gun flashes on, making me squint.

"We arrived there shortly after it started and got a lot of it on tape," Debra says. "It was a terrible fire. Did you know the old man?"

"Yes." I tell her about Mr. Kellock and the pigeons he kept on the roof. Occasionally I look down at the microphone she extends toward me or up at the camera. It feels odd to be in the middle of a television interview when I'm in a hospital bed. Yet there's something natural about it, too; it's not as disturbing as it should be because there's part of me that believes I have lived my whole life on the cusp of a local TV news interview, that we *all* do, and that it's just a matter of one tipped-over candle, one misstep off a curb, one drunk driver, before the inevitable happens and we find ourselves in the strangely flattering position of having the camera turned on us and someone we've only ever seen on TV asking us for the proper spelling of our name.

"And what about the guy who saved you?"

That makes everything stop, including me. She can see that I have *stopped*.

"The one who carried you out. We're trying to find out who it is. We've talked to the neighbors but nobody seems to know him." When she sees I'm still unable to speak, she turns to the misshapen silhouette at the foot of the bed. "Don't we have it on tape?"

"I caught it getting B roll."

A tension comes into Debra's voice. There is a change in her momentum. "Can we show it to her? Maybe she'll recognize him."

"She could watch it on the viewfinder, I guess."

Debra flutters her hand in the air as if to tell him to hurry up. The cameraman slides the lump off his shoulder. The sun gun beam sweeps across the ceiling, then snuffs out. The three of us are in darkness for a moment, waiting for the light from the street to shine up and adjust our eyes. Through it all I hear the clicking and snapping of a tape being changed.

"The audio might be a little rough," the man says, turning the camera around and setting it on my lap. "But the pictures should be okay." He flips a rubber eyepiece off the camera and I see a small, square screen with a shifting black-and-white image on it. He gives me a gray earpiece, which I fit into my ear. There is something playing on the screen. I have to squint and lean closer to see what it is. It is a moment before I realize it's a jostling shot of running shoes on wet asphalt.

"Can you get this?" says a voice from a little speaker on the camera—Debra's voice, compressed and tiny. The image zooms upward, panning quickly from the running shoes across a set of dark archways, which I recognize as being the doors of St. Francis, and above them, the unblinking eye of the stained-glass window. The shot swings across something vast and black into a tumbling gray-whiteness and down onto a large white hand with fingers straining upward. But no, not a hand. It's the fire. Between shoots of flame, as the fingers separate and reach, I make out the placement of a window, familiar brickwork. It's my building.

I hear Debra's tiny voice again. *"This is good right here . . ."* The camera steadies, pulling out to a medium-wide shot of her standing in front of the building, holding a microphone, looking undaunted by the chaos behind her, the fire engines, the streaming water, the firefighters hurrying back and forth. Debra squares her shoulders. Clears her throat. *"Take one, in three, two . . . Debra Wilson for NY4 News on Sullivan Street in SoHo, where an apartment fire is still burning out of control. . . ."* I have now adjusted to the size of the screen. It seems to have usurped my whole field of vision. I could be watching IMAX.

"I'm gonna get some B roll," says a man's voice on the small speaker. The camera jostles down to the ground again. Debra seems to fly out of frame. Things focus and unfocus. Glints of fire engines. Ambulances. Great ropes of water shoot toward the flames. Bystanders, some of them wearing pajamas, seem stunned, holding themselves.

"It's coming up," Debra says, leaning over. "There." She taps a manicured fingernail to the screen. A murky scrawl of images moves from right to left then away. "Did you see it?" I shake my head. The cameraman tells me he'll "slo-mo" it for me. He starts the tape again. I lean closer to the frame. I see the bulky coats of the firefighters, the hoses seeming impossibly heavy in slow motion, the water frustratingly slow against the fire.

"Here," Debra says.

A blur of images appears in the right corner. I curl my knees up, cupping the edges of the screen to block out the light. I see a black-and-white smear move onto the right side of the screen. It's the dark figure of a man, hunched over. . . . No, not hunched over. He's carrying something in his arms. I make out an arm dangling. A stream of fair hair. The dark figure turns once to face the camera as if sensing he's being watched, then disappears off the left side of the frame. I motion for them to play it again. The tape rewinds. I watch the dark figure materialize once more—one long, determined stride following the next. He doesn't seem to struggle with the weight of the pale form draped lifelessly in his arms. He seems graceful with it; it seems easy for him. The cameraman hits PAUSE. The screen freezes.

"So?" I hear Debra's voice. "Do you recognize him?"

I remain still. I see the jut of cheekbone. The slash of jaw. Dark eyes staring back at me. Surrounded by fire. I watch him for so long, the individual images on the screen begin to separate and blur beneath the sting of tears.

"Sally . . ." Debra's voice again.

I push the camera away. "I'm sorry, no." My voice breaks. "I don't know who he is."

"Too bad. We wanted to find him. Someone saw him go back into the building. We guess to help other people. But he never came out."

I swallow a soft gasp.

"Well, whoever he was," she says, yanking her tote up onto her shoulder, "he's a real hero. He saved your life."

I feel my eyes heat up. "I know."

FORTY-SEVEN

And he laid hold on the dragon,
that old serpent, which is the Devil, and Satan,
and bound him a thousand years.

REVELATION 20:2

"I have expectant-mommy-proofed the place," Gus says, unlocking her apartment door after I get released from the hospital. The curtains are open, sunlight streaming across healthy plants and comfy furniture. "There's no coffee, no alcohol, and no tobacco around. And there *won't* be, either," she says. I follow her down a short hallway to a small, bright room.

"It's not much," she says, "but it'll do for a while."

The walls of her extra bedroom are banana yellow. The carpet is gray tweed. There is a single bed against the far wall with a flowered bedspread, one window with a crisp white blind, and the usual things that end up cluttering even the tidiest extra bedrooms: an ironing board, a laundry basket, an exercise bike. A poster at the head of the bed has a little kitten clinging by her front paws to a tree branch, and reads: "HANG IN THERE, BABY!"

"Do you like it?" she asks.

"It's perfect," I tell her, trying to smile.

She exhales in relief. "Oh, good. You can stay as long as you like.

Mi casa, su casa. There are just a few ground rules. Do not, under any circumstances, take my migraine tablets. That's not for your protection—that's for mine."

"No problem."

"Do not hang your skinny-girl under thingies from my curtain rod."

"No problem."

"Not that you'll be a skinny girl much longer," she says, nudging my abdomen. "And one other thing."

"What?"

"You still have to go to auditions."

I stare at her.

"I'm serious, Sal. You're a talented actor. . . . You can't let this—or anything—stop you." She's looking at me with such seriousness, such earnestness, that I almost don't recognize her. "Now, let's not get too sappy here. I'm going to run down to the store and pick up a few things. Do you know if you were taking enough folacin before you got pregnant?"

"Um . . . falla what?"

"Never mind. I'll get some anyway." She dashes out into the hall and I hear the front door open and slam closed, the security system beeping.

I look around the room. I drag my feet to the bed and sit down, putting my head in my hands. I feel an ache in my heart so intense I'm not sure I can endure it.

Where is he?

What happened to him?

I kept expecting to see him at the hospital. I kept thinking he'd be on the street outside, leaning against his black car, waiting for me when I got released. He'd be holding a dozen long-stemmed red roses. He'd have a big grin on his face. "Didn't think you could get away from me that easily, did you?" he'd say. Or something like that. Then I'd run to him and throw my arms around his neck and tell him, "I'm sorry . . . I know what it means now . . . that I'm on your side. . . . It means I love you . . . it means you can count on me . . . and I can count on you always." We'd laugh and kiss and then hurry through rush-hour traffic to get to City Hall before the end of the day, where a justice of the peace, a smiling man with gray hair and a kindly way, would marry us. Then we'd take a cab to the airport and fly somewhere warm and lie on a beach for two weeks. I'd sip virgin piña coladas while he stroked my tummy and we talked about baby names. My shoulders would burn and my nose would peel and I'd get a pedicure every other day in colors I'd never dream of wearing in New York. He'd turn nut brown in the sun and only shave twice and dried seawater would turn chalky white on his brow after he went swimming. We'd eat dinner outside, feeding each other fresh fruit with our fingers, chunks of mango and papaya slices, and meat straight off the bone; we'd buy cheap silver jewelry we'd only wear while we're there and a terra-cotta pot that will crack the minute it drops below zero when we get back to New York. On the flight home, we'd wear flowers around our necks and not take them off until we cleared customs. Then we'd pick out paint colors and rocking chairs and cradles and spend the next fifty gray winters arguing about college tuition and retirement funds.

That's what was supposed to happen. Not *this*. Not crashing at my agent's apartment, unemployed, pregnant—and alone.

GUS comes back from the store with a plastic bag of groceries. She has a stricken look on her face. She tosses a newspaper over to me. "Jack Weaver is missing," she says.

I freeze.

I'm not sure I've heard his name spoken out loud. I've been repeating it so often in my head—*Jack WeaverJack Weaver*—that it feels like my respiration, something that couldn't exist apart from me.

"He was supposed to go out to L.A. for the new job," Gus says. "He never got there."

She watches me for my reaction. "WEB PREZ VANISHES" declares the headline. I sit down and read the article. There aren't many details. Agnes MacGregor says he didn't decide whether he was flying or "taking the scenic route," meaning driving. The only thing they know is he never arrived.

I try not to cry. I don't *want* to cry. I'm afraid if I start, I'll never stop again.

FORTY-EIGHT

And lead us not into temptation,
but deliver us from evil: For thine is the kingdom,
and the power, and the glory, for ever. Amen.

MATTHEW 6:13

I don't know when I actually make the decision to keep the baby. I'm not sure it even happens consciously. Like all the biggest moments in our lives, something seems to club us over the head and we're not sure we can cope. We spend some time adjusting to it, and suddenly it's *ours*.

The first few weeks at Gus's place are a strange combination of sifting through the classifieds for day jobs, screwing up the nerve to go to auditions, and waiting for news about Jack. Gus keeps me apprised of the rumors circulating in the business. Some people think Marty Fletcher's death affected him more deeply than anyone thought and that he just couldn't deal with it anymore; others think, like a lot of executives, he just burned out and took off, not leaving a forwarding address. Nobody seems to draw a connection between the mysterious hero caught on a piece of B roll and the sudden disappearance of a powerful TV executive. Even Debra Wilson moves on, as preoccupied with a string of robberies uptown as she seemed to be with anything else. If the rumors about Jack's disappearance include me in any way, nobody says anything except to tell me that they're sorry: They knew we used to be close.

I find myself thinking about him constantly. Dreaming about him. Sometimes I even think I see him on the street. Or in a restaurant. Or driving by in a black car. Then a few hours will go by and I realize I haven't thought of him at all. I guess the rest of my life will be like that. Waiting for the hours to turn into days. I know that will happen. I just don't know when.

THIRTY-ONE weeks later, Jake William Carpenter is born, a healthy baby boy with all the right numbers of toes, fingers, and other appendages. No tails, in other words. Gus sat through the delivery with me, reminding me to breathe, and saying things like: "You sure you don't want an epidural?"

When they hand Jake to me, pink and warm and stretching out his curled body, I'm trembling with relief and joy. His small hands are clenched tightly. He has dark hair, like Jack's. He opens his eyes almost immediately and looks up at me.

I move into a small studio (emphasis on small) in Chelsea, which I paint all white. Not exactly a Mediterranean mansion with one whole closet just for shoes, but it's bright and clean. I was able to afford the deposit after getting a couple days' work during my third trimester. I got a part on *Sex and the City* playing a woman in Miranda's prenatal yoga class. During a particularly strenuous position, I look at Miranda, wincing and groaning. "Would somebody pass the Chitos?" I say.

The apartment feels like one big nursery. Gus brings something new over almost every day, Fisher-Price toys and mobiles and a bouncy seat. Not wanting to seem too sentimental, she shrugs it off, saying "It was on sale" or "I just happened to pass it in a window" (when I can see very well that she's gone out of her way—in one case, ordering a custom-made bassinet from a craftsman in Vermont). She even insists on baby-sitting when I go to auditions. I bring Jake to her office, where she's set up a playpen in the corner where the koi pond was supposed to be. She complains about changing diapers and tripping on rattles half the day, but I know she loves it. She almost started bawling out loud when I asked her if she'd be the godmother.

It seems strange, I know, but I'm having him baptized. I wonder what Jack would think of that. I don't think he'd mind. I bet he's amused by all the things we do to protect ourselves from sin.

THE yellow cab pulls up in front of St. Francis de Sales. It's a crisp afternoon in November, a little chill in the air. Jake is in his white christening gown, the top corner of a powder-blue blanket partially covers his sleeping face. I pay the driver and get out of the cab, looking at the church first, and then the big stained-glass window. I take a deep breath and turn around. It's been so many months since I've been down here, I expect to feel a flood of memories, the pang of nostalgia, a surge of melancholy, and yet . . . what I get is confusion. *Is that my old building?*

It takes a moment before I completely understand. Yes . . . my building . . . but all the windows have been changed. They're gleaming and uniform with white vinyl casings—the landlord must have replaced them after the fire. They have no character, but great insulation properties, I bet. The brick itself, once painted over in so many colors it seemed to be dripping with candle wax, has been sandblasted down to its original brown, the mortar lines white as chalk drawn on with a ruler. I can't believe I actually *lived* here. That I used to look out that window. Walk through that door. It's as if the physical changes to the building have disconnected me from the details of the past. Maybe that's for the best. Maybe it's okay that things keep changing, never allowing us to go back. Memories make things easier for us. The best and worst of our lives can be made manageable that way: a white ice cream truck. The feeling of someone's hand on your back.

The inside of the church is chaotic with parents, gurgling babies, altar boys, and nuns dotting the pews. I hadn't been to a christening in so long, I didn't realize that in large parishes more than one baby is baptized at once. I always pictured a moody, sepia-toned scene, like the one with baby Sophia Coppola in *The Godfather.* I thought the archbishop would speak in Latin and anoint only my son. But there are four babies getting christened today. I don't mind. There's a sense of occasion about it.

"Where have you *been?*" Gus says, marching down the aisle toward me. She's wearing a winter-white crepe skirt suit and a matching wrap flung over one shoulder. Her hair is freshly done, the pale streak winding like a mountain road.

"Just checking out the old neighborhood," I say. She takes the baby from my arms, touches his nose with her fingertip, immediately forgetting that I'm there.

I look toward the front of the church, where the other families have collected—some on pews, some near the altar, everyone chattering excitedly.

Two people stand up in the second row and move uncertainly into the aisle. I walk toward them, feeling a swell of emotion. Paul and my mother. I haven't seen either of them in so long. Paul, who was nervous but flattered when I asked him to be the godfather, is wearing a gray flannel blazer, a plaid shirt, and a burgundy tie that—*somehow*—work together. He looks rugged and healthy, his cheeks windburned. His hair is not as long as Van Halen's anymore, but it still reaches his collar in back, a thick, dark mullet that obviously still sees its fair share of blow dryers and mousse. But his eyes are clear—meaning he's given up his adolescent pastime.

"All the way from Alaska, huh?" I remark as we embrace.

He juts out his jaw and runs his fingers under his chin. In a raspy voice he says, " 'You made me an offah I couldn't refuse.' " We both laugh.

My mother steps out from behind him, her hands clutched in front of her, a nervous smile on her face. She's wearing a turquoise suit and a navy overcoat, both of which look brand-new. I don't think I've ever seen my mother in everything *new*. But then—ah—there's a black vinyl purse I remember from years ago. When we hug, there is none of the awkwardness between us there usually is. I don't know why. Maybe it's because she feels so *small*. Slight as a bird.

I had been so afraid to tell her I was pregnant. If she thought playing a nun on TV was in bad form, what would she think of *this*? But there comes a point where your family starts surprising you. I don't know what happens to them. Maybe they just get tired of being a certain way—or maybe they were never that way in the first place. Whatever the case, my mother, now fifty-eight and still a salesclerk in the JCPenney women's hosiery department in Tecumseh Falls, did the unexpected when I told her I was going to be a single mom. She whooped for joy. I was still staying at Gus's apartment when I made the call. I was already three months pregnant at the time.

"I thought it would *never* happen!" she exclaimed. "I thought you were going to be like all those other Hollywood mothers and wait until you're forty or forty-five. I was so worried. I might have been *gone* by then." Of course, she asked the inevitable question. "What about the father?"

"He's not in my life anymore."

She let out a resigned sigh. "Well, I guess that's okay. I raised the two of you practically by myself. What was he like?"

"He was . . . amazing, Mom."

"Do you think *I* would've liked him?"

I considered how best to answer that one. "Let's just say, he was a little hard *not* to like."

It was my mother who, tentatively, brought up baptizing the baby. "I know you think it's silly, Sally, but I believe in it . . . it'll make me feel better."

And I said, "I don't think it's silly, Mom. It'll make me feel better, too."

And somehow it does. Attending classes and the occasional Sunday mass while I was pregnant, establishing myself as a member of the parish. Because the nuns at the convent are so active with single moms, I felt comfortable here. Sitting on the pews, listening to the priest, it reminded me of the mornings my mom used to take me to church. I remember watching her pray and say the rosary and cross herself, being so impressed by her. There was something soothing about doing it again by myself. Of course, I haven't been to confession yet. I wouldn't know where to start.

"Where's my grandson?" my mother asks, looking toward the back of the church.

Gus comes down the aisle, grinning proudly. My mother's eyes turn wide and bright as Gus transfers the little bundle to her arms.

"You guys already met, I guess?" I ask, motioning between my mother and Gus.

"We introduced ourselves," my mother says, rocking the baby.

"How could they miss me?" Gus asks. "You told them to look for the one with a white streak in her hair."

I shrug helplessly. "Was I wrong?"

"Jake William Carpenter," my mother says, letting the baby wrap his tiny hand around her finger. "You're beautiful."

"Do you want to hold him?" I ask Paul.

"Not yet. I'm too nervous. Let me get used to the idea first."

"He has your eyes, Sally," my mother says.

"I know." I always used to think it was silly when people said of babies that they had their mother's eyes or their father's nose. As far as I was concerned, if babies resembled anything at all—other than Cabbage Patch dolls—it was other babies. But not Jake. He has blue-gray eyes like mine. His smile, of course, is Jack's. Slightly crooked and mischievous. A devilish smile. There is no other word for it.

My mother straightens the white skirt of the christening gown; it's supposed to be a symbol of purity and innocence. The priest told us this during the baptism preparation classes I had to take about raising a child in a devout home. There were a lot of rules and rituals. I found some of them hypocritical—a *lot* of them, in fact. Many of the other young parents seemed to agree, sharing knowing looks with each other as the priest spoke. But there was still something comforting about listening to these ideas, about knowing they were there and that some part of us still strives to preserve them. Because no matter how ridiculous the rituals or how pitifully short we may fall, at the heart of it, our different faiths are about trying to be good people, about trying to do the right thing, and that's okay with me.

My mother smiles at Jake. "That dark hair—that must be from his father."

"It is," I say, running my hand gently over the baby's head. He looks so content in my mother's arms. It strikes me for a moment how odd it is to be standing here in New York with my mother and brother. It feels as though a frayed piece of thread is finally stitching me, haphazardly maybe, to all the things I left behind—or thought I could. Bad memories and good. Fears and hopes. And this baby—tiny and innocent and unable to walk or talk or do anything for himself—has miraculously accomplished something that, so far, nothing else in the world has been able to do. He actually got my mother to come to New York.

A door on the side of the church opens and the priest walks out, wearing a long white robe. My mother, a conscientious Catholic, hands me the baby and moves to a nearby pew. The parents, on cue, gather with the godparents at the front of the church. The priest begins the ceremony, asking us if we understand the solemnity of the occasion.

We murmur back our practiced responses.

I admit that I'm nervous. I look up at the ceiling, making sure there aren't any fissures that could crack open, letting in fire and brimstone. I glance down either side of the church—no large urns to fall and split open . . . no suspicious cracks in the floor.

As the ceremony continues and the candles are lit and the babies, one after the other, are anointed with oil and cleansed with water, I find myself relaxing.

I think about Jack.

It's been almost a year since the night of the fire and I'm still thinking about him all the time. That's the way I refer to it now, "the night of the fire." We all have our ways of dealing with the unthinkable, of living with our sins, playing them up or down, like imperfections in our face. The rumors that circulated in the business after his disappearance quickly began to feel like modern myths.

"He's in England drumming up money for an independent film. . . ."

"He's in the south of France working on a book. . . ."

"He's living in Tibet, becoming a monk. . . ."

People seem comfortable with stories about him. They always have been. It is as if stories are all we ever wanted from him. The only reason he existed in the first place.

As for me, I'm not sure what happened to him or where he went. After the fire, he must've moved on somewhere. To another battlefield. Another boardroom. Maybe just another bed. Even now it makes me jealous to think that. When I imagine him with someone else, I feel the sweet, pointless tug of possession. Maybe I wasn't the only one he ever loved. Maybe there were thousands of souls just like me strewn throughout his grim and ancient past. Lovers. Victims. Whatever we can be called. Then again, maybe, like most of us, the Devil really only falls in love once.

The priest approaches our little circle with a kind smile on his face. Gus and Paul nervously take their vows as Jake's sponsors. The priest dips a shallow silver bowl into the font and gently lets the holy water flow over Jake's forehead and crown three times. In a soft voice he says, "I baptize you in the name of the Father and of the Son and of the Holy Spirit." The priest then anoints the top of Jake's head with oil. Paul comes forward, holding Jake's white candle in his trembling hand. "Receive the light of Christ," the priest murmurs as the candle is lit. Jake squirms in my arms and gurgles, but that's about it. There are no collapsed ceilings. No cracked floors. When the priest steps to the next couple, I have my own special reasons for exhaling in relief.

"What a good boy he is," Gus coos, tickling Jake under the chin.

It's then that I see him, in the very back pew of the church, beyond the other families in their Sunday best. Beyond the men in their suits and ties. Beyond the restless brothers and sisters standing on tiptoe to get a better view. Beyond the nuns sitting quietly and the women who still wear hats to church. A man with dark hair, wearing a black coat, sitting alone in the very last row. I feel my heart beating very slowly. He is watching me.

I narrow my eyes. Try to get a better look. *Do I know him?*

Jake makes a noise, as if to get my attention. I glance down only for a moment to make sure he's okay. When I look up again, the back pew is empty and the church doors have swung open. The man's figure is silhouetted in the light from outside. He descends the stairs quickly, his black coat billowing out behind him. The doors hover open for a moment, bringing with them a gust of wind that rushes down the aisle, swirling a cloud of dried leaves and dust from the sidewalk; it ruffles the hair and shirt collars of the people sitting along the pews. Some of the women must put their gloved hands on top of their heads to keep their hats from blowing away. As the wind reaches the front of the church, the long white hems of the christening gowns begin to flutter. The flames on the many white candles tremble wildly, then all at once, in one quick huff, are blown out.

The relative darkness that follows is momentarily disconcerting. People look around in confusion.

The priest speaks first, chuckling good-naturedly. "Well, it seems as if we've really made an impact on someone today."

The congregation erupts with laughter, the tension released. The altar boys scurry around to relight the candles and the ceremony resumes. When the last baby is baptized, the congregation claps and cheers.

"I hear that's a positive sign," my mother says as we make our way back down the aisle toward the doors. "When the candle blows out at a christening. Like rain on your wedding day. It's good luck. Not that

I'll ever get the chance to see a wedding I suppose," she murmurs under her breath.

We emerge into the sunshine. The sky seems endless today, blue and cloudless. I catch myself staring up at it so much lately. I'm aware of the sky now, the same way I used to be aware of the forbidden territory around me. But the space around me now seems limitless. I reach into it, unafraid. There is room to move. I have walked and wandered, and still not found a wall. Maybe there isn't one. Maybe there never was.

My mother turns to me. In a shy voice, almost a whisper, she asks, "Would you mind if we took a picture? Just the family? Maybe Gus would do it."

"Love to!" Gus exclaims, overhearing.

My mother rummages through her purse and retrieves—naturally—the old Kodak Fiesta. My brother and I exchange a look.

"I guess we know what to get her for Christmas," he mumbles to me.

"Everyone get close together," Gus says. She moves down a few steps, toward the sidewalk. "I'll take a few shots. Just to be safe. Annie Leibovitz I'm not." She adjusts her positioning, trying to find the best angle.

I feel my brother and my mother move in on either side of me, the soft pressure of their shoulders against mine. It's been so long since we've posed for a family photograph . . .

My gaze moves briefly across the street to my old apartment building, with its gleaming windows and freshly cleaned brick. Everything seems so new. So different. Jake squirms gently in my arms, as we all face the camera and smile.

ACKNOWLEDGMENTS

There is a long list of people who helped get this book—and occasionally *me*—off the ground. First of all, I feel incredibly grateful to have had the opportunity to work with Greer Kessel Hendricks, who is not only a smart, inspiring, and creative editor—but one of the most amazing people I've met. I also want to thank Helen Heller for all her hard work on my behalf and for taking a chance on me in the first place. Thanks also to Suzanne O'Neill, who was invaluable throughout the entire process. And because I know how lucky I am to have landed such a great publisher, special thanks to Judith Curr, not just for the title, but for her confidence and enthusiasm every step of the way.

For all the years of support and for never telling me to get a real job, thanks to my mother and my brother, Gary. Thanks also to my wonderful second parents, Allan and Erlene McInnis, for their love and guidance. For shoulders to cry on, encouragement, and/or individual expertise, big thanks to: Linda and Michael Cranston (Marla and Todd too), Judy Steer, Marilyn Guest, Roseanne Agasee, Meredith Kelly, Ivan Fecan and Sandra Faire, Michael Levine, Alison Reid, Raymond Morris, Joe and Lisa Woolf, Melissa Musen-Gerstein, Sean McInnis and Jennifer Pepper, Michelle Hoeg and Craig Norris (Abby, too, for her timely christening), and, since one's greatest influences sometimes happen in the strangest places, for all those Saturday mornings at the

Burger Pit, thank you Archie Tzortzis, for teaching me to question—everything. Much love to Sia Petropoulos for always keeping the faith—and Tracey Lowther for loving stories so much when we were kids.

Like all first-time novelists I feel indebted to many different authors. But I'd particularly like to thank Elaine Pagels for writing *The Origin of Satan*. I won't pretend my book trespasses on even an inch of the vast territory she covered, but I couldn't have confidently undertaken writing it without her. And of course I'm beholden to the many late, great writers quoted throughout the book (and to their families) for elevating my prose.

Huge thanks to the public affairs departments and press desks of the FDNY, the NYPD, and the New York Medical Examiner's Office. Anything I got right is because of them. Any mistakes I made are mine alone or, like Meridien's Bible, "for effect." Likewise for effect is the uppercase D on *the Devil* throughout the text. My apologies to, among others, the editors of *The Chicago Manual of Style*. (Though I should probably be apologizing to them for a lot more.)

When it comes to my wonderful husband, Mark, I can't list all the ways I'm grateful to him without registering a separate ISBN number, so let's leave it at thank you, darling! I love you!